THE PURVEYOR

THE PURVEYOR

KARELIA STETZ-WATERS

SAPPHIRE BOOKS

SALINAS, CALIFORNIA

Dedication

For Fay

Acknowledgements

Thank you to the P & C Committee – Paul, Terrance, Chris, Robin, Rob, and Jane– and to all my friends and colleagues at Linn-Benton Community College.

Thank you Sean Mishra for being the first to read The Purveyor.

Thank you Rod Carter for taking me shooting. Thanks to all the friends who make my life so bright.

Thank you to Chris, Schileen, and everyone at Sapphire Books for helping make my dreams come true.

Also, thank you to my parents, Elin and Albert Stetz, for supporting me and supporting my love of writing since I was a little girl. You gave me everything.

Finally a big thank you to my wife, Fay Stetz-Waters for believing in me for so many years. I could not do it without you.

From the diary of Charity Kimball

I'm writing this diary in my mind because anything I write down will be seen, confiscated, and held as proof of my disobedience. Obedience is the path of the True Reckoning. Like the Israelites I am in bondage, but it is my Lord who has enslaved me, and I can never be free, for even my blood is not my own.

Prologue

The Purveyor ducked her head to avoid the blades of the helicopter, then shielded her eyes from the sand thrown up by its departure. Then she was alone. The cement landing pad was the only sign of modern habitation on the small Caribbean island. Her instructions were to follow the foot path east to the main lodge. She set off. She was not accustomed to meeting clients in their homes, nor did she travel without a body guard or yield to the whims of her customers. That was what her girls did. That was what the clients paid for. However Harlow Galloway was an opportunity she could not resist.

A sandy path took her through a sea of reeds, past a turquoise lagoon worthy of a postcard. At the end, the path opened on an equally photogenic beach and a low, flat building on stilts over the water. With no reference to anything but sea and sky, it looked like a pleasant summer house, but she had researched the square footage and considered the value, to which she had added the value of the island, assets, and company holdings. The sum was practically incalculable but by conservative estimates it made Harlow Galloway the twelfth richest man in the world. A man who had everything, except what she—if she liked his terms— was selling.

She walked the long boardwalk to the front door. Before she could knock, a servant in starched livery met her at the door and invited her into a palatial sitting room overlooking the sea.

Galloway was seated on a sofa, his back to her. "Good afternoon," he said without turning. "Be careful of the leopard."

The Purveyor was momentarily speechless. She was used to wealth. There was no car, no chandelier, that she herself could not buy, but Galloway had bought the sky. He had bought the sea. He owned the island and, in an unprecedented deal with the government of Antigua, owned exclusive rights to the ocean and airspace within a fifteen mile radius around his home.

"Please don't move too quickly," he said in a voice that was stillness itself. "She is nervous."

Slowly, the Purveyor looked around, and indeed there was a great dappled cat lying alert by the plate glass window that looked out over the sea.

"An Amur leopard. There are less than fifty left alive," Galloway said. "Please sit." He motioned to a chair several feet away.

The Purveyor sat but said nothing. It was best, she believed, to let the client begin negotiations. It either made men uncomfortable or it made them boast. Either way, she learned all she needed to know in that moment.

Galloway sat, his hands folded in his lap. He had the ageless complexion of mixed parentage, perhaps Swedish and Syrian, yet his English was flawless, touched only by a slight, British accent. "She takes her beauty from her singularity," he said finally.

Behind Galloway, in the corner of the room where the plate glass met the wall, stood a man in a white caftan with a rifle held across his chest.

Following her eyes, Galloway said, "If she attacks

me, he will shoot her. If she has already struck, he will shoot me, so I do not feel the pain. He has his orders. The Amur always bites the throat. They can feel your pulse. Even from here, she can smell the valves of your heart opening and closing."

"How exceptional." The Purveyor arranged her face to reveal nothing.

"She is alone, as am I," Galloway said.

The Purveyor knew about lonely men and their needs, but Galloway was different.

"You are a wealthy woman," he went on. "But not wealthy enough, I think, to be without peers."

She tucked a strand of hair behind her ear, as she glanced over at Galloway. He wore loose linen, but beneath the fabric she could make out a lean, muscular frame.

"I am not as wealthy as you," she said.

"And you have taken up an unusual profession." A faint smile played across his handsome face.

She met his eyes. "I have built an empire," she said, lest he think she was a servant he could dress in Turkish robes and place in the corner like a palm plant.

"So you, too, are alone," he said.

She shrugged.

"There is someone more lonely than you and I, more unique than the leopard. Priceless beyond measure." He withdrew a piece of paper from his shirt pocket and held it out to her, a faded magazine article with black and white photographs. The Purveyor looked at the photograph and then back at Galloway, her face set in an expression that said…*so?*

"I would like them. For my collection." He gestured toward the window, the sweep of his hand taking in the sea and the sky and the leopard.

"It would be a monumental undertaking for my company." She paused. "We are not in the habit of this kind of selection, particularly of such a unique…" She paused, searching for the word Galloway would use to describe his prize. "Individuals."

"I would prefer that we do not lower ourselves by negotiating. You are a woman of the world, and you have your price." His voice grew fierce.

The Purveyor leaned forward. "How much are they worth to you?"

"There is no price that you can conceive that I cannot pay in triplicate." Galloway held a hand up. "To own something so rare is beyond calculation." He looked up, his eyes almost black against his sandstone complexion, a striking contrast to his thick white hair. "Can you put a price on the cell dividing only once along this line? Can you put a price on God?"

"I can," said the Purveyor. "It is my calling."

Chapter One

In Adair's dream, Helen was walking in the gentle surf of a Provincetown beach. White ruffles of ocean water were lapping at her feet while her sandals dangled from one hand. The sun was high. A breeze off the ocean cooled the air. The shore was littered with starfish. Adair stopped and picked one up to toss it back into the ocean. The underside of the starfish was gray and covered in mucous, a thousand foreshortened tentacles writhing in her hand. She dropped it.

Helen screamed. "Get it off me!" The starfish had landed on her foot and stuck. She kicked frantically. "It hurts!"

Adair seemed to move in slow motion as the words, "I'm sorry," drawled out of her.

Now the whole beach was seething with starfish. Helen screamed again and ripped at her leg where they swarmed, but when she tore at them they sank deep into her flesh. Her eyes were wide and dark with terror. "It hurts!"

Suddenly Helen was very far away, just a speck on the horizon, but her scream was close.

Adair jolted awake and blinked at the dim light. In front of her, suspended in the air like an apparition, a frantic green line beat across a black screen. She reached for Helen's warm body in the bed beside her. She felt a stab of pain in her arm. Then her hand connected with cold metal. She tried to speak, but she couldn't breathe. There was something in her throat, gagging her. Frantically, she tore at it. Pain stabbed through her hand again. A needle hit her bone. Slowly her situation became clearer…an IV…a tube in her mouth. He had her!

Marshal Drummond, the serial killer who had terrorized Pittock College, had found her, caught her, drugged her. She kicked her legs. The movement sent a sickening wave of pain through her body, but at least she still had her legs. He had not amputated them as he had tried to do to Helen Ivers…at least not yet. And where was Helen? This was not their inn by the beach. This was not the high, soft bed in which she had made love to Helen and Helen had whispered declarations of love to her.

With her free hand, Adair pulled out the IV. With both hands she fumbled with the contraption at her lips. It was some kind of a mask taped to her cheek. She tongued the tube in her mouth, retching as her throat tried to expel it. She pulled at the tape and then the tube. She felt it scraping deep inside her body, abrading her throat until she had pulled out a foot or more of tubing, the end of the tube disgorging a thick brown substance that smelled of protein powder and bran.

Above her on the ghostly green monitor, a red light flashed. Although Adair was not aware of a door opening, a second later a woman in a white uniform rushed to her bedside. Adair tried to rise.

"No, no, no," the woman said, pressing a hand to Adair's chest. The woman looked very young, a child really, with the dark complexion and narrow eyes of the Mung or perhaps an indigenous South American people. She held Adair down easily, although her arms were as thin as bird bones.

"Where am I?" Adair asked. A wave of nausea rolled over her. She tried to rise again, but could only manage to turn her head, vomiting more of the brown substance on her pillow.

"No, no," the woman whispered. "Shh. No move." She looked anxiously around the room. From somewhere beneath the bed, she grabbed a box of wet towelettes. She swabbed at Adair's face and mouth, all the while whispering "No, no, no," as though she were frightened of some unseen force.

Adair let her clean her face, but when the woman tried to reinsert the feeding tube, she struck her hands away.

The woman tried again, but her movements were as tentative as her heavily accented English. After another failed attempt she wrapped the tube around itself and tucked it away. A second later, Adair felt the sting of an auto-injector. Then the world went black.

❧❧❧❧

Adair woke after what felt like hours, but it might have been days, or perhaps only minutes. She was in a large parlor. Heavy tapestry curtains shrouded high windows. The walls were lined with inset bookshelves and heavy, leather-bound tomes. The ceiling above her head displayed an intricate filigree of hammered tin, and the crown moldings were carved like a Victorian rendition of pineapples. She lay in a hospital bed, the aluminum rails at odds with the antique décor. Someone had returned the IV to her arm but not the feeding tube. She was also aware of a catheter between her legs.

Primarily she was aware of the pain. It was like nothing she had experienced before. It was not the sharp agony of a broken bone from a riding accident. Nor was it the feverish, cleansing pain of hunger that had beset her after her mother had died and she had stopped eating. It was a pain that lived nowhere and everywhere. It was in the very fluid of her spine, in between vertebrae, in her blood, and in the air around her. It moved through her, and it reached deep inside her. She felt hollowed out in a way that was all body and not body at all. It was as though her soul had become an empty skin. Now someone scraped it with a cold stone and hung it up to dry, unrecognizable. She wanted to move, but moving was agony. She wanted to sleep, but sleeping and waking had blurred together.

"Help," she whispered.

She was drowning. She was dying. Marshal Drummond had poisoned her, and this was the end. Polonium. Dimethylmercury. Hemlock.

Even in her incapacitated state, she recalled Helen's dark eyes, her auburn hair. The slight imperfections of the skin of her hands, a freckle, a wrinkle, proof that she had lived. The vision cut through the pain. She had to find Helen. She had to find out what happened! "Help me!"

A moment later, a door opened. Adair held her breath waiting for Drummond's familiar face to appear.

"Merrill!"

It was her middle name, the name only her family called her.

A moment later, her sister-in-law, Cecelia, stepped into view. "How are you, Merrill?" Cecelia said with unnecessary cheer. "You're home. Do you know that? Do you recognize the West Parlor?"

Adair's eyelids drooped closed. She had not recognized the room, but now she associated it with some distant memory. Her mother. A Christmas party. A college girlfriend with long, black hair. The memories swirled behind her eyes, imperfect and grayed out, like a film that had been cut and bleached and spliced back together. It was too hard to think. Then Helen's face flashed across the screen, and her eyes flew open again. "What happened?" she whispered.

Cecelia pulled up a chair. In one hand she held a glass of water with a straw. "Try a drink."

Adair's throat constricted. She coughed, and the water spilled down her neck. Cecelia set the glass on the bedside table and touched Adair's chin with a tissue.

"What...?" Adair tried to signal her questions with her eyes.

Cecelia watched, her dark hair haloed by light from an amber light fixture above. She wore bright red lipstick. Adair closed her eyes against its brilliance. She had known Cecelia her whole life. They had been in boarding school together. They had broken a horse together, a vicious Arabian named Take Five Sterling. Cecelia had given her her first taste of cocaine. They had been other things to each other as well. Lovers, some people would call it, although that was never a word Adair used. Then Cecelia married Cyrus and became inextricably, eternally part of the family.

Now she and Adair were here, and Adair could not make sense of the pain.

"You've been ill." Cecelia smiled at her tenderly.

"You're on a special kind of drug therapy. That's what the IV is for. We're taking good care of you. You don't have to worry about anything. Just rest."

Adair felt sleep pulling at her, dragging her down, but when she closed her eyes, she saw Helen. She forced her eyes open. "Where is she?" She held onto the image of Helen's face. If Drummond had killed Helen, if he had hurt her, Adair would have to rise out of the hospital bed.

She felt a surge of adrenaline push the pain away. She could rise. She did not need the heart monitor to chart the pounding in her chest. If she was indeed in the Wilson estate, she could limp to the gun safe where she kept the arsenal her brother Cyrus had bought for her over the years. The tiny Seacamp. The Kel Tec shotgun. Ridiculous gifts for a thirty-something theater professor with family money and a job at a sleepy Berkshire college. Had he somehow seen into the future? Foretold that provost Marshal Drummond would fixate on Helen, would "love" her in his own sick way, and that Adair would have to remove the Kel Tec, load the magazine, and try to remember the lessons Cyrus had given her when she was just a girl shooting hay bales late in the summer twilight? She would remember. Even as the pain gutted her belly, she remembered. She would kill Marshal Drummond.

She rolled over and vomited onto her pillow again. "Please." Her whisper was thick and wet.

"Helen is at Pittock," Cecelia said, her voice icy.

"Is she…okay?"

Cecelia glanced away. "I presume."

Adair searched her profile for a lie. "And Drummond?" Adair's mouth burned. "Did he get her? Did he hurt her?"

Cecelia turned back to her and laid a cool hand on Adair's cheek. The sharp smell of Cecelia's perfume caught in Adair's throat.

"Drummond is in the State Hospital." Cecelia's lips were the bright red of a do not enter sign. "Nothing happened to Helen Ivers."

Relief flooded Adair's eyes with tears, and with the tears her strength ebbed.

"Rest." Cecelia stroked her face.

Adair fell back into her writhing dreams.

Chapter Two

When Adair woke again, she was surrounded by people. She sensed that they were discussing her. She forced her eyes open, and her vision cleared. Cecelia stood by the side of her bed again. Beside her stood Adair's eldest brother, Montague, and beside him stood, their middle brother Cyrus. At the foot of the bed stood a tall man with the sun-bleached hair and light tan of a surfer or a marathoner. He wore a white coat and checked the papers attached to a metal clipboard with practiced efficiency.

"The doctor is here to see you," Cecelia said.

"How is she?" Monty asked.

Cecelia touched Adair's forehead.

Cyrus fidgeted with the sleeves of his suit which were too short. His arms were also short and ape-like. It seemed the tailor exaggerated his proportions.

"You're probably wondering what's going on here," the doctor said to Adair. He stuck out his hand, but she did not have the strength to lift hers. He squeezed it. "It's called Persistent Complex Pain Syndrome or PCPS. You're one of the most interesting cases I've seen." He sounded excited.

Cyrus coughed into his fist.

The doctor lowered his voice into a gentle drawl. "Don't you worry. We're going to take good care of you. How much do you remember?"

Adair shook her head slightly.

"That's probably for the best," the doctor said. "Do you want me to explain? Do you feel up to a little conversation?"

Adair nodded.

Cecelia pulled up a chair for the doctor. He sat beside Adair and took her hand again. His hand was cool, and his touch made her bones ache.

"Persistent Complex Pain Syndrome is a very rare form of Complex Regional Pain Syndrome. Have you heard of that? Most people haven't. It's an amplified musculoskeletal pain syndrome. It usually occurs when someone has suffered an injury, particularly a crushing injury. We see it in industrial accidents. What happens is that the actual injury heals, perhaps by way of an amputation. But the body keeps responding as though the trauma is new." The doctor kept his voice modulated, professional. "The limb swells. There is pain. Heat. Often the skin thins or becomes brittle. The symptoms spread. There is neurogenic inflammation, vasomotor dysfunction, and maladaptive neuroplasticity."

The recitation went on. Adair tried to follow the litany of technical terms.

"It happens when the brain changes and adapts to the constant pain signals. Persistent Complex Pain Syndrome occurs when those symptoms are present and affect the internal organs and the connective tissue. It's an amplified version of the syndrome."

Adair pulled her hand away from the doctor's cool grip. "How?" she whispered.

"We think it's related to your injury."

Adair could not remember the days between Provincetown and the West Parlor, but she clearly remembered the day Marshal Drummond shot her.

The case had been closed. Drummond's son, Ricky, had been arrested for the murder of Adair's student, Carrie Brown, a homeless woman named Crystal Leigh Evans, and old Professor Lebovetski. On paper, everything was resolved, but Helen had been skeptical. She had returned to the abandoned Pittock Asylum on a hunch, hoping the building would yield its secrets. Drummond had followed her. He would have imprisoned her in the basement of the asylum and amputated her legs with his crude instruments, except that Sully the Fortuneteller, the town's resident madwoman, had warned Adair.

Adair had been sitting outside the Craven Bar and Grill with her friend Patrick. Sully appeared, reeking of alcohol and ranting. "He has your lover under the grate. The isolation ward. They pluck out your soul. The syringe. It's filled with water, and when they pull it out, it's filled with your soul. Hurry! He will cut her."

The waiter had tried to push her away. "I'll call the cops, Sully." Everyone in town knew her.

"Call them!" Her yellow eyes flared open. "He has the saw."

Adair knew what Sully was saying. She yelled for Patrick to call the police. Then she ran. She flew up the stairs to her penthouse at the nearby Grandville Hotel, praying she remembered the combination to the small gun safe. It had been years since she handled a weapon. When she opened the safe, the magazine felt like a toy, a Pez cartridge jammed into the handle of her Glock. Was it enough? Could it possibly be enough? She was fit, and she ran all the time, but it was over a mile to the Asylum, and her heart was exploding as she careened through the open door to the main foyer.

Helen and Drummond looked up. So poised. So calm. Drummond in his sport coat. Helen in a trim, high-waisted suit. A portrait of respectability.

"Adair, I know this has been hard for you," Drummond said, all false compassion.

A moment later he shot her.

The body armor, another odd gift from Cyrus, had saved her life.

Now the doctor with the sun-bleached hair spoke to her with the same paternal care. "Your friend, Ms. Ivers, she said you were feeling ill, so she brought you back to the estate. Your family wasn't overly worried. You had been through so much. But the next morning, you didn't get up. Mr. Ubol, the house manager, sent a woman servant to check on you. He thought perhaps you had had too much to drink the night before."

Adair scanned the faces that hovered above her. Cecelia, Monty, and the doctor had arranged their faces in a look of calm sympathy. Cyrus crossed his arms and glowered.

"Your kidneys were failing," the doctor said, matter-of-factly.

"What can you do for her?" Cyrus asked, moving his bulk into the doctor's space as though he needed to threaten an answer out of him.

"Prior to now, the prognosis would not have looked good, I'll be honest. But we have reason to be hopeful." The doctor smiled at Adair. Then he stood and examined the IV bag that hung beside her bed. "We're testing a new drug. A high dose of Trando Sodium Veraluronate or Texidol, delivered straight to the bloodstream. Your sister-in-law has worked tirelessly to get you on the trial." He glanced at Cecelia. "She wouldn't take no for an answer. It has taken her months."

"Months?" Adair rose up on one elbow, nausea washing over her. She felt the catheter, pulling at the soft flesh between her legs. "How long have I been…?"

"She needs to rest," Cyrus said.

"How long?"

"Almost three months," Cecelia said.

"I need to call Helen. I need a phone," Adair said.

Cyrus reached into his pocket. "Use mine."

"Cy!" Cecelia took the phone from her husband's hand and returned it to her own pocket. "She's not a child. I think she needs a phone she can keep. I'll get you one, Merrill. I don't know where yours is, but I'll have your number switched to a new one."

With that, the foursome exited the parlor.

❧ ❧ ❧ ❧

Sometime later, Cecelia returned with a phone. She sat down in the chair the doctor had vacated, her hand resting on the bed rail. "Who are you going to call?"

"Helen."

Cecelia turned away. For a moment, Adair thought she was not going to give her the phone.

"Please, Cecelia. She has to know."

Cecelia ran two fingers down Adair's cheek and along her neck, across her collar bone, under the collar of the loose, white shirt the nurse had tied around Adair's body.

Adair tried to recoil. "You're married to my brother!"

Cecelia let her fingers linger. "But I remember you."

"We were kids," Adair said, closing her eyes. She could not escape the imprint of Cecelia's bright red lipstick searing into her retina.

"We were twenty," Cecelia said. "I helped you. I could help you again."

Before Adair realized what was happening, Cecelia threw the sheet off her, and gripped her nipple through her thin shirt. She pressed it between knuckle and thumb, squeezing and twisting. "You're in so much pain," Cecelia whispered. "I can help you."

"Stop," Adair cried. She saw Helen's face float across her vision just as the pain of Cecelia's pinch turned the world orange. "No." But this time, her voice was nothing more than a sigh, because the pain of Cecelia's touch cut a bright, hot line across the pain of her illness. A real pain. A sharp pain. The pain of PCPS covered her soul with cold ashes. Like a parasite, it consumed her until it alone occupied her body and mind. This pain brought her back to herself. It outlined the place where her soul lived. It reached through the animal body and made her soul flare up in rage.

She knew that pain. She knew Cecelia's face flushed with triumph.

When Cecelia released her, she felt a moment of clarity before her illness clouded her mind again. "I can't, Cecelia. We can't do that. You married my brother. I have to call Helen."

Cecelia stood, the phone in her hand. She looked toward the window. "I don't want you to call her, Merrill."

Adair did not want to fight. "Please."

"It's not what you think." Cecelia gave a sharp laugh. "Maybe it's that too, but...oh, Merrill." She sat down again. "I know how much you care about her.

          Karelia Stetz-Waters

You cried out for her when you were so sick. And you were right not to marry me. I make a terrible wife." She cradled the phone in her hands. "We're all terrible here. Me and Cyrus and Monty. You wanted a real love, someone you didn't buy, someone who didn't love you for all this." She glanced up at the crown moldings. "You wanted your *own* life."

"What is it, Cecelia?" Adair felt inexpressibly weary.

"She came here, Merrill!" Cecelia's voice was suddenly taut with anger. "She saw you. God! You were hooked up to so many tubes and fluids and machines. She stayed for a day. We offered her a room in the house, but she said she needed to think. She got a hotel. I called her." She brushed at her eye. "We thought you were going to die. I called her to see if she would come to say goodbye. She said she would, but she never did. I called Pittock College a few days later, and her secretary said she was there, but she was too busy to talk."

"Patrick?"

"I don't know. She never called back." Cecelia paused. "She doesn't want you broken, Merrill. She doesn't want this." Cecelia's gesture took in the hospital bed, the bottles of prescription pills on the end table, the smell of urine. "I'll have a nurse come clean you up." She set the phone on Adair's chest, then stood and left without another word.

When Adair dialed Helen's number it rang directly to voicemail. Patrick's did also.

Chapter Three

No one told the Purveyor when Galloway's first payment went through. It was too expertly done. Some of her off shore holdings rose in value. Three Cayman Islands accounts were merged into one and, in the process, tripled in value. Last year's interest on an IRA was adjusted making the net profit well over $250,000. Many small sums. Handled discretely. Galloway had convinced her he could do it.

She called him from an encrypted laptop he had given her. It had no recognizable operating system, only a black screen on which she typed a few lines of code. The screen cleared to reveal an interface like Skype, but without the friendly bubble font and sidebar of contacts. A few minutes later Galloway's face appeared, slightly pixilated. The Purveyor could see nothing behind him. She too had cleared her surroundings of identifiable marks, choosing to make the call from a garret office hidden behind a fake wall.

"I'm impressed," she said. "You've handled the transfer very gracefully."

"You didn't think I would run a million dollars in cash through some Indian casino, did you?" Galloway smiled. "I'm not the mob."

He was more powerful than a mob. He was also very handsome, even through the pixilation. Had he simply wanted a woman, he could have had a thousand beauties. There was nothing he could not acquire on his own, except for this.

"Do you have them?" Galloway asked.

There was no impatience in his question.

"We have not acquired them yet," the Purveyor said, equally calm.

The Purveyor had dealt with men who were impatient, desperate. She had heard them grunting as they jerked off, even as they tried to command her over the phone. Business men rutting like animals. She never visited these men in their anonymous hotel rooms. If she sent an emissary it was Bolo, her henchman, as she had come to think of him. She did not fear attack as much as she loathed their sweat.

Galloway was different.

"I much prefer you handle this slowly and carefully," he said. "I trust you are in no hurry for the rest of the funds. No great debts you must pay off?"

"Mr. Galloway, I'm not in the mob." She let a smile slip across her face, and Galloway returned it. They were flirting, but it had nothing to do with sex.

"I do not want a media scandal following their disappearance," Galloway added.

"I can't imagine that the media could reach you."

It was easy talking to Galloway, but she knew she could not manipulate him like the other men she sold to. So many of her customers tried to play the good husband, the good father. They doted on their families and then bought their daughters' likeness a hundred times over. It made them weak. They were forever standing beside a live wire. "How is your wife?" the Purveyor would ask. "How old is little Angelique now?"

Such innocuous questions, but they were the end of every negotiation, as surely as a knife to the jugular. Galloway had no family. He did not pretend.

"The media," Galloway said, "is like a picture frame hung crookedly. It is such a small thing, but it mars a room." The pixilation on the screen increased. For a moment Galloway disappeared. "The issue that is beyond negotiation is their safety. I want them whole. Physically. Spiritually. If I find that someone has tampered with them, I will find that man and have him killed."

The Purveyor raised her hand. "You did not hire me because you think my men would assault these girls."

"Indeed, I did not. But yours is a rough trade, no matter how fine the salesman."

The Purveyor felt the warmth of his compliment.

"I do not want them traumatized. I do not want them thrown in the back of some airless van." Galloway put his hands together as if in prayer, resting his lips on the tips of his fingers. "But we have already talked of this. I trust you. Just remember, I want their souls intact. I did not ask you for a seashell. I asked you for the ocean."

Chapter Four

The days passed like marks carved on a prison wall. The Wilson estate was gorgeous in the fall. Adair rose a few times to see the colors flare on Wyatt's Bluff, wheeling the IV beside her. Then she fell back into her hospital bed, pulling the railing up like a security blanket. Cecelia visited her every day, and Adair often had the impression that Cecelia watched her while she slept, but she could never be sure. Except for the few times she leaned on the windowsill and looked out at the hills, she could not tell if she was waking or sleeping, living or dead. Cyrus visited her occasionally, standing at her bed like an awkward suitor, hands clasped behind his back. "Are you in pain?" he asked each time he visited.

"Yes," Adair breathed.

Unlike Cecelia and the sun-bleached doctor, Cyrus never said anything cheerful or comforting. For that Adair was grateful.

❧❧❧❧

It was early winter by the time Adair was finally able to get up for more than a few minutes at a time, more than a few days in a row. She didn't feel better, but she felt stronger. It was as though her body had adjusted to the constant pain by dampening all her senses, or perhaps it was the Texidol. The Texidol worked—if one could say it worked at all—in a cycle of numbness and withdrawal. First, her body would be suffused with the alien pains of the PCPS. Then the doctor would replenish the IV bag. The Texidol would knock the pain into a distant region of her brain where it was bearable, but with it the Texidol took all sensation. Sounds were muffled. Her skin felt thick. Everything tasted metallic. Only her sense of smell remained. And those were the good times. There was always a point when the pain would return, moving through the numbness.

Adair had come to imagine the cycle like a seesaw. Every day she walked up and down the inclined plain of the seesaw. She would be feeling better, at least feeling dead instead of feeling pain, then suddenly the pain would return, breaking through the numbness, as though she had just stepped over the halfway point on the seesaw and crashed to the ground. Then there was nothing to do but repeat the dose and increase it.

Cecelia had offered her three lines of exceptionally pure cocaine on a Tiffany & Co. hand mirror, and Adair had accepted, although she had always disliked the way Cecelia snorted cocaine. She hated the way Cecelia touched her nose furtively but obsessively. It made Adair think of the blood pounding beneath the thin membrane of her septum. It was like watching a needle pierce the skin. She didn't care now, but whatever receptors had once accepted the drug into her brain were dead or dying. It had no effect on her.

She rose and dressed and sat by the window holding her mother's hardbound copy of the complete works of Shakespeare. Outside, the grounds lay blanketed under snow. Adair wondered if the first snow had arrived at Pittock. Classes were always canceled for the first snow. She could almost see the students racing from their dormitories, their scarves flapping, their mittens scattering. Some of the boys would wear bathrobes over their winter clothes, and the girls would laugh at them, and they would beam. Winter's Table the celebration was called. The dining halls served pancakes all day, and the students raced elaborately decorated sleds down the hill near the Pittock Asylum.

Adair remembered standing on the edge of the race with a few of the younger faculty members, chatting and bumping each other's shoulders and pretending a great rivalry over the sledders from the Ventmore Dormitory, and the science majors from Boston Hall. There had been a film professor, a woman about her age, who had brought cognac. They passed it back and forth and laughed each other into tears with their melodramatic attempts to hide the flask from Bruno Duffy, the dean of Arts and Humanities.

Now, looking across the Versailles garden shrouded in white, she could not remember her colleagues' names. Even if she could, she realized they could not be friends. There was no common ground on which they could stand—the professors and their bucolic life, her and her pain.

She took the cell phone out of her pocket and dialed Helen's number again. It rang to voicemail. Then she rose, holding onto the windowsill for support. The room spun. Her stomach heaved with a nausea that was deeper than food and bile. She edged her way around the room, passing each of ten windows, touching each window ledge for balance. On the other side of the parlor her laptop rested on a large roll top desk. It had been a gift from Cecelia, wrapped in a cream-colored box and tied with an enormous gray velvet ribbon. She had only used it for one thing, and Helen had not responded to any of her emails. Now she sat in front of the black screen, her finger hovering over the power button.

What could she possibly type? What could she beg of Helen when an army of mute nursing staff worked day and night to rid the parlor of her smells? When her mouth tasted of metal and her body ached inextricably and she could not concentrate enough to read plays she had once memorized? What could she ask for? If Helen came back, she would bar her from the sick room.

At that thought, she dropped her face in her hands and sobbed, wracked by a bone deep sadness for all the things she would not experience again. She cried for Helen's beautiful body, the slight softness that settled around her hips and belly, the line of blond hair that bisected Helen's stomach, her lips, her sex. And she cried for her own body, whole and strong, for the smell of good sweat, for the flush of running, for the heat of summer and for the clean ozone smell of snow. For the speed of a sled racing downhill, for her students laughter, for her lips damp on a friend's flask because no one cared about germs or sickness. For the spring.

Which she knew, suddenly and entirely, she would not see.

꧁ ꧂

And then it was late winter, the snow melting off the rooftop, crocuses breaking through the ice, the anniversary of her mother's death. Adair understood that she had been waiting for it the way geese remember the south. She had barely kept track of the weeks, let alone the days. But there it was. She did not have to consult the calendar. Her body knew.

She sat down at the desk and pushed the laptop aside. Slowly, she pulled out the top drawer. Her mother's fountain pen lay inside, the ink long dried. There was also a stack of creamy stationary and a Mont Blanc ballpoint that the nurses used to make notes on her chart. She scratched the pen to life on the blotter and began:

> *Dearest Helen,*
> *Why have you forsaken me? I loved you. I needed you. I woke up and you were gone, and I was afraid. They say PCPS is an autoimmune disorder. I thought that if you could only have held me somehow my body would not have betrayed me.*

She wrote for a long time, her words slanting off the page. Then she crumpled the paper and threw it in the trash. She tried again.

> *I am glad that you did not stay to see what has happened to me.*

She thought of the IV, the feeding tube, the bouts of nausea, and worse of all, the sense that she was barely present in her own mind.

> *In the end, I suppose it is best that you did not stay. I wanted you to come to me, but I don't now. I know how deeply your sister's death affected you. I know you felt responsible. Please know that you are not responsible for what I am going to do today. This is not the slamming closed of a book. The book that was my life ended with Drummond's bullet. Everything has burnt to ash. This is but a shred of paper drifting over*

the flames.

Please be careful. Marshal Drummond is an evil man, and he is powerful. He will find a way out, and he will come for you again. My only regret is that I do not have the strength to go after him and to kill him. If there was anything left of the woman I once was, he would be dead. Know that I have loved you deeply and that your memory is the only good thing remaining to me.

Yours,
Adair

PS: If you are curious, my family can explain the details of my medical condition to you. I prefer that you do not know, but I will not be there to protest.

Adair addressed the envelope to Helen Ivers at Pittock College, Pittock MA. She had forgotten the zip code, so she added "Berkshire County" beneath the state. She sealed the envelope, tucked it in her pants pocket, then pulled the needle out of the IV port that the doctor had planted in her arm.

Dressed in a heavy wool overcoat, Adair trudged along the slushy paths of the Versailles garden, down to the stables. Inside, the large building was warm and smelled of hay. The stable master was gone, and a young man of about twenty lounged behind a makeshift desk, thumbing his phone. He jumped to attention when Adair entered.

"Can you ready a horse for me?" she asked.

"Yes ma'am. Right away."

He didn't seem to recognize her as anything more than part of the family. She was relieved. The nursing staff would have alerted Cecelia the minute she stepped outside, but the boy just smiled and asked which one.

"Do we still have Naples Peach?" It occurred to Adair the old Clydesdale might have been sold or shot. It had been several years since she rode out from the Wilson's stables.

"Yes ma'am."

"How is she?"

"Slow ma'am, and stubborn."

"Fit?"

"She'll outlive me." He smiled.

"Saddle her up then. A western with an extra saddle pad."

A few minutes later, the boy returned, leading the giant horse.

Adair lifted her hands to the horse's massive head and pressed her lips to its nose. She closed her eyes holding back the tears.

"Where you going?" the boy asked.

"Nowhere. Just getting out to enjoy the air," Adair said, but she had chosen the exact location. Wyatt's Bluff. A flat, hilltop meadow open on one side to the valley with a forty foot drop.

"Be careful how you tie her," the boy said. "She's a real Houdini."

"I know, but she's a good girl," Adair said, pressing her cheek to the horse's neck.

"She always finds her way back home." That was why Adair picked Naples Peach. The horse was wise enough not to follow her over Wyatt's Bluff, wise enough to simply wander back to the stables, the reigns neatly tied up behind the pummel so they would not tangle in any loose branches on her solitary walk home.

"One last thing," Adair said. "Will you post this letter for me? It needs to go out today.

Chapter Five

Helen Ivers sat at her desk in Meyerbridge Hall. It was a bleak spring day in the Berkshires. The temperature was warm enough to turn the paths on the Pittock campus to slush. The quad was still covered in piles of dirty gray snow. The oak trees were bare, and the cherry blossoms had been knocked down by the previous night's storm. Around the edges of the academic halls, crocuses lay crushed beneath the weight of the snow that slid off the roofs.

Helen opened her calendar screen and scanned the day's events. A conference call with the University of Massachusetts about their new transfer compact. A meeting with the president of the local community college. Lunch with the accreditation team. Two hours budgeted for negotiations with the faculty association. She sighed. Every day was different, yet it was still boring.

Helen opened the window behind her desk and took out a pack of cigarettes. She drew in a breath of smoke. It was an old habit left over from her teenage years when she had taken up smoking on the porch at night to avoid her sister Eliza.

Feebly, Helen's mother had pleaded with her not to smoke.

"Then get her out of my room," Helen had countered because at night Eliza would stand over Helen's bed while she slept, clutching a Bible.

"I know. I know," her mother said, but the two inch deadbolt her father installed in her bedroom door lasted only a week. Eliza crashed through it one night, dislocating her shoulder and sending a shard of molding across the room with such force it had cut Helen on the forehead and left a fine, white scar. So Helen had smoked every night from age fifteen to seventeen, then gave it up the day she left home. She had not smoked again until the day she knew for certain that Adair had left her.

Even now, she felt her fingers reaching out to dial Adair's phone number. How many times had she called in the past months? A hundred? A thousand?

"That shit will kill you," her friend and secretary, Patrick Jaycee, yelled from the front lobby. "Don't think I can't smell it just because you opened a window." She heard Patrick get up and open the door to Meyerbridge Hall. He greeted the mailman as he did. They exchanged "nice days," and then Helen heard the slap of a large stack of mail hitting Patrick's desk.

The sounds were so familiar, she could picture the entire scene from her seat at her desk.

"This one's addressed to Helen Ivers. Pittock College, The Berkshires," the mailman said, undoubtedly holding it up for Patrick's perusal.

"Oh, one of them!" Patrick said. "Let me see it."

The mailman carried on with his pleasantries, but Patrick fell silent.

Helen finished her cigarette, crushed the embers out on the sill of the open window, and put the butt in a mason jar in her desk drawer.

She wandered into the foyer of the chapel-turned-administrative building. Sometimes the renovation still struck her as sacrilegious. At other times, she saw Patrick resting in the glow of the stained glass rose window and thought it was perfectly appropriate. A slightly balding angel, a purple shirt over his barrel chest and tucked into khaki cargo shorts, a matching purple Bluetooth in his ear. She had been raised catholic. She knew the Bible. Angels never appeared as people expected them. "What have we got today?" Helen asked wearily.

Patrick looked up. "You can't smoke in the building. You gotta quit that shit." He didn't seem to have his heart in the anti-smoking campaign. He looked back at an envelope in his hands.

"Another nut case?" Helen asked.

They had both been on edge. Marshal Drummond's arrest and sentencing to the State Hospital, under an insanity plea, had not alleviated the anxiety that hung in the office like Helen's cigarette smoke. The students seemed impervious to it. Even some of the faculty seemed to dismiss the events like any other college scandal. But Helen was always scanning her inbox for threats, the mail for odd letters. The blinking voicemail light on her phone still filled her with apprehension. Sometimes she wondered if she actually wanted another crisis, something to relieve the monotony of waiting.

Patrick looked worried.

"What is it?"

"Helen Ivers. Pittock College. The Berkshires," he said, holding up the letter.

Helen felt as though the blood had drained out of her body. "It's her handwriting." She had only known Adair Wilson for a few months, had only known her intimately for mere days before she disappeared. But she had noticed Adair's writing on a stack of student papers and been struck by the hand, both masculine and Victorian in its flourishes. Like the handwriting on the envelope.

"I'm sure it's not," Patrick said, handing her the letter.

Their eyes met.

"I…" Helen could not finish the sentence. It had been almost a year since Adair had commissioned a limousine to drive Helen from the Cape back to Pittock and a helicopter to fly herself back to the Wilson Estate in New Hampshire.

"I just need to see my brothers for a few days," Adair had said, cheerfully, casually. "Make sure Cyrus doesn't do something dumb and heroic."

"Like shut down Pittock College?" Helen had asked.

Adair's shrug said *maybe*. "He worries about me. He always has. He just doesn't know how to do it right, you know?" She smiled. "He's like a big dog that bites your date because they hug you. I'll be back in a week."

Helen could still see Adair silhouetted against the chopper, and behind that, the flat blue infinity of the Atlantic Ocean. Adair wore black slacks, spike heels, and a short-sleeved shirt made of black calfskin leather, with a silver zipper up the front. It would have been a bizarre outfit on anyone else, but it was stunning on Adair.

Two days later, Helen had received an email from her saying she would be staying in New Hampshire a bit longer than expected. Her responses to Helen's emails were curt. She did not return Helen's calls. Finally, Adair wrote to say she would not be coming back to

Pittock College. She hoped Helen would forward her resignation to HR. She did not even mention their relationship. After that, every email Helen sent was returned "undeliverable." Every phone call she placed rang to an impersonal computer greeting reciting the number.

When Helen drove up to the Wilson Estate, a stern Asian butler told her Miss Wilson was traveling. He did not know when she would return. Helen had driven an hour south before she started to cry. Then her tears were a deluge. She pulled over to the side of the highway, insensitive to the semi-trucks that hurtled past her. She had been a fool. She was just a working-class girl from a sad Pittsburg family. The daughter of a house painter. Her sister's caretaker. She had become one of those plain, bitter, dutiful women who mortgaged their life for others or for position, then ended up alone, taking Saturday crafting workshops at Jo-Ann Fabrics, talking about "me time." She had met women like this, even in the higher echelons of college administration, and she avoided them as much as she could, as though their loneliness would rub off on her. Then, in the horror and feverish excitement that surrounded the Pittock murders, she thought that she could be Adair's lover. She thought that was the life she had been moving towards.

But she had meant nothing to Adair. A fling. A dalliance. A one night stand. A mistake. Adair had not fallen in love with her, Adair had fallen in love with the adrenaline that coursed through the campus, the excitement whose absence left Helen as bored as she was anxious.

These realizations had broken her heart and left her whole body flushed with shame.

Now Helen stared at the envelope on her desk. She lit another cigarette. Her hands trembled. It was probably just an old woman writing to complain about the students tromping across her lawn, or a goth kid with pretentious handwriting. She smoothed the surface of the envelope. It felt like cream. She lifted it to her nose, but she could only smell the cigarette smoke on her fingertips. Then Helen did what she had always done and moved inexorably forward into duty. Open the letter. Read it. Discard it. Accept the call from UMass. Try to forget.

She slit the edge of the envelope with a letter opener, pulled out the letter, and froze.

Dearest Helen.

It was like finding her sister Eliza again. She stared at Adair's careful, imperfect handwriting.

I am glad that you did not stay to see what has happened to me.

For a moment, a calm voice inside Helen's mind said, *this is incorrect, and I will fix it. I will call her and tell her that there has been a mistake.* All crises were solvable. Even Eliza's death had, in some way, been a solution. Even Carrie Brown's death was just a mystery to be solved. She would just…"No," Helen said aloud.

Please know that you are not responsible for what I am going to do today.

Then for the first time in months, Helen heard Eliza's voice. *Help me, Helen!* She grabbed the letter and the envelope and ran for the door of Meyerbridge Hall. She didn't care who saw her as long as they did not try to stop her.

The book that was my life ended with Drummond's bullet.

She ran across the main quad, slipping on patches of ice, then ran past the library, between the science building, and past the frozen fountain in the science courtyard. She nearly fell as she raced down the steeply sloped service road that led to the playing fields. It didn't matter. She crossed Barrow Creek, ran the length of the rugby pitch and then half ran, half clambered, up the hill that led to the asylum. She stopped only when it came into sight, three stories, four wings, all arranged in perfect symmetry, a beautiful, monstrous palace dusted with snow, rising out of its own ruin, the windows shattered, the leafless ivy pulling at its turrets.

Helen fell to the ground in the overgrown rose garden. She knelt in the snow, insensitive to the ice beneath her knees, clutching the letter to her chest as though to staunch blood from a wound.

Adair had waited for her, and now she was dead.

Her mind reeled. Had she misread Adair's curt emails? When the messages started coming back undelivered, had she somehow forgotten the address? Mistyped it a hundred times? Had Adair called out for help? When she had phoned Adair, had she misdialed? Called a work number? An old cell phone? Had she made some terrible mistake? All the time she had spent reaching out for Adair, had Adair been reaching out for her too?

My only regret is that I do not have the strength to go after him and to kill him.

For a long time, Helen was aware of nothing but her own breathing and her grief. It was possible that a pair of joggers had run by and waved to her. There might have been a trio of students who whispered, "I think that's the president." She did not know. The first thing to bring her out of her own mind was the weight of Patrick's hand on her shoulder.

"Let me see it," he said.

Helen was still gripping the letter. She did not move. She couldn't. She had hallucinated before. After her sister's suicide, she had seen Eliza everywhere. Perhaps she had dreamed the letter. As long as she held it, the words might not be true. They might not be there. She might unfold it, and see "Dear College President...an invitation...the next annual conference."

Patrick reached over and touched the paper.

"No!" Helen's voice echoed off the walls of the asylum.

"Helen," Patrick murmured. "What is it?"

"She's dead." Helen sobbed, a raw, animal cry. "It was Cyrus. He kept me from her." She pushed the letter at Patrick, suddenly loath to touch it. "After Adair was shot last fall, I went up to the Wilson's house. You remember. You told me to go after her. I went up to their mansion, and her brothers treated me like some sort of interloper. Her older brother, Monty, told me he didn't want me to see her, but it was Cyrus who hated me. I could tell. He looked like a brute, like some bouncer who was going to take me out back and beat me if I didn't do what they wanted. He must have kept us apart. You know I tried to call her. You know I did. I did everything I could." She wasn't pleading with Patrick. Maybe she was pleading with God. "They told me she was traveling. They made their butler tell me she was gone, and now she's dead."

Patrick unfolded the letter and read it silently. Then he sighed and nodded.

"She's dead!" Helen's voice was shrill.

"I know."

"Did you know before now?"

"No, but…yes." Patrick put his arm around Helen's shoulder. She stiffened, but he pulled her closer, closing his other arm around her. "I didn't know, but when we didn't hear from her…I knew." He reached into his cargo pocket. "I brought your cigarettes," he said producing the pack. He even held the lighter for her. She smoked until the heaving in her chest subsided.

"I have to call Terri. He'll be able to find out what happened to her. I have to know. I did this to her," Helen said. "She needed me, and somehow I didn't know it. I couldn't reach her."

Patrick nodded again, but it wasn't a *yes*. "Adair's always had problems," he said finally. His voice held none of its usual jovial lisp. "You only knew Adair for a little while. I loved her too. Shit. But there was never a time when I didn't think this would happen eventually. Adair's always been in trouble. You haven't seen that, because that time at Pittock, before Marshal Drummond, that was the best time of her life. That was the happiest and strongest she had ever been, but she had a lot of problems, and people like you and me, we couldn't help her." He took her hand. "Listen to me, Helen. Don't think that you could have saved her."

From the diary of Charity Kimball

I remember.

We were seven years old and running with a shotgun clutched in my sister's hand.

"Do you want to eat venison again?" Mother called after our protests.

We didn't like shooting rabbits even though Mother cooked them with acorns and the house smelled of stew and woods, and the dogs played with the pelts. Prudence always loved the dogs, especially the gray giant named Blue that Daddy rescued from the fights because he said Blue had Christian eyes.

So we ran down the mountain, our arms spread wide, the shotgun in Prudence's hand, the bullets in my left pocket. It was February and the air was cold, but I didn't feel it because I had Prudence. And we ran, laughing and stumbling, and it was like our arms were laced around each other's waists, closer than lovers, although we did not know that word yet.

Then Prudence stopped.

"Charity, there!" she said.

She saw a rabbit. I thought it was too far, but Prudence said I was the best shot in the fold. We wedged the rifle against her shoulder. She eyed the scope. I steadied the barrel with my hand. She rested her index finger beside the trigger. I braced for the explosion that always frightened me, although Prudence said it was like God coughing, and we should never be afraid of anything that came from God. Even the cold, or the coyotes howling, or the dark look that got into Blue's eyes sometimes. Not even the squall of blood and entrails when we hit a rabbit.

"God provides for the lilies of the field," Prudence said as she scooped up the animal and put it in the bag Mother gave us. "He provides. But we can't wait for him to chew our food for us."

I knew Prudence had learned that from Mother. It bothered me that she recited it so quickly. But then, we were seven. Everything was recitation.

❧❧❧❧

A moment later, Prudence pulled us up short. She eyed another rabbit on the horizon. She cocked the rifle. Then she stopped. I was waiting for the blast.

"Come on," I whispered. "Shoot."

"No," Prudence said. "See?"

She moved forward, drawing me with her. When we got close enough for me to see, I saw that, along with its two hind legs and two front legs and its head, there was another, smaller head. That head had no ears, but it had brown eyes that looked at us in fear.

"Just shoot it," I squealed.

"Shut up," Prudence said. Then she reached over and did something she had never done before. She pinched me, hard on my upper arm where only I could feel it. She pinched with her nails until I looked for blood to come through my jacket, even though our plaid coats were thick.

I started to cry, and Prudence looked at me sideways. We could never really face each other, and I was aware of that suddenly, for the first time.

"What is it?" I asked, afraid, feeling that the rabbit was more than a rabbit. It was like in church when Pastor would read us stories from the Bible. He told us that they meant more than they meant, and that there were no good stories, except the stories that pointed to God. "Is this a story that points to God?" I whispered.

"Yes," Prudence said and turned so quickly, I felt our pelvic bones cry out in pain as her torso shifted away from mine.

"Where are we going?" I asked.

"Home."

"Without the rabbit?"

"Without *that* rabbit."

Chapter Six

From her seat on a bale of hay, Adair watched Cecelia as she leaned back and forth in the saddle of Shen Yun, a massive black Andalusian stallion, testing the saddle's give. Back at the estate, Montague and Cyrus were at work in the large hall they referred to as the board room. Another merger. A real estate deal gone sour.

It's wrong. For the thousandth time Adair remembered the seconds she had spent at the edge of Wyatt's Bluff and wished that she had jumped. *It's wrong.* The familiar pain ground away at her spine.

"Well, Merrill?" Cecelia asked. "Are you coming?"

Cecelia's dark hair cascaded out from beneath her riding helmet. In one gloved hand she held the reigns; in the other she gripped a riding crop, tapping the leather tip against her boot.

Slowly, Adair mounted Fête d'Or, a small, uncharacteristically docile Arabian.

"I'm beginning to think you don't like me," Cecelia said.

Adair let her eyes glide up Cecelia's leg. Her riding pants showcased her lush body. *I hate you.* Adair steadied herself on Fête d'Or's back. The horse whinnied. Adair stroked its silver-gray mane. "Come on," she said.

They rode for thirty minutes, climbing steadily

toward Wyatt's Bluff. When they reached the familiar spot, Cecelia and Shen Yun veered off the path and into the forest, now shrouded in a canopy of maple, birch, and ash. Adair followed her into a little clearing. When they were hidden from the bluff, Cecelia rose off her saddle, and struck Adair across the shoulder with her riding crop.

Adair sighed. The blow was not enough to dispel the pain that ground into her bones, but there would be a moment when the pain of Cecelia's crop would release her from all other suffering, she knew. She dismounted, tossing her shirt to the ground, waiting for Cecelia's crop to bite her bare skin.

The ritual was familiar to both of them.

❧ ❧ ❧ ❧

Cecelia had come to her the day she road Naples Peach to the edge of Wyatt's Bluff. Adair had tied the reigns and then sent the horse home with a kiss on its nose and swat to its massive haunch. Below, the valley was thawing, patches of green broke through the snow. A red barn glistened like a tiny train-set replica.

She remembered clamoring up these hills as a child, her long hair flying behind her, her clothes covered in dirt and smelling of leaves. She had licked the stamens of wild honeysuckle and drank creek water. She remembered taking her college girlfriend, Soledad, to the bluff. She remembered Soledad in her brightly striped sweaters, knit by a Mexican grandmother who could not fathom why anyone would leave the barrios of LA. As she stood on the bluff, she remembered Helen's body, and how she had dreamed of taking her hiking in the forest surrounding the estate. She had

had so many dreams.

Then she had lifted her boot to take the last step off the bluff, but she had hesitated and in that moment, Cecelia had found her, alerted by the scraps of her suicide note emptied from the trash by a conscientious maid. In the distance, a helicopter roared.

Cecelia came toward her with outstretched hands. "You can't do this, Merrill. We'll find a way. Remember when your mother died? You thought it was the end, but it wasn't." Cecelia squinted into the light of the valley.

"That was different," Adair said. Her voice sounded far away, as though she was already falling.

"No. It wasn't. You were starving yourself because you thought you couldn't bear the pain, but you did. I helped you."

Adair remembered. "I don't want that anymore."

"I know." Cecelia stepped closer. She was not wearing the violent lipstick, and her dark hair was pulled back into a simple bun. "I know none of this is what you want, but you don't want to die."

The buzz of the helicopter drew closer. Cecelia pulled a two-way phone out of the inner pocket of her riding jacket. "Get back, Cyrus," she barked. "I've got her. Just give me a minute."

Cecelia had almost reached her. Adair knew she had only a second in which to fall backwards into the valley, and she knew simultaneously that it was too late. Cecelia grabbed her hand and pulled her away from the edge and into the forest. Beneath one of the evergreen pines, Cecelia released her. "On your knees!"

The crop had struck Adair's back. Almost without volition she had slipped out of her coat and lifted her shirt. She had wept as the pain of Cecelia's crop released her from the pain of her illness.

❧❧❧❧

Now Cecelia removed the leather straps from the saddle pouch. Stripped naked, Adair lay down. Cecelia bound one strap around Adair's wrists. She secured it to a maple sapling. She repeated the process with Adair's ankles, pulling the second strap tight. Adair's back arched. Her arms strained. It was too tight. Her shoulders burned. But that was the point. It was a knowable pain.

Cecelia stood above her, straddling her, fully clothed, her crop raised. Adair felt her skin burn where the leather connected. "Again," she whispered. "Harder."

The crop struck her arms, her thighs, her breasts.

"Do you deserve it?" Cecelia demanded.

The leather snapped again.

"Yes." Adair closed her eyes, the leafy canopy above her disappearing. When she opened her eyes, Cecelia was naked except for an enormous, handcrafted leather dildo that hung off her hips, as long and black as the stallion's penis. Adair took a deep breath, waiting.

Behind Cecelia's head, the golden maple leaves sparkled. Every leaf was lit with sunlight. They sung with green, with life, with spring. Some part of Adair's mind—the woman she had once been—recognized that. Then the thought disappeared.

Cecelia's hips pressed down. The leather straps bit Adair's wrists. Adair felt the pressure of Cecelia's cock stretching the walls of her dry sex. The saplings bent.

"Yes." Cecelia clamped her hands on Adair's hipbones, rocking back and forth. "Oh!"

For a moment, with Cecelia pressing her down into the sharp rocks, Adair felt a curtain lift, as though the real pain finally dispelled the phantom agonies that tore her apart without leaving any mark. It was not release. She never came with Cecelia. But for a second she could feel the gold in the leaves above her. *It's wrong,* she thought. *Cyrus, I'm sorry.*

Cecelia climaxed. Then she rose. "I've rented us a flat," she said conversationally, staring down at Adair. "It's rather a squalid little place, horribly middle-class, but it'll do."

Adair tried to remember the glimpse of gold she had seen as the rocks cut her back, but the scene was nothing more than a paper cutout from a faded calendar page. "No," she said, offering no further explanation.

"If this is about Cyrus, you're being childish." Cecelia planted her hands on her hips, the dildo still hanging erect in the open air. "I'm not cheating on him any less because you insist on getting moss in your hair. Not that I mind, he's *your* brother. It's *your* conscience."

Adair closed her eyes. She did not have the energy to explain to Cecelia that she wanted to stay near the edge. She never wanted the plunge to be too far, that even as she bared her body, she was planning her descent.

"What will we do in the winter?" Cecelia asked. Cecelia bent down and kissed Adair on the lips. She loosened the ties at Adair's wrists.

Adair sat up, rubbing the marks on her skin,

while Cecelia untied her ankles. "I won't do this in the winter."

"No!" Cecelia's eyes grew dark and hot. "I won't let you leave me."

Adair stood, dusted the leaves off her naked body. "I've already left, Cecelia." She put on her shirt. For a moment, she thought she would run for the edge and leap, like a child leaping into a pool, but her knees ached and her vision clouded. "I think you know that." Adair pulled on her pants, then sat for a moment with her head between her knees, waiting for the dizziness to pass.

Cecelia was silent for a long time. Finally she said, "Why is that, Merrill?"

Merrill. The family name.

"What?" Adair asked wearily.

"Why do I love you, and you never love me back?"

"You love this." Adair gestured to the clearing. "That's all."

❧ ❧ ❧ ❧

That night, Adair took the tiny Seacamp pistol out of her safe and cleaned it with a cloth and bottle of Ballistol. She tried to catch the familiar smell of the gun oil, but the Texidol had begun to dull even her sense of smell. The only thing that was familiar was the feel of the gun, 13.25 ounces fully loaded. She remembered Cyrus's lesson. At close range, one never needed a large gun.

From the diary of Charity Kimball

There was a night when we were still very young. It is the last night I remember her being stronger than me. First, we prayed with Mother and Daddy and Billy, and afterward we said our own prayers. Then Prudence made me get out of bed. She told me to take off our night gown.

"But that's a sin," I whispered.

"Nothing that God makes is a sin."

So I pulled off my half of the gown and she pulled off hers, and we stood in front of great-grandma's mirror, and I saw it for the first time. I don't know how I could not have seen it before, but I hadn't.

"Do you know what Billy looks like?" Prudence asked me.

"No."

"Do you know what Mother and Daddy look like?"

I said "no," although of course I did know what they looked like with their clothes on, but that was not what Prudence was asking.

"Do you see it?" she asked, looking into the mirror.

"Because we have our arms around each other," I said. It was part of a story Mother had told us. "We love each other so much that we always have our arms around each other, forever and ever."

"Then let go." Prudence's voice was cold.

"I can't." I felt the first tears. I pulled away a little bit, but of course, I could not pull away from Prudence, not then, not ever.

"It's God's will," Prudence said, and she pulled the gown back over her head.

❧ ❧ ❧ ❧

As I grew, I learned about cities. They are like great congregations of people who live without God. And I learned about doctors. I dreamed of going to a city where I could kill her, and they would excise her from my body. I would lose her arm. I would limp unbalanced forever. I would fall out of God's love. But I would be free!

They say we were made in the image of God's inseparable love. We are bound to each other as we are bound to God. That is what Prudence believes. But I think it is because we are so different from everyone, so lonely. That is how we are like God. I feel His loneliness like the stars. We are one. She is pure light, and I am pure darkness.

Chapter Seven

Helen Ivers watched the overgrown bushes that lined Patrick's yard. Fireflies blinked on and off in the boxwood. Behind that, in the empty lot that bordered his property, her sister Eliza—dead now three years—shuffled and twisted, not an object but an intention, her voice a vibration in Helen's bones.

At her side, seated in a matching plastic lawn chair, Patrick raised a can of beer. "Cheers," he said, waiting.

Helen said nothing.

"Do you see her?" he asked.

"No."

Eliza reappeared, closer this time, and then disappeared faster than a blink and as intimate. In the pocket of her blazer, Helen's phone rang with a shrill, standard-issue ringtone. She had not silenced it since she called her friend Terri two weeks earlier. Now she froze when she saw his name on the screen. "I'm sorry," she said to Patrick. She stood and walked to the end of Patrick's gravel driveway. The sky was clear but the moon had not risen yet, and it was very dark. Helen accepted the call. "Terri?" she whispered. She could hear Terri sigh on the other end of the phone.

"I looked into your friend Adair, like you asked."

Helen held her breath. He was bracing her for the news.

"I looked up death records in New Hampshire and the other forty-nine. I put my best intern on it."

"And?"

"These systems aren't perfect, Helen."

"She's really dead."

Terri hesitated.

Helen glanced back at Patrick who remained seated in his plastic lawn chair, although his whole body was focused on her. In the house behind them, the radio played Bruce Springsteen. Patrick's husband, David, called after their adopted niece. The child laughed.

Helen turned away. She did not want Patrick to see her when Terri delivered the news. A day. A place. A method. Suddenly she couldn't bear the image of Adair's cold body. She didn't want to know. She wasn't sure why she had called Terri and begged him to discover the details. "Closure," her therapist would have called it, but she had stopped seeing Irene Thompson-Hasseldorf the day she received Adair's letter.

"We couldn't find a death record." Terri sounded worried.

Helen laughed, then covered her mouth. She felt tears welling up behind her eyes.

Terri continued. "We also couldn't find any record of her in the past three months. Helen, I want you to listen to me. It is very possible that the family sealed the death records. They're a prominent family. It was a suicide. It wouldn't even be a bribe, just a fee to keep it out of the public databases. Almost every database has a privacy fee. It's time consuming to hit them all, and expensive, but the Wilson's have plenty of resources. It's also possible she died abroad. There's no record of her death, but there's no record of her life after she left Pittock. Almost everyone leaves an internet shadow, especially a woman like Adair Wilson."

"What are you saying?"

"I'm saying be careful. You've been through so much. Even if she is alive, ask yourself if this is what you want, what you need. You lost your sister. Don't try to fill that void with Adair Wilson."

"This is different," Helen said.

"Are you sure?"

"I love her." She said a perfunctory goodbye.

Patrick rose to meet her. "What did he say?"

"He said she's probably dead."

Patrick's brows drew together in a frown.

Helen pulled a pack of Parliaments out of her pocket and lit one with trembling hands.

"Come on, Helen. That shit'll kill you," he said quietly.

The firefly blinked off as though deferring to the greater flame.

"I don't care."

In the frequency that only dogs can hear, Eliza repeated, *Help me, Helen.*

"You should," Patrick said.

Helen exhaled. She looked at Patrick. He had aged in the past two years. His hair was thinning and graying around his temples. He had put on weight, but his face had lost its baby-round softness. "He said she was probably dead, but there's no record of her death." The cigarette smoke burned her eyes in the place of tears. "But Terri is good at finding things. He runs a PR firm. That's his job…finding things and covering them up. I've never known him *not* to be able to find something…if it exists."

Ulysses, the mastiff Patrick had adopted when it was clear that Adair was not coming back to Pittock, lumbered out of the house. The dog found a dirty bone in the lawn and began chewing loudly.

"I am still in love with her. Am I crazy?"

"Yes," Patrick said. "No."

"Terri's worried about me. He thinks I'm trying to replace Eliza with Adair."

Patrick shrugged.

"I have to know what happened to her." Helen took a fast drag off her cigarette and coughed. "If she's alive, I have to find her." Helen was waiting for Patrick to repeat Terri's cautions or his own vague diagnosis… Adair was troubled. Helen didn't know. He did.

Don't think that you could have saved her. She met his eyes, willing him to understand. "I have to find her." Helen expected Patrick to enfold her in his warm, gentle bear-hug.

Instead he clasped her once, quickly, then slapped her shoulders and released her. "Yes, you do."

⁂

The gates to the Wilson Estate were beautiful wrought iron. The wall that enclosed the property was twelve feet high at least, and shrouded in hedges. Helen marveled at the length. It went on for acres, and, from where she sat in her car, she could barely make out the mansion at the end of a long driveway of faintly rose-colored gravel.

She unrolled her window and pressed the intercom button.

A man's voice greeted her. "Wilson Estate. How

may I help you?"

Helen stopped for a moment. She had left Pittock first thing that morning. The drive to New Hampshire seemed to have passed in mere minutes. She had not thought about what she was going to say. "I'd like to speak to one of the Wilsons."

"Concerning?"

"I'd like to speak to Adair if she's there."

"I'm afraid Miss Wilson is not accepting visitors."

"So she is there?" Helen's heart beat faster. "May I leave a message?"

"You may dictate a message," the voice said in a way that made the promise of its delivery patently uncertain.

"No. I don't want to leave a message. I need to talk to someone. I'd like to talk to Adair, but if not her then one of her brothers." Helen remembered her frightening encounter with the Wilson brothers, men Patrick described as the NRA crossed with the GOP crossed with the mafia. She loathed the idea of facing them again, but she was ready. "To whom am I speaking?"

"My name is Ubol. I am the house manager."

Helen was not sure if Ubol was a first name or a last name.

"I don't want to make your job more difficult… Ubol. But I am ready to sit here in my car for as long as it takes for someone from the Wilson family to come out and see me. I know they don't want to, but I promise I'll leave if they can provide a few very simple answers to my questions." She knew it was only half true, and that if the Wilson brothers deigned to speak to her, they would only give her half-truths.

"I am not authorized to facilitate such an arrangement," the man said.

Helen withdrew her finger from the intercom button, hanging up on him. If she could not persuade him with her words, she would persuade the Wilsons with her presence. She would sit in her car until one of the Wilsons spoke to her, or the police forced her out of their driveway.

She brought her tablet and scanned through her email. There was plenty there to keep her busy for hours. The athletic department wanted an emergency grant to re-sod the rugby pitch. A student who spelled Helen's name "Iverns" complained that Dean Bruno Duffy had offended her as a feminist. The New England Council of Women in Banking asked if she would give the keynote at their annual meeting. She checked her voicemail. There was nothing from the Wilsons and more of the same from her constituents, including a rambling message from the director of admissions, a nervous woman who wore patterned leggings and jumpers and did not seem to realize that part of her job was turning people away.

"I think this is something you really need to hear," she began, alerting Helen to the fact that it probably was *not* something she needed to hear. "We got a call from an attorney in Utah or Nevada or something."

Or something. Helen sighed, but she had nothing else to do besides listen.

"She said she has this client named Peter Reynolds Barr. There are two girls, sisters, and he wants to give them a scholarship to Pittock, but he's concerned that they may not be academically ready, and he is willing to pay for their remediation."

Helen had heard these requests before. The sons of rich politicians who had failed out of their private high schools but would love to attend Pittock College to the tune of a $10,000 donation.

"I know we don't do this," the director of admissions went on. "But he's offering a million dollars. He's offering five thousand if we'll send a recruiter just to *talk* to them. He says their parents don't want them to leave home, but he thinks…"

A knock on the car window startled Helen.

The woman at her door seemed to have appeared out of nowhere. There was no sign of a car or a golf cart, but Helen could not imagine the woman had walked the entire length of the rose quartz driveway without her noticing. She rolled down her window.

"Ms. Ivers?" The woman stepped back so that Helen could see her.

She was wearing an impeccably tailored coat, of a subtle shade between taupe and gray, the perfect accoutrement for an early morning in a New England spring. Her hair was pulled up in a French twist. Her make-up was both provocative and professional, a kind of come-hither, get-back warning. Pale lips. Dark eyes. Pearls at her ears and her throat. Helen stepped out of her car and surveyed the woman from head to toe. It was a look Helen had emulated, but she could see that this woman *emulated* nothing. She *was*.

"Cecelia Beaucharnel." The woman held out her hand. "I'm a family friend."

At Cecelia Beaucharnel's suggestion Helen drove them to a small café attached to a country grocery store that advertised "organic arugula" and "Burgundy wines" on their letter board. The décor was rustic, but Helen had the sense that the diners all came from the

Wilsons' echelons, even if some of them were playing at college hiker in their neon windbreakers and cargo pants.

Helen ordered a coffee. Beaucharnel ordered a bottle of Volvic water.

"Dr. Ivers, you are…?" Beaucharnel gestured to the table between them. Her hands were as smooth as marble. Helen wondered if she was younger than her elegance belied. "At Smith College?"

"Pittock," Helen corrected.

Beaucharnel shrugged slightly. "I'm sorry. I don't know it. You are here because you wish to speak to Adair Wilson."

"I'm here to find out if she's…dead." A finger of sunlight crept across the table, illuminating Helen's hand in bright relief. The bones stood out and her veins throbbed blue. She folded them beneath the table.

"No. She's alive." Beaucharnel managed to make the statement sound patronizing. "She's just been preoccupied."

A voice in the back of Helen's mind chanted *please, please be true.* "I'm not sure I believe you."

"Why not?"

Helen took a sip of her coffee. She could not imagine what it meant to be the "Wilsons' family friend." Still, this was the closest she had gotten to Adair since they parted on the beach in Provincetown, half a year ago. "I received what appears to be a suicide note from her. Several weeks ago. But I couldn't find any record of her death online. Adair and I were friends." They were all "friends," Helen thought grimly. One euphemism for all life's complexities. "I realize the Wilsons may want to keep this quiet, but I have a right to know." Helen's voice trembled. She glanced out the window at the parking lot with its cavalcade of Audis and BMWs. "She worked at Pittock College. We have a life insurance policy."

"I don't think the Wilsons need a life insurance policy," Beaucharnel said. "But since you've come all the way up here…" She followed Helen's gaze out the window.

For a long time she was silent, and it seemed to Helen there was more truth in her silence than in her speech. Finally Beaucharnel said, "All right. She's been ill. She may have sent you that note, but she didn't go through with it."

Helen let out a breath she did not realize she had been holding.

"It happened shortly after she was shot," Beaucharnel said, spreading her perfect hands out on the table before her as though revealing a hand of cards. "It's an autoimmune disorder, and the prognosis isn't good. She's very sick and any emotional upset or agitation makes it worse. Her brothers are very careful to keep her in a perfectly controlled environment. Even reminding her of her illness or her job, her old life, can trigger an attack. Even things that you and I would think of as positive—the birth of a niece or nephew, or a party—can be just devastating for her. We have to be very, very careful. The Wilsons have to be very careful, but they have the resources to keep her at home which is a blessing."

Helen wanted to cover her face with her hands, but she remained rigid, staring slightly past Beaucharnel's shoulder. "What's the disease called?" She did not know if it was joy or grief that turned her voice into a strangled whisper. Adair was alive, but she was ill. She was suffering.

Beaucharnel rattled off a list of medical terms and acronyms. When she had finished, Helen could not remember one word, not even the name of the disorder.

"I'm sorry," Helen said, trying to compose herself. "I'm…that's very sad news."

"But there is one thing."

"Yes?"

Beaucharnel straightened her shoulders and poured the rest of her Volvic into her glass. When she caught Helen's eye, her smile was wan but genuine. "Just between you and me, I think she's bored. She's not used to being an invalid. Of course, she can't work. It's too late for that. I wish there was something though. The doctor can change her medication for a few days, and that helps with the pain, although it's not good for the long term prospects. I wish there was some small, meaningful thing she could do to give her purpose. Do you know what I mean?"

Purpose. Helen's calendar was full of things to do, but none of them gave her purpose anymore. She thought of the director of admissions. "Would I be able to see her…if I had something for her to do for Pittock College?"

"I don't know if her brothers would let her see you."

The waitress appeared and asked if they would like anything else. Beaucharnel slid a credit card onto the little tray that held the receipt and the waitress disappeared.

"Please," Helen said. "Pittock is courting a new donor, but he's asked us to send a recruiter to talk to some prospective students. Adair was always…Ms.

Wilson was always our best faculty recruiter. She grew the theater program from nothing, and when she was there she could attract the best students from across the country. It would mean a great deal to Pittock College, and it might provide a diversion for Ms. Wilson."

"You want her to recruit the students to Pittock College?"

"It's a one-time thing. It's not a job. It's just a…special situation." She could almost imagine the politician with his two, spoiled daughters, probably both racking up MIPs and DUIs in whatever desert town they terrorized. Kids who worked for nothing, earned nothing, deserved nothing, and were going to buy their way into Washington where the best hope was that they only married politicians and didn't try to become them. Their father had probably tried Harvard, Stanford, Yale, and Amherst and been turned down. They did not want to go to Pittock, but he wanted them out of the house. He wanted Pittock to convince them. Ordinarily she would have let the college bankroll bleed into the red before she accepted students like this, but Beaucharnel was already signing the credit card slip. She was standing up. Helen did not have time to think of anything else. "Please let me call you with the details," Helen said.

Beaucharnel pulled a business card out of the inner pocket of her coat.

"I can't promise the brothers will agree," she said. "But I'll ask."

From the diary of Charity Kimball

Another letter came. We were washing dishes, Prudence picked up a dish and held it as I ran the dishtowel over its surface. I rinsed. In the living room, Daddy bowed his head before Father Apostle.

"Did you solicit this?" Father Apostle asked.

Father Apostle has the only postal box in Oquat, and he reviews our mail for the devil's intrusions. It is a necessary precaution, he says, especially for converts, like Daddy, who are forever tempted to return to the wicked world. That's what Father Apostle says. That is what Prudence believes.

Father Apostle waved the white envelope. "I told you to scrive them an answer."

"I have," Daddy pleaded. "As you instructed. I would not give my daughters away like chattel."

I could tell that Prudence was not listening because it was not right to listen. I could hear her thoughts in prayer, like the sound of water in the Basemath Creek. But I was listening. Someone had written a letter (and now another one!) calling us away from Oquat.

The water had grown tepid. I hated the oily feel of the dishwater.

"Eavesdropping is a sin," Prudence whispered, because she could hear my thoughts.

I wanted to cry because I was not even allowed to want to know what Father Apostle held in that envelope, which was as white as snow in heaven.

Chapter Eight

Adair sat in the western facing parlor where the staff had installed her hospital bed. She had returned to the family mansion on several occasions in her youth, but she had not expected to return as an adult, not when she had a life in Pittock, not when she had imagined a life with Helen. But here she was, drawn back into the family as though she had never left. Her eldest brother, Monty, his wife Belinda, and their children–when they were home from boarding school–inhabited the north wing. Cyrus, the middle brother, and Cecelia lived in the east wing. Her youngest brother, Blaine, had not been seen in years. He was in Bolivia or Argentina. No one spoke of him. Presumably he would take the south wing, if he ever returned. Four points on a compass: Monty, Cyrus, Blaine, and Merrill. It was like living in a stage version of Upstairs Downstairs, except the stage was over thirty-thousand square feet, and her role, as the invalid daughter, was simply to sit and stare out the window.

Behind her, the door opened. Cecelia strode in, looking fresh but wearing her riding gear.

"I'm not going with you." Adair turned back to the window. "I can't."

"Are you feeling ill?"

Adair shot her a look. "I can't do this to Cyrus."

Cecelia snorted. "That's not why I'm here." She

held her phone in one hand. "Conference call." She placed the phone in Adair's hand, then strode over to the landline on the desk. She pressed a few buttons. "Are you there? Yes. Okay. I'm going to transfer you now, and I'll stay on the line. Do you remember what we talked about?" She paused and glanced at Adair. "Okay."

Adair raised the phone to her ear as though it might bite. "Hello?"

"Adair."

Adair felt a lump rise in her throat. She covered her mouth to capture a sob. It was Helen. And it was not Helen. It was the college president with her blazer button tightly over her heart. It was the administrator. Helen spoke quickly and cheerfully. "We've been approached with a very attractive proposition for Pittock College. A wealthy donor has offered us a significant sum if we pay a recruiting visit to two prospective students. We hope you'll be willing to lend your talent to this endeavor," she said, as though Adair had not kissed the very center of her sex.

"Helen…" There was so much she wanted to say, to beg. She felt Cecelia watching her.

"The girls live in a rather isolated community in Utah," Helen continued. "I suspect they think Pittock is beneath them. I don't know a lot about them, but I know you're an exceptional recruiter."

"Ms. Ivers," Cecelia murmured into the phone. "I suspect Miss Wilson is tired."

Helen's voice was perfectly modulated. "It would be a great honor for Pittock College to employ you in this capacity. Given the events at Pittock College…"

"No," Cecelia cut her off.

Helen tried again. "I hope it will be a quick and

enjoyable trip."

Adair felt like her throat had squeezed shut. Helen's polite appeal was even more final than her absence. *She doesn't want you broken, Merrill.*

"If you say yes, your friend, Ms. Beaucharnel, has agreed to make all the arrangements through our Admissions Office."

Adair wanted to cast the phone to the floor and run out across the Versailles gardens, through the forest, up to Wyatt's Bluff, and over. Nothing, but the split second of impact, would match the pain in her heart. But she could barely stand without growing dizzy, and Helen was still talking, even as Cecelia moved her finger to the base of the landline to hang up.

"Please say yes," Helen said.

Then the line went dead.

❧❧❧❧

At dinner that night, Monty and Cyrus sat at each end of the table, like tarot card opposites. Monty was as graceful as a crane. Cyrus had removed his jacket to reveal sweat stains beneath his massive arms and a holster strapped to his chest. The women—Monty's wife Belinda, Cecelia, and Adair—had taken their usual places at intervals along the table, all beyond touching distance, like the points of an irregular pentagram. Without the head butler, they would have had to stand to pass the silver terrines. Someone poured a Chateau la Tour.

Cyrus's eyes fixed on Adair. "I am worried about you, Merrill."

Belinda laughed nervously. "What have you

heard from the doctor?"

"Merrill." Cyrus did not take his eyes off Adair. "Is it worse?"

"The doctor has decided to take her off the IV for a few weeks," Cecelia answered. "He has to cycle the drug, so she doesn't build up a tolerance. He'll put her on a lower dose she takes by mouth."

Adair felt as though a weighted band had been placed on her head, squeezing her temples until the pain ran down her spine. It did not matter if Helen loved her or not; she had to leave. She had to leave forever. She was broken, and she had sinned, and she could not risk the chance that the pain would drive her back into Cecelia's arms. *No, not her arms, her whip.* "I'm going on a trip," she said.

"You're not well enough," Cyrus growled.

"It will be good for her." Cecelia sipped her wine. "It's only for a day or two. The drug takes a toll. It will be good for her to move about while she's on a lower dosage."

Adair wanted out of the room. She needed to fall into a deep, death-like sleep. She needed to put days and then weeks between her and Cecelia, so that she could look at her brother again.

Cyrus turned to Cecelia. "Is this your idea?"

"No." She smiled. "Merrill's little friend from Pittock asked her for a favor."

"I don't like it." Cyrus scrapped at the immaculate tablecloth with his thumbnail. "If Merrill isn't here with us, she should be in a hospital. There's a beautiful facility in Zermatt."

"You'd put her under a bell jar," Cecelia said.

"She's not your concern," Cyrus snapped back.

"She's my family."

"Not by blood."

An electric chill ran through the room as though every particle coming through the central air had been ionized.

"That's enough." Monty had inherited the same pale blue eyes that Adair had, only his eyes had grayed over the years, until the blue had disappeared entirely. In the fading light of the west window, they looked fiery white.

"Merrill isn't your property, Cy." Cecelia's smile curved into a knife. "You don't own her."

"Neither do you." With that, Cyrus stood, threw his Damask napkin on the table, and left without a word.

❧ ❧ ❧ ❧

A few days later, Adair eyed the clerk at the car rental in the Salt Lake City airport. He was clean shaved, with rosy cheeks, and a blond crew cut. "Yes ma'am! Welcome to Express Rent-a-Car where we serve our customers like family." He was already pulling out a stack of rental agreements.

Something about his bright smile and cheerful "Yes ma'am" made Adair want to reach across the counter, grab him by the lapel, and say, "Do you understand that you are going to die?" but she didn't have the energy.

"I'd like a BMW. Whatever you've got."

Rosy Cheeks ran though the paperwork, his professionalism in overdrive. Then he retrieved a set of keys.

"Where will you be going, ma'am?"

"Oquat."

He shook his head. "Never heard of it."

"I guess it's a commune or something, east of here. Near something called King's Peak. Almost at the Wyoming border."

"Up in the mountains? You'll want a truck then. I got a Dodge Ram outback. You don't want to take a city car way up there."

Adair had already picked up her key and turned her back on the boy. He had probably never driven a BMW in his life, unless it was to move it from one side of the rental lot to the other. She, on the other hand, had spent much of her adolescence—at least those days when she was home from boarding school—careening around the curves of the Monteith Speedway, speeding past senators' sons and NASCAR retirees.

❧❧❧❧

Adair followed her GPS for what felt like hours. She exited off Interstate 80, to Route 189, to Route 150. From there she took a state highway and finally turned onto something called West Old Highway. West Old climbed and climbed, until Adair's ears popped, and the temperature in the car dropped. Fir trees encroached on the road, brushing the car with their branches. About a mile farther, the cracked concrete gave way to gravel and then to a rutted dirt road.

"Continue on foot when safe to proceed," the GPS told her in a soothing woman's voice.

Adair turned off the GPS and consulted the instructions Helen had emailed her. They said nothing about the forest she saw before her, uniform and dark, each tree rising above its neighbor, as the land clawed upward. The ground beneath the trees was bare, except for a few large rocks that jutted out of the earth.

A few meters farther on, the BMW tilted on the rutted road, then stopped, its wheels spinning. Adair rocked the car gently as she would on New Hampshire ice. Pull forward. Rock back. On the third try she felt a rock dislodge. The car dropped another inch. She heard the axle grind against stone.

She got out. The air was surprisingly cold. She looked behind her. True to its reputation the BMW had given her the smoothest ride possible. She could now see that the road was much rougher than she had guessed. Deep ruts scarred its surface as though the last travelers had been pioneers in covered wagons. Pioneers, Adair thought, who had probably died from drinking poisoned water, whose bodies were buried under lonely wooden crosses.

Laying down on the ground to look under the carriage, she could see radiator fluid leaking into the dust and a rock wedged beneath one axle. She pulled out her phone, but there was no reception. She sank down in the driver's seat again, hugging her arms to her chest. The sun was almost directly overhead, but when she released her breath she could see a hint of mist. She was wearing only a silk T-shirt. The summer in New Hampshire had been oppressively humid, and nothing in the dry heat of Salt Lake City suggested she would need a winter coat in Oquat.

She wondered what Cyrus would do. He carried himself like a man who could handle any physical challenge. He had tried to give her that knowledge over the years, always in blunt, monosyllabic lectures. He had taught her how to shoot, how to handle a car, how to break a horse. But what was Cyrus when stripped of his toys? What was she? For a panicked instant, Adair wondered if Cyrus had discovered her secret and planned this. Had he sent her out here to die? But, no. It was Helen who had asked her to go. It was Cecelia who had made going inescapable.

She huddled inside the car for what felt like a very long time. When she finally looked up and squinted into the trees, she thought she saw a movement in the distance. She blinked. A shadow moved, darting from one tree to another. For a second, she thought she saw two faces peering around a pine trunk. A minute later, she was certain she caught a glimpse of two women. Then they coalesced into one. Then broke apart again, two young women with white bonnets tied over their hair, the brown of their clothing perfectly blended with the tree bark. A mirage. Two pioneer women dead these past 200 years, now making their way toward Adair to claim her bones for their grave.

She rubbed her eyes. When she opened them again, the figure was standing beside the car. First she noticed the white apron and the tip of a rifle pointed at the dirt. She looked down and saw two ugly boots planted in a wide stance, braced to shoot. Her eyes followed the front of an apron to a wide waist, a torso, and then two faces. One leaned slightly to the right and one leaned slightly to the left. Both bore the same face, sun-browned and rough, but beautiful, like a modern rendition of the Virgin Mary painted in duplicate.

She opened the door and stared. "I'm dreaming," Adair said to the vision.

Chapter Nine

A re you all right?" one of the Virgin Marys asked. The two-headed figure moved closer to Adair and stared at her with four dark eyes.

"She is suffering apoplexy," one of the faces said.

"She has been struck by the Lord," its companion answered.

Adair closed her eyes again.

"Let's get her back to the trailer."

"But she is from the outside." The voice was breathless and quiet, as though even the words might conjure some anticipated evil.

The other voice said, "*But a Samaritan, as he traveled, came where the man was; and when he saw him, he took pity on him.*"

Like a school girl reciting a lesson reluctantly learned, the other voice said, "*Which of these three do you think was a neighbor to the man who fell into the hands of robbers?*"

"*And Jesus told him, 'Go and do likewise.'*"

Adair felt a gentle hand on her shoulder. "Who are you?" She reached out and touched the hem of the figure's skirt. It felt real. It looked like denim.

"I'm Charity," the louder head said.

"I'm Prudence." The head on the left looked down shyly.

Adair stared. The figure had two arms, two hands clasped in front of a dingy apron. For a second she thought it was a costume, two girls in a large dress. When she looked down, she saw that there were only two boots. The girls' cheeks were pressed together, and Adair could see the place where their necks met in a single U-shaped curve.

"What...?"

"It's God's gift," the one named Prudence said quietly. "So we're never alone."

"Dicephalic parapagus twins," Charity pronounced each syllable carefully.

"I..." Adair stammered. "Charity and Prudence Kimball?"

"Yes. What are you doing here?" Charity asked.

Adair swallowed. "I'm looking for you."

Prudence shook her head. "No. That can't be. The Apostles are invisible because we are blessed."

"I don't know..." Adair began.

"Shh," Charity said. She scanned the distance, near a craggy rock formation. "Over there."

Slowly, but in perfect coordination, they picked up the rifle.

For a second, Adair thought they were going to shoot her, point blank, without an expression on either face. But they turned away before balancing the rifle between their heads. Prudence leaned away so Charity could rest her chin against the stock. The hand on Prudence's side held the barrel. Charity's hand release the safety and squeezed the trigger slowly. The sight was only a metal wedge mounted above the muzzle. A second later the shot echoed off the distant mountains. Adair saw a puff of dust where the bullet hit.

Without a word, the girls set down the rifle and the leather sack they had been carrying and walked over to the settled dust. When they returned, they carried a dead rabbit. They knelt, an odd, heavy motion, like a camel dropping to its knees, and opened the sack. Inside, were three other rabbits, identical to the one they had just shot. Adair gagged at the sight, for each rabbit had been shot through the eye. The one they carried was the best preserved. In the bag, one had lost the top of its skull, one the front of its face. Adair turned away as the girls scrabbled around in the bag.

"It's not our rabbit," Prudence murmured.

"Not ours, not this time."

Adair had the sense that they had spoken these words before. It was a liturgy, but she did not understand the meaning. When they closed the satchel, Adair turned back to them. "I've been sent to personally invite you to attend Pittock College," she had said those words before, to hundreds of prospective freshman at magnet schools and theater camps across the country. Now they came out of her mouth like a refrain from a past life. "You don't have to say anything. You're probably not interested."

"We can never leave," Prudence said. "Our family is here. We are waiting for the True Reckoning. We live in faith, and God has chosen this place for us to meet Him."

Prudence and Charity had the same face, a closer match than any identical twins Adair had ever met. Still, there was a difference. Prudence's eyes were wide and guileless. Charity squinted, appraising her.

"We have heard of Pittock College," Charity said. "There was a letter."

"Shh," Prudence cautioned. "Father Apostle destroyed it."

Adair shrugged. "I'm following up. I don't know what to say."

"Beware. *For Satan himself is transformed into an angel of light,*" Prudence said.

At this Charity turned her head and shoulder away from her sister, quickly. Prudence let out a little gasp as though she had been stung.

❧❧❧❧

"When is the True Reckoning," Adair was finally alone with the twins, sitting in a small trailer. Their father, a snake-thin man with large watery eyes, had come and gone, promising to find someone at the prayer meeting who would help lift Adair's car off the rocks. Their mother had gone with him, trailing two young boys, and toting a baby wrapped in gray swaddling clothes. The twins stayed to take care of Dorothia, a child who lay on the sofa in a fever, occasionally rising to cough desperately into a pail.

Everything about the trailer was meager, but carefully tended. The rag rug was worn thin, but the linoleum floor around it was swept clean. The furniture was faded, but each arm chair wore a lace doily on its back and two more on the arms. The enamel on the white two-burner stove was chipped, but the stove was clean. An ancient metal pot simmered beneath an ill-fitting lid, releasing the smell of rosemary. On the kitchen table rested an enormous leather-bound Bible.

"The True Reckoning will occur in God's time." Prudence held her head high but cast her eyes modestly down as she spoke.

"It was supposed to be June 16, last year," Charity said.

Adair thought she heard irritation in her voice.

"It was a test of our faith." Prudence spoke with

utter sincerity. "The weak in faith turn away in their disappointment, but the true apostles understand that God separates the wheat from the chaff. Our joy will be tenfold because our faith was strong."

On the sofa, Dorothia moaned. Adair rose from her seat at the table and placed a hand on the girl's forehead. Her skin was hot and damp, and Adair felt a shiver run through the child's body. "She needs a doctor."

"The Lord will provide for her. She knows her prayers." Prudence did not sound as certain as she had been about the Reckoning.

"Our aunt sent for a doctor once," Charity said. "He gave her some pills, and she was better. It was a *miracle*." The bitterness in her voice was undisguised.

"It was the devil's work," Prudence said.

Adair looked in the bucket. The sides were splattered with blood. "It could be tuberculosis." She pulled her hand away instinctively and wiped it on her pants. "You can't pray that away."

"Jesus lifted Lazarus from the tomb," Prudence offered.

"Are you Jesus?" Adair said.

Prudence looked away.

Adair checked her cell phone for the hundredth time. She did not get enough reception to send a text. She sat back down.

After several minutes, Charity spoke again. "Father Apostle Eldon does not approve of apostles mixing with the wicked world." Charity sounded mournful. "That is why we can never go with you."

"Wicked, eh?" Adair leaned her chin on her hand.

"The world is steeped in sin," Prudence added.

It was cool in the trailer and colder outside, but suddenly Adair wanted to see the stars. "How long is the prayer meeting?"

The girls shrugged in unison.

"I'm going outside."

"Can we come with you?" the girls asked together.

Surprised, Adair nodded.

Outside, the sky had faded to navy. The Kimball's trailer was located in a small valley between craggy peaks. In the darkness, Adair could make out a vegetable garden and beyond that a meadow. Higher up in the mountain she could see patches of snow. The air smelled of juniper.

The twins retrieved two rusted lawn chairs.

"Tell us about where you come from," Charity said when they were seated.

"You mean how wicked it is?"

"Is it really that wicked?" Charity seemed intrigued.

"No." Adair looked up at the sky. The whole arm of the Milky Way was visible like a powder of diamonds. "It's not wicked. I come from...I used to come from Pittock. It's a town and a college."

"What is a college?" Charity asked.

"What is a college?" Adair guessed they had never been to a campus, but she assumed they knew the word. "It's like a little town," she began. "Everyone there is your age, eighteen, nineteen, twenty. They live in big houses, built of bricks, and every day they go to class."

"Like Bible study?" Prudence asked.

"Yes. Only they study everything. They study the stars." Adair looked up. "They study books and stories, and they ask questions."

"Are they Christians?" Charity asked.

"Some are. The school was founded by a Christian. Jedidiah Pittock. The school motto is *Ego quoque angelos vidi et tremui.* I too have seen the angels and trembled." Adair tried to remember what her mentor Professor Lebovetski had told her about Pittock, but she could not remember the historical details. Instead, she told them about Josa himself, not his death at the hands of Marshal Drummond, but how he loved history and all its minutia. She told them about the old professors who carried a world of arcane knowledge with them and yet answered the simplest questions with bright-eyed delight. She told them about the Night of Peace, when the campus was hung with lanterns from all over the world, and the choirs took turns singing on the library steps. She told them about ice skating on Arcadia Pond and the bull frogs that filled the edges of the pond in the spring, croaking their songs in unison like a heartbeat.

"And then there was Helen," she said, more to the night sky than to the girls. "She was the president, our…what did you call him? Father Apostle? She was our leader."

"Why did you come to find us?" Charity's eyes were wide.

"She asked me to."

"To convince us to come?" Charity asked.

"Yes." Adair leaned back in her chair. "There is a lot you could learn there. And there are things that would not happen at Pittock that happen here." Adair glanced back at the trailer. "We wouldn't let a girl get sick like that. You wouldn't have to share a trailer with six other people."

Prudence had been so quiet Adair thought she was sleeping or rendered speechless by her disapproval. Now she finally spoke. "Does it snow?"

"Snow? Yes. Of course."

"I love the snow," Prudence said. "It reminds me of God's purity."

"In Pittock it always seems to snow at night," Adair said. "Maybe that's just because the nights are so long in the winter. But you go to bed, and it is dark. Black. Raining. Then it snows. On the morning of the first snow, the chapel bell rings, and all the classes are canceled. We call it Winter's Table." She closed her eyes. She could see the students running from the dorms, some wearing down coats over their pajamas. "The cafeterias serve pancakes all day. The students race sleds they've been decorating throughout the fall. The professors walk to campus through the snow and watch."

She had a sudden vision of Helen standing on the sidelines of the sledding slope, her camel-colored coat buttoned up to the neck, a cup of coffee steaming in her hands. How wonderful it would be to stand beside her, their love a barely-kept secret. How wonderful it would be to draw Helen in from the cold, into her office in the theater attic. She would bolt the door, turn up the radiator, and lay Helen down on the Persian rug. A restless pain skittered up her spine, and Adair had to stand and pace until it subsided.

"Are you sick?" Prudence asked.

Adair turned back to where they sat. In the darkness, their eyes were like four perfect bullet holes. "I'm very sick."

"Would you like to pray about it?" Prudence asked.

The last time Adair had been inside a church she was seventeen, home from boarding school, and her father was wooing a Baptist congressman. Still she said, "Okay," and sat back down. A moment later, Charity reached across the gulf between their chairs and took her hand.

She heard Prudence's voice, "Dear Lord, who is at the beginning and end of all things, decide for our sister Adair what is right and good in your eyes, and lead her to righteousness, and comfort her, for the road you set before us is steep. And now we shall pray."

Apparently this was a cue to pray silently. The twins both bowed their heads, so Adair bowed hers and thought about Helen, her face framed by her auburn hair, her eyes smiling.

❧❧❧❧

The next day after deliberations that seemed to involve the entire church, eight men arrived at the trailer. Their faces were so stern Adair feared they planned to put her out of the world, not just out of the ditch in the road. She gave the twins an awkward hug, whispering to Charity, "If you can get a doctor in to see your sister, do it."

Adair followed the men across the meadow and down a rocky path to her car. Silently they circled it and bent their heads. She thought they were going to pray the car out of the rut, but after a moment each man took hold of the undercarriage. Their wiry arms strained. Their grim faces grew grimmer. Then the BMW was on the road again.

"You'll need to get some coolant at the next

service station," Charity's father said. "Godspeed." It did not sound like a benediction.

The men watched as Adair turned the car around.

"I'm going. I'm going," she grumbled, as she made a six point turn.

The men had disappeared behind a bend in the road and Adair had driven several more miles before she felt hopelessness descend upon her again. She had felt oddly at peace sitting in the darkness outside the Kimball's trailer. She remembered how much she liked being around students that age. She liked their freshness, their curiosity, and the seriousness of purpose with which they went about everything.

Now she was back in the car, headed to Salt Lake City to explain to the rental car agent that she would buy the car's repairs—or replacement—on her credit card, as long as they didn't have to talk about it. She didn't want to sign forms or apologize. She was thinking about Dorothia, lying beside a bucket of blood, waiting for God to heal her.

Adair's phone beeped, signaling that she once again had reception. She slowed to a stop and searched for the Utah Department of Human Services. After ten minutes in a phone-tree where every button led back to the same phone-tree in Spanish, she got an answering machine that promised to take messages regarding suspected child abuse. She left as many details as she could and her phone number. She was starting the car, when something caught her attention. Someone was running, awkwardly, arms flailing, through the woods. She recognized the two-headed silhouette immediately.

"We want to go with you," Charity gasped when

they arrived at the car.

"You, too?" Adair looked at Prudence.

She nodded, mute, her eyes frightened.

"Good," Adair said. "We'll make that happen. Classes start in August, but the donor is going to arrange for you to visit the campus before school starts. He'll help you get anything you need in the way of clothes or books, and he'll send someone to escort you to campus before fall semester starts. What is the best way to contact you and arrange..." She looked at the girls. Prudence carried a small, plastic suitcase. Charity clutched a single tattered Pittock College flier like a talisman. They hadn't come to give Adair a message. They had escaped. "You can't go back, can you?" Adair knew the answer before the girls spoke.

"We're not even supposed to talk about you," Charity said. "You have been unborn."

"Unborn?"

"You have become that of which we shall not speak," Prudence said. "And it shall be as before the birth of the offender. May the family strike all remembrance from their hearts and tongues."

"But we want to go with you. It is God's will," Charity said, her voice growing stronger.

"Shit," Adair said. "You better get in before they 'unborn' you." She leaned over and opened the door. "What made you change your mind?" she asked as the girls settled nervously into the seat.

"Dorothia," Charity said.

From the diary of Charity Kimball

The sad woman with the pale eyes appeared like a baby sent down the river in a reed basket. Prudence said she was the devil, but I knew I would follow her. I told Prudence that God's signals were difficult to decipher. They were in the wind and in the heart. It was prideful to expect a burning bush every time.

"She has come. It is a sign," I whispered as Prudence slept. "God has grounded her until we are ready. We are his messengers."

She did not want to leave.

I spoke in her prayers. "Has there been another sign since the rabbit? God gave us the rabbit to show us who we are, but there are no others like us and the rabbit. We are fashioned in the image of his love. Do you think he intends us to live here forever? Does he not want us to share his message with the world?"

She turned away from me in her heart, but we are of one heart, and she could not escape.

I took Dorothia's hand while she was still cooling. "Her death is on our heads. He is punishing us for your refusal. Do not forget Job who lost all comfort through no sin of his own. How much more powerful is the wrath of God against those who disobey him?"

"I'm scared," Prudence said.

"He has told me that He will kill our brothers if we disobey," I lied.

So we put what we owned in the tiny suitcase father had brought with him from the wicked world, and we ran. When we saw the sad woman with the pale eyes, I thought perhaps I had been right. God had turned my lies into truth, as he turned water to wine, for I saw something in her face of our loneliness, which is also God's loneliness.

But there was something wicked in my words. I dared to speak for the Lord God. I knew He would punish us for my pride. *"For no one knows the thoughts of God except the Spirit of God."*

Chapter Ten

The Purveyor met Bolo at the private shooting range as he had requested. It was early. A slight mist hung over the field behind the range. The leaves on the trees were very still. She was restless. She hated these hours in which there was nothing to do but wait, especially this time, when the prize was so great.

She spotted Bolo's Maybach pulling up the gravel road. He parked a few paces away and stepped out, dressed in a ridiculous baby-blue suit and fedora. She moved toward him, then stopped in midstride. He was not alone. He opened the passenger door, and a woman got out, dressed in an equally theatric 1920's style cloche hat and drop-waist skirt, also in shades of blue. They looked like the middleclass lovers from some Merchant Ivory period piece.

"Who is this?" she asked when they reached her.

The girl was barely twenty, probably half Bolo's age. She clung to Bolo's arm.

"This is Ashley Payten," he said proudly.

"Miss Payten," the Purveyor said without extending her hand.

"It's Ashley Payten Brennan," the girl said with a little giggle.

"They're hyphenating first names now?" the Purveyor asked.

Sarcasm was lost on the girl. "It's not hyphenated.

It's just Ashley Payten. And my sister is Madison Mosley. And my brothers are Jacob Garret, John Bosworth…"

"How wonderful for you. You are thoroughly named," the Purveyor said.

"This is my sister-in-law," Bolo said in a rush, "who I've told you so much about, and who is such a wonderful business woman she practically runs the family. I mean she's the brains behind the brawn." Bolo flexed the arm of his blue linen suit and the girl laughed again. "And this is Ashley, who I told you about."

The Purveyor shook her head. "You did not."

"Yes, I did." He looked upset. "I told you I'd met someone."

The girl stuck out her hand shyly. "More than just met." The purveyor noticed a cheap, brand name diamond in a setting of rubies and sapphires that made it look fake, glittering on the girl's finger. "Bolo." Her voice was a glacier. "Come with me. Miss Ashley Payten Brennan, excuse us for a moment." She took Bolo by the arm and marched him into the gun lodge.

The gun master came out from behind his counter to shake Bolo's hand and offer him a weapon.

"Leave us," she said.

When he was gone, she turned to her henchman. "Who is she?"

"My fiancé."

"Who are her people?"

"She's Michael Brennan's daughter."

"The senator?"

Bolo looked down.

She wanted to crack him across the temple with the butt of her vintage Makarov pistol. "And how old is she? Sixteen?"

"She's twenty-one, and she is very mature for her age."

"And you think you can get married?" she said, her hands tightening into fists. "You think you can do what we do and still marry little Ashley Payten? Have a couple of kids? Maybe you can send Ashley to private school, too. What are you going to tell her you do?"

"I told her we were in business."

"In about ten years she's going to be old enough to wonder what that means."

"I'll tell her."

Now the Purveyor did pick up the Makarov. "The hell you will!"

"You're married," Bolo shot back.

Of course she was married. It was how she got into the business. It was her best investment and perhaps her most expensive. "What part of my marriage looks like you and that child from the cotillion dance? You will break this off."

"But I love her." His lip was actually trembling.

She raised the pistol to his head. If he had half a brain he would see the magazine was missing, but, of course, there could always be one in the chamber. He gasped as the metal touched his temple.

"Tell her you're gay. You're sorry. You can't live a lie. You know this is hard for her, so you vow never to see her again."

"We've already picked a date. She's going shopping for a dress."

"And if you carry on this little charade, there's going to be some icy night after Girl Scouts when Ashley Payten's little pink Cadillac just slips off the road." She pressed the gun hard against his temple. "What a tragedy."

"You can't."

"You don't get to love people," she said, slowly pulling the trigger.

Bolo's whole body jerked at the sound, but of course the gun was empty.

"Get her out of here." She slipped a pair of noise canceling head phones over her ears and headed toward one of the indoor shooting alleys. She slipped a magazine into the pistol and fired five holes into the bull's eye.

Love. It was not permitted in their profession. Bolo would get over Ashley Payten. He was too soulless to die of unrequited love.

As for herself, she was not so sure. For more nights than she could remember, she had had the same dream. She stood at a great height, on top of the world as it was drawn in *The Little Prince* picture book she had read as a child. Her lover stood before her naked, arms open, framed by stars. The Purveyor understood, as one understands in dreams, that her lover finally knew everything, blessed everything. They had become like ancient Gods, their fingertips stirring the affairs of men, their hearts in the sky.

Chapter Eleven

Adair rounded the last bend before the gravel road turned to pavement. Behind her, the mountains lay in shadows, although it was not yet twilight. In the passenger seat, Charity and Prudence sat quietly, Prudence staring at her lap as if in prayer, Charity gazing wide-eyed out the window.

"We've never been this far down," Charity said.

"Not to go to school or to go to the doctor?" Adair asked.

Prudence looked up. "Everything the faithful need is provided by God."

Charity added, "There used to be a doctor who would come."

Prudence opened her mouth to speak, then stopped. Up ahead, a black shape, like an onyx boulder, blocked the road. On the side of the road in a turnout, three similar shapes hulked beneath an expanse of granite that had been sheered to make way for the road.

Adair blinked. The simplicity of Oquat had rubbed off on her. For a moment she did not recognize the shapes: three SUVs and a limousine. She slowed to a stop before the SUV blocking the road. The driver's door opened, and a man emerged. He had a ruddy complexion, a fine suit, and impenetrably dark sunglasses.

"Who is he?" Charity whispered.

"I don't know," Adair said, peering at the man.

The windows of the other vehicles were as dark as the man's glasses.

Prudence started praying again.

"She thinks it's a sign," Charity said. She sounded scared. "Father Apostle says the power of the True Reckoning is immense."

"You think these people are from your church?"

Prudence spoke louder now, although not to Adair or her sister. "*And the great dragon was cast out, that old serpent, called the Devil, and Satan, which deceiveth the whole world. And I heard a loud voice saying in heaven, 'Now is come salvation, and strength, and the kingdom of our God....And they loved not their lives unto the death.*"

The man approached the car slowly, his hand raised.

Out of the corner of her eye, Adair saw movement. She checked the mirrors again. A window in one of the other SUVs had retracted. Now she could see a telephoto lens extend from the dark interior of the vehicle. "Fucking paparazzi!" She squeezed the wheel. "Hold on." She swerved around the SUV. The BMW fishtailed in the last scattering of gravel on the pavement, then the tires gripped the road. The man ran for his vehicle. The other SUVs lit up in a flash of parking lights.

Adair had the advantage of a head start, and a moment later they were whipping around the bends on the curvy mountain road. On one side, a cliff rose to meet the sky. On the other, a forested canyon promised a hundred foot plunge. But this was the sports car's natural habitat and the road was not unlike the Monteith Speedway where Adair had raced as a teenager.

For a moment, she felt a little bit of her former self invigorate her limbs. The pain receded. Her vision grew clearer.

The SUV fell farther and farther behind.

Eventually, Adair came to a side road, took it, turned left, and took another side road. "If they find us now, it'll be dumb luck," she said.

"What are they?" Charity asked.

"Paparazzi." Adair sighed, remembering the many galas she had attended in boarding school. She had never been the focus of their attention, but there had been enough senators' daughters, enough movie star progeny, to attract photographers. "They make their living by taking pictures."

"Of you?"

It occurred to Adair that the minute the twins stepped out of the car, they would become a media spectacle. "No, of you."

"Because we are a symbol of God's inseparable love," Prudence said, wonder filling her voice.

✿ ✿ ✿ ✿

At seventy-five miles per hour on a straight, open road, Adair felt the pain reclaim her body.

An autoimmune response to trauma.

If Helen had stayed, she wondered, if Helen had held her the way the girls wrapped their arms around themselves, around each other, would her body have rebelled so completely? Was there not a possibility that Helen's presence could have calmed whatever animal terror caused her very cells to revolt?

There was no use thinking about that now.

Helen's calm, modulated voice on the phone had told Adair everything she needed to know. She was indifferent. She was gone.

"The man who gave you the scholarship," Adair began. She felt very tired. "He thought you would come to school later. He was going to send everything you needed, and then get someone to come get you. But we left early and someone must have told the paparazzi."

"And now?" Charity asked.

"There will come a time, when you'll have to come out. You'll get a lot of attention, and you want to be ready for that. They'll want to put you on television."

"What's television?" Charity asked.

Adair shook her head. "It's a waste of time. It's the wicked world. We'll get a hotel in a couple of hours, after it gets dark, and I'll show you one. It will be hard to convince people that you're just…who you are. But you'll have a good life at Pittock. It's a good place."

"Will you stay with us?" Charity asked.

Adair felt Charity's eyes searching her face. "No. I'm going to make sure you're safe, and you have everything you need, and then…I'm going to go away."

"For a long time?" Charity ran her hand along the dashboard, as if trying to trace the edges of her new world.

"Forever," Adair said.

"With God?" Charity asked, cocking her head.

"I don't know about God."

Charity touched Adair's hand on the steering wheel, a soft, probing, unselfconscious touch—like the touch of a small child. Prudence kept her head bowed and her hand balled in a fist in her lap.

"I think we are always with God," Charity said. It sounded like a question.

≈≈≈≈

Adair was surprised by how good she felt as she walked the familiar path across the quad, between the science buildings. It had been winter in the Oquat Mountains, but it was warm in Pittock. Green tinted the oak trees. The daffodils were in bloom, a thousand variations on the yellow flute. A strain of cello music drifted from a practice room in the music hall. As she crossed the quad, Adair caught sight of her former student, Marcus Billing. He walked with a group of friends, probably heading to a three thirty seminar.

He caught sight of her and called out, "Dr. Wilson!"

His friends pulled him away. "We're going to be late," they complained.

He blew Adair an extravagant kiss. "I love you, Dr. Wilson."

She watched as Marcus continued on his way, remembering the shy, bovine creature he had been when she first met him. Now everything about his body language exuded cheer. She loved that: watching awkward freshmen grow into confident young men and women.

A minute later, she was at the Ventmore. The theater was fashioned in Elizabethan style, and Adair noticed it had been repainted. Inside was brighter than she remembered. Looking up she saw a new arrangement of houselights. She walked down the center aisle, brushing her fingertips along the seat backs.

She had made love to Helen in this theater, their backs against the heavy, velvet curtains. Helen had cried out, her voice projected by the acoustics of the empty theater. She had been so beautiful, so tormented. And Adair had been so in love.

"Excuse me." A man of about thirty, with stringy, blond hair lumbered down the aisle. He stopped in front of her and readjusted his glasses on his nose. "Can I help you?"

"Who are you?" Adair asked.

"I'm the new theater program director."

"What?"

"Andrew Slater." He paused, as though waiting for her to recognize the name. "From Rutgers," he added.

Adair felt nauseous. She had built the theater program from a box of musty pinafores to one of the best theater arts programs in the country. "Boot camp for Broadway," one article had called it. "No one but Adair Wilson could do this," another columnist had written. "It is not through arduous selection that she produces the best young actors in America, it is through the grace of her teaching." But she had been gone for months. Of course, they would rehire. *Her* last half year had been eaten away in a blur of pills, but the rest of the world had kept living. The magnitude of her loss left her breathless. "What happened to the last theater director?" she asked.

The man squeezed his lips into a little sneer. "She was some debutant, left her job in the middle of the year for no reason, so they fired her," he added as though this fact was ridiculously obvious. "She's probably crazy."

❧❧❧❧

Adair opened the door to Meyerbridge Hall. Patrick was seated behind his desk, glaring at his computer screen. At the sound of Adair's entry, he looked up. A smile that was half shock and half joy lit his face. "Oh my God! Adair! You're alive." He leapt to his feet, his arms outstretched. "Holy shit. You actually came back." He raised his voice. "Helen! Get out here."

A moment later, Adair was pressed in Patrick's robust hug. Pain seared through her ribs.

"Let me go," Adair gasped, stumbling out of his grasp. "Don't touch me."

"Fuck you," Patrick said, joy converging with anger. He folded his arms across his broad chest. "Where have you been?"

"I got the twins."

"I called you a thousand times. What the fuck was up with that letter?" His face softened and he rubbed his forehead. "We thought you were dead until Helen went up to New Hampshire. Did you mean it…? Were you really going to…?"

Adair stared at him. She knew she should embrace Patrick. She should tell him that she was sick, tell him to hug her gently, tell him she missed him. But she felt too tired to explain. "Where's Helen?"

"She's in a meeting." He pointed toward the conference room.

Everyone in the meeting looked up as Adair burst through the door. Helen froze in mid-gesture, her hand raised above her laptop.

Adair felt Helen's beauty like a physical blow.

Her auburn hair was pulled back in a twist. A few tendrils had come loose and curled against her cheeks. Her eyes were dark. Her slightly parted lips were the color of rosewood, a lipstick perfectly chosen to compliment her hair, or perhaps just the blush of her own blood beneath the skin. "Adair," she gasped.

"Excuse me. We are in a meeting," Bruno Duffy, the dean of Arts and Letters said. His close-set features drew together into a grieved pout and his voice came out in a whine, both pleading and hostile. "This entry is inappropriate."

"I need to talk to Helen."

"You may schedule an appointment with her secretary."

Her secretary. The president. As if Adair had not known Patrick since he was a scholarship kid nearly bullied to death at her prep school. As if she had not drunk Helen's body. "Helen, I brought the Kimball twins," Adair said. "They're at my apartment. I have to talk to you. Do you know what they are?"

"Who is this?" one of the women at the meeting whispered.

Another woman whispered back, "Adair Wilson."

There was a murmur around the table.

Someone said, "Helen, if you need to take a minute, we can get back to this next time."

Helen was still staring.

"You asked me to get them," Adair said.

"Miss Wilson, I'm going to ask you to leave," Duffy said. "You…"

"Did you fire me, Helen?"

"Do not interrupt me." Duffy stood.

Adair took a deep breath. The pain that circled her ribs was reaching a critical intensity. Soon it would move to her spine, and no heat, no pressure, no movement, would keep it from leaking out into the rest of her body. She heard the doctor's voice: *Stress is a significant contributing factor.* She had to talk to Helen before the pain overcame her.

"Dr. Wilson," Duffy said, pushing his chest forward. "This intrusion is inappropriate especially given your recent dismissal. I would like to remind you of college policy concerning decorous behavior including…"

In one quick movement, Adair swiped her arm across the table, sending a pile of papers, crashing into Duffy's lap.

"Patrick," Duffy yelled down the hall. "Get Wilson out of here."

"Not my job," Patrick called back.

Adair felt a swell of affection for him.

Suddenly she was aware of Helen at her side. Her grasp on Adair's arm was gentle but irrefutable. Adair felt the room around her disappear as she watched Helen's beautiful face crease with worry. "Please, Adair. Come with me."

Moments later they stood in the Carrie Brown Memorial Garden. It was just a corner of the campus, a little nook between the greenhouse and the social science hall. A gravel path outlined the eastern edge of the garden. In its half circle, it held Carrie's shrine, an oak, a cluster of rhododendrons and some ornamental grasses.

Helen still held Adair's elbow, as though afraid Adair might run back to the conference room and further abuse the dean. Slowly she released her grip. "I'm so glad you're here."

"You fired me?" Adair reeled toward Helen.

"Was it convenient? Were you relieved?"

Adair knew her questions weren't fair.

"Adair, of course not."

"I saved your life," Adair went on. "When you went into the asylum, I went after you. I didn't wait for Thompson to show up with a police escort. I didn't stand on the sidelines, I went after you." The exertion of speech intensified the pain in her side and Adair clutched her ribs. "And you couldn't even hold my job?"

"You disappeared. No one could reach you." Helen's face had gone pale.

"Was I just too inconvenient? Your little dyke lover. It doesn't fit, does it?"

Two students hurried past them on the gravel path, glancing and then glancing away. Adair did not lower her voice. "You can send me to the middle of nowhere to round up your precious twins, but you couldn't take me to the alumni dinner, not with Bruno Duffy breathing down your neck about 'decorum.' You–"

"Adair, please," Helen broke in. "I tried to save your job, but the president doesn't have any control over hires. The bylaws are very clear."

"The bylaws? I would have died for you!" She remembered Helen standing on the periphery of the crime scene, cameras flashing in her face. Adair had loved her with an immediate fierceness that was all raw intuition. She also remembered Helen standing in her bedroom, gazing down on her, saying, "You're lovely. You really are. But I have to put the college first."

"I called. I wrote. I stood outside your door," Helen pleaded. "Your servants turned me away." She was crying now.

Adair knew she should stop, but watching Helen cry was like feeling the sting of Cecelia's crop. She stepped forward, projecting every word into Helen's stricken face. "I loved you."

Helen looked at her. "I *love* you." Her eyes were wide. Mascara streaked her cheeks. "I love you. I would never leave you." She clasped Adair's cheeks.

The pressure made Adair salivate and her throat constrict. A second later Helen pressed her lips against Adair's. It wasn't a kiss so much as an exclamation.

Helen ground her lips against Adair's closed mouth. Then she drew back, her hands still squeezing Adair's face. "Adair?"

"You left me." Adair grabbed the lapels of Helen's blazer. For a moment they stood, like wrestlers locked together, neither strong enough to win or break free. *She doesn't want you broken.*

"I tried!" Helen tightened her grip. "I'm sorry. I don't know what you've been through, but I know you've been sick. I got your letter. I'm *here* Adair. Talk to me."

But Adair could not talk because Helen tried to kiss her again. Only this time, the pressure of Helen's touch on her face made a hot needle of pain shoot down her spine. Her mouth filled with bile. She pushed Helen away and turned her back, swallowing the acid so that Helen would not see her vomit on the grass.

Helen put a hand on her shoulder.

"No," Adair choked, and stepped away so that Helen would not smell the sickness on her breath.

"What happened?" Helen asked softly.

Adair felt deflated. There was no point in reminding Helen of the countless messages she had left, no point in sorting through Helen's story and her own half remembrances. "It doesn't matter." Adair dropped onto a bench. "I'm sorry."

Before them, Carrie Brown's shrine looked aged. The New England weather had warped the contents: a photograph of Carrie, a few clippings from the school paper, and a typed summary of Carrie's life that discretely left out her struggles with Body Identity Integrity Disorder and her death at the hands of Marshal Drummond. *Carrie blossomed under the tutelage of theater professor, Adair Wilson,* the obituary read. "It's so little," Adair said. "After everything Carrie went through, that's all she gets. Her picture in a box."

Helen still stood. "I wanted to put in a sculpture, something in bronze, but the budget…"

"No one really wants to remember, do they?" Adair asked. She expected Helen to protest, but Helen only nodded.

"Not really," Helen said. Carefully, as though approaching a wild bird, she sat on the very edge of the bench, as far from Adair as possible. "What happened?" she asked again.

Adair sighed. "It's called Persistent Complex Pain Syndrome. PCPS."

Helen waited.

"It's an autoimmune disorder." Adair ran her hands over her face. "It's very rare. There is a localized version where only the area of the injury is affected: Complex Regional Pain Syndrome. It's like the body is constantly reliving or recreating the trauma. For me, it's my whole body."

"Because you were shot?"

Adair nodded.

"Are you in a lot of pain?"

Adair nodded again.

"There must be a treatment. Have you been to specialists?"

Adair felt tears welling up behind her eyes. "The best specialist in the country." She laughed bitterly. "I have access to the latest drugs."

"Is it…fatal?"

Adair felt like the space between them expanded, as though an ocean had filled up the garden and they were floating apart, the ocean of chance and what could have been instead of what was.

A breeze rounded the corner of the social science hall, blew into the garden waving the grasses, then died down. Somewhere a fountain gurgled. Adair closed her eyes. "It's complicated."

"Because of the letter?"

"Yes."

"You can't, Adair." Helen turned toward her, gripping the bench. "You have to promise me. You won't try again."

Adair nodded.

"Adair," Helen pressed. "Promise me." Helen reached for her, but Adair stood and walked into the shade of the newly leafed oak tree that sheltered Carrie's memory.

"I did this to you, didn't I?" Helen asked, looking up at Adair. Helen's lips had lost their lovely rosewood blush. Her eyes were as dark and frightened as they had been that day in the asylum when Drummond took the gun from Helen's hand and shot Adair in the chest.

"Marshal Drummond did this to me," Adair said, looking away from Helen's penetrating gaze. "There's nothing else. You don't have to feel guilty."

"Promise me!"

Adair wanted to cling to Helen. "The twins are at my apartment," she said instead. "They had to leave with me. Their family wasn't going to let them go. They're conjoined twins. Did you know that?"

"What are you talking about?"

"Dicephalic parapagus twins. Two heads. Two arms. Two legs. Two unique personalities."

"I had no idea." Helen shook her head.

"As soon as they step outside, they're going to be a media spectacle." Adair sighed. "The paparazzi already know. They tried to catch us as we were leaving Oquat, but I dodged them. I got the girls here without anyone seeing them. But the minute they step outside the Grandville Hotel, every reality TV show in America is going to be on campus. You have to protect them. They're sheltered. They'll need a therapist, but they don't even know what that is. They're very religious, at least Prudence is."

"I'll have Patrick take care of that," Helen said.

"Have him call me when you want me to bring them onto campus."

"Adair I…"

Adair felt her gut contract as though the sheath of tissue that held her body in place was writhing. "Go, Helen. I need you to leave me."

Helen stood, one hand raised as if to touch Adair. Then she withdrew it.

"Now!" Adair said.

When Helen was out of sight, Adair doubled over and vomited. Adair was still doubled over, when a voice startled her.

"Not really your finest moment, is it?"

She looked up. Cecelia stepped from the shadow of the oak tree, dressed in tight leather pants and a fitted jacket.

"What are you doing here?" Adair asked.

"I was worried about you. I knew how much you wanted her to remember you."

"Of course she remembers me."

Cecelia held out her hand and pulled Adair into an embrace. "I didn't mean like that," she whispered.

Adair let her forehead sink onto Cecelia's shoulder.

"Come on, baby," Cecelia said quietly. "I'm sure you know someplace where we can be alone." She grabbed Adair by the back of the head, clutching a fistful of Adair's hair, and pulled her closer. "Helen, doesn't want you sick. She never will."

※ ※ ※ ※

Adair walked home slowly, feeling more than usually battered by Cecelia's attentions. Cecelia had taken her to a secluded bend on the Barrow Creek, tied the leather thongs, and whipped Adair savagely across the shoulders until Adair feared she would bleed. When Cecelia finally released her, Adair dressed without speaking and started back toward campus without waiting to see if Cecelia followed.

She almost knocked into a cluster of weekend tourists as she walked. The Pittock murders had devastated college enrollment, but they had been good for tourism. She kept moving, her head down, only looking up when she heard a fire engine pass by.

It was not until she rounded the bend on Main Street that she realized it was not on its way to pick up an elderly woman who had fallen or to put out a hay fire in one of the barns outside of town. Sirens were converging from all directions. People were pouring out of the surrounding buildings pointing down the street toward the Grandville Hotel where Adair had left the twins sitting by the window, clutching their Bible.

Chapter Twelve

Helen bypassed the cafeteria counter. The offerings were the same as always-boxed tuna fish sandwiches, anemic salads, a grill that could deep fry anything and did. The students made a sport out of talking the short order cook into trying new recipes. Fried Rice Krispie treats were the latest favorite. She filled a paper coffee cup at the urn. The coffee smelled like it had been sitting since noon. Still, Helen liked the anonymity of the cafeteria. The professors ate at the Faculty Club House by Barrow Creek. The administration ate at the new bistro near campus. No one over the age of twenty thought the cafeteria served real food.

She reached the cashier and Duffy, who had been following behind her, darted forward with his sandwich. "I'll get this." He pulled out his wallet, pointing to Helen's coffee.

"It's fine," Helen said to the student clerk. "It's on account HHCI9."

The girl looked back and forth between Duffy's wallet and Helen's glare.

Duffy pulled out a fifty dollar bill. "I don't think this is college business," he said, handing the bill to the clerk.

Helen wanted to rip the fifty dollar bill out of his hand. His idea of college business was whittling down his division's materials and supplies budget and diverting the money to his dry campus campaign. His idea of college business was writing and rewriting the campus bylaws. She said nothing. Duffy paid and shot her a self-satisfied look.

They took their seats at a table near the window. The room looked out at the physical sciences building. *Deus in astra choris. Homo in studiis invenit scientiam,* the motto read, carved in stone above the entrance. *God, in the stars dances. Man, in pursuit, finds science.* That was college business.

"Have the ADA auditors done Boston Hall yet?" Helen asked as they settled into their plastic seats.

Duffy answered at length. Helen watched the cafeteria reflected in the window behind his head. The room was almost empty, caught in the lull between late lunches and early dinners. When he stopped talking, she asked about a new part-time hire in music.

Duffy looked at her. "Did you hear what I just said?"

"Sorry?"

"That was some fiasco this morning."

Helen did not want to talk about Adair, although Adair was the reason she had invited Duffy to dine with her.

Fiasco.

Adair had looked terribly sick. Her skin was pale, her face slightly bloated, her movements jerky as though she walked, barefoot, across an electrified grate. But her eyes were the same, the ozone blue of heaven's outer reaches. "We need to talk about Professor Wilson," Helen said.

Duffy reached for Helen's hand, but she withdrew it. "This bothers you, doesn't it?" he said.

"Of course it bothers me. One of our most

talented faculty members was instrumental in solving a serial murder on campus. She saved *my* life, and Pittock rewards that by firing her, gutting the program she grew from the ground up, and replacing her with a part time professor with the charisma and the talent of a sponge."

Duffy nibbled his sandwich, then daubed his lips. "Well, let's look at this from all sides." That was his preamble to everything, although Helen had never seen him take another opinion into consideration unless he was bullied into it by the other deans. He checked his cell phone. His eyebrows rose a fraction of an inch. Then he set it face down on the table. "Adair Wilson has been gone for over half a year without an email, without a leave request, without a Post-it note as to where she was or why."

Helen had never shared Adair's resignation letter, as though keeping it a secret would keep Adair at Pittock.

"If she was on Family Medical Leave Act," Duffy continued, "or a sabbatical…but she wasn't. She just didn't show up."

"She almost died." Helen paused. "What if she did fill out FMLA paperwork?"

"She didn't."

"But what if she did?" Helen wished she could throttle Duffy. Barring that, she wished she could pull rank, but she knew what all college presidents learned eventually–her power was illusory. She was a figurehead, a symbol, a fund raiser. Her job was to eat tapas with wealthy alums. When it came to the actual day-to-day running of the college, Patrick had more clout.

"The college charter is very clear on this," Duffy

said. "Deans have the final say in hiring. I told Andrew Slater a renewal contract was almost a guarantee."

"Why would you rehire him? Slater has done nothing but mount the worst production of *My Fair Lady* that I have ever seen."

"And that's why the president doesn't get to make faculty hiring decisions. This isn't about your personal taste in theater or in *other areas.*" Duffy paused significantly, pushing his wire framed glasses up a nose that managed to be both petit and bulbous. He checked his phone again. "That is the purview of the deans and the department heads. And may I remind you, Adair has not expressed any interest in returning to Pittock unless you count that ridiculous outburst at the meeting."

Helen pressed her fingers to the bridge of her nose, hoping to forestall a migraine. She had not slept the night before.

Duffy folded his hands and looked at her over the rims of his lenses. "She's not interested, Helen. I hope you are not trying to use your position to make arrangements in your personal life." Duffy's smile was neither professional, nor friendly.

"She was here today," Helen pleaded, "and she was devastated by the loss of her job, and this has nothing to do with me. This has everything to do with the humane treatment of a woman who should be a campus hero."

"So get her a plaque. We can't have people like her just disappear and then think that they'll get their jobs back."

"There are no *people like her,*" Helen spat.

A student worker tidying the recycling station glanced over. A freshman, Helen guessed, the girl would not have known Adair. She would never have seen one of Adair's spectacular performances, never have looked across the quad to see Adair suddenly turn a cartwheel in the grass. She would never have sat in on one of Adair's lectures, lectures that were so good the Teaching Company recorded them. Helen had bought the set, but she could not bring herself to watch it, certain that the sight of Adair on the Ventmore Theater stage would break her heart.

Duffy checked his phone again. This time he typed something before setting it face down on the table. "Wilson is gone." His eyes slid down the V of Helen's blazer. "I think it's time you woke up and saw what's in front of you." Duffy picked up Helen's phone from the table. A fleck of tuna fish clung to his finger. It transferred to the phone.

"Excuse me." Helen reached for her phone.

He ignored her, tapping something into the phone. Then he turned it so it faced her and placed it back on the table. "It started about fifteen minutes ago." He stood, leaving his tray on the table despite signs reminding him to bus his own. "Sorry, Helen."

Helen wiped the phone with a paper napkin. On the screen, she saw a reporter's face frozen in an awkward grimace. Behind the reporter, the spray from a firefighter's hose blasted a window. Helen touched play.

The video buffered for a moment, then the reporter spoke. "I'm here outside the Grandville Hotel in Pittock Massachusetts where firefighters have responded to a fire of dangerous proportions. Initial reports say the blaze began in a boiler and quickly spread throughout the basement and parts of the first floor. Areas surrounding the building have been evacuated as firefighters battle what could become the fire of the decade."

Helen leapt up. She dialed Adair's cell phone. *Be there.*

It was no use. As Helen expected, Adair's cool alto voice instructed her to leave a message.

❧ ❧ ❧ ❧

Helen approached the Grandville Hotel at a breathless run. It was only 5 p.m., and the sun was still high, but Main Street was twilight-dark with smoke. Her eyes burned. Her lungs, already tight from running, expelled the smoky air in violent coughs.

On the street, the people of Pittock seemed to be of two minds. Half were fleeing, pushing children in front of them, T-shirts pulled up over their noses, while the rubber-neckers were running toward the blaze, clamoring against the police barricade, and snapping pictures.

The scene before her did not look real. All the windows on the east side of the Grandville Hotel and half the windows on the north side were on fire. Flames billowed out, blackening the white brick. Two fire engines were already spraying the lower windows, but it seemed a futile gesture. The Grandville was six stories high, with vaulted ceilings at every level.

Beyond the sawhorse and tape, she saw Police Chief Thompson. She called to him. He had one hand on his shoulder-mounted radio; with his other he directed an EMT crew. "I can't," he mouthed back.

"Adair. She might be in there!" Helen yelled. Panic gripped her. Adair was sick. She was weak. Helen had already lost her once, she could not lose her again.

It was like watching a traffic accident in slow motion. At that exact moment, Adair could be alive, huddled on the floor, crawling away from the flames, and in minutes—seconds—the balance between oxygenated air and smoke would tip. "No!" Helen screamed. "Adair! She's in there."

But of course, anyone could be in there. The police and the firefighters all knew that. Helen clutched the sawhorse in front of her.

From deep within the fire, Eliza whispered, *help me, Helen.*

Slowly Helen eased along the outside edge of the barricade, keeping close to the building behind and out of the way of the firefighters. Closer to the fire, the heat was devastating. It seared her eyes. She was drowning and her lungs were on fire, but still she called into the heat and the noise. "Adair!" She could barely see. Her eyes wept from the smoke. Every breath drew in hot ashes. But somewhere inside the embers, she could feel Eliza singing, *ashes, ashes.*

"Did everyone get out?" Helen screamed to a man with a bullhorn, but he did not hear her.

Another fire engine pulled up. Three firefighters leapt off the back of the truck and began unfurling a canvas hose. Another pair of firefighters donned oxygen tanks and an even heavier layer of protective clothing. Everyone was yelling. Even the onlookers seemed frantic.

Suddenly, Helen saw her.

Near the blaze, Adair was arguing with a fireman. She looked almost paramilitary herself in her heavy boots and white tank top smeared with soot. On her face, Helen read the same fear she had felt. For a moment, she thought Adair must be looking for her.

"Over here!" Helen called

The fireman grabbed Adair's wrists.

Helen could hear him yell, "You can't go in there!"

"I have to get them out," Adair yelled back. "They wouldn't know. They would have stayed."

"We're doing everything we can."

"Let go of me!"

"You have to get back. It's too late." The fireman punctuated his words with a chop of his hand. "It's too late!" His voice was almost as anguished as Adair's.

Helen held her breath and ran forward. She felt, as she did in dreams, as though she waded through a thick ocean. Around her the sirens blared. The bullhorn screamed, "Emergency personnel, pull back."

All the first story windows were gone. Inside was a wall of undifferentiated flame. There was no way to dodge past burning curtains and falling beams. There were no "places" inside the inferno, only white hot noise.

Over the back of Helen's shoulder, Eliza whispered, *It's so hot.*

Then Adair caught sight of Helen and looked, it seemed, almost directly over her shoulder at Eliza. Eliza hissed and disappeared into the cacophony.

"Helen!" Adair stopped struggling with the fireman. "What are you doing here?"

The whole town was there, either watching or cowering a few blocks over. Helen grabbed Adair's arm. "She's my friend," she said to the fireman. Then to Adair, she said, "I came for you."

"You have to move back." The fireman pushed the barricade back. "It's going to collapse."

"Helen," Adair said again. "Please. The twins are

in there."

A deafening crack ripped through the sounds around them. Inside the fire, something was giving way.

Helen grabbed for Adair's hand and held it tightly.

The fireman yelled, "Run!"

Helen felt like no time had passed since Carrie's murder. She was back in the terror and the strange exhilaration of the days before Drummond's arrest. She felt the sting of embers touching her skin. A shower of sparks landed in Adair's hair. Then their feet were pounding the pavement in unison as they fled. Behind them, Helen heard a crash. One of the floors had collapsed. She followed Adair.

Adair did not stop until they were standing in an alley three blocks from the fire. In the narrow space the air was cooler and less smoky. She leaned against a wall, breathing heavily. "The twins were in there."

"The alarm must have gone off." Helen reached out but stopped before her hand touched Adair's arm. "They would have gotten out."

"They wouldn't understand." Adair rested the back of her head against the brick wall behind her. "They didn't know what a fire alarm was. They didn't even know how to work the elevator. Hell, they hadn't seen real stairs before they came here."

Adair's face was covered in soot, and her eyes were paler than ever.

"I should have been there. I was…going to go home. I should have gone home. They would have waited for me. They sat there waiting for me." Adair turned, leaning her side up against the wall, her face pressed to the brick. "Oh, God, it's my fault."

"You don't know that." Helen's throat felt raw. "None of this is your fault." She started to cough. When she tried to speak again, her voice was an indecipherable rasp. Because she could not speak, Helen opened her arms. She expected Adair to turn away, but Adair fell into her embrace, clutching her, pressing her face to Helen's shoulder. Helen caught the words.

"...dirty...not again...he was good to me..." Slowly, Adair's words faded into sobs and then into gasps. Helen cradled her, pressing her lips to Adair's hair. For a long time, she held her, tight and motionless, feeling only the weight of Adair's body leaning against her.

"Are you all right?" Helen whispered when her voice finally returned.

"No." Adair spoke quietly. Then suddenly she pulled away. "I did that, Helen." The tears were gone. "And they're dead now."

As if on some kind of cue, a large, black sedan turned down the alley, its massive side-view mirrors barely clearing the brick walls. It stopped in front of them. A door opened. Helen caught a glimpse of a woman with black hair. Her severe beauty printed on Helen's retina like the flash of a camera, and it took Helen a moment to remember the face...Cecelia Beaucharnel, the family friend who had greeted her outside the Wilson's estate.

Beaucharnel extended a hand to Adair. "I've been looking for you."

Then the door closed, and Helen quickly pressed herself against the wall to avoid being crushed by the side of the sedan. And they were gone.

From the Diary of Charity Kimball

I smelled the smoke before Prudence. It was like the smoke from Father's burn pile, the time he burned the tires from his truck because Father Apostle said the wicked world would call him to leave and he must prepare accordingly.

Prudence asked me what we should do, and we agreed we would wait for the sad woman with the pale eyes. But a man came in her stead. He opened the door. He said, "I am your friend." I knew he was a false profit. His eyes were quick and empty. But the smoke grew thicker. Prudence began to cough, and it was Dorothia's cough.

Then the man said, "I don't have time for this," and he grabbed Prudence's arm and dragged us toward a staircase. It was dizzying. It went down and down and down. The smoke got thicker and thicker. Finally, we were underground. Red lights flashed through the smoke, and something wailed like an unholy bird. The man kept pulling us. Prudence kept coughing. I could barely see. And I thought perhaps we had descended into hell for the sin of my lie. It did not seem fair that Prudence should be punished with me.

Then the man shoved us into a car and closed the door behind us. A moment later, we were on the street. I tried to roll down the windows so that Prudence could breathe but the windows were locked and the glass was very dark. I pressed my face to it, but the people on the street could not see us, or, perhaps, they were too busy running because there was a great fire behind us.

The man said, "Hold on. I'll get the air conditioning running." Only it wasn't really him. It was his voice coming through a disc in the wall. There was a window between us. I could not touch him, although I could see the back of his head.

"She can't breathe!" I hit the window.

The man said, "I've got the fucking air on. Just wait."

A thin stream of clean air, trickled out of a hole in the wall, like spring water in a dirty pond.

Prudence coughed and coughed, and her coughing jerked our body and wracked my chest, and I thought, *maybe she is dying.*

I could hear her prayers. *Lord, I abase myself before your judgment. I have sinned and strayed from the True Path. Return me to my home, oh Lord.* She was so fervent. She was so good. Even as her breath slowed and she drew her air from my air, she loved God.

I could feel my heart—which is her heart—pounding, and I knew I would rip it from our chest before I returned to Oquat. I would go back into that burning building before I would go back home.

❧❧❧❧

The car stopped after many hours. I could tell it was night by the stillness on the street, although the windows of the car were so dark they made even daylight turn black. Prudence thought it was a sign. The man spoke to us through the disc in the wall of the car and told us to remain silent. Then he came to the door of the car and opened it and threw a cloth bag over our heads and shoulders. "Keep your head inside the bag," he whispered. "If anyone sees you, you're dead."

I missed the sad women with the pale eyes. She was of the wicked world, but there was no wickedness in her. I had asked Father Apostle about that once. What happens to the babies who are born without the True Reckoning? How will they avoid the fires of hell, if there is no one to teach them? Father Apostle told me that a woman's questions were the root of sin, and then he said they would burn. "We are not punished for what we have done," he said. "We are punished for what we are." I understood that then. I understand it now. I felt a tear slide down my cheek. Prudence wiped it away.

Pray with me, Prudence whispered in my mind.

She prayed as the man opened his car door and slammed it shut. She prayed as he stomped around the car to our window. She prayed as the man pulled us out of the car. I did not. I only stared at the ground at our feet, then at a flat wooden door like the door of a tomb. Inside there was a staircase. At the foot of the staircase, beneath the ground there was a place with many pipes running along the floor which was sometimes dirt, like a root cellar, and sometimes a hard floor, like the butchering patio where Mother used to take the chickens.

I did not pray, although I tried to comfort Prudence in my mind. I made a mind-picture of our false friend, with his blond hair which had been combed to silk like the hair of a vain woman. *His jacket shines like his hair,* I spoke to her mind. *This man cannot war against God's creations.*

Prudence kept praying. God kept silent.

I heard the man unlock a door. He pushed us. Then he pulled the bag off our heads. "Don't make a sound."

The room was very dark. A little bit of blue light came through a high window with thick, opaque glass, but that was all. As my eyes adjusted, I could see a bed and a toilet. The man watched us.

In my mind, I whispered, *see, he has provided for our requirements. He cannot mean us any harm.*

Prudence turned away from me because she believed I had given false witness. I had taken her away from the mountains, from Mother and Daddy, from our brothers, from Blue, from the Apostles and the little white chapel, from the ground that held Dorothia's body.

"Is it not arrogance," I quoted Father Apostle, "to claim to know the purpose of God's plan?" I spoke out loud. I wanted to see the false friend's face as I spoke the words of the True Reckoning, but he did not recoil from the word of God.

He watched us, fiddling with a small, dark object, like an idol or a talisman. I did not know what he would do next. Father Apostle never put words to the wickedness of the world, lest the tempted converts return to their old ways.

"Okay, here's what's going to happen girls," the man said.

Prudence coughed, deep inside where her air and her blood mixed.

"We need a doctor," I said, but I was not thinking about the time the doctor visited Dorothia and, for a few months, she was cured.

The man continued to lay his eyes on us. Prudence hid her face.

"Listen, you're gonna make a call," the man said. "If you do exactly what I say, I won't hurt you. Nobody's gonna touch you. Mr. Galloway's made that clear."

Prudence coughed again.

In the dimness of that wicked room, I heard Prudence's thoughts in her very breath, in my breath.

Sister, why do you not love me?

I touched the tears on her cheek and thought of Father Apostle.

It is not what you have done; it is what you are.

Chapter Thirteen

Helen set out two glasses and a bottle of merlot. Then she poured herself a shot of vodka. She felt sick. Everything in the Pittock House, the college president's historical residence, reminded her of Adair. When Adair was first courting her, Adair had acquired the key to Helen's residence. In an overblown gesture of affection, she had redecorated the mansion. Removing the Turkish rugs and horse hair sofas, she had installed a white velvet sofa, white velvet arm chairs, and a white marble coffee table. In place of Jedidiah Pittock's portrait she had hung an oceanscape painting of such gorgeous subtlety it still took Helen's breath away.

The whole project had been the result of Helen's offhand comment that she wanted her house decorated in white. Helen had just been making small talk, sifting through her memory for a blueprint of everyday conversation. What did normal women say? What would she say if she had not spent her whole life caring for her sister Eliza? If she had ever had friends? If she had not opened the kitchen door into a pool of her sister's blood? If she did not see her sister's specter in the shimmer of birch leaves? If she had not felt, even then, that the young professor with the alien blue eyes was somehow her savior?

She poured another shot of vodka and knocked it back. She saw Adair's face in her mind's eye.

Beautiful Adair, her face darkened by smoke and her eyes as wild as a winter storm. Helen knew what she should do and what was forbidden by all the rules of professional decorum. The doorbell rang. She moved toward the door as if in a trance.

"You wanted to see me, Helen?" Bruno Duffy carried a stack of folders under his arm, probably records of faculty who had ordered more than their allotted number of dry erase pens. Behind him the campus was dark.

Helen knew he had had a late meeting. She knew it would run long. She had seen the agenda on his calendar. Now it was after eleven "Come in," she said.

The Pittock House was surrounded by bushes. She could feel Eliza shivering up their stems.

Helen took the folders from Duffy and placed them on an end table by the door, touching his hand in the process. He smelled like damp paper, sweat, and old linoleum. "Let me take your jacket." She slid his blazer off his shoulders, running her fingers down his back.

He turned, surprised.

She smiled. It was so easy. "Let's have a glass of wine."

"I...well..." he stammered.

He had a wife, a prudish, saintly, ash-blond woman who wore gingham dresses and ruled over their brood of five children with a saccharine fist. Helen had seen her at campus picnics smiling at Duffy's colleagues and pinching her children when she thought no one was looking.

Helen led Duffy to the kitchen and poured two glasses of merlot. She motioned for Duffy to take one of the chairs at the kitchen table.

"That was quite some fire today," he said.

Reluctantly, she placed her hands on his shoulders and massaged. He groaned under his breath.

"You're tense. Relax," Helen said. Her own body felt like it was squeezed in the jaws of a vice. She massaged his shoulders for several more minutes, then ran her fingers through his thick, gray hair. Tiny flecks of grease caught under her nails.

"Helen, you surprise me," he said.

She reached around him and picked up her wine. "Oh, I don't think you'll really be surprised." She tried to keep rage out of her voice. She wanted to wrap her hands around his neck, to press her thumbs into his arteries. She wondered if that was how Marshal Drummond felt. Was it this easy?

She pulled her fingers from Duffy's hair, resisting the urge to wipe her hands on her slacks. She took a seat across from him. This conversation had to be conducted eye to eye. "You said I should pay attention to what was right in front of me," she said. "I think I know what you want."

"Mmmm." He closed his eyes as if he were still savoring her fingers in his hair.

Helen stretched her leg so it rested against Duffy's.

"And you know what I want," she added.

His eyes opened.

"Don't be obtuse." She leaned forward, holding his gaze. "It's very simple. The answer is yes." She dropped her voice to a husky whisper. "And the price is Wilson."

"I can't just…"

Helen touched his lips with the tip of her finger. "Yes you can. You don't give a shit about Andrew

Slater, and his contract is up at the end of the semester. Reinstate Wilson."

"I would have to run that by the other arts faculty."

Helen slipped her foot out of its shoe and slid it up Duffy's leg. "They love her." She stood and held out her hand. When Duffy stood, she reached for the sag in his pants and squeezed gently. He sighed. She felt him stiffen.

"Do we have a deal?" Helen asked.

"I…"

She released him for a second. Reading his face, she guessed his wife had lain down only five times, once for each of their blond children. She tried again.

This time he groaned loudly. "Yes."

"Yes? Yes, you will reinstate Adair Wilson? Yes, you will tell her that you have renewed her contract? Yes, you will do everything you can to encourage her to come back?"

Duffy reached for the back of a chair as Helen continued her ministrations.

"Yes," Duffy said, his voice strained.

"And do you understand that if you don't, I will tell everyone about our little arrangement?"

His eyes bulged open, his face torn between pleasure and distress. "You wouldn't!"

Helen released his zipper. "I won't have to."

For a fraction of a second, Eliza's face appeared in the window behind Duffy's head, one eye staring, the other socket gaping black. Then she was gone, a subliminal frame spliced into the film.

"It would be very bad for your career," Duffy said. "Anything you did to me would come down on you tenfold."

She slid her hand into his boxers. He trembled. She moved her hand up and down, all the while watching the window for Eliza's face. But Eliza had disappeared. When Helen felt Duffy's legs tremble and his belly tighten, she squeezed just below the head to abort the orgasm. She withdrew her hand. She wanted his full attention. "You see Bruno, the difference is that I don't care what happens to me."

Chapter Fourteen

Cecelia had wanted to take Adair back to the Wilson Estate, but Adair had refused, instead calling one of the family's secretaries and asking her to book a hotel room near Pittock. The Motel 6 had been the only option, and Cecelia had complained, "Now you're just being stubborn." Adair simply shrugged and ordered the driver to take her to the small, squat hotel at the edge of town.

There she called the police department's non-emergency number and asked about the twins. The dispatcher said it was too soon to identify all the casualties. Adair explained the twins' situation, but she knew how pain and fatigue slurred her words. She knew how she sounded. She ended the call and turned on the television. If the twins had escaped, the media would be swarming. A two-headed girl! But there was no mention of them. She had doubled her dose of Texidol and passed out.

❧ ❧ ❧ ❧

Now it was dark. She had no idea how long she had been lying unconscious. Something was moving on the table beside her. She jumped. It was her phone, vibrating across the glass surface. "Hello?"

"Hello."

It was Prudence!

"Where are you?" Adair asked, suddenly awake.

"We've decided to go home. I'm sorry for the trouble we caused you. We are going back to Oquat to be with our family. It is the right thing to do. Father Apostle has to come get us, and he is going to take us home."

"Wait." There was something familiar in the way Prudence spoke. Adair had heard that tone a thousand times before. It was the voice of a new theater student reciting her lines. Flat. Barely memorized. "Tell me where you are. Don't hang up."

There was a scuffle on the other end of the phone.

"Please do not try to find us. We do not want to see you again. We are Apostles of the True Reckoning, and we must go home."

Adair thought she heard a man's voice in the background. Then Prudence added in a rush, "Sister Dorothia said to say hello. She said she is looking forward to seeing us. We are going to be with her."

Then the phone went dead. When Adair called back, she got a message saying the number had been disconnected.

❧ ❧ ❧ ❧

Adair slipped into her leather jacket, tucked the Seacamp in the inside pocket, and stepped out into the cool night air.

When she arrived at the Pittock Police Department the dispatcher greeted her. "The chief is on the road."

"I have to speak to him." Adair noticed the sign. *Surrender all weapons at front counter.* She pulled the Seacamp out and put it on the counter. "Call him now," she said. "Tell him Adair Wilson is here to see him."

The dispatcher grabbed the gun and put it in a locked drawer. "You can wait there." She spoke into her radio. "Ten-nineteen station, ten-ninety-six. Copy?"

A few minutes later, Thompson appeared, looking concerned. "You'd better come on back." He led Adair down a narrow corridor to a small room, bare except for a table, two chairs, and a silvered window that, presumably, allowed people in another room to look in. "What is it?" Thompson searched her face. "Are you all right? Here, sit." He pulled out a chair for her.

Adair told him about the twins' phone call. Thompson listened, his long fingers folded on the table before him. He nodded after each sentence, but there was something wary in his expression.

"They said they were going to see their sister, Dorothia, but she's dead. They were trying to give me a message," Adair went on. "There was someone else in the room, and then they just hung up. Tyron, you've got to trace the phone call. You've got to do something."

When Adair had lived in Pittock, she and Thompson had been casual friends. Before Carrie Brown and Marshal Drummond, they would drink beers at the Craven and tease each other for noticing the pretty college girls who fluttered into the bar. She had met his wife. He had given her her dog, Ulysses, when he rescued the enormous beast from an animal hoarder. It was an easy, simple friendship. It was another life.

Thompson hesitated. "Has something happened

Adair?"

"Yes!"

"I mean besides this?"

Adair caught her reflection in the mirrored window. Her hair was matted. Her bottom lip was still swollen where Cecelia's kiss had become a bite. Her eyes looked wide and flat and gray. She remembered Andrew Slater's words. "*She was some debutant, left her job in the middle of the year for no reason, so they fired her. She's probably crazy.*" Was he wrong? Could her body be this sick and her mind not break a little bit? "I've been sick." She wanted to tell Thompson it was none of his business. The twins were no less gone because she was sick. But it mattered. She had learned that over the past months. Her words weighed less because her body was failing.

"We tried to call the Kimball family," Thompson said slowly, "after you left your message with dispatch."

"They don't have a phone," Adair balled the cuffs of her jacket in her hands.

"I know," Thompson said. "So we called one of the police departments down there and asked them to send someone out to talk to the next of kin. It took some doing to find them, but they did."

"And?"

"There aren't any twins."

"That's wrong." Adair placed her fists on the table before her.

"We checked."

"They must have gone to the wrong community. There are probably dozens of people living in those mountains."

"They found the Kimballs. They actually had some ID on them which was surprising. But they never had twins. We corroborated with other people in the village." Thompson shook his head as though it pained him to say the next words. "We asked about you. They had no idea who we were talking about."

Adair thought for a moment. "I've been unborn."

"Pardon?"

"Unborn. They do that when someone shames the community. They write them out of the book of life. They erase them. The whole cult is in on it."

"Okay." Thompson sat back in his chair.

"You have to trace the call." Adair leaned forward, trying to fill the space Thompson had vacated. "Whoever has that phone, has the twins." She could hear her own voice going shrill.

"Has anyone in Pittock talked to them?" Thompson pronounced each word carefully, as though pleading with her to weigh her answer carefully.

"You have to believe me. It must be a cover-up. Someone wants it to look like the twins were killed."

"It doesn't look like anyone was killed. It was a miracle, really. A fire that big, that fast. And no one was even hurt…that we know of."

"That's the point!" Adair said. "They were there, and they weren't killed, and now they're gone. I know they didn't die in the fire. You have to do something. They were good people. They were *children*."

"I'll put out a bulletin. I'll let my people know, and I'll talk to the chief in Oquat."

"That's just paperwork." Adair wanted to scream.

"We're exploring every avenue. We've not ruled out arson. You can leave your phone with us, and we'll trace the call."

"No! You don't believe me."

"I don't have any reason to think you'd lie," Thompson said, but his eyes told another story.

She's probably crazy.

        ❧❧❧❧

It was after eleven when Adair exited the police department. A few minutes later she stood before the Pittock House. The exterior of the saltbox had not changed much since she had seen it last; it had not changed much since Jedidiah Pittock built it in 1890. But Helen had planted some annuals in wine barrel pots by the front door. At the base of one pot sat a concrete statue of a kitten rearing up on its hind legs. At the base of the other, was a collection of stones and shells. She had been to the beach. She had come home with a little shoe box of treasures.

She moved on.

She doesn't want you broken.

Adair pulled out her phone which she had refused to relinquish to Thompson—not that he fought much. *Focus!* She had to get information about the girls, the scholarship, the donor. It was all wrong. Scholarship hopefuls had to apply. Donors did not simply invite homeschooled girls living in remote communities to attend college, and offer them large sums of money.

She dialed Helen's number, but as always it rang and then went to voicemail. She ended the call. The house was silent, but there was a light on in the bedroom.

"Helen?" Adair called into the still air.

Chapter Fifteen

In her upstairs bedroom, Helen kissed Duffy for a long time, delaying the fate she had chosen for herself. The windows were curtained. The overhead light fixture, which she almost never turned on, shone a bleak, white glare on the bed.

Finally Duffy pulled away and said, "You're not at all what I expected."

Duffy's face had lost its affected pout. His pants flapped open and his erection pushed at his cotton boxers. He had always been arrogant, only now it showed through. Helen's hands felt greasy from Duffy's hair. Her mouth tasted of his kiss.

"Take off your jacket," Duffy said.

Slowly, Helen slid out of her suit jacket and hung it over a chair.

"Hurry up." He hitched up his pants and shuffled over to Helen's bed, examining the contents of her bedside table. She moved in front of him quickly, but not quickly enough. He picked up the small, framed photograph.

She had printed it from the website–Adair's faculty profile photograph. Then she had put it in a small, gilt frame. There was a gold heart soldered to the top of the frame and "XXOO" etched on the bottom. It was tacky. It was simple. No one ever saw her bedroom, so it did not matter.

Duffy gave a sharp laugh.

Helen felt like a teenager caught in some ridiculous masturbation fantasy.

"This is what it's all about." Duffy sneered. "You want to fuck Adair Wilson."

I love her.

"You and half this college." He slapped the photograph down on its face. He pushed his boxers down and pulled out his cock. "I'd like to watch that." He laughed again. "She's a fucking dyke."

"Of course she is," Helen said.

"You think this is going to make her want you?" Everything obsequious and bureaucratic about Duffy seemed to have slipped away, leaving only the pride Helen had always sensed behind his pinched smile and his wireframe glasses. He pulled on his cock, two long, slow strokes, closing his eyes as he did.

For a year after Eliza's death, Helen had had the same dream. She had done something innocuous: left a light on, opened a window in Eliza's house. Suddenly she was on the freeway driving to her old job at Vandusen, and she realized what she had done because in dream-logic it was terrible, unthinkable. She tried to turn the car around, to get back to the house. Everything moved in slow motion, but she always made it back and the outcome was always the same–Eliza in a pool of blood on the kitchen floor. How had she not known? How had she forgotten?

She felt the same panic now. Duffy stood before her naked, expectant.

"No," she said abruptly. "No, it won't work."

"It better." Duffy stepped toward her.

"You're right. She doesn't want to come back here. Why would she?" Helen dodged around the bed. "Neither of us want this, Bruno. We have to work together. You have to think about your wife. And Adair doesn't want me." The last words escaped her lips before she realized she had thought them.

Shh, Eliza whispered at the window.

"No, she doesn't," Duffy said. He lunged toward her.

Helen darted for the bedroom door, but Duffy grabbed her, surprising her with his strength. "We're not done here." He shoved her onto the bed, then pressed a hand to her mouth, pushing her head back against the covers. She smelled his groin on his hand. She struggled. With the other hand, he tried to unzip Helen's slacks. For a second he pulled his hand away from her mouth.

"No!" she yelled. "Get away. Get off me." She kicked at his knees.

In the house below, she heard glass break. They both froze. There was a second of silence, then a door squeaked open. Very softly, almost beyond perception, Helen heard footsteps moving down the hall. Cautious. Stalking.

"That's security," Helen lied. "I called them."

"You didn't."

Helen shoved Duffy's shoulders and pushed him with her feet. He rolled to one side. She leapt up and ran for the stairs. Whatever danger, whatever disaster had entered her house, it was not of her making. It was not her fault.

Chapter Sixteen

Adair rushed in, then paused halfway down the hall to listen for Helen's voice. Helen was upstairs. Adair pulled the Seacamp from her jacket. She moved slowly toward the back of the house, her back against the wall, the gun pointed upward as Cyrus had taught her when she was a teenager. "When will I need to know this?" her teenage-self had protested. "When you shoot," Cyrus had said, turning away from her so his face was hidden, "shoot for the head."

Adair swung quickly into the kitchen at the end of the hall, scanning the entire area in one fast sweep that would have made her stomach turn if it were not for the adrenaline coursing through her gut, masking the damage her illness had wreaked on her body. A second later, she heard footsteps. She saw the stairwell at the back of the kitchen. Someone was descending at a run. She lowered the tip of the pistol, trained it on the entryway. She braced her arms. The footsteps slowed.

"Stop," she yelled.

The footsteps froze.

"Adair?" It was Helen's voice.

Helen took another step forward and appeared in the doorway. She was wearing slacks and a blouse, but the shirt was untucked and her hair was tousled. Adair caught a glimpse of her breasts beneath the silk blouse. Helen clasped her hand over her mouth as if to abort a scream. They stared at each other.

When Helen finally spoke, her voice was a whisper. "You're bleeding."

Adair looked down. A shard of glass had cut her hand when she punched through the diamond-patterned casement in the door. The pain barely registered. There were drops of blood leading across the kitchen.

"What are you doing here?" Helen asked.

"I thought I heard you scream."

"How did you get in? You have a gun. Oh god, you're here!" Fear crossed Helen's face, but behind her wide eyes there was something else. She crossed the room in two strides and touched Adair's face. "Adair, you need to leave."

"Is there someone here?"

Helen's eyes darted to the doorway through which she had come, then shook her head.

"Are you okay?" Adair asked.

"Yes." Helen looked at the stairs again. "Please. You've got to go."

"I need to talk to you. It's about the twins and the Grandville. I need to know who gave them that scholarship. Thompson isn't investigating. It's probably too late, but I need to know."

"Adair, you need to *leave.* I...I want to talk to you, but not now."

Someone was moving around upstairs. The realization dawned on Adair. A lover.

"You said you loved *me,*" Adair whispered.

"I do!"

Helen stood very close. Adair could feel the heat from her body. She felt pain reassert itself in her spine. She heard Cecelia's voice. *She doesn't want you broken.* "Who is it?"

"No one."

Someone was coming down the stairs. Helen winced with each step. Her hands were shaking. "It's not what you think," she whispered.

❧❧❧❧

A moment later, Bruno Duffy entered the room, his little pot belly protruding over an open zipper, his face pulled into the same officious question mark it wore at Pittock meetings.

"Duffy!" Adair stared at him, the gun still clutched in her hand. "You left me for Bruno Duffy?" Rage cut through the pain that was seeping out of her vertebrae and into the muscles of her back. "I would have thought you could do better. Someone, anyone…a woman…*any* other man on campus."

Duffy had never even been worth despising. He was such a wincing paper-pusher, a bureaucrat stabbing his tiny pencil into the backs of his colleagues, most of who barely noticed. The students called him Dean Stuffy or Mr. Tea for his repeated efforts to make Pittock a dry campus. The other deans planned meetings without telling him. Facilities had moved his office next to the boiler room.

"Is that what you wanted?" Adair demanded.

"No." Helen glanced behind her at Duffy. "I don't want this. I didn't…it's not what you think."

"It's not safe? It's not easy? It's not the perfect accoutrement for the college president?" Adair spat.

All Helen's pleading in the Carrie Brown Memorial Garden had been a lie. The kind of lie people tell the terminally ill, because they can say anything to the dying and, because they feel guilty.

"He's nothing to me," Helen pleaded. "Nothing."

"A little, tiny dean to take to the Spring Social and the Winter's Table races. Perfectly acceptable. No threat to anyone. Is that really what you wanted? You bitch." The last word came out so softly, it was almost an endearment.

"Tell her to get out," Duffy said.

"You get out," Helen shot back.

Adair shook her head. "Get me the information on the twins, and fuck this life you're living with Bruno."

Adair turned to go, but Helen grabbed her hand.

"He tried to force me," Helen said.

"That's a lie," Duffy yelled.

"He broke in." Helen sagged against Adair's chest. "He said it was business. He dragged me upstairs. You heard me cry out. I was calling for help."

"You bastard!" Adair moved Helen aside. A second later she was on Duffy, the Seacamp pressed to his neck.

"Don't," Helen cried.

"You raped her!" Adair kneed Duffy in the crotch. He doubled over. She trained the gun on the side of his head. "I swear to God I will blow your fucking brains into your asshole!"

"Stop! Adair," Helen cried. "I got away before he could. Don't kill him."

Adair released a string of obscenities, pressing each one onto Duffy's temple with the end of her gun. She wished she had brought the Glock. All she could see was Duffy's naked back and a wave of red rage.

Behind her, Helen was yelling, "Don't shoot. You'll be arrested. He's not worth it."

Finally, her words reached Adair. She released

Duffy, pushing him against the kitchen counter. He staggered and flailed his arms, sending a vase of daffodils crashing to the floor.

"Wilson!" Duffy straightened. "I'm calling the police. Helen, where's your phone?"

"No, you're not," Helen said. "If you call the police, I will tell them you raped me. She heard me scream and broke into the house to save me."

Duffy sputtered. "I didn't. You wanted me here. They'll know you're lying."

"I was so ashamed." Helen's voice was matter-of-fact. "I showered and washed it off me."

"You liar."

Adair glanced back and forth between them.

"Bruno, leave us," Helen said. He looked like Napoleon posturing in his boxers. Helen leaned against the kitchen counter as though the whole situation suddenly wearied her. "Get out of my house."

"I'm reporting this," Bruno shot back. "She's a psychopath."

Adair did not need a mirror. She saw herself in Duffy's expression. *She's probably crazy.*

"It's my house," Helen said.

Adair felt a wave of love for Helen, for her calm power and for her weariness.

"Go," Helen said to Duffy.

Duffy backed toward the door. On his way out the front door he called back, "She broke your window."

"It's my window," Helen said quietly.

Then the door latched behind Duffy.

Adair glanced around the kitchen. Helen had not removed any of the decorative touches Adair had added. The still life with fruit. The white ceramic bowl filled with silver apples.

"Your hand." Helen reached for Adair's injured hand and held it in her own, examining the cut. "Hold on." With one quick, decisive movement she spread the cut open, releasing a fresh stream of blood. Then she flicked a shard of glass from Adair's skin.

It seemed to Adair there was more intimacy in her blood on Helen's fingers than in anything she had ever done with Cecelia.

"Rinse that and put a towel on it," Helen said. She turned away, and Adair had the impression that she was hiding her face. "Talk to me about the twins."

"We have to get you out of here," Adair said. "What if Duffy comes back?"

"He won't."

"I could rent you a hotel room."

"He won't come back. Tell me about the twins. Those girls are my responsibility, too." Helen's voice lacked conviction.

Adair had the sense that Helen was trying to distract her. "What is it?"

Helen pulled out a chair and motioned for Adair to sit across from her at the kitchen table. "What happened? Why did you come here in the middle of the night?"

Adair relayed the same story she had told Thompson–the phone call and her sudden suspicions about the scholarship. "Do you know who sponsored that scholarship?" she asked, trying to keep her thoughts focused on the twins and not on Helen. "I need to know."

"Those are confidential college records. I can get them from HR by tomorrow." Absently, Helen reached behind her head and pulled her hair into a ponytail and then let it drop. She sighed.

Chapter Seventeen

The Purveyor met Bolo in a small bar on the outskirts of Jamaica Plain. It was the kind of place Bolo hated—full of cheap plastic décor, and rank with the smell of stale beer and grease. Several black men leaned against the bar, their thick arms and muscular ribs bared by loose fitting basketball jerseys. She hated the place as much as Bolo, but she had done business with the bar owner. Plus, it was worth it to see Bolo cringe in his zoot suit. It was almost iridescent.

The Purveyor ordered a cosmopolitan. It tasted like grenadine. She gestured toward a corner table. An inflatable Corona bottle the size of a kayak hung from the ceiling. Bolo rolled his eyes.

When they were both seated, the Purveyor leaned in. "What the fuck was that?"

To the men at the bar, it would look like a lovers' quarrel.

"What?" Bolo turned toward the soccer game on television.

"You know exactly what I mean."

The sheen of his iridescent suit did not reach his face. His eyes looked darker than she remembered.

"You said, 'don't leave a trace.'" He folded his arms across his chest, still not looking at her. "This is not my fault."

"You were supposed to get them in Oquat. You were supposed to have them before they came down off that mountain. How the hell did you miss them?"

"They got away." He shrugged like an angry teenager.

"You had four vehicles," the Purveyor persisted.

"You said not to shoot. My driver could have taken out her tires at a hundred meters, but you said no guns, no wrecks. You said not a fucking scratch."

"And now you've burned down the Grandville Hotel." The Purveyor took a gulp of her sugary drink. "Every cop in western Massachusetts is crawling over the ruins trying to claw their way up to deputy chief. Did anyone see you coming out of the Grandville?"

Bolo did not dignify her question with a response. The men at the bar were watching them, not staring but eyeing them as their eyes glanced from television to television–two overdressed whites in a black neighborhood bar, fighting.

Bolo sipped his beer, made a face, and slammed it down. "If you had let me go to Oquat, they'd have been out a week ago and no one in the fucking world..." he drew a circle over the table, "...would have any idea they ever existed."

"Galloway didn't want you coming in and dragging them out in the middle of the night. This isn't some raid in Dagestan."

"If you had let me go to Oquat like I wanted to..." Bolo's voice had lost its adolescent whine. He leaned in. "...Galloway would have them by now."

"I know my job," the Purveyor said.

"Do you?"

The Purveyor stared at Bolo. He was right. She saw that now. When Bolo traveled abroad he worked alone. He had killed. She saw that, too. Suddenly. Simply. For a moment, the Purveyor saw the man the girls feared: lean, sharp-eyed, mean. "You're right." She ran her hands through her hair, trying to untangle her thoughts. "I know you're right. But how did you miss the cell phone?"

"I didn't miss it." He sounded cavalier. "I gave it to them."

"What?"

"To save your ass. Now everyone thinks they've gone back home, and luckily home is in the middle of fucking nowhere with no phone, no internet, no TV, no nothing. They're gone, but if you ask me, we should send in a clean-up team. Round up all those cult members, drag them off to some cave or something. Tell them Jesus finally showed up. And waste them."

The Purveyor stood. "No! Galloway would never have that."

"Fuck Galloway," Bolo drawled. He took another swig of beer and turned back to the soccer game.

She leaned down so her lips almost brushed his ear. "Galloway is our future. Galloway is the fucking New World. Galloway is everything." But he wasn't, of course. She closed her eyes for a split second, and in that private darkness she saw her lover silhouetted against the night sky full of stars.

Everything I've done for you.

She sighed. "Next time you have a plan, you run it by me."

"Next time you need something done right, you let me do it alone," Bolo shot back.

Chapter Eighteen

Early the next morning, Adair called the family's secretary, Elena, from her hotel. Like all the Wilson's staff, Elena was at work early, efficient and courteous. Adair asked her to find the number to Anderson Investigations, a small firm the Wilson's used to track down delinquent accounts and to get information on future business partners. A minute later, Elena connected the call.

"Anderson Investigations," a man's voice answered. "We're not open yet."

"This is Merrill Wilson."

The gruff voice on the other end smoothed itself out. "Ms. Wilson, what can I do for you?"

"I'd like to trace a call placed to my cell."

"Of course. I can help you with that. Can you bring the phone to the office in Springfield?" He gave her an address. "I have an associate there. He can take a look at it."

"I'll be there."

It was after dawn by the time Adair arrived at the street Anderson had indicated. The associate, a grizzled man in a forest green tie with grease stains, took the phone and disappeared into the back office. An hour later, he handed her the address with an apology. "I don't know if this will be what you're looking for. Looks like the call you got came from a pre-paid. Address could be anywhere from three hundred feet to a mile from here. But this is my best guess. Mulligan Street, Jamaica Plain. ”

When Adair arrived on Mulligan Street, she could see another reason to be pessimistic. The street ran along a freeway. Chicken wire fencing kept the local kids from taking the twenty-foot plunge down to the road. If the trace was correct, the caller had probably called from the road. Nonetheless, she walked the length of Mulligan Street, knocking on dilapidated colonials with sagging porches and shutters askew.

For the most part, she was greeted by parents readying children for school as they stumbled into their own work uniforms. On one porch, a pair of old Cuban men talked at length, but they were so full of pronouncements Adair could tell they knew nothing. When she had visited every house on the block, she crossed the street and leaned against the chicken wire, watching the cars below. She could smell the exhaust rising from the road.

The freeway noise was loud enough that Adair did not hear the woman approach. She did not notice her until she felt a finger poke her arm. She jumped. A small black woman stood at her side. She had her hair tied in a green scarf. Though her skin was unlined, she carried a cane and her eyes were blued by cataracts. “I heard you was looking for some girls with two heads?” The woman shook her head, coughed and spat over the concrete wall. “I haven’t seen them.”

Adair sighed.

“I saw nothing. Just saying, though, if you’re looking for something that ain’t right, I’d try them.” She jerked a stubby thumb in the direction of the end of the street.

The last house on the block was the nicest. It

was tucked back on a large shaded lot. In the side yard stood a play structure made of four-by-four lumber. Adair had already knocked on that door, and a white woman in a sweater-set had answered, glancing nervously to the right and left before stepping onto the porch. She said she knew nothing.

"It's not right," the black woman said again. "That whole house ain't right. That nice gym, but they ain't got no children. And they don't let none of the neighbor kids play on it either. Not that I want my grandbabies playing over there. Not with those kind of people."

Adair laced her fingers through the fence and rested her forehead against the metal. It was not hard to identify the stock characters in this production. The grandmother who had watched the neighborhood kids grow up. The new-moneyed couple with their big lot and their optimistic swing-set, probably waiting for the right moment to have their only child.

"I've lived here all my life," the woman said. "Didn't never used to be people like that around here."

Adair said nothing. She was thinking about Helen standing on the edge of Carrie Brown's crime scene, her face pale and grieved but not surprised. That was what had struck Adair. Everyone else had been shocked, but Helen's eyes asked, simply, *why are we always here?*

The woman said, "I know 'cause my daughter don't like me smoking in the house."

Adair had lost the train of the woman's conversation.

"When I can't sleep, I come out here, have a smoke and watch the cars. I know where some of them is going." She nodded her head toward the far lot. "Cars coming and going all night long. They think don't nobody notice. I notice."

Adair woke from her reverie.

"Thank you." She clasped the woman's shoulder.

A moment later, she was on the porch again, knocking on the door. "Hello?" She hit the door with the flat of her hand. "Open up."

Nothing moved inside. For the first time, she noticed a security camera watching her from above. Behind her, a navy blue Lexus glided down the street, made a three point turn and parked.

Just as Adair was about to strike one final blow, the door opened. The woman in the sweater-set appeared with the same wary glance. "What do you want?"

Adair stumbled into the house, pushing with her shoulder and knocking the woman out of the way.

"Stop. I'll call the police," the woman cried.

The front door opened onto a shadowy sitting room connected to the rest of the house by way of two doors, one on either side of the room, both closed. Adair stopped short. Silk palm trees stood in the corners. On one wall, a large flat-screen TV showed a blank face. On a coffee table rested a large book titled *Impressionist Masterpieces*. She listened. Although she could not see beyond the living room, she sensed movement. The house was breathing around her.

"Get out!" the woman yelled. "I'm calling the police right now."

"Fine. Call them."

The woman held the phone in her hand but made no motion to call.

"Call," Adair urged.

The woman watched her.

From somewhere above them, Adair heard a sudden creaking, the fast, frantic beat of a bed scraping against the floor while someone rutted their way to orgasm. "What is this place?"

"This is my home," the woman said, "and you are a trespasser. I could have you arrested."

One of the connecting doors opened, and a teenage girl slipped into the room. She was wearing a cheerleader's outfit, complete with pom-pom tassels on her shoe laces. "Everything okay, Mom?" she asked, her head tilted to one side, ponytails swinging.

Too perfect, Adair thought. It was the fatal flaw of inexperienced costumers; they got everything too right. The tassels matched the insignia on her sneakers which matched the red in her skirt which matched the letters on her shirt. A real cheerleader would wear scuffed sneakers or have a Band-Aid on her knee or half a sandwich in hand.

Adair looked around. The room was a stage set. "Call the police," Adair said.

The woman looked at the cheerleader. "Go back to your room." To Adair she said, "You must be looking for your husband. Have a seat."

Adair sat slowly.

The woman sat beside her. "I'm sorry." The woman's look of sympathy was as staged as the room.

Adair picked the coffee table book up. Inside, were not impressionist paintings but vintage pornography. "What is this place?" she asked.

"I like to think of this as a private recreational facility." The woman sat back, wrapping her sweater a little bit tighter around her chest. "The modern man experiences more stress than ever before. In 1940 he was king. He ruled the world, inside the house and out, and he could ask his wife for anything." The woman flicked red nails toward the book. "And frankly, I'm too busy, so he comes here."

Adair tried to hide her disgust. "A brothel?"

"I can assure you our girls are extremely careful about protection," the woman went on. "The way I see it, Harold, my husband, is going to do what he's going to do."

Adair was certain that there was no Harold.

"If he comes here, I know he's safe. No street hooker is going to give him a VD, and no college coed is going to cry rape." The woman smiled. "I always use his little visits as an excuse to hit the Coach outlet."

Adair said nothing. She was thinking about the twins running across the mountain meadow, their hopes pinned on escape, on her, on the possibility of a new life. She was thinking about Helen's beautiful body stretched before her, naked and willing, in the moonlight of her past life. She was thinking about the teenage prostitute dressed up like a cheerleader she would never be, gasping under the weight of whatever bored business man or lonely trucker visited the house. She wanted to slap the woman, to pull open the doors and tell the girls to run, to call the police, but she didn't.

She scanned the room. If the twins were here, she didn't have time to call the police or mount a public protest. She had only that moment, the tiny Seacamp, and her art. She had been in the theater since she was twenty. Adair took a deep breath and allowed the character to well up from her belly, then said, "I'm not looking for my husband."

"No?" The woman raised an eyebrow.

Adair draped her arm over the chair's back and

crossed her ankle over her knee. Her hand rested on the inner seam of her jeans, near her crotch. "Actually, he told me about you." Adair chuckled.

The woman's eyes went cold. This was Adair's script, not hers.

"This is a gentleman's club. I'm very sorry," the woman said.

"I can pay."

"We don't cater to women." The woman stood.

"You don't like dykes?"

"I am sure that you will be able to find facilities that cater to your needs, but…wives will say anything to get to the woman their man is sleeping with. I've had girls audition just so they could meet their own husband."

"Do I look like I'm trying to teach my husband a lesson?" Adair leaned back on the sofa. She could feel the woman's gaze travel from her cropped hair, down the sleeves of her leather jacket, her loose jeans, her motorcycle boots. It was an outfit she would never have worn at the Wilson estate where anything less than Dolce and Gabbana would have seemed churlish. But she had slipped back into her old style before setting off for Oquat. It fit the part perfectly.

"Everything your husband has done on this property has been filmed," the woman said.

Adair felt the adrenaline of opening night course through her once more. "I'm not worried, and I'm not threatening you. I'm just saying, I'm a very rich woman, and this is America. Tell me there's one place in America where money can't buy everything, and I'll take a picture. Like the last fucking buffalo."

"What kind of service are you looking for?"

Adair gave a sharp laugh. "I'm not looking for

some twenty year old gigolo to tell me I have beautiful eyes." She moved her finger tips along her inner thigh, looking up at the woman intently. "I'm bored."

"We can't help you."

"I think you can." Adair rose. She could feel her every gesture animated by the woman she had conjured. Arrogant, impatient, hungry. "I am... what would you call it...a collector. A virgin nun in Guatemala. A vet, just back from Iraq, in a coma. You know a man can still maintain an erection when there is no brain function at all?" Adair laughed too loudly. "My husband and I understand each other. He said you would be able to help me find something."

"You need to leave."

"Ah, but you see, I won't."

"Go."

Adair studied the woman. She saw now that the woman could be a madam. The sweater-set was a conservative burgundy, but the low neckline revealed heaving cleavage. Her pants were skin tight. She wore spike heels. Beneath the smooth canvas of her make-up, she was younger than Adair had guessed, twenty-five instead of thirty-five. The woman kept glancing at the corners of the ceiling, suggesting to Adair that there were security cameras hidden in the crown moldings.

"Are you waiting for someone?" Adair asked casually.

"If I give you a number, will you go?" the woman replied.

"Someone who can help me?"

"Yes."

"How do I know you're not just giving me the number to the nearest Dunkin' Donuts?"

The cheerleader popped her head in again. "They'll be here in a couple of minutes," she said.

To Adair, the woman said, "Look. If I give you a fake number, you'll come back. I know that."

"I better like it," Adair said. "Because if I don't, I might just give you a bad customer review. Who do you think would be interested in a review like that? Boston PD, maybe? The Center for Missing and Exploited Children?"

"If you're a customer, you're just as guilty," the woman whispered.

Adair rose. "Ah, yes, but you don't cater to women do you? I was just coming by with my Mary Kay, and something didn't smell right."

"No one would believe you. You're a fucking dyke." The woman's voice lacked conviction.

Adair took a step toward the woman, so that the front of her jacket nearly brushed the woman's protruding breasts. The woman held her ground for a second, then stepped back.

"Do you know what I own? You cannot even imagine..." The character Adair had invented dropped away as she spoke the truth. "You cannot imagine the resources I have at my command to ruin you, and I will, even if it's the last thing I do."

It will be the last thing I do.

❧ ❧ ❧ ❧

The address the woman had given Adair belonged to a drab, single-story hotel in Watertown. On the far side of the parking lot, large pieces of concrete lay in a pile as though awaiting a cosmic broom and dustpan. A sign mounted on a tall pole glowed red against the darkening sky *America's #1 Extended Stay Comfort Plaza.*

A moment later, Adair found Room 12. She knocked.

"Who is it?" a woman's voice called, harsh and commanding.

"I got this address from Mulligan Street."

Inside, a chain lock released with a clatter. "Come in." The door swung open revealing an ordinary hotel room.

The interior was surprisingly bright. The only thing to distinguish it from any other extended stay hotel was the rack of clothing…no costumes…parked against one wall. She saw the puff of an Elizabethan sleeve, the sweep of a red cape. An apron dangled from an end of the rack and several lacy garments draped over its top. For a moment, Adair thought she was hallucinating. She had taken her students on tour and they had stayed in hotels like this, turning the rooms into costume lofts and practice rooms. Adair could have paid for better. She could have simply installed her students in the nearest Josslin Heights. The Wilson's owned controlling shares in the company, and Merrill Wilson was always welcome gratis. But she had been determined to make the program self-sufficient. "This program has got to keep going when I'm gone," she had told Patrick, never thinking the end would come so soon.

Chapter Nineteen

Helen knew better than to bother Chief Thompson the day after a major incident, but she could not wait. She had been up all night, replaying her encounter with Duffy and Adair in her mind. Duffy had been buzzing around Meyerbridge Hall all morning, slamming doors and muttering about "conduct" and "values."

"What's up his ass?" Patrick asked, leaning against Helen's office door watching Duffy storm by for the third time.

"I don't want to talk about it." But she knew she would have to. Duffy would file a report. He should have filed it already. A former employee put a gun to his head—that was grounds for a full campus lock-down. Everyone should be in their dormitory, their office, or safely off campus until Adair was apprehended.

She had to talk to Thompson before it all exploded. "I'm going to go see the chief," she said. She rose and grabbed her briefcase.

"He's gonna love you today," Patrick said.

When she arrived at the station, Thompson was out.

"You can guess where he's at," the dispatcher said with a shrug.

Helen walked the remaining block to the rubble that had been the Granville hotel. The area was eerily clear. The dark flank of the Pittock Hills was suddenly visible, as was the charred side of the 7-Eleven behind the hotel. Singed trees lined the green space to the south. Helen thought of Adair's penthouse with its beautiful silk scrolls, the bed where she had explored Adair's body. All gone now.

The entire area had been cordoned off. Within the yellow tape, the investigation crew moved slowly, their eyes glued to the ground, their feet covered in white boots. Helen saw Thompson surveying the work. He caught sight of her and crossed the area carefully, lifting the tape so he could slip his lanky frame beneath it. He was still as skinny as ever. His large eyes set against his dark skin still gave him the same wide-eyed look Helen remembered seeing on the young cadet. But everything else about him exuded competent authority. She was glad he had been promoted.

"Dr. Ivers." He shook her hand.

"Chief, I'm sorry to bother you. I know you're busy."

"It's all right." He gestured toward an edge of the green space that had not been cordoned off. "I think I know what you've come to ask about." He dusted off a seat on a park bench and offered it to Helen. "Adair Wilson?" he asked kindly.

Helen's breathe caught in her throat. Had Duffy already talked to him? "Yes."

"There are certain things I won't be able to discuss because of the investigation," the chief said, "but I'll try to answer what I can." He looked apologetic.

He didn't know. Not yet. Helen stared at the pile of blackened rubble. "Is Ms. Wilson all right?" she asked.

Thompson hesitated. "I spoke with her last night." The fatigue in his voice suggested that he had been up through the night. "She appeared to be unharmed by the fire."

"Did she tell you about the twins?"

"Yes." Thompson seemed surprised. "What do you know about that?"

Helen told Thompson what she knew about the twins and about Adair's concerns. He listened, his head bowed. When Helen finished he nodded, then took a deep breath. "That puts things in a new light," Thompson said slowly.

"How so?"

"Adair came by the station last night. She reported receiving a call from these twins. She said that the content of that call led her to believe they had been abducted."

"Abducted?" Helen asked.

"I was…skeptical. Ms. Wilson seemed to be suffering some mental distress which is reasonable given what just happened." He motioned to the blackened wreckage. "But we followed up with the family, naturally. We called the police department closest to Oquat, Utah. They couldn't find any record of the twins in the town she mentioned or the surrounding area. No one had ever heard of anything like she described."

"Are you sure they weren't killed in the fire?"

"We've excavated a good part of the rubble. If they were on the top floor, as Adair said, we would have found them by now."

"Were there any casualties?"

Given the rubble, it looked like no one could have survived the fire, but Thompson said, "Not that we know of."

The air still smelled of smoke. Helen watched as

two men in clean suits lifted a charred beam from the rubble and carried it to one side.

"It went up so quickly," Helen said. "Was it arson?"

"Our preliminary findings suggest it was. The Grandville Hotel had a state of the art sprinkler system. Ms. Wilson had it retrofitted after she bought the building. Something like this should never have happened."

"It could have malfunctioned," Helen suggested.

"In case of malfunction, the fire department would automatically have been alerted. The only way around the system was to turn it off. Someone had the pass code and knew the system."

Helen felt her stomach twist. *She's always been in trouble.* "Who do you think it was?"

Thompson spoke gently. "The insurance company will certainly try to suggest that Adair set it herself, for the money. If you know her family, that's not going to carry a lot of weight. We'll know more when we recover the black box from the alarm system. We're interviewing all the tenants and anyone who routinely visited the Grandville. "

Helen stared at the wasteland before her. It had gone down so quickly, two hundred years of New England history—and her history with Adair—gone in an afternoon. If Adair did not return to Pittock, there would be no trace of her left in the town. In two more years, the last of her students would graduate, and she would become part of an urban legend, a sideline to the story of Marshal Drummond.

"My office. Now," Helen said to Patrick upon entering Meyerbridge Hall. He looked up from his computer. "What? No *'please'*?" He followed her anyway.

In her office, Helen gestured to a wingback chair, one of the antique throwbacks she had not had time to replace. Patrick sat, but Helen continued to pace. She could still smell the smoke from the fire. The smell hung in the air and caught in her clothing. "You said Adair had always been in trouble, but people like you and me couldn't help. What did you mean?"

"Sit." Patrick held up his hands. "You're making me nervous."

Helen strode across the room and stood before him. "I just talked to Chief Thompson. He said someone tampered with the sprinklers at the Grandville. He thinks it might be arson. If you know something, you need to tell me." She was daring him to accuse Adair, so that she could argue with him.

"Helen." Patrick stood and put his hands on her shoulders. "Sit down."

"Do you think she did it?" In the back of her mind, a tiny voice whispered, *it doesn't matter.*

"If I knew something that would help Adair, I would tell the world," Patrick said in answer to the question Helen had not asked out loud.

"I'm sorry." Helen took a seat in the facing arm chair, her heart racing. The air in the room felt thin. At that very moment, Bruno Duffy could be calling the police. He could be meeting a police officer in the foyer of Meyerbridge Hall, directing them to her office. "Talk to me, Patrick. What did you mean?"

Patrick sat and tapped the arm of his chair. "I didn't mean anything." He seemed to be sizing her up. "Adair was born into a family where the men are men and the woman are…decoration. And she's gay as the day is long. And before she admitted that, she thought she could starve her way to heterosexuality. Plus, her first girlfriend—love of her life, you know the story—lured her to San Francisco, loved her for a half a year, then turned her out on the street. Literally locked her out without a bag and never said a word about it. No explanation. Ever. Somewhere in there her mother died of a drug overdose. Then she *really* stopped eating. She was hospitalized.

"But Adair pulled through. She went on Broadway. She was a rising star. She saw her name in lights. Until her brother Cyrus got the reputation for ruining everyone who crossed her. Someone gave her show a bad review and suddenly they lost their job at the New Yorker. Adair auditioned for a part and didn't get it. Suddenly the production lost its financial backing. Half her friends wanted to fuck her for her money, and the other half left her because they were scared shitless by her brother. She finally gets a job at Pittock. She's happy. She finds herself. Then her student is hacked to pieces in the woods. That's a boatload of shit. But that doesn't mean someone set the Grandville on fire."

"Are you sure?"

"It was an old building."

Helen could hear the hesitation in Patrick's voice. She could feel him watching her. "What if Thompson thinks it's her? What if he decides she turned off the sprinklers?"

"Did he say that?" Patrick asked.

Helen pulled at a thread that was unraveling from the arm of her chair. "He didn't *say* it."

"She loved that building." Patrick shook his head. "She took care of her tenants like family. You know half the little old ladies who lived there weren't paying a cent in rent. She installed a fire escape that dogs could get down. She's crazy, but there is no way she set that fire."

"I know."

"Tyron Thompson knows that too."

"I know," Helen said again.

"Plus, didn't the fire start about the same time she was storming in here threatening to rip Duffy's balls off?"

"She didn't…"

"I'm joking."

Outside the office, two phone lines rang simultaneously.

"But what if someone was trying to get to her?" Helen asked, twisting the thread in her fingers and breaking it off.

"I told you. It wasn't that kind of trouble."

Patrick's young assistant, Stephanie, knocked on the door. "There's a call?" Stephanie ended every sentence with a question mark. "Channel 22 News wants your opinion on the fire? And Dean Duffy called? He said he needs to see you in his office?"

Helen thanked Stephanie.

"What's up with Duffy?" Patrick asked after Stephanie left.

"Duffy is an asshole." Helen stood and crossed to the window, staring out at the quad so that Patrick couldn't see her eyes.

"Duffy's always been an asshole." He left his question hanging in the air.

"I can't do this right now."

"Does this have something to do with Adair?"

"How long can you keep me off the radar, Patrick? Vacation. Family Medical Leave Act. A conference. I don't care."

"Helen?" Patrick's voice lost its cheerful lilt.
Helen turned.

Patrick watched her for a full minute before speaking. "Are you going after her?"

"Yes."

"Okay. The Women Administrators Association is holding their annual symposium. You said no, but no one knows that. I'll put it on your calendar. It's in San Antonio. It runs until Thursday. Is that enough time?"

"I don't know."

"Okay. Living relatives?"

"What?"

A slight smile returned to Patrick's face.

"We'll say 'aunt.' Close enough that you have to go to the funeral, but distant enough that no one expects you to have talked about her much. Plus, if you already mentioned your aunt's death, no problem. You can have as many as you need. Never say parent. That's a rookie mistake."

"Where did you learn this?" Helen asked.

Patrick grinned. "Our students, of course." He opened his arms, and Helen stepped into his hug. "Go find her, Helen. Bring her back here."

Chapter Twenty

Adair surveyed the hotel room and jumped when she noticed a young woman sitting in an easy chair. She wore skinny blue jeans and a pink lace T-shirt that revealed a turquoise bra. Her hair was blond and over-processed, and an inch of dark roots showed. She wore a thick layer of make-up, as if for the stage.

"So…" the girl said. "You've got a fantasy." Her voice had the tremor of a girl with stage fright.

"No," Adair said. "I've got a question."

Like an amateur improve comic, the girl tried her line again. "You've got a dirty fantasy that you can't tell anyone." She stood up and walked to the costume rack. "Maybe a…pirate?" She pulled out a shapeless black tunic. "Or maybe a school girl? Two school girls practicing kissing?" She dug through the rack. As she turned her back to Adair, Adair saw that the seat had been cut out of her jeans, revealing her pale bottom and a hot pink G-string. "I can be anything you want," the girl said without looking at her.

"Please sit down." Adair held her side. The familiar pain had returned to her ribs. While the girl's back was turned, Adair quickly removed a pill and swallowed it dry.

The girl turned back to her, pulling on a mask with zippers for the eyes and mouth. "Maybe you've been naughty and you need someone to spank you,

you fucking whore."

Adair sighed. Cecelia would never have resorted to masks and swear words. Adair could see Cecelia's face in the dappled sunlight, thoughtful, even tender.

What will we do in the winter?

Die.

Adair shook her head. "Take off your mask."

The girl pulled the leather off her face. She pushed her breasts out, tipping her head back with a sneer that looked more frightened than arrogant.

Adair reached for the string that drew the curtains.

"Don't!" the girl said.

Adair raised an eyebrow.

"If my boyfriend sees the curtains open, he'll kill me." The girl looked at the door as if it might swing open at any moment.

"Your boyfriend?"

"Yes. My boyfriend!" the girl said defensively. "Anchor. He's right outside."

"Right." Adair pulled a chair from the small desk and lowered her body onto it gingerly.

"Are you the cops?" the girl asked.

"No, but I might call them if I don't find what I'm looking for here."

The girl sat in an arm chair and pulled her knees up to her chest, wrapping her arms around them like a child on the edge of a cold swimming pool.

"I just want some information." Adair reached into her back pocket and peeled two one-hundred dollar bills out of her wallet. She handed them to the girl. "I'll pay you for your time."

The girl snatched the money.

"I'm looking for two girls. Charity and Prudence.

They're conjoined twins."

"What's that?"

Adair explained.

"A chick with two heads? Get the fuck out!"

Adair wasn't going to quibble about definitions.

"And you think they're hooking?" the girl asked.

"They were abducted. I think they were at the house on Mulligan Street, at least for a little while."

"I haven't seen them."

"Have you heard about them?"

"No." The girl chewed on a strand of her hair.

"You sure?"

"Yes."

Adair regarded the girl. "How old are you?"

"Twenty-five."

"I'd guess seventeen," Adair said, softening her voice as if she were talking to a student.

The girl shook her head. "Am not."

Adair was certain she was no older than eighteen. Transfer the girl to Pittock College, and she could be a freshman on her way to her first showing of the Rocky Horror Picture Show. Perhaps one of the scholarship students from a tough neighborhood, not quite as pretty as the other girls. Eighteen, but not quite as young as she should be.

"Are you from a church?" the girl asked.

"I'm…I was a college professor. I convinced them to come to my school." She let her distress sound in her voice, hoping to elicit the girl's honesty in return. "They were very young and very sheltered, and they were abducted. The police traced their cell phone to the house on Mulligan Street."

"So?" The girl pouted her lips. "What the fuck do you want me to do about it?"

"A woman at the Mulligan Street house sent me here."

"Yeah? I'm sure they didn't send you here to talk. Even if I did know anything about it, I wouldn't tell you. If they're in the life, they're in the life."

"These girls don't want to be prostitutes. I don't think you do either." Adair watched the girl's face for a reaction. "Charity and Prudence are very religious. They don't know anything about this." Adair glanced around the room.

"Are those even their real names?"

"Yes."

The girl snorted.

"What's your name?" Adair asked.

"Scarlet."

"What's your *real* name?"

A loud knock on the door interrupted their conversation.

"What the fuck's going on in there Scarlet? You fuckin' sleeping or what?"

"That's Anchor. You better go. He doesn't like me talking to clients. That's not what I'm here for," the girl said. In a louder voice she yelled, "Leave me the fuck alone."

"Come with me," Adair said. She had not known she was going to say it before she spoke, but as the words left her mouth, she knew it was the only thing she could say. "I can help you get out of here, get back on your feet. If you have family…"

"My family." The girl's cheeks flushed as she held back tears. "At least I get paid here. At least I don't do it for free."

"Okay. Forget your family. We'll find you an apartment, a real job. Maybe you can go to community college."

The girl stood, looking around as though she had misplaced something important.

"This doesn't have to be it, Scarlet."

Anchor hit the door again. "Ten minutes!"

Adair did not relish the idea of confronting Anchor outside. She did not like the idea of spending several hours in a car with Scarlet either, but Scarlet was barely more than a child. She couldn't leave the girl here.

The girl rose, glanced out the spy hole, then fumbled through the pockets of a coat hung on a hook by the door.

"If you are on drugs, I can get you help," Adair said.

"I'm not going with you. I don't like girls."

"I'm not propositioning you! You're a child."

"I'm more woman than you will ever be." Scarlet pushed her small breasts forward. A few tears squeezed out of the corners of her eyes. "I don't need you."

The girl retrieved a spoon and a glass of water from the small kitchenette. Then she opened a dresser drawer and pulled out a cigarette packet from which she removed a syringe, a cotton ball, and a tiny packet wrapped in foil.

"Don't please…" Adair said.

The girl tore off a tiny piece of cotton and rolled it between her fingers.

The pain that had been located in Adair's chest, now spread down her arms and legs. Her stomach contracted. She didn't want to look at the needle, but she couldn't look away. She had the impression she was watching the girl walk out onto a distant stage. The theater was full. The critics seethed in the darkness, writing in blood. The girl was about to deliver the wrong lines from the wrong script.

"Don't," Adair whispered.

The girl struck a lighter, warmed the spoon, dropped the tiny cotton wad into the drug, and pulled the liquid up into the needle.

"Wait." Adair felt the need to stall her, to stall the needle.

"What?" The girl braced her arm against the edge of the dresser. "You a junkie?"

Adair thought of the Texidol in her pocket. "Not like that."

For a second, the girl met her eyes. "If you really want to find those girls, I'd try Maine."

"Maine?"

"Anchor took me up there once. He said we were going on vacation. Some vacation. There was this club. He said we could make more money. So he drove me out to fucking nowhere, fucking freak show. Amputees. Some girl with no arms. All these creepy Johns who are into that shit. But those fucking perverts didn't want to play dress-up. They want something sick…fuckin' sick shit happened up there."

"Where was this place?"

"I told you. Maine." The syringe shook in the girl's hands. Her arm remained braced against the dresser, the vein a deep blue.

"What city?" Adair asked.

"I don't know."

"How can you not know?" Adair pressed.

"I just don't. Anchor doesn't like me to know where we are. It was some big hotel in the woods. Looked abandoned. Outside a big city. The girls called it the Ashfelt Club."

Adair felt as though the temperature in the room dropped. "You think someone took the twins there?"

"Maybe."

"I'm calling the police."

"You can't."

"Why not?" Adair demanded.

"It won't help. The Johns just get out, you know. Down the rabbit hole. Then the cops take us girls downtown, and it's all our fault. And that place up in Maine, it's not like me and Anchor, just trying to get by. They know when the cops are coming. They got all these ways out. I was there when a girl stole her John's phone and tried to call for help. Ten minutes later, we were all in the bottom of some boat. I don't know how long they had us out there in the ocean, but when we came back that girl was gone. They said the police knew everything, and if we tried to call them, it'd happen to us. That's when I told Anchor he had to get me out."

"I can get you out now," Adair said.

The girl shook her head. Her whole body was trembling. Adair thought she would drop the syringe.

"It's too late."

Then, before Adair could stop her, the girl injected the drug, as expertly as a trained phlebotomist. Her body remained perfectly still as she pressed the plunger. Then her eyes closed, and she slid to the floor murmuring something about Anchor and a holiday and a big hotel.

Outside, a man sat on the hood of a dingy white sedan. Adair hurried past him. She called the police as soon as she was off the hotel lot. "I don't know that there's much you can do," she told the dispatcher after relaying her message.

"Can you tell me what you were doing at the hotel?" the dispatcher asked.

Adair thought of the twins and of Scarlet. *They know when the cops are coming. They got all these ways out.*

"I was just walking by," Adair said. "I just happened to look in."

Chapter Twenty-one

The Purveyor brought Bolo with her to the holding pen, as they called the house in Jamaica Plain. It made things easier with the girls. Even Marta, the queen bitch, whose job it was to break in the new girls, still thought it all had something to do with men and women. The Purveyor could have disabused her of this notion with a fist, her fingers, or just with a fat roll of hundred dollar bills. But Marta was not worth the time. All the Purveyor needed was for Marta to know that someone owned her. If it was easier for Marta to believe it was the blond haired man in the shiny suit, so be it.

As the Purveyor had instructed, no one had seen Bolo install the girls in the small basement room. No one would see them while they were there. No one would see them leave. Now the Purveyor followed Marta and Bolo to the basement. It was an old house. The basement was little more than a dirt floor, but there was one room with electricity and running water.

"You can go now, Marta," the Purveyor said as they approached the closed door.

Marta paused, pulling her sweater around her enormous breasts. The Purveyor did not like her anxiety. She and Bolo were there to instill fear in the women, but there was something else vying for Marta's attention. "What is it?" the Purveyor snapped.

Marta looked at Bolo.

"Well?" he said.

Marta glanced behind her and then at the closed door. "She's been asking for a Bible."

Marta had no way of knowing what kind of treasure lay beyond the door. She must have heard them begging for a Bible, but the Purveyor had given her strict instructions not to open the door. She knew Marta would obey.

"I didn't know what you'd say." Marta stumbled over her words. "I have one here." She held it out.

The Purveyor could tell this was not the source of her anxiety. This was not why her hands had been trembling when the Purveyor and Bolo first entered the house. Lots of girls asked for bibles or crucifixes when they arrived. There was nothing like the first glimpse of the life to send them scurrying, momentarily, back to God.

"Give it to me," the Purveyor said.

"Why the fuck would we give them a Bible?" Bolo said. *Them.* It was a slip, but Marta did not appear to notice. "Pretty soon all you girls will be asking for something. I'm not fucking Santa Claus."

He played his role well...dumb pimp. It wasn't hard for him.

"It can't hurt." The Purveyor pretended to argue with him. "She can't even read."

"I don't want her getting ideas," Bolo grumbled.

The Purveyor took the Bible from Marta's shaking hands. "Now go." The Purveyor knocked on the girls' door.

"Can I come too?" Bolo asked.

"No."

"I've already seen them."

"Then you're not curious."

"How much is Galloway offering?" Bolo asked.

"More than you can imagine."

"For them?" Bolo's face looked bovine in its confusion. "To fuck?"

He was as dumb as Marta. He still thought it was about the pouch of skin between his legs. "He's a connoisseur," the Purveyor said. She pushed open the door and closed it on Bolo's vacuous face.

The room inside was clean but bare. A bed. A chair. A sink. A mini fridge. A small alcove that contained a toilet but no door. A narrow window, no larger than a shoebox, let in a little bit of light from an airshaft. In this wan light, the twins sat on their single chair, their hands folded, their faces identical. They still wore a long denim skirt and white hair nets. They looked up in unison, their expressions neither fearful nor angry, as though they had brought the calm of the mountain with them, the peace of rocks, and the fresh incalculable beauty of wild flowers.

Yes, they are worth it.

"Hello," she said. "May I sit?" She pointed to the bed. It was a stupid question. Her face felt hot. It took her a moment to realize she felt nervous. They were so still. Only their eyes followed her. "Do you know why you're here?" she asked.

"We've been called by God."

"What's your name?"

The girl who had spoken said, "I'm Prudence, and my sister is Charity."

Their faces were identical but she saw, now, that their eyes were not. Prudence's eyes were as simple as an open horizon; behind her beatific face, Charity had the eyes of a trapped animal.

"May we have a Bible?" Prudence asked.

The Purveyor handed her Marta's Bible.

The girls took it. Their hands moved like one person.

"I'd like to introduce you to someone," the Purveyor said.

The girls said nothing.

The Purveyor pulled out her tablet and waited for it to find the secure cell phone signal she used to communicate with Galloway. It was sluggish, but eventually she connected. His face appeared pixilated at first, then clearer. She handed the tablet to the girls, who watched the screen with the curiosity of primitive people. The Purveyor wondered if their loveliness came through on the small screen.

Finally Galloway spoke. "*For the Lord says, I am the truth, the life, the way, and all who trust in me shall have eternal life.*" He had done his homework.

"Amen," the girls said in unison.

"I have been waiting a very long time to meet you," he said.

The girls reached out and touched the screen, their finger leaving a momentary pool of color. The Purveyor had the sense it was Charity's curiosity that moved the hand.

"You are very special," the words, though banal, sounded like a benediction in Galloway's smooth British accent. "Do you know how special you are?"

"We have been called by God," Prudence said. "We are an image of his inseparable love."

"I too have been called," Galloway said. "I have been looking for you for a very long time."

What woman could resist his power?

"Have you ever seen the Caribbean Ocean?" he asked.

The girls shook their heads.

"Have you seen the ocean at all?"

"No," Charity said. There was a hint of anger in her voice.

"It is like looking into the mind of God," Galloway said. "So vast. So blue. So bright."

"God cannot be made manifest on earth except in the form of Jesus Christ our savior," Prudence said.

"But he made you." Galloway's voice was gentle.

"We are only messengers," Prudence said. Their hands tightened on the tablet.

A misstep? the Purveyor wondered.

"How can you tell the dancer from the dance?" Galloway asked.

"Who are you?" Prudence asked, her voice cracked, finally showing some of the fear that was like air in this house. The trembling lips. The tears. The Purveyor had seen it so many times. Usually it drew nothing but her contempt. Now she felt her own eyes well up in sympathy.

"A father. A helpmate. A bridegroom." Even through the blur of the tablet screen, Galloway's gentle smile was clearly visible.

"The Lord is our father in heaven," Prudence said.

"We have a real father," Charity said, but her voice was a door opening. The Purveyor could tell she was considering something that Galloway had not said. A tear slid down Prudence's cheek. She turned away. Charity remained dry eyed, her gaze fixed on the screen.

"In a few days, I am going to come for you," Galloway said. "I do not want you to be afraid. No one will hurt you because if they do, the wrath of God will reign down upon them."

That was a warning, and the Purveyor heard it.

"What about the woman?" Charity asked.

"The woman?" Galloway asked.

"The woman who found us, who is so sick, the sad woman. What will happen to her?"

Chapter Twenty-two

Adair checked into the nearest Josslin Heights Hotel and dropped down on the bed, wondering how many Boston hotels lived a secret life behind closed doors. The Josslin Heights at least was safe. The Wilsons owned controlling shares in the luxury chain, and though the hotels had never been as profitable as Monty had hoped, they were convenient.

There was one in Paris, she remembered. When she came out in college, Cyrus had offered to give her the penthouse. "Isn't that where you go?" he had asked. "Women like you."

"Yes," Adair had scoffed. "All lesbians live in Paris. It's like Mecca only we can't leave."

Now she wondered if Cyrus had been right. Maybe she should have gone. Living in a penthouse in Paris she would never have met Helen. She would never have been shot.

She closed her eyes. She could see Notre Dame. Inside, the cathedral pillars rose like great trees. Outside, the towers touched the sky, a miracle of architecture and perseverance. Were the exterior walkways still open, she wondered, with only the low balustrade to keep the penitent from falling? When all this was done, and the twins confirmed dead—because lying on her bed in the hush of the hotel she could not imagine another ending—might she still climb those stairs as thousands had before her? Would she have the courage to jump? Would she have a choice? She swallowed a dose of Texidol and slept for a few hours. When she woke, she checked her cell phone. The battery had died, and the charger had been destroyed in the fire. She called the front desk and asked them to search for Helen Ivers's work number and ring it. "If her secretary says she's busy, tell him it's Adair. If she's already gone home, get her cell number."

The clerk connected them a second later.

"Adair, where are you? I've been calling you all day." Helen sounded relieved.

"Did Duffy come back?" Adair asked, the previous night suddenly rushing back to her. "You should get out of that house."

"I'm fine."

"If he tries to hurt you…"

"He won't, Adair. He won't."

"I could buy you something." Adair twisted the phone cord around her hand. "A house in North Canaan or a flat somewhere, maybe a gated community. You can't just wait for him to come back."

"I didn't wait," Helen said sharply. "And that won't solve anything. You're sweet." A sadness crept into Helen's voice.

In the silence that hung between them, Adair's mind raced through the little villages around Pittock. There had to be someplace beautiful and safe.

"How's your hand?" Helen asked.

Adair looked down at the gash on the back of her hand.

"It's fine." She paused. "Did you get the information on the scholarship?"

"I know the donor's name is Peter Reynolds Barr. At first I thought he was trying to get his own daughters into the college, but he's not. He doesn't know Charity and Prudence. He just knows *of* them. He wants to give them a scholarship because his sisters were conjoined twins. They died. I'm sure it was all very sad."

"Thank you." Adair drew in the breath that would say "goodbye" to Helen."

"Wait," Helen said. "What are you going to do?"

"My family works with this guy, Anderson. He's a debt collector. He's a blowhard. If someone crosses a state line, he loses them. But he traced the call." Adair told Helen the bare outlines of her encounter at the house on Mulligan Street and the hotel.

"If this is true," Helen said slowly. "If they were kidnapped, and the fire was a cover-up, it's a matter for the police."

"The police won't do anything. Thompson will write a bulletin. Look what happened with Hornsby. Hornsby stalled the Pittock investigation for weeks because Drummond had paid him off."

"Hornsby was desperate," Helen said, her voice gentle, "in a way you can't imagine because you've always had money. You don't know what it's like to watch someone suffer and not have the money to help them. That doesn't mean you can't trust the police. If what you're saying is true, you could be killed."

"Maybe." From where Adair sat at the desk she could look out the window at the city as it transitioned from work day to Friday afternoon. She had loved that time once, loved setting out in the evening with friends from her theater troupe in New York and later with her students in Pittock, walking down Main Street, conversations bouncing between them like a dozen silk scarves kept aloft by their breath.

Another life.

She looked out the window. Like a theatergoer in cheap seats, she was too far away to decipher individual faces, but she could follow the story. A couple kissed on the corner. Two business men vied for a parked taxi. She longed to be among them–to strut out into the night with Helen; to find the tiniest, steamiest restaurant in the North End; to eat pizza with fresh basil and not taste metal. "I have to do this," she told Helen.

"No." Helen spoke with a force that surprised Adair. "Let the police look...or not. Do what other people do. Just feel bad about it. A hundred thousand awful things happen every day, and they're not your fault or your responsibility. They just *are*, and you have to grab a little tiny bit of happiness around the edges." She paused. "With me."

Adair rested her forehead on her palm. The drug was wearing off. As it did, she felt the fog lift from her mind. She felt her soul re-solidify, and with its return came the pain and the certainty that after she found the twins there was only one solution. "I can't."

"Then with whoever you choose, Adair," Helen whispered. "Don't do this. Please. Don't do something reckless. This isn't your problem."

Adair did not have the energy to explain that she knew it wasn't, but she *wanted* it. A question. A quest. Something to put between her life and the inevitable plunge.

"Goodbye, Helen."

"Wait..."

Adair held the phone away from her ear. On the other end, Helen kept talking, unaware of the dead air that listened.

I'll never see her again.

Adair stared at the receiver. Finally, Helen must have realized no one was listening. Adair heard her pause. Speak. Pause. She did not need to hear the exact words to know what Helen was saying. *Are you still there?* She hung up the phone.

It was after hours, but it was not difficult to reach one of the Wilson family's attorneys. Adair described the house she wanted for Helen.

"When will you be available to sign the papers?" the attorney asked.

"Not me. Helen Ivers. I won't be around to sign anything."

From the Diary of Charity Kimball

Prudence prayed and coughed, but I only listened. There were many voices in that place and many footsteps. I thought perhaps there was a large family living above us. Perhaps it was a congregation of devils. We were underground. I imagined we were tangled in the roots of a bush. I imagined the whole building was enmeshed in its roots. I did not know. I did not know anything except for the voice of Prudence's heart which was always praying. It was like the sound of the river thawing in spring, her praying. The sound of something breaking apart with grief.

For myself, I did not pray. I did not pray when the men took us from the sad woman's beautiful room, and I did not beg for a Bible as Prudence did. I do not need pages to hear God's voice, and I could never substitute pages in a book for His silence. We lay in the little room underground for many hours. Perhaps it was days. Prudence could not get the smoke out of her throat. I told her "You have a bubble of smoke in your throat."

She asked me if I felt it. I said no, but I remembered Dorothia's coughing, and I felt the sickness because Prudence's chest is my chest. Her heart is my heart.

Then the new woman showed us a tiny window, a tablet, she called it. Like Moses' tablets, there was more inside it than on its surface. A man looked out at us. He spoke to us. He was as beautiful as sunlight and clear water on stone, unlike any man I have ever seen. Like the sad woman, he had the skin of a youth, the clean white teeth of a child, but the eyes of an old man. He spoke through the ether of an island where everything is blue. Prudence believes he is our savior, a messenger from God, our Gabriel. Perhaps he is.

He did not speak like Father Apostle who knew everything and did not ask questions. He did not speak like Mother, who always told us to be silent and then looked away. Nor did he speak like the dark haired woman or the false friend who spoke in codes and seemed to know everything about this world and nothing of the next. Even Prudence loved the sound of his voice. She hid her coughing, and she smiled at him like a bride smiles through a veil.

When he said goodbye, he left the image of an ocean lapping at the tablet's surface. He told us this was his home. After that, Prudence fell into a death-like sleep that did not break even when she coughed, so I...I interfered with myself. She always hated it when I tampered with our body, even the wellspring that came at the end. I know that he will touch us like that.

Chapter Twenty-three

Helen stared at the phone in her hand. *Call ended*, the screen read. She dropped her head back against the white sofa in the Pittock House living room. She had begun, "Whatever you're going through, I can help you. I can be there with you." She had heard only silence, not even a breath on the other end of the line, still she had continued. "I love you." She had stumbled over her words. "I haven't loved other people."

I haven't been loved.

There was no time, not growing up with Eliza clawing at her parents' souls, and not afterward. Helen heard her mother's hospital bed plea...*please, don't put her in a home.* She remembered driving the streets of Pittsburg searching for Eliza lumbering in the alleys. Somewhere in the walls of the house, Helen could hear Eliza scratching at the insulation, pulling out tufts of pink fiberglass and rubbing it into her eyes. *Helen,* she whispered.

"Adair?" Helen hated the desperation in her voice. "Are you there?"

She had listened to the silence for a long time. Finally, a click on the other end told her that her confession had been rejected. She rested her face against a sofa cushion. She stayed like that for a long time, listening to the sound of her own breathing. Finally, she stood and walked onto the front porch.

She dialed her friend Terri's number but hung up before it could ring. A minute later Terri dialed her back. Reluctantly, she answered.

"Where have you been, young lady?" Terri said.

Terri had been general counsel at Vandusen College when Helen had been a young dean. They had struck up a friendship despite, or perhaps because of, the thirty year gap in their ages. Terri claimed to detest all young professionals. Helen had little patience for the banter of women her age. Her life had been so different. She had forced medication down Eliza's throat with a plastic syringe, had cleaned Eliza's excrement off the walls. She had nothing to say about the PTA auction or the merits of Pilates. Now Helen was at Pittock and Terri ran a PR firm in Los Angeles, but they stayed in contact.

She took the pack of cigarettes from their hiding place in the eaves over her porch and lit one. She guessed Terri was also on his porch, by the blare of Mexican rap music that faded in and out as cars passed on his end.

"You still living in the ghetto?" she teased.

His house was worth over a million.

"Keeps me in touch with the people. How are you, Helen?"

"Fine." Helen tried to follow with small talk. How was the firm? Was there any news of the wild fires in Inyo County?

"Helen," Terri stopped her. "What's wrong?"

"Nothing."

"Are you sure?"

Helen stared at the darkening campus beyond her porch. The Barrow Creek. The playing fields. The Pittock Woods. It was supposed to be idyllic. She took a drag on her cigarette. "She came back."

"And what happened?" Terri asked.

Helen told him about Adair's illness, the fire, the twins, Adair's phone call. She did not tell him about Bruno Duffy. "Adair wants to find the twins." She sighed. "It's like she thinks this is all her fault. She doesn't trust the police. I thought Eliza was the worst thing that would ever happen to me. Then there was Drummond, and now this. I just want her to be okay."

"Oh, Helen," Terri said. "I'm sorry."

He had approved of their relationship, as much as he could approve from three thousand miles away. An expert on finding and hiding the indiscretions of the rich and famous, Terri had set his researchers to work on Adair as soon as Helen mentioned Adair's advances. He found nothing untoward. "Trouble has a way of finding Adair Wilson," he had said. "But that's not to say she *is* trouble."

"I'd be okay if she was happy." Helen drew her thumbnail along a crack in the paint of the porch railing. "If she'd shown up looking like a million bucks with a beautiful wife on her arm, it'd be okay."

"Really?" Terri drew the word out.

"I'd be sad, but it would be okay. But she's sick. When she moves, God, it reminds me of Eliza." She had not put the thought into words before, but now it seemed utterly true. Everything about Adair's body language exuded fatigue, and yet in the few minutes Helen had seen her she had been constantly in motion, shifting her weight from side to side as though trying to escape some internal pain.

"Eliza died. Don't fill that gap with Adair Wilson." Terri was firm.

"Will you look into it for me?" Helen said.

"Anything you can find out about Adair."

Terri's sigh traveled across the country. "What do you want to know?"

"Just find out…I don't know. Find out if there is anyone who can help her." Helen supplied all the details she could remember about Adair's diagnosis.

"You aren't going to do anything rash, are you?" Terri asked.

Helen thought of Duffy mounting the stairs to her bedroom.

"Helen, do you promise me?"

"I'm not going to kill myself if that's what you're asking." Helen stubbed out her cigarette and went back into the house. Her face looked haggard in the hallway mirror. She forced herself to smile, hoping the smile would reach her voice. "I'm sorry, Terri. I'm fine. I really am. The fire at the Grandville…it just shook me up. Don't worry."

As soon as she hung up, she returned to the recent call list, looking for Adair's call. Although Helen did not recognize the number, she knew its place in the list. She touched the call-back icon. The phone rang for a long time.

Then a woman's voice answered. "Josslin Heights, Boston."

"Could you connect me with Adair Wilson?"

"What room?"

"I don't know."

"I'm sorry ma'am. For our guests' privacy, I can only connect you by room."

Helen wondered how many rooms there were in the Josslin Heights. Hundreds probably.

Chapter Twenty-four

The Purveyor had just sat down to dinner in the North End. The restaurant was small and dimly lit with lanterns hung from exposed wooden beams.

"Would you like to see the wine list?" the server asked. "May I recommend the house Trebbiano?"

The Purveyor glanced at the menu. "A bottle of the Gianfranco Soldera Brunello."

"Brunello pairs very nicely with the oysters," the server said, gliding away.

The Purveyor was about to open her menu when her phone vibrated on the table. All calls rang to this phone, but an asterisk beside the word "unlisted" told her the call was ringing to the private number known only to the inner circle of the business. And to one other man. She lifted the phone to her ear. "Yes?"

There was a moment of silence that sounded like the ocean in a seashell. Then she heard Galloway's voice as cultured as the finest wine. "Do you know who this is?" he asked.

"Of course."

"They are ill," he said. "You must tend to them immediately."

"What? How do you know?" The Purveyor remembered the tablet. Galloway had asked her to leave it in the twins' room so that he could watch them, and they could communicate with him if they wanted to.

"If they die," he said, "I will destroy you and everything you have ever loved. Do you understand me?"

Before the Purveyor could respond, Galloway hung up. A second later all record of the call disappeared from the phone's log.

The restaurateur returned with the Brunello, but the Purveyor was already leaving. She had left the twins in their monastic cell with enough food and water to last a week, although she planned to collect them within forty-eight hours, and move them to the rendezvous point where Galloway would meet them. She had locked their room with a padlock to which only she had the combination. It was a risk. The house could catch fire. There could be a raid. But leaving them unsecured was a bigger risk. If one of the girls saw them, even for a second, it would be over. The girls would cue up to look at the freak show, and one of them would surely see the opportunity. It wouldn't take much to alert the media. A contraband cell phone. A few photographs sent to an old friend. A John with an ear for a peculiar story.

The risk was too great.

No one could visit the twins except her, but Galloway had been talking to them on the tablet. She sped through the streets of Boston and into the grassy side streets of Jamaica Plain. "Keep everyone upstairs," she barked to Marta as she headed for the basement. At the door to the twins' room, she glanced around to make sure none of the surveillance cameras were pointed in her direction. Then she released the padlock.

Inside she breathed a sigh of relief. The scene

before her was so peaceful it was almost surreal. The girls lay in their narrow bed, their hands folded over their chest as if in prayer. A little bit of street light filtered through the airshaft window. The only other light came from the tablet that rested on the bedside table.

As Galloway had instructed, the Purveyor had loaded the device with religious music, an electronic version of the King James Bible, and a secure connection that allowed him to look in on the twins from his island paradise. This had apparently been left on. The screen displayed an ocean so perfectly still and blue, it took the Purveyor a moment to realize she was not looking at a screensaver but at a live feed of a window in Galloway's mansion. As she watched, a tiny roll of white crested the smooth ocean surface, moving forward then disappearing. Suddenly the screen was eaten up by a blur. It was only after the screen cleared that she realized what she was looking at–the Amur leopard was pacing.

The Purveyor turned back to the girls. The moonlight made them look pale. Too pale. The shadows beneath their heads too dark. She crossed over to them. She was about to touch them when their eyes flew open simultaneously. They sat upright quickly. Their movement startled the Purveyor, and her heart responded with a frantic staccato beat. Then they released a cough so loud and violent she could not believe that it had ushered from their delicate, bifurcated body. All she knew was that suddenly the white blanket that covered their bed was soaked in blood.

The Purveyor sat in the back seat of her car, shielded from view by tinted windows and the night. The location, a side street in a wealthy residential neighborhood, was chosen at random. She would never return there. "I know a doctor." The Purveyor held her laptop in her lap. She spoke to Galloway's face, pixilated but still beautiful, glowing in the dark interior of the car. Even through the ether of satellite space, she could see the concern etched in his sandstone complexion. And something darker in his eyes. "Someone I trust," she added.

"How quickly can he be there?"

"A day, maybe two. I haven't asked him."

"He must be there tonight," Galloway said. "Immediately. They have probably been infected for years. If the disease has compromised their vascular system, they could bleed to death. One cough. Only one of them has to die, and the other will pass within minutes."

"If you are worried about the transactions…" the Purveyor said.

The tablet crackled as Galloway raised his voice. "I think you have sold in bulk for too long. I am not returning a suit! I do not want a refund with a receipt! You will save their lives or you will forfeit!"

Everything. Galloway did not need to explain his power. The Purveyor knew. She felt a shiver of fear run through her legs, urging her to flee.

"This doctor of yours, what is his name?" Galloway demanded.

"Chastain. Ronald."

"Let me know when they are well, and I will arrange for him."

"No," the Purveyor said. She could not sign Chastain's death warrant like this. "I need him. I trust him."

"I think you can buy your valium on the black market." Galloway's voice had lost its smooth flirtation. He was mocking her. "I'm sure they have street corners where you are."

"Drugs," the Purveyor spat. She drew away from the screen. "You chose me, Harlow, because there is no one else, not one person whom you could even *ask* to do what I have promised. Now, will you let me run my empire?"

"Yes." Galloway bowed his head. "Call your doctor. Do what you must."

Chapter Twenty-five

"Checking out?" the hotel clerk asked.

Adair had not brought any luggage, although she had gone out the night before and bought a change of clothes. "Can you make a reservation at the Josslin Heights in Portland? Top floor. Put it on the Wilson account." She recited the account number.

"The Executive suite or the Honeymoon suite?" the clerk asked.

"Is there a difference?"

"The honeymoon suite comes with chocolates in a heart-shaped arrangement and a complementary bottle of champagne." The clerk looked about twenty, but he had a wry, world-weary way of delivering his lines. Adair liked him. "What a choice," she said. "I'll take the executive suite. I hate chocolates in a heart-shaped arrangement."

The hint of a smile pulled at the clerk's deadpan face. He added, "There are a few messages for you. We don't transfer calls unless the caller knows your room number." He handed her three slips of paper, each in a different handwriting.

Adair pulled out her phone. She had bought a charger from a convenience store down the street. The screen showed the usual icons. No messages. She glanced at the papers. As she expected, they were from Helen. She crumpled them in her hand and swallowed her tears.

She rode the elevator down to the bottom level of the parking garage. Downstairs, the garage smelled of subway rubber. Her footsteps echoed between the concrete walls. Halogen lights lit some areas too well, while the far corners remained in shadows. It was in one of these shadowy corners, behind a pillar, that Adair had parked her BMW. She hurried toward the car and then stopped short. The silence was louder than her footsteps. Someone was sitting beside the car on the low concrete curb that prevented drivers from over-shooting the parking-spot. The figure sat doubled over, arms folded across its knees, its head in its arms. For a moment, Adair thought it was a homeless woman, but the woman's camel-colored coat was too clean for the streets. Beneath the coat, the woman's ankles emerged from graceful tan heels. And Adair knew the sheen of auburn hair. Almost blood red. "Helen." Adair wasn't really surprised.

Helen looked up with a start and struggled to her feet, morphing—even as Adair watched—from lost soul to the prim administrator. She straightened her coat and smoothed the front of her boiled-wool skirt. "I'm coming with you." Helen took a step forward and placed her hand on the car. She carried a large purse that could double as an overnight bag.

"You don't know where I'm going," Adair said.

Helen kept the fingertips of one hand on the car as she moved around to the passenger side. "It doesn't matter."

"You have a college to run. You have a life, Helen." A frisson of pain seared down Adair's neck, through her shoulder, and into her gut. Her whole body jerked. She leaned against the side of the car. Now in proximity to the door, the key in her pocket sent its invisible signal to the locks, and they clicked open.

Without waiting for an invitation, Helen opened the door and slid into the passenger seat, staring at the wall in front of her.

Adair stared at the roof of the car. Helen didn't move. Eventually Adair took the driver's seat. "This really has nothing to do with you."

"The twins?" Helen answered without looking at her. "No. They have nothing to do with me."

"You don't have to come, Helen. I'm not going to find them. I know that. I just have to try."

"I want to be with you."

Adair heard Cecelia's voice. *She doesn't want you broken.* Then wondered, *what if she does?* "I'm sick."

Helen turned to her. "I know, and I still want you. Even if you're sick. Especially if you're sick, I want to be with you. I don't know much about relationships, but that's how it works. I know that."

Adair could almost feel the rush of the cathedral catwalk, the outline of the Seacamp. "We barely knew each other, Helen. How long were we...together?" Her voice caught on the word. "A week? A couple of weeks?"

"It was enough." Helen's voice was calm and certain.

Outside the car, the garage looked overexposed, like a washed out photograph. In the shadow of the car's interior, Helen's eyes looked very big. Adair took a deep breath. "There is almost nothing left..."

"Left?" Helen echoed.

"Of the woman I was."

"I'll take care of you." Helen touched Adair's knee gently.

"I don't want you to see me like this."

"I doesn't matter how you look, or if you're sick, or if you're imperfect, or if you have problems you haven't told me about. In case you haven't noticed, I don't like a lot of people, and they don't like me." Helen offered a self-deprecating smile. "I don't have a lot of friends. I don't have anyone I *love*, except you. Oh, I love Terri, but he's far away. That's so different. I lived my entire life alone until I met you, and I would rather be with you in the worst situation than go back to Pittock and pretend that any of that matters without you in my life."

"It matters," Adair whispered. "It matters how you see me..." She didn't know how to tell Helen about Wyatt's Bluff and the bite of Cecelia's crop.

"I'm sorry." Helen turned away.

Adair felt Helen's sadness in her own throat. She paused. "I'm going to Maine. But first I'm going to see my family in New Hampshire to see if they can help." *The last time I'll see my family.*

"Please let me come with you," Helen said without looking at her.

Adair remembered Helen's kiss in the Carrie Brown Memorial Garden. She remembered her own bile spattering the dirt at her feet. She tasted the blood-like taste of Texidol in her mouth. She started the engine. "I can't be with you like that again." Adair blinked back tears.

Helen nodded. "Okay."

❧❧❧❧

They drove in silence for almost an hour. Adair knew she was driving too fast, dodging around the slower moving cars, accelerating to almost a hundred when the road straightened and the traffic thinned. The adrenaline kept the pain at bay. The concentration kept her mind clear of the Texidol fog and her eyes clear of tears.

Soon it would be summer vacation at Pittock, she thought. They should have been idling along a coastal highway. *Another life.* She was vaguely aware of Helen's occasional gasp as they slid in between two semi-trucks or darted ahead in the right lane.

Finally Helen cleared her throat. Adair expected her to tell her to slow down, but she said only, "Is that why you never called me? Because you didn't want me to know you were sick?"

Adair shook her head. "I called you." *I thought you could save me.*

"Give me your phone," Helen said suddenly.

"Why?" Adair asked, but she reached into her pants pocket and handed it to Helen. Out of the corner of her eye, Adair saw Helen fumble with the two phones. A moment later, she put Adair's phone on speaker and rang a number. The phone buzzed and then Adair heard Helen's familiar voicemail instructing her to leave a message. Helen waited for the beep and then ended the call. She held her own phone up to the window as though it would receive the voicemail faster.

Outside, the highway rushed by in a blur of trees and ordinary cars.

"It didn't call me," Helen said finally. "You got my voicemail, but there's nothing on my phone. No missed called. No message."

"Maybe it's the reception."

Helen tapped something into her phone.

"Dialing." A pleasant woman's voice said. A moment later Adair heard her own voicemail.

"It didn't ring," Helen said. "Mine doesn't ring to yours. And yours doesn't ring to mine either. You hear my voicemail, but I don't get the call." She tried a few more numbers. "Or Patrick or anywhere at Pittock. All your calls go to voicemail, but I don't think they're reaching the people you call. I didn't get your call until you called from the hotel in Boston."

"Cyrus." Adair sighed. "Cyrus and his fucking toys." He was always trying to play the big brother, always trying to solve her life. Close this theater. Sue that critic. Buy the flat in Paris. Block Helen's calls. Adair clutched the wheel. Her teeth ached.

"Don't you see, Adair? Someone's tampered with your phone." Helen's voice was full of hope.

Adair could almost read her mind; she thought it mattered. She thought all Adair needed was a reason to forgive her. All she had to do was prove her faithfulness, and they could step back into the life they had almost tasted. "It doesn't matter," Adair said very quietly. "Not anymore." But she took Helen's hand. The Texidol numbed her sensations, and Helen's hand felt like rubber, but she clasped it nonetheless and held on for a long time.

From the Diary of Charity Kimball

I did not know how loud Prudence's voice was until it stopped. Even after she slipped into unconsciousness, she whispered fleeting prayers that only I heard and dreamed dreams that I saw behind my own eyelids. They were strange half-images, fragments of our past, like shards of a broken bowl: Dorothia when she was just a babe in swaddling, staring up at the ceiling with the dark blue eyes of infants. A stew pot bubbling. The chapel in cold sunlight. And always interspersed with these images, were images of running. In her dreams, we ran like coyotes, not like rabbits lumping forward, one hop at a time. We were graceful, long-legged creatures in her dreams. It was almost as though we were flying.

Even though she was sick, I wanted to shake her. I wanted to remind her of the rabbit. I wanted to tell her that we were the Leviathan, the Behemoth. We were the monster created out of God's loneliness. But then she dreamed that she was holding me. It was late at night in Oquat. We were looking up at the stars, our arms around each other. Two arms. One embrace. She dreamed that Mother came outside.

"What are you doing?" Mother asked.

"We are looking for God," Prudence said in her dream.

No.

She said, "We are looking *at* God."

Then she fell silent as though the images in her mind scattered like leaves blown by approaching winter. Perhaps she simply pulled a curtain between her life and mine, giving me my dreams alone. It was so quiet. The only thing I could hear was the tiny window they called a tablet. On the other side of it, our savior read to us from the Bible.

"What? Know ye not that your body is the temple of the Holy Ghost which is in you," he read, *"which ye have of God, and ye are not your own? For ye are bought with a price: therefore glorify God in your body, and in your spirit, which are God's."*

I listened to his voice, and I listened to the ocean, and then Prudence's illness pulled me under.

Chapter Twenty-six

Chastain wore a long-sleeved athletic top over jeans, his pectorals clearly visible beneath the silky microfiber, his arms as big around as her waist. He was everything the Purveyor hated in a man–large, cocky, and not powerful enough to possess real grace. But he had a voracious gambling habit, and that was all it took–one weakness.

"So you need a favor," he said, strolling along the Boston harbor with her, glancing at her hungrily, although her aggressively tailored suit was designed to repel that kind of attention.

"Yes."

He thought he owned her. She hid her disgust.

"I know two very special girls," she began. "They are sick. I think it's TB. But they are in danger of becoming a media spectacle, and I can't allow that."

"You want them treated out of the public eye," Chastain concluded.

"Indeed."

The harbor water lapped against the concrete walkway. On the other side, the towers of Boston sparkled in the sun. A couple walked by, pushing twins in a double stroller. Chastain grinned at them. "Bet they're a handful," he called out to the young mother.

"They sure are," she said.

"Don't worry. Before you know it, they'll be sixteen and asking for the car." Chastain and the father chuckled. The family kept walking. "What are the terms?" Chastain asked her when they were out of earshot.

"I would have thought, with your retainer, I would not need to negotiate with you." His retainer was exorbitant. On several occasions she had considered firing him. But the service he provided could not be bought on the black market, as Galloway suggested. Chastain was more than a drug dealer.

"The new drug resistant TBs are very hard to treat," he said.

The Purveyor felt her throat constrict as she remembered the spray of blood from the girls' cough. She had washed it off her hands, a fine mist like spray paint. "One hundred and fifty thousand," she said.

"Two-hundred and fifty thousand."

"Two-hundred and fifty if they live."

Chapter Twenty-seven

Despite everything, Adair felt a familiar pride as she turned the car onto the shaded lane that led to the Wilson estate. As a young woman, she had brought her first girlfriend, Soledad, home from college, imagining that Soledad would see it as Jane Austen's Elizabeth had first gazed on Pemberley, falling in love with the owner because she fell in love with the house.

Adair glanced over at Helen who sat upright, clutching her bag.

"Are you sure this is a good idea?" Helen asked. "I can wait for you at a bar or a hotel."

"There's room." Adair motioned to the house, now clearly visible at the end of the lane. "Forty-two rooms, if you count the servants' quarters. We won't be long."

Helen shot her a wry smile. "I'm sure you could find space. But I don't think your brothers want me here."

"You mean the phone?"

Helen raised an eyebrow. "The phone. The fact that I begged them to let me see you, and they wouldn't let me through the gates. And the first time I was here, after Drummond shot you, they told me they would ruin me and everything I worked for." She paused. "Not that I didn't deserve it."

"You didn't."

Helen smiled sadly.

Adair drew up in front of the gate and typed the code into the key pad. The gate swung open. It was a beautiful vista. The sky was overcast, but the crushed granite drive still sparkled with little flecks of pink mica. Beyond the driveway, on the top of a gentle rise in the land, the Wilson estate stood in stately grandeur.

"It's Modern Palladian," Adair said. "But one of the original owners remodeled it with a touch of Colonial Revival."

Even at a distance, the house showed its size. Someone might have called it "sprawling" except that it was so controlled, so precise. It occurred to Adair, as it often had, how masculine the house looked. It wasn't just the heavy leather furnishings that filled it. The very blueprint, with its ninety-degree angles, its rows of identical windows, and its black trim painted in sharp contrast to the white walls, reminded her of her father and her brother Monty.

"Who lives here?" Helen asked as they approached.

"Besides the servants, my brother Monty and his wife Belinda, their kids–Grace and Bronson, when they come home from boarding school–Cyrus and his wife…" She paused. "My father used to live here but he passed on in…" It had happened while she was sick, but she could not remember the month. "We weren't close."

At the front of the house, Adair stepped quickly out of the car, confusing the footman whose job it was to open her door. Then she led Helen up the marble staircase and into the grand foyer. The space was empty except for an enormous arrangement of fall flowers. Helen looked up at the domed skylight.

A thousand pieces of cut glass looked down on her, casting her face in a glow that was neither daylight nor lamplight.

"Come. I need to change before I talk to my brother," Adair said. She led Helen to the third floor wing, still referred to as the nursery, and opened the closet in one of the bedrooms. "I will call housekeeping and have them bring something up. What do you want? Coffee? Cognac?"

"I'm fine," Helen said. She looked nervous.

Adair stepped into the walk-in closet, chose a pink crepe dress, then pulled the door closed behind her and changed.

Helen was still standing by the window, looking at the grounds, when Adair emerged. Adair felt Helen's eyes travel the length of her dress.

"Fancy," Helen said.

Adair felt suddenly shy. She smoothed the crepe, trying to articulate why it didn't matter to Monty whether she wore Dolce and Gabbana or jeans, except that it did. "It would just look…childish if I came in that." She pointed to her leather jacket tossed over a chair.

Helen smiled with only a fraction of her mouth. "What a life."

✦ ✦ ✦ ✦

"Merrill!" Monty feigned surprise when Adair entered the parlor. She knew the house manager had informed him of her arrival. He held out his arms to embrace her. "I was worried about you."

"Hello, Monty." Adair kissed the air beside his cheek. There was no time for pleasantries. "I need your help."

Monty adjusted the steel framed glasses on his nose. The last softness had gone out of his face, and now he looked like pictures of their father as a younger man. "Are you all right?"

"Yes." *No.*

"Cyrus is worried about you," Monty went on. "He didn't want you going off on that wild goose chase...and then the Grandville. That was a tragedy, but it was well insured." He gestured toward two chairs by the window, and they sat. From a decanter on an end table he poured a snifter of cognac and offered it to her. Then he poured one for himself. "Cyrus said he had Elena book you a flat in Paris, just until you find something that you really like. Did he tell you?"

Monty swirled his cognac and raised it to his nose, then lowered it without drinking.

"I'm not going to Paris," Adair said. *Not yet.*

"Paris is lovely in the spring."

"I'm here about the twins." Adair took a gulp of her drink. It splashed as she set it back down. "They've been kidnapped. I think they might be in Portland. We need to hire someone. You must know someone who could help."

"The twins...?" Monty regarded her as a father might regard a favorite child who had rushed into the room recounting a wild flight of imagination.

"Yes. The twins," she pressed. "You have to help me find someone who can track them down."

Monty smiled obligingly. "We'll put Anderson on it."

"Anderson is a phonebook bounty hunter, Monty." Adair was sick of his paternal smile. She wasn't a child. She had never been a child. There were no children in the Wilson house, only perfect, silent, little men and women in crepe and black ties. "We need a professional, CIA, FBI, someone with real training. I don't know where to find someone like that, but you do." Adair leaned over the arm of her chair, trying to draw her brother's attention. He held his cognac up to the light. On the other side of the garden, Adair saw a figure on horseback. She recognized Cecelia's hair billowing out beneath her riding helmet, as thick and dark as Shen Yun's mane.

Had Cecelia told him? Had Cyrus guessed? "If you help me, I'll go to Paris if that's what you want."

"That's what Cyrus has always wanted." Monty sipped his drink. "Camus Cuvée 3.128. You know this is one of the finest cognacs. It's made from three different eaux de vies, aged forty-one, forty-three, and forty-four years respectively. Hence the name one hundred twenty-eight years in the making. You need a family to run a business like that. One generation can't do it alone."

"What do you want from me, Monty? What do I need to say?"

"Anderson is a good man," Monty said decisively. "We'll have Elena call him and get this all settled." He pressed the intercom button hidden discretely beneath the top of the nearest end table. He rattled off a list of instructions, then added, "Have Anderson call me back in about half an hour in the west parlor."

"I've already talked to Anderson," Adair pleaded. "I need someone better."

"I don't think I know anyone better than Anderson."

Adair was just about to call Monty on his lie, when the door opened behind them.

"But I might," the newcomer said.

Adair turned. Behind her Cecelia stood with her riding helmet and crop tucked under one arm, her dark hair cascading over her shoulders.

"What are you offering in exchange?" Cecelia shot Adair a cat's smile, then cut her eyes over to Monty. "I might strike a deal with Merrill. What do you say, Monty?"

Monty glared at Cecelia. "That's enough."

"If we were going to stop at 'enough', Montague, we would have stopped years ago." Cecelia tossed her head. "Come on, Merrill. Take a turn with me."

❧❧❧❧

The stable was warm with the smell of horses and fresh hay. Cecelia had sent the servants scurrying. "Will you ride with me?" she asked.

"No." Adair lowered herself onto a straw bale covered in a rich brown, Pendleton blanket. She felt Cecelia's eyes follow the curve of her breast in the crepe dress.

"Fine," Cecelia said. She unbuttoned her riding jacket and tossed it onto the blanket beside Adair. Deftly, she stripped off her blouse and dropped that too. A moment later she stood before Adair topless. She kicked one foot up behind her and draped her arms over Shen Yun's stall, her breasts jutting out over cream-colored ribs.

Adair had only glanced briefly in the mirror the night before, but she knew her own body was marked with deep purple bruises from Cecelia's crop.

"Is the medication helping?" Cecelia asked, stretching her arms wider, then patting Shen Yun's glistening black flank.

"No."

"You look lovely though," Cecelia said. She took a step toward Adair.

"I won't..." Adair could hardly bring herself to say the words, "Never again, Cecelia. Do you understand? I'm done."

"That's a funny thing to say, right before you ask me for a favor," Cecelia said, shaking her lustrous, black hair over her shoulders.

"I'm not asking for me. I'm asking for two innocent girls."

"How touching." Cecelia reached out and ran a finger down Adair's cheek. "Are you really done with me? I saw your little secretary creeping into the house, like Cinderella looking for her slipper. She's really rather pretty, in a bowl-cut, Midwestern sort of way."

Adair said nothing.

"She thinks you're horrid," Cecelia added in a conversational tone. She leaned back against the wall, eyeing Adair. "You know I'm right, Merrill. The middle class always do. All this..." Cecelia's gesture took in the stable, the line of pure bred horses snuffling in their stalls, the wall of hand-crafted saddles, "and you never worked for any of it. What does that look like to your little Helen?"

Adair said nothing.

When it had become clear that she was not going to take the bait, Cecelia added, "Tell me about your little dilemma. I might know someone."

Adair stood, wincing. "Who is this person you know? Do you really know someone who could help?" She walked a few paces and stopped beside Naples Peach.

Cecelia followed her. "He's a retired general. Worked in secret ops for years, oversaw a lot of covert missions. Then he got a desk job at the FBI, worked there for a decade solving serial murders."

"What's his name?"

Cecelia picked up a brush and ran it over Naples Peach's back. "You know we've known each other for over twenty years." She set the brush down and roped her arms around Adair's waist before Adair could protest. Their hipbones touched, and Adair could smell Cecelia's perfume, an Attar of Roses derivative that Cecelia bought in little glass bottles from a distributor in Murano. Adair tried to pull away, but Cecelia held her tightly.

"Send her away," Cecelia said. "Stay here with me. You're done now. You went on your little quest. Be with me, Merrill." Cecelia reached up and stroked Adair's cheek.

Adair pushed her away, stumbling slightly on the straw covered floor. "You're married to my brother. It's wrong."

"You're just carrying a torch for your little secretary. At least I'm a lesbian. That's more than you can say for Cinderella."

"Will you help me find the twins or not?" Adair tried to step back, but she was trapped between the stall and a heavy worktable on which the stable hands polished the horse tack.

Cecelia grabbed Adair again, clasping her to her chest. "Your brother. My husband. It doesn't matter. What we have is so much bigger than my marriage. We're the same, Merrill. Take me right here. You can tie me up, if that's what you want. You can do anything. I need you." Her fingernails dug into Adair's back, offering the promise of pain.

It would be easy to give in, to let the sharp sting of the whip ignite the welts already on her back. Then she remembered her own blood on Helen's fingers, the excision of glass. Helen had moved quickly so as not to hurt her. Adair wanted that tenderness, and she wanted to salt the cut on her hand and suffer. "I'm running out of time," she said. "Who is this man? Let me call him."

Cecelia leaned in and bit Adair's lower lip hard enough to send a jolt of pain through her face. "You need something from me, and I need something from you," Cecelia whispered.

The air seemed suddenly sharp and cold. Adair tasted blood in her mouth. "You blocked her calls," she said, wrestling out of Cecelia's grip and pushing her away.

"No," Cecelia drawled, as though Adair had just jumped to a conclusion so obvious the whole world had seen it before her. "You didn't need to get dragged back to that awful school."

"You sent her away. I needed her."

Cecelia shrugged.

Adair felt her face flush with anger. "PCPS can be triggered by stress." Adair's words came out in a gasp. "It broke my fucking heart when she didn't come back for me." Adair wanted to wind back her fist and punch Cecelia in the face, but the pain in her side was spreading. Before she even realized she was going to be sick, she doubled over and white bile flecked the straw at her feet. "She could have saved me."

"Don't try to rewrite history," Cecelia said, stepping away from Adair's sickness. "Little Helen Ivers isn't going to love you back to good health. That's not how it works. You know she would have left you within the year. How long did you fuck? A week? Was she really going to drive up to New Hampshire every weekend to see you like this?"

Adair closed her eyes as she heaved again. She could not bear to look at the ground before her, the spattering of half-digested food and something that looked like a sliver of pink tongue, as though her body was expelling itself, clawing away piece by piece.

"You were her fantasy," Cecelia went on, "so young, so rich. She doesn't want you broken. But I love you. I'll take you even now. Wipe your lips and fuck me, and I'll save your precious twins."

Adair stood. Her throat burned. Her eyes felt bloodshot. She drew her hand across her lips. "Never."

"Who else would have you, Merrill? Who else deserves you?"

Through the blur of tears, Adair could see Cecelia standing before her, her hip cocked, her hands on her trim waist. She was smiling.

"I won't bargain with you." Adair stumbled toward the door. "I'm not your whore, and I'm not going to do this to Cyrus." She wrenched the door open and stepped out, blinking against the brighter light of the day.

Behind her, she heard, Cecelia call out, faint but clear, "You already are, Adair Merrill. You already are."

Chapter Twenty-eight

After Adair left, Helen explored the suite. It was lovely in a way that did not invite enjoyment. Each room seemed to be staged for a tour of historic houses. All the furniture was antique, but unlike the hulks that filled every hall at Pittock College, these were carved masterpieces, each brass rivet and every inch of dark wood polished to a luster. She tiptoed into one of the bedrooms. A four poster bed stood in the center of the room, hung with an embroidered tapestry depicting the medieval hunt for the unicorn. *And this was the nursery,* Helen thought, running her hand along the surface of the coverlet.

She was surprised when, about an hour and a half later, someone knocked on the door. "Come in," she called, worried that it might be a servant uninformed of her visit, and surprised to find a stranger in the nursery.

The door opened and a tall Asian man with a stern face greeted her. "Ms. Ivers?"

"Yes."

"I am Ubol, the house manager. Cecelia Beaucharnel would like to see you in the gazebo. Please follow me." He offered no other explanation.

Helen hesitated. "What is this about?"

"I wouldn't know, ma'am," the house manager said. "This way."

As they exited a back door to the mansion, it

struck her that even the air was rich. Cleaner. Cooler. As though a great fan had blown in the faint smell of lavender. She followed the house manager along a path of crushed granite, and through a garden of hedges and gladiolas staked with military precision. As they rounded the corner of the estate, Helen saw a smaller garden with a pool and a replica of the famous Winged Victory. Beyond that was a white gazebo. She could just make out Beaucharnel sitting in its shade.

"She is there," the man said and walked away without further conversation.

Beaucharnel turned at the sound of Helen's footsteps. "Helen Ivers," she said without rising.

Beaucharnel wore a dress of butter smooth yellow. A string of pearls accentuated her graceful neck. Her dark hair fell from a loose upsweep, revealing opals in each of her ears. A flash of bright red lipstick was the only ostentation, and even that had a classic, old-world flare, like a touch of hand-painted color on a sepia toned photograph. Still, Helen had the vague impression that the outfit had been hastily donned.

"I've startled you. I'm sorry," Beaucharnel said. "Please come here and sit with me."

Slowly, Helen mounted the gazebo steps and extended her hand. To her surprise, Beaucharnel pulled her down into a hug.

"I'm so glad you're here," Beaucharnel patted the pristine white bench beside her.

Helen sat.

Beaucharnel crossed her ankles. Her cream colored heels were impossibly high and yet elegantly conservative. "Have you been enjoying the grounds?"

"They're lovely."

"Merrill's mother always loved to garden."

Helen looked around. She could not imagine anyone gardening there. It would take a small army of professionals to maintain the grounds.

"She planted those over there." Beaucharnel pointed to a hedge of well-contained roses. "Fairy Spirit." She laughed. "They give them such funny names."

Helen nodded.

"Merrill is a lot like her mother," Beaucharnel said.

"Merrill?"

"We all call her by her middle name. Only her mother called her Adair." Beaucharnel folded her hands in her lap. "I wanted to talk to you about Merrill…Adair."

Helen felt a cold thread of sweat slide down her side. She straightened.

"What has Merrill told you about me?" Beaucharnel asked.

"Nothing."

Beaucharnel dipped her chin, her face half hidden by her curls.

"Should she have told me something?" Helen asked.

Beaucharnel looked up and drew one finger beneath her eye as though wiping away a tear. "I should never have let her go on that trip to Utah. She wasn't well enough. I thought it would…help her, but it didn't, did it?"

"No," Helen said quietly.

Beaucharnel rose and walked to the opposite side of the gazebo, staring out at the garden. When she turned back, her face had lost its perfect composition. She teetered on her high heels. "Merrill and I are lovers," she blurted out.

Helen was so surprised by the suddenness of her confession, that it took her a moment to understand the words. *Merrill and I are lovers.*

"It's more than that," Beaucharnel went on. "She's my only love. There is no one else. The sun doesn't shine without her." She wiped at another tear.

In the distance, a peacock called its panicked cry. *Help, help.*

Merrill and I are lovers. Helen felt a trap door open beneath her heart. *I'd be okay if she was happy.*

"And she's sick," Beaucharnel said. "She's so sick." She sat back down. All pretention drained from her face. She pushed a strand of hair behind her ears. "It started after she was shot. We thought she had rallied…then…she just gave up."

She's always been in trouble.

"I thought if I could get her interested in something, if she felt needed, then maybe she would pull through."

Helen's mind reeled. *We're lovers. She's so sick.* "How long have you been together?" she asked, anger biting into her voice.

"Since forever." Beaucharnel smiled sadly. "Of course, not really, but our families have known each other for years. We grew up together. We kissed at boarding school. We fell in love in college."

Helen felt as though the air had been knocked out of her lungs. She saw it all now. It had been the threat of the Pittock murders and the intensity of those weeks before Drummond was caught that had drawn Adair to her. In those strange, feverish days, Adair had betrayed her lover, her wife. Now Adair was sick, and she risked losing Cecelia. Of course, Adair did not want any contact with Helen. Even an apology or an explanation could destroy her relationship with Cecelia Beaucharnel. Helen wanted to scream, *I fucked her too. Your Merrill. I loved her too.* But she loved Adair still.

She looked at Beaucharnel's perfect face. "Goodbye, Ms. Beaucharnel."

"Before you go," Beaucharnel called after her. "Talk to her. Please. Get her to stop. I was wrong to send her away. She's too weak. She needs to be here where our doctor can see her. Don't let these girls become her obsession. They're not worth it."

Chapter Twenty-nine

The sun was setting as Adair rode into the stable. She had not gone directly back to the house, but had taken Naples Peach up to Wyatt's Bluff and looked out over the valley. When she got back to the estate, the house lights were glowing in the purple twilight. Monty and Cyrus would be closing their Mac books and revisiting the cognac. Soon, Monty's wife would appear, dressed for dinner in a Burberry skirt. Cecelia would take her place next to Cyrus. Ubol would bring sherry for the women, and then they would proceed to dinner. She knew she should go back and find Helen, but something in the twilight kept her outside. She found herself riding toward the Versailles garden where she had strolled so many times with her mother.

It was strange, she thought, she had barely noticed her father's passing, but her mother's death felt as fresh and raw as the night it happened. She longed to be a child again and curl up in her mother's arms. But her mother had set out a row of pill bottles and drank them down, one by one.

***

When Adair finally returned to the nursery wing, Helen was sitting by the window under the light of a Tiffany lamp. She had a book in her hands, but it was closed.

"You can't do this," Helen said by way of greeting.

Adair dropped into a Victorian finger-carved armchair on the far side of the room. She didn't want Helen near her. Despite a quick shower in the stables, she felt sweaty and flushed, her breath still sour.

"Monty wants me to call Anderson." Adair did not mention Cecelia. She sighed. "Anderson's an ass."

"You have to stay here." Helen held the book to her chest. Adair caught sight of the title: *Le Recherche de Temps Perdue.* A leather bound first edition, part of her late mother's collection.

"You know those are just for show. No one actually reads them." Adair tried to smile, but the familiar pain beat behind her eyes.

"Why didn't you just tell me?"

"What?"

Helen rose, crossed the room, and stood before Adair's chair, her posture both angry and tentative.

"I met your girlfriend."

It took Adair a second to understand that Helen meant Cecelia. "Shit."

"Is it true that you've been together for years?"

Adair hung her head. "On and off."

"I didn't realize you had someone. When you and I…"

Helen sounded so pained. Adair could almost see the image Cecelia had painted in her mind. Cecelia, the faithful girlfriend, making peace with Helen for Adair's sake. She could see it now, Cecelia leaning forward, perhaps taking Helen's hand. None of Cecelia's scorn would show through. In fact, she would imbue her words with a hint of awe. *A college president. I always wanted to work at a college.*

"Cecelia is a snake," Adair said.

"She says she loves you."

"Did she tell you how she's connected to my family?"

"She's a family friend." Adair let out a sharp laugh. It occurred to Adair that she had never mentioned Cecelia's name in conjunction with Cyrus. My brother's wife. Cecelia. They were two different people, except that they weren't.

"Why didn't you tell me you had a life here?" Helen asked.

Adair saw Cecelia's fiction reflected in Helen's face. She could tell that Helen had already rewritten the nights they had spent together, drawing an outline of Cecelia over their bed.

"Did you think I would out you? Did you think I would race up here and tell her everything just because…" Helen's voice caught. "…I was jealous."

Jealous. Adair searched Helen's face.

"Did you think I would try to destroy your life with her if I knew you were sick?" Helen asked. "Is that who you think I am? Don't you trust me enough to tell me the truth?"

Adair turned away from Helen's gaze. It didn't matter. Even if Helen was jealous, the woman who had made love to Helen on the stage of the Ventmore Theater, who turned cartwheels in the quad, that woman was as present as the characters in the leather bound volume Helen still clutched in her hand. "I've got to go up to Maine," Adair said. "There's just a tiny chance that Prudence and Charity are there, and alive, and that I could find them. Monty and Cecelia won't help, but I have to do this. They're only wherever they are because I went after them."

Helen knelt by Adair's chair. Then Helen's hands were on Adair's cheeks, their faces so close together Adair thought, for a moment, that Helen was going to kiss her.

"Don't," Adair said, although a stupid childhood version of herself thought *maybe she could save me,* like Sleeping Beauty risen from the dead.

"Listen," Helen pleaded. "What can I do to make you stop?"

Adair shook her head and shook free of Helen's touch. "I didn't go get them because I cared about Pittock College or because I needed a hobby if that's what Cecelia told you. I want you to know that. I went because…" She thought of Cyrus, seated across from her at the dining table, sweat staining his shirt beneath the holster of his gun. "Because you asked. Because I wanted to see you once more."

Helen opened her mouth and then closed it without speaking. Adair felt a wave of tenderness for Helen so palpable, for a moment the pain in her heart eclipsed the pain in her chest. She took Helen's hand.

"If you go to Maine," Helen said, "I'm going with you. We'll look, and we'll do whatever we can to find the girls, but then you have to promise me you'll come back here. Even if we don't find them, even if they've gone somewhere else, will you promise me you'll go back home?" Something in Helen's voice— usually so calm and fluid—broke apart as though she was stumbling over a field of boulders. "You'll be here where she can take care of you."

Helen still knelt by her chair. Adair watched her for a moment. Then Adair put her arm around Helen in an awkward embrace and kissed the top of her head.

"I'll never come back here," Adair said. "I'll never

go back to Cecelia."

❦ ❦ ❦ ❦

Adair and Helen arrived in Portland around ten in the evening. The city was still alive with dock workers grabbing a pint after a long shift and office workers hurrying home from after-work dinners.

"I have a reservation for the executive suite." Adair felt the concierge examine her. "I'll take the Honeymoon Suite for her." She gestured toward Helen. "Put it on the Wilson account."

Each suite took up half the top floor. Adair handed Helen a key card. "That's yours." She pointed to the Honeymoon Suite, then unlocked her own door. She guessed by the smell of new carpet, that the Executive Suite was hardly ever rented. It had four bedrooms and a proliferation of pastel seascapes that looked nothing like the rough, gray ocean that beat at the docks.

Helen followed her in, hovering behind her as though wanting to speak and losing the courage.

"They both look the same," Adair said. "You can have this one if you want."

She watched Helen cross to the window with its sixteenth-story view of the Portland harbor, then do a three-sixty before saying, "This place is amazing. Do you own this too?"

Adair shrugged. "A corporation called Insurant National Supplies Inc. owns the Portland Josslin Heights."

"And who owns Insurant National Supplies?"

"On paper? My brother Monty."

"Of course," Helen said, shaking her head.

"I'm going to lie down," Adair said.

"Sorry." Helen moved toward the door as though she had just realized where she was. "What happens next?"

"Just wait for me," Adair said. When the door closed, she took a double dose of Texidol and fell into a sleep that felt like death.

⁕⁕⁕⁕

It was late afternoon the following day when Adair woke, her body stiff and her mouth dry. She splashed some water on her face, took another dose of Texidol, and called Helen to tell her that she would be resting. Then she slept for another five hours.

The next time she woke, it was evening. She dressed and checking the spyhole in the door of her suite to make sure Helen's door was closed. Then she slipped her keycard in her pocket and tiptoed down the hall to the elevator. In her car again, she asked the GPS for strip clubs in the Portland area.

"Calculating," the GPS said.

The first club she visited was a small store front in between an all-night pharmacy and a pawn shop. A letter-board outside advertised, *Beautiful girls! 24/7!* Inside, men ate plates of tacos and yelled at a game on the television above the bar. A stripper moved lazily around the pole in the far corner, not really dancing, just exhibiting herself. A man in a wheelchair handed her bills at a steady rate. No one else was watching.

Adair ordered a gin and tonic and drank it quickly, glowering at the stripper without really seeing her. She considered asking the bartender if she knew anything about human trafficking in Portland, but paused. The bartender wiped the clean counter with a dirty rag. The stripper pressed play on a stereo behind the stage and Lady Gaga blared over the speakers. No one spoke, but Adair could feel the room assessing her. A tourist. A dyke.

There was no way to break into this world as Adair Merrill Wilson. She left the club and wandered into the all-night pharmacy and bought hair dye, an electric razor, athletic tape, a cane, and a Maine Sea Dogs sweatshirt.

Back at the hotel, she dyed her hair a shade of brown the box identified as "Walnut 002" but which looked in life like orange-tinted mud. She shaved a half inch of hair away from her forehead, creating a slight receding hair line, just enough of an indentation to signal hair loss without so much gone that an observer might notice the faint stubble. Next she wrapped the athletic tape around her breasts until she could feel her nipples crush against the edge of her rib cage. Even with a heavy dose of Texidol the pressure of the bands reawakened the pain in her chest, and it echoed through her body. She pulled harder, wrapping the tape around and around her chest until there was no sign of the woman she had been. Then she threw on the cheap sweatshirt with its mockish dog face emblem.

The cane was the final touch. It was not the cane of an old man, but the cane of a young man injured in a fight or an accident. She took twenty minutes to practice her character: a man of about twenty-eight, brutish, wealthy but without class, a man who was used to pretending, who got away with things because of his perchance for violence, a man who got things done but who was imminently forgettable. Finally, the transformation was complete. Adair swallowed one more Texidol and set out again.

Chapter Thirty

Chastain leaned over the twins, swathed in a mask, surgical gown, and safety glasses. "For the blood spray," he explained as he donned them. He pressed a stethoscope to their chest with a gloved hand.

The Purveyor hated him. Perhaps because the blood had touched her hand and not his. Perhaps because their lives were worth so much more than his.

He straightened and pulled the stethoscope off as though afraid of contaminating his gown. "How long have they been down here?"

The basement room that had looked serene before, now looked dank. The Purveyor noticed a water stain near the window. The air smelled of mildew. "Not long."

"You've got quite a specimen here," Chastain said, removing his gloves. "Do you know how many conjoined twins are born in a year? One for every 500,000 births, and most of those die within a day. But these girls! They're so perfectly formed. There's usually some deformation. One twin takes over more of the body, but these two are perfectly symmetrical."

They both turned as the twins stirred. Charity's eyelids fluttered and then opened. Her eyes had sunk deep into her cheeks. "Dorothia?" she asked. She seemed to wait for an answer, then she laughed. "Blue has run off again. Father says he's chasing bears. He'll be back with a rabbit."

At this, Prudence opened her eyes and traced the ceiling frantically. "It's our rabbit!"

The smile fell from Charity's face as she whispered, "No, Prudence. It's the consumption."

A dribble of blood escaped the corner of Charity's mouth, and the Purveyor loathed Chastain for not wiping it away, although she made no motion to do so herself.

Then the twins' eyes closed simultaneously, and they settled deeper into their pillow.

"Where did you find them?" Chastain asked.

"It doesn't matter. Can you treat them?"

"With a proper hospital. X-rays. A course of antibiotics. If it's drug resistant, we may have to collapse a lung. This isn't a case of chlamydia that's going to clear up with one prescription from CVS pharmacy."

"But can you do it?"

Chastain stroked his chin. "This is more complicated than I expected."

The Purveyor felt Galloway's presence in the room. He had insisted that the tablet be left on, so he could monitor the girls. The screen showed only the familiar oceanscape, but the Purveyor knew he was listening. He didn't need the tablet to listen. He was like a God.

"Money is no issue," she said. "I will get you anything you need, and I will pay whatever you ask."

Chastain grinned. She could almost see the casino lights flickering in his eyes. The high rollers table. The wheel of fate turning.

"Once they get where they're going, they'll have all the care they need," the Purveyor said, "but I need them well enough to travel."

"I have an IV bag in the car, fluids, antibiotics, but a hospital would really be the best setting."

Chastain would blackmail her. She knew it. But it didn't matter. Once the final transfer from Galloway's holdings went through, no sum Chastain could ask for would matter. "No one can know about them," she said. "If one photo gets out, you're a dead man."

And so am I.

Chapter Thirty-one

The next strip club Adair visited was a glitzy franchise in the suburbs. The lights were too bright and the waitresses too quick to offer appetizers or to upgrade her drink to a double. The next two clubs were smaller and darker, with more wharf men and fewer business men.

The bands around her chest made Adair sick, but she let the pain lend authenticity to her character. She twisted her foot inward and allowed almost no weight to rest on it, so that each time she stepped she fell a little bit. It was a magician's gimmick, a slight of hand. Look at my beautiful assistant and you will not see me take the card out of my pocket. Watch and wonder how such a young man ended up with a limp and you will not notice his soft face, her shifting eyes.

The last club on her list billed itself as Portland's finest gentleman's club. Inside, chairs circled different stages of differing sizes, each speared with a bronze pole. Most of the seats were full. Men were cheering. Dollar bills fluttered in the air around the girls. It was one in the morning.

A woman in black panties and stilettos sidled up to her almost immediately. "Can I help you find a seat? Perhaps in our Crystal Lounge?"

Adair shook her head.

"We also have a private, twenty-seat lap dance room. It's very intimate." The woman brushed against her. "My name is Aubrey." Then she flitted away, winking at Adair over her shoulder as she left.

Adair took a seat in the corner by the smallest stage. From there, she could watch the entire room, while appearing to watch the muscular woman hanging like an inverted crucifix from the pole. Within an hour, she had identified the woman she wanted, a tattooed stripper with aggressively goth make-up. She had danced twice on the small stage, her eyes moving over the crowd as she worked. When she was done with her dance, Adair beckoned to her. "Is there someplace we can go?" Adair's voice was a growl.

"You want a lap dance?"

"Maybe."

"What's your name, honey?" The word "honey" sounded strange coming from her black painted lips.

"Len," Adair said.

"I'm gonna call you L-Man." The stripper pronounced it *el man*. "The man," she added. "I bet you're the man."

Adair nodded.

"Want to come up to the lounge?" The girl took her hand. Adair squeezed her hand hard, hoping the girl would not notice her smooth skin. The stripper led her into one of the back chambers. Dim, red sconces lit a room lined with three rows of heavy, leather chairs. Like pews, each row was a solid piece, but between each seat was a thick, wooden partition. In several of the seats, men sat grinning or gasping as women gyrated against them.

"What do you do, L-Man?" the stripper said as she settled Adair into one of the seats.

"Imports," Adair said.

"You work on the docks?"

"At a desk on the docks, yeah." Adair crossed her legs as the girl reached for her crotch.

"You playing hard to get, honey?"

"I'm not really looking for a dance."

"Whatcha looking for L-Man?" The girl swayed her hips in front of Adair.

"You're pretty, but you're not what I'm looking for."

The stripper pretended to pout, batting long, purple eyelashes, but her face was much harder than her act. Behind the eyelashes she looked angry. "Then why'd you ask me back here?" She sucked on her finger tip.

"I'm bored," Adair said. "If you know what I mean." She cast her eyes across the girl's leather half corset, her pierced nipples, her dragon tattoo. "I'm looking for an adventure."

"You looking for some take out?" the girl asked.

Adair let fatigue slur her words. The stripper probably thought she was drunk. "My buddy Jason…" The power of a script was in the details, Adair knew. Details anchored the story in people's imagination. "He took me to this club down in Boston. Wasn't really a club, it was more of just a meeting spot. This old house near the freeway. The girls there were good. They were different, you know. Not just regular girls, no offense. They were like collectors' items. There was this one girl…she was a freak show. I'd tip anyone who could find me a girl like that. Jason told me there was a club like that up in Portland called the Ashfelt Club, told me he'd use his connections. Then his wife caught on and said she'd fucking divorce him the next time he went with a hooker. You never heard of the Ashfelt Club, have you? The Ashfelt girls are real curios, you know, like freaks of nature."

"I could be your freak of nature," the stripper purred.

"I'm not talking about you." Adair closed her eyes.

"How much are you paying if I can get you something like that?"

Adair opened her eyes took a money clip of crisp hundreds out of her back pocket and flipped two off the roll. "Here's for asking around." Adair returned to the main room and stayed for another hour, then drifted out so as not to appear too eager. She went down the street, tried to eat something at an over-lit diner, but the Texidol had turned her stomach, and the burger smelled like the flesh it was.

She tried not to remember the many nights she had spent at the Craven pub surrounded by her students wolfing down burgers, laughing at their antics, and teasing them cheerfully until the whole table wept with laugher. Each year she had thought the students could not be more charming. Each year at Pittock had been the best until Marshal Drummond took over the college and Anat al Fulani disappeared and Carrie Brown died. And even then the nights held their own dark magic, like a vein of silver in black rock. There had been Helen, so beautiful from afar, and so profoundly captivating in the flesh. She tried not to remember.

Then she returned to the club. As she had suspected, the stripper had noted her departure. As she had hoped, the woman was waiting for her to come back. "L-Man," the woman said. She had dropped the pouting girl routine. "So I may have a little something for you." She flicked a card between two claw-like nails.

Adair whipped out another hundred and passed it to her.

"Call first, and tell her Spider sent you. That's not me," the girl added. She waved vaguely in the direction of the dance floor. "That's my friend over there. She said, if you go, you better be serious."

Adair snatched the card. "I'm always fucking serious."

It was almost three by the time Adair returned to the Josslin Heights. By then, she really did need the cane for support. She stumbled into her bedroom. The Texidol had worn off on her drive back to the hotel. Now pain existed in every tendon, every bone, and yet nowhere at the same time. She pulled off her sweatshirt and released the bandage around her chest. Her hands felt numb, the air thin. The edges of her vision closed in, blackness eating up the room. Then she passed out.

From the Diary of Charity Kimball

The false friend with the shiny clothes and the silky hair came to visit us again. This time he was full of nervous laughter. He kept saying, "You think you run this company? You think you get to call the shots in *my* family? *My* house?" But I knew he was not talking to us.

He tried to make us stand, but Prudence is still silent. Eventually he disappeared and returned with a chair on wheels. He dragged us into it and made me hold the bag of water attached to the needle in Prudence's arm. I reached out for the window they call a "tablet."

The false friend said, "You won't need that anymore." Then he dropped it on the floor and stepped on it.

I could not believe he would destroy such a beautiful object, but I knew that our savior, who calls himself Harlow, lives far away. The tablet is only a portal. I tried to whisper to Prudence. *Harlow will come for us.*

Then the false friend threw a blanket over us and wheeled us outside. I tried to smell the fresh air through the blanket, but I could not, or perhaps the air was not fresh at all. I felt as though all the blood had drained from my body, like one of the venison carcasses Daddy let hang. I knew it was Prudence's illness.

A moment later, the false friend lifted us, blanket and all, and pushed us into a large box or maybe it was a room, or maybe it was another car. We lay on the floor in the awkward way that Prudence hates, on our side, with my head resting on top of her head. A door slammed. An engine started. It was entirely dark. Since Prudence was not there to pray to God for us, I prayed to Harlow Galloway.

You are so beautiful. Save me. Save me. Save me.

Chapter Thirty-two

Adair woke late in the morning. She rose slowly, limping to the bathroom. Her face in the mirror was drawn. Her soft, blond hair was now an ugly brown. Some of the hair dye had stained her skin. The receding hairline was convincing. The slightest hint of a smile crossed her lips. She had always been good at make-up. "You have a gift for transformation," one of her professors had said, his tone a mix of admiration and concern.

She was staring at the mirror when she heard a movement behind her. She whirled around. Helen stood in her suit and pumps, fresh and professional, as though preparing for a Pittock College board meeting.

"How did you get in?"

Helen held out a cup of coffee. "I asked for an extra key. What happened to your hair?"

"How long have you been here?" Adair asked, taking the coffee and sipping it tentatively.

"I came looking for you."

"This morning?"

"It's afternoon."

Adair sat down at a table by the window. "I was out last night."

"You're sick. You were supposed to rest. What happened to your hair?" Helen said more gently.

Adair lowered herself into a chair by the window. She recounted the night's events, starting with the drugstore costume and finishing with the card pinched between the stripper's black nails. "This might be it," Adair finished, pushing the card across the table.

"Oh, Adair." Helen sat across from her. "Are you going to call the police?"

"I told you what Scarlet said." Adair took the business card back and studied it for a moment. "If I call the police, the whole operation disappears."

"So what are you going to do?"

"Call this number."

"And?"

"Go where they tell me?"

"Adair! What if it's a trap?"

Adair gazed out the window. Below them the city moved in miniature. Tiny cars and tiny people moving about their ordinary lives. "It doesn't really matter."

"It matters to me," Helen said. "Why don't you talk to Thompson? He can call Portland police."

"We can't."

"Just because Hornsby took a bribe doesn't mean you can't trust the police."

"I trust the police." Adair took another sip of her coffee. "But all it takes is one disgruntled dispatcher, one guy who scans papers all day in a back room. A tip-off. Just one person who wants to make a thousand dollars by sending a text message, and the whole thing is shot."

Helen tucked a strand of hair behind her ear. "You have to trust someone."

Adair was about to tell Helen what Monty had always said. That institutions were for the poor, networks the legacy of the middle class—the rich had no need of governance—but instead she said, "I trust you."

Helen's hand rested on the table, and Adair covered it with her own. She thought of the Seacamp, the bluff, the cathedral catwalk, the bottles of oxycodone which did nothing to ease her pain but which, in sufficient quantity, could end it. "I'll call this morning," Adair said. "If I can get a location, I'll go after them today. Go back to Pittock. Go back to your happy life." She stroked her fingers along Helen's hand. "I'm not going to risk your life…and plus, you'd never pass."

"Pass?"

"As a man. You're too pretty." Adair felt a sad smile pull at her mouth. "I could give you a full beard and a set of balls as big as Texas, and no one would believe you were a man."

Helen laughed and for just a moment Adair felt like the sun had come through a window.

Then Helen said, "I won't let you go alone. I'll call the police first and tip them off. This is stupid and foolish and dangerous, and the least I can do is go with you. And Adair…" Helen leaned forward. "I'm not happy."

Adair called the number she had received from the stripper. She was greeted by silence. "Spider told me to call. I'm looking for an Ashfelt girl."

At the table across from her, Helen sat watching her, clutching her coffee mug in both hands. Behind her, the penthouse window showcased a view of the Portland skyline.

A voice came on the phone. "Name?" The voice had the fake quality of a drag queen or an old woman trying to sound breathy.

"Len," Adair said, her own voice an octave lower

than usual. There was a long pause, then the voice delivered an address which Adair scribbled quickly onto a hotel note pad. "When should I come?" she asked but the phone line had already gone dead.

"Now what?" Helen asked.

"Find this on a map." Adair handed her the address. "I'll get a costume."

Adair grabbed her leather jacket and her wallet and left the suite before Helen could say anything. She had half a mind to simply get her car and disappear. And yet she found herself walking toward a costume shop she had spotted when she first arrived.

"Looking for anything in particular?" the clerk called from behind the dusty counter, where a small black and white television showed security footage.

Adair moved through the aisles piled high with misshapen boxes and filmy plastic bags full of wigs. As she wandered through the store, breathing in the smell of mildew, she thought, *you can't take Helen. This isn't about her.* The thought repeated in her mind like a distress signal broadcasting from the end of the world.

Almost without volition, Adair picked up a plastic shopping basket from the end of one of the aisles. She dropped a turquoise wig in the basket, then a vinyl miniskirt, a leather choker, leash, and a bottle of scarlet nail polish. Finally, she selected a box bearing a photograph of a woman in a corset. She took the garment out of its box and held it up, but she was not sizing it for herself. She was remembering the curves of Helen's body, the weight of her breasts.

Chapter Thirty-three

The Purveyor stood a few yards from the landing pad on the roof of the long defunct Briggs & Folston Textile Mill, several miles outside of Manchester on the Piscataquog River. Below her, the ruins of the industrial revolution lay in collapsing piles of brick and rusted iron. The only sound was the distant cry of doves.

The Purveyor felt nervous. Bolo usually handled exchanges alone or pawned them off on one of his underlings, but this was too important. If Harlow Galloway spoke to the right circles, this could be the beginning of a new era, a new business. No more Thai whores in grimy fishing boats. No more Russian girls ripped from their stony villages. But if Galloway talked to the wrong people, if a nosy reporter from Vanity Fair found their way onto his island…the risk was as high as the payoff.

She looked around. Bolo should have been there already, and delay was not acceptable. There were other clients she would make wait simply to flex her muscle. *I own you*, her tardiness would say. Not Galloway. She listened for Bolo's SUV. He would not have brought the twins on foot, not after they had been sick. He could not be that stupid.

She heard nothing until she heard the first rumble of Galloway's helicopter. A minute later, she saw the speck of the helicopter appear through a break in the trees.

Where was Bolo?

She called his phone. Nothing.

She could now recognize the helicopter–a modified AgustaWestland. A moment later, she could see the pilot, a black man in a dark suit. A second later, the blades were churning the air, sweeping dust into the sky. Galloway stepped out ducking below the blades.

There were two other men in the helicopter besides the pilot. Both wore identical suits and sunglasses. The Purveyor felt fear run the circumference of her ribs. Her breath felt shallow. They would kill her if he commanded. Looking at Harlow's gracious smile and easy stride, she realized she would never recognize the signal when it came. They would be gone beyond the reach of the law before the bullet had cooled in her chest.

"My dear," Galloway said, as the noise of the helicopter died down. He extended his hand.

Who did she have? Who could she trust? The Purveyor glanced around, trying not to stare at the entrance to the stairwell through which Bolo was supposed to have emerged. "My brother-in-law, Bolo, has been detained," she told Galloway. She could smell her own fear like blood on iron.

Galloway squinted slightly, anger making his chiseled features even more handsome. "We had an understanding."

"Yes, I was concerned about their health." She knew it was a gambit. If Bolo appeared in the next minutes with the twins in tow, she was a liar.

Galloway raised a hand. "Their price is beyond measure." He spoke casually as though commenting on the weather, taking her arm and leading her away from the helicopter, to the edge of the parapet. "We're not buying diamonds. If you have hurt them, if you have frightened them..." He stepped away, gazing down at the river below them. "I will destroy everything you love."

"Love." The Purveyor tossed her dark hair over her shoulder. They were still flirting, in a way. Even the bullet piercing her vest would be part of the seduction. He would select the finest Nigerian-made depleted uranium penetrator enclosed within soft copper. Cupid's arrow, straight to her heart. "What makes you think I would go into this business and be foolish enough to love something?"

Galloway gazed at her. "Your land perhaps? Your husband?" It was a test. He was watching her pupils dilate, waiting for her body to give her away. "Or is there someone else? A child? No. A lover, a young man somewhere?"

They remained frozen, staring into each other's eyes. Behind them the helicopter was a heartbeat.

"You are a man of the world," she said, taking his arm now. "That it is imperfect should come as no surprise to you. The twins were not well enough to be moved. I thought they would be, but they aren't." She was standing beneath the gallows. "I made the decision at the last minute with the help of our doctor. You can threaten me all you like, but it is you who demand their safety. Ordinarily, I would lock them in a freight carton with a gallon of water and ship them to you by boat."

Galloway held up his hand as though her words had a faint but unpleasant scent. "I will return in a week," he said, turning toward the helicopter. Then he stopped. He turned back to the Purveyor and fixed her with his gaze. "Your recruiter. The woman you sent for the twins."

"What about her?" The Purveyor felt her eyes dilate.

"Adair Merrill Wilson. You love her."

How had he seen it?

"I've been watching you for years." He rested a hand on her shoulder, his flirtation taking on a paternal warmth. "Don't be naïve, Cecelia. I didn't choose you for your strength. I chose you for your weakness."

❧ ❧ ❧ ❧

"Where the hell are you?" Cecelia Beaucharnel demanded when she finally reached Bolo on his cell phone. She was sitting in the upstairs office, behind the false wall, the room in which she kept documents that could not be sufficiently encrypted. A room that could be locked and sealed in case of a raid. A room even Bolo could not access. "Galloway was here. He was waiting for the twins. How could you possibly have fucked this up?" There was a long silence. "Bolo?"

"I'm sorry," Bolo said. "I love you like a sister."

There were no windows in the office. Clearly. They were not careless enough to be caught by a junior police officer counting windows and rooms. Even though the space was large and well-appointed with original Stickly furniture, it felt claustrophobic.

"I really do," he whined.

Cecelia wished she could reach through the phone lines and strangle him. She had always thought it advantageous to have one family member dumb enough to take the risks she and her husband, Cyrus

Wilson, would not take. To fly to the Ukraine to collect a shipment of girls left stranded when two of their local bottoms got in a fight and shot each other. To negotiate terms with military agents in the Congo. To beat and to fuck when necessary. To kill. But there were disadvantages also, and his stupidity was one of them. "You were supposed to be there," she said.

"I love you, but I love Ashley Payten too," Bolo said, "and we want to start a life together."

"Ashley Payten? You left me on the gallows for Ashley Payten? Because I wouldn't let you fuck the Girl Scout?"

"She's not a Girl Scout, and I want to marry her." Bolo's voice trembled. He was forty, but he acted like a child.

"Well you can't."

"Have you heard of Bi Jiao Hui?" Bolo asked.

"What?"

"Samuel Buchanan?" he went on. "He's from Texas, but he changed his name when he moved to China and set up some of the first electronics factories, right after China earned most favorable trade status. He's worth billions."

"What is this about, Bolo?" She tried to tame the rage in her voice.

"He found out about the twins. I don't know how."

"What the fuck!"

"He offered me three million."

Cecelia slapped her hand on the table in front of her sending a Monte Blanc pen skittering across the desk. "That's nothing! We have a contract with Galloway. We honor that contract."

"That's your contract," Bolo said. "My contract is with Bi Jiao Hui."

Chapter Thirty-four

When Helen heard Adair knock on her hotel door, she realized she had not really expected her to return. Everything Adair did had a kind of finality to it. But there she was, her hair damp from the rain that had been hitting the city on and off throughout the afternoon. She had several shopping bags in her hands.

"Do you still want to do this?" she asked.

Helen nodded.

"I'll need to do your make-up."

It struck Helen that Adair looked shy.

"I remember how," Adair added.

At Pittock, Adair's transformations had been legendary. For several years, she had made a habit of greeting her students in costume on the first day of class. Once she was an old janitor bent over her cleaning cart. Once she burst through the theater door dressed as a man and complaining that Professor Wilson had not shown up for work. The older students made a sport of helping Adair fool the freshman, and everyone had marveled at her gifts.

"Sit here." Adair pulled out a chair. She placed an assortment of bottles and pencils on the table beside them. Her hands trembled and jerked as she arranged her tools. She dropped a powder compact. When she opened it, the power inside had cracked into crumbs. Helen looked away.

"I'm sorry," Adair said.

"It's fine."

"I'll start with a foundation." Adair shook the bottle. "Remember the goal isn't to accentuate your beauty, it's to mar it."

Your beauty. Helen had never thought of her appearance as anything more than an asset to leverage. It was important to be polished. It was important to be attractive but not sensual, healthy but not young. Now she longed for Adair to look at her. *See me,* she pleaded silently.

Adair picked up a sponge and daubed at a bottle of foundation and then at Helen's face, her gestures furtive and uncertain. She worked for several minutes applying different shades and textures. When Adair's hand brushed Helen's hair off her forehead, Helen jumped.

"I'm sorry," Adair said again.

"Please don't be," Helen whispered.

Adair set down the sponge. She traced the curve of Helen's cheekbone with her thumb, her hand more steady than it had been before. Helen closed her eyes. Adair ran the fingers of both hands along Helen's jaw, along her cheeks, across her earlobes. The touch sent a frisson of pleasure down Helen's spine and into her hips. For a long time, Adair rubbed light circles over Helen's ears, the make-up forgotten. Helen felt like there was nothing in the world except Adair's touch and her own body waking. Helen wanted to squirm and press herself against Adair and beg for her touch. She wanted Adair's hands to slide down her neck and across her breasts and clutch her. She felt as though all the grief-stricken longing of the past six months had settled in the flesh behind her clitoris, and if Adair would gather her sex into her hand, her mouth, the relief would be like a rebirth. But Helen did not move. She was not sure if she was even breathing, afraid that any movement would startle Adair back into the fugue state she seemed to inhabit.

When Helen finally opened her eyes, she saw that Adair's eyes were closed, her face set in a look of concentration, like a blind sculptor, like someone trying to remember. Helen felt certain that Adair was saying "goodbye." Suddenly the hot dampness between Helen's own legs felt as mournful as tears.

As if sensing Helen's gaze, Adair opened her eyes and jerked her hands away. "I'm almost done," she said.

Helen released her breath.

❧❧❧❧

A half hour later, Adair stepped away from Helen and admired her work. "Do you want to see?" she asked.

"Not really," Helen said but walked to the mirror and stared for a long time.

Adair had dusted her face with a heavy cake of powder. She had applied dark make up around Helen's eyes and a touch of red lip liner to their inner rim. Then she had shown Helen how to tilt the wig over her tightly wound hair. Adair had pushed the last strands of auburn under the nylon mesh. "Are you ready to change?"

Helen nodded. A few minutes later, she emerged from the bathroom in heels, skirt, tights, wig, and corset.

"It takes real talent." A smile crossed Adair's

face.

"To do what?" Helen asked.

"To make you look bad."

For a second, Helen saw the brash, flirtatious woman who had wooed her at Pittock. Then she was gone, and the woman before Helen stood sad and stoic.

"You don't have to do this," Adair added, but the words meant nothing because Helen knew she would follow Adair anywhere.

Chapter Thirty-five

Adair changed into her own costume. A few minutes later, they were in the car. The sun had not yet set, but the drizzle had turned into a storm, and the sky was black with rainclouds. The rain spattered the windshield as they turned onto the forested highway that ran along the coast. A minute later, the thunder clapped and the rain poured down as though the sky were a bowl of water cracked open. The wiper blades slashed back and forth. Adair could barely see the road. She glanced at the GPS. They were getting closer. She looked at Helen, but she could read nothing in her profile. Then, Helen who had been staring silently out the window, pointed. "Is that it?"

Through a break in the trees, Adair could see the ocean and, in the distance ahead, on a promontory above the waves, a sprawling white structure. It disappeared behind the trees and then reappeared a minute later like a specter, pale against the navy sky. On third glimpse, Adair noted that the bottom story of the hotel seemed to be crumbling into the ocean. The waves lapped at the building's pilings, as though ready to tear it off the rock.

"It looks abandoned," Helen said. "How close are we?"

Adair checked the GPS. "That's got to be it."

They rounded another rocky outcropping, the guard rail only a fragile ribbon between the car and the forty-foot drop to the sea. The hotel was clearly visible now. Adair caught sight of a light in one of the windows.

The GPS said, "In 500 meters turn right on Pines Lane…Pines lane in 400 meters…prepare to turn right."

Adair felt a chill go down her back.

From the main road, Pines Lane looked like a driveway to a private residence, but the gravel road led to a sprawling white hotel. Despite its obvious disrepair, the building still had a grandeur about it. It reminded Adair of her family's estate. The main entrance was graced by an empty fountain. The statue of a woman pouring water from a basin stood like a sentry in the middle of the blue tiled basin. Behind her, the hotel exuded a bygone elegance. The double doors were ornamented with carvings and frosted glass in large oval panes. Adair looked up. All the windows were intact. She turned off the car.

"Are you ready," she said without looking at Helen. She could see that Helen's hands were shaking, and she could see Helen steady them. I should never have brought her, Adair thought, but the thought was just a record playing in an empty room. She *had* brought Helen. "They are probably watching us already," Adair added.

"I know."

"I'm sorry." Adair exited the car, walked around to Helen's side, opened the door, and grabbed the chain that hung from the leather choker at Helen's neck. She wrapped it angrily around her fist. "Move bitch," she said, loud enough for her voice to pierce the rain.

A light came on inside. Adair took a few limping

steps forward. She held the cane in one hand, the leash in the other. With each step she yanked Helen, cursing and grumbling as she moved toward the building. At the door they were greeted by a large man in jeans and a black T-shirt. His arms were massive and his neck stretched the cotton fibers of his shirt. Adair saw the familiar bulge of a gun tucked into the back of his pants when he turned.

"Yeah?" He stood in front of the open door.

Adair guessed that this was his welcoming stance. They were expected. The unexpected guest would probably be looking into the barrel of a rifle.

The man eyed Helen. "Pick up or delivery?"

Adair pulled the chain until Helen was standing right next to her. Helen did not look at Adair or the man, her chin turned up angrily, her hands hanging in limp defeat at her sides. She was a good actor, Adair thought.

"I've come to teach this bitch a lesson," Adair said in the voice of the character she had conjured. She had thought the scenario through the night before, and outlined the basics to Helen without giving her a script. The worst thing one could do to a novice actor was give them one read-through before curtain call. Better to push them out into the lights unprepared than to feed them a few melodramatic lines on which they could choke. For her part, Helen had asked nothing and offered nothing, following Adair with a silent docility that made Adair feel like she was moving through a dream.

To Helen she hissed. "Do you hear me, you jealous bitch? You're gonna watch and then you're gonna lick my come off another trick's boots. Do you hear me?"

Helen said nothing.

Adair gave the chain a sharp jerk. Helen cried out. Adair worried that she had hurt her, but she could not break character now. "You listening?"

"Yes," Helen choked.

Adair turned back to the man in the doorway.

"Spider said I could find something different here. An Ashfelt girl. I want to show this bitch I'm not her fucking husband. I want to show her shit she can't ever do for me." She grit her teeth. "Ever."

"Name?" the man asked.

"Len."

"Last name?"

"That's all you fucking need to know. Spider sent me, and my name's Len."

The man seemed to accept this, because he stepped aside and ushered them in. The front entry led to a large ballroom that looked out on the ocean.

"I'm going to pat you down." The man took the Glock that Adair had retrieved from her gun safe at the Wilson estate. He even turned it over appreciatively. "Customized," he said, then he grunted at Helen. "Her to."

It was clear when Helen removed her coat that there was nowhere for her to conceal a weapon, but the man ran his hands along her breasts anyway. When his hand dipped between her legs and squeezed, Adair feared Helen would protest reflexively, but she just scowled.

"I'll get Angel." The man took Adair's gun with him and exited.

Adair's heart raced. Adrenaline coursed through her, pushing the familiar pain to the periphery of her body. Despite the Ace bandage binding her breasts, she could breathe. She straightened. She looked at

Helen who was staring at the ocean, her face set like a stone. *I should never have brought her.* But it was too late to rethink anything. Adair stepped toward the door where the man had exited. Then she pressed her ear to the wall.

Helen snapped around, her eyes terrified. *No,* she mouthed.

Adair was already listening to the conversation in the other room.

"Says he's here for an Ashfelt girl." It was the man's voice.

"Name?"

"Len."

"Who sent him?" The woman had a faint Spanish accent.

"Spider."

"Damn her. We don't have a Len."

"He asked for an Ashfelt girl."

"I'll look at him."

Adair leapt away from the wall. A second later, the door opened. A woman in a long black evening dress emerged.

"It will be just a moment more," the woman said to her. "Can you tell me what you're looking for?"

Adair hesitated. "I told your man. An Ashfelt girl."

The woman gestured vaguely toward the ocean. "I don't know what you're talking about."

"Yes you do." Adair cast Helen's leash to the floor as though the mere act of holding it frustrated her. "I want to fuck like I've never fucked before." She was riding an adrenaline high. Pain disappeared. Only her performance—only *everything* for which her life and her profession had prepared—could save her. "I want something fucking twisted. Some fucked up shit, not just some tired bitch in a collar calling me daddy. I want to go out on the edge." She limped toward the plate glass window. Outside it was so dark she could no longer see the rain. She could only see the crests of the waves where the sea ended and the sky began. "That dark." Adair let her voice go deeper. "I want the night. I want to drink it up. I want to see things go wrong. I want the chromosome split. I want the uranium bride. I want the Cyclops. I want Lazarus back from the grave." She turned to meet the woman's eyes.

"What was your name?" the woman asked.

"Leonard Thomas Brown."

The woman pulled a pistol out of a slit in her dress. "What's your real name? And don't lie, because I can see it in your eyes."

The performance had been masterful. Adair did not need a bouquet of roses in cellophane to tell her that. But the woman had found a flaw. The woman wanted a truth.

"Wilson," Adair said. "Last name's Wilson." She did not tremble on the outside.

The woman studied her.

"First name?"

"Adair."

"Okay, Mr. Wilson. I'll be right back."

As soon as she exited, Adair flew to the wall. Through the wall, she heard the woman speaking to her thug.

"It's a fucking sting," the woman said.

"Who is he?" the man's voice asked.

"PD. FBI. How the fuck should I know? He said his name was Adair Wilson."

"That's not possible."

"No, it's not. Get them out of here."

Adair did not have time to register anything but the threat in the woman's voice. She grabbed Helen's hand.

"Run."

"What is it?" Helen broke character.

From overhead, and simultaneously from everywhere in the building, a siren sounded. Adair and Helen ran to the front door through which they had entered the Pines, but the driveway was now flooded in bright lights. Several men in ski masks were running toward the hotel, appearing from the woods like mythical creatures.

Adair looked at Helen. The only way out was through the building. They ran to a door on the far side of the room. Together they careened through the door, finding themselves in a long hallway lined by closed doors. The hallway was brightly lit in a way that suggested a sudden flood of light, not the normal lighting for a hotel. Every few feet, a siren blared from the ceiling. The hallway seemed to lengthen as they ran. Adair cursed. There were no turns. She tried a door as she passed, but it was locked. As soon as someone opened the door behind them, they would be in plain sight. Easy targets.

Adair did not dare look back.

At the end of the hall, they came to a door that opened onto a staircase. They flew down the carpeted stairs and then through another door that opened onto a cement staircase. That staircase eventually opened onto a third set of stairs. This time the stairs were wood and encased in a wind-blown wooden structure. It was as though the hotel was disintegrating as they ran through it, its grandeur falling away. Adair could smell the ocean air blowing through cracks in the slats around them.

Finally, they reached the bottom of the last staircase. There they stood in a room, like a covered pier. Through the knotholes in the wooden floorboards, Adair thought she saw the ocean crashing beneath them. A door stood open, letting out onto yet another hallway.

"It's a trap." It was the first thing Helen had said since they entered the hotel. "Those doors were alarmed." She nodded in the direction they had just come. "They could have locked any one of them. It's standard procedure in a school shooting. Minimize the damage. I recognize the model on the alarms."

Adair was about to speak, but the sound of footsteps above them stopped her. The wooden structure shook. They had no choice but to run down the final hallway. This hallway was as ragged as the rest of the hotel was stately. The right side of the hall was made of warped Plexiglas windows, as though someone had tacked a plastic windbreak to an open-air walkway. Through the salt-stained Plexiglas, Adair saw a tangle of blackberries and, beyond that, the sea.

On the other side of the hall were rooms. The windows to the rooms were covered by stained curtains. The locks had been drilled out of the doors and the door knobs had been removed, leaving two holes in each door. Here the siren was almost mute, and the hallway felt inhabited in a way the others did not. Through the roar of the ocean and the blood in her ears, Adair heard a woman's moan, then the slap of hand on flesh.

The brothel. It was here, not in the decaying

splendor of the hotel above.

She beckoned for Helen to follow. "There has to be a way out," she whispered.

They raced down the hall. The cries of sex and protest grew louder, as did the footsteps in the stairwell above them.

"Where are they?" someone yelled.

"You take the second floor. We'll go down."

They froze. Helen held Adair's gaze with terror in her eyes and something else, something Adair could not place. It was as though looking into Helen's eyes she looked beyond the raging surf, down to the stone floor of the ocean.

Adair tried one of the doors, pulling at the hole where the doorknob should have been. Inside she saw a woman's legs flailing beneath a large man. "Get out," the woman gasped.

In the next room, a man knelt in the fetal position so thoroughly bound it seemed there was more leather than skin. She pushed the door closed quickly before the woman standing over him noticed the intrusion. In the third room, she caught a flash of red, a corset, a shoe, and a glimpse of a woman's face.

The voices were drawing closer.

Adair tried the next room. It was empty. She pulled Helen inside. There was no time to explain. She ripped Helen's blue wig off and threw it under the small bed in the middle of the room. She threw her cane after it. "Fuck me," she whispered. Then she pushed Helen against a wall. Awkwardly, frantically, she pulled Helen's skirt up around her waist and raked her hands down Helen's thighs, dropping her underwear to the floor. Helen's eyes were wide. Adair dropped her own pants and boxers. She knew her body. From behind, in motion, her lean buttocks could easily belong to a young man. She pinned Helen to the wall.

"Put your legs around me," she instructed. She felt their pubic bones touch. "Your face in my shoulder."

Adair picked Helen up and pressed her back against the wall. Helen wrapped her legs around Adair's waist.

The limp was not only a disguise, it was also a lizard's tail: something to drop when in danger. The voices in the hall were chasing a gimp and a prostitute in a blue wig. In the room, stood a young man strong enough to hold a woman on his hips. From the vantage of the door, Helen would be only a cascade of auburn hair.

Adair pumped her hips into Helen's. Together they slammed against the wall. Adair thought she felt the whole room shake. She thought she felt the moisture of tears as Helen buried her face against her shoulder. But she could not stop. The footsteps were converging. She heard her pursuers checking the rooms, coming closer. From one room, a man's cry of protest. From the next, a woman's languid "go away." A door slammed and then another.

She beat her naked hips against Helen's. She could feel where their pubic bones connected, hard on hard, but at the edge of that grind was the softness of flesh, the hair thickened and curled. Adair could feel the skin of her hood melding into Helen's, and she remembered…suddenly…pleasure.

PCPS had not only steeped her body in pain, it had erased even the simplest possibility of pleasure. Now one singing chord of flesh remembered. She felt the pressure of Helen's pubic bone pull at the skin around her clitoris and despite everything, she felt herself go wet. She tried to shift, to pull away, to keep up the rhythmic beating of her hips without feeling the pleasure to which she had no right. To make it all an act and not rape. But the voices were upon them now. She plunged her body against Helen's, the fictitious cries of a John in angry lust blending with the tenor of her own heart, as her mind screamed, *I'm sorry. I'm sorry. I'm sorry.*

The door behind them flew open.

She felt Helen's legs tighten around her waist, Helen's hips buck against her body, Helen's lips press her neck, muffling a cry.

"Get the fuck out!" Adair bellowed to the men she could feel behind her. She slammed Helen against the wall. "Out!"

Helen's teeth sank into her shoulder.

Behind her, a man's voice called, "Next."

The door closed.

Adair continued to beat their bodies against the wall until the voices of the search party receded into the stairwell again. Then she stopped. Listened. The hall was silent except for the sighing of the other patrons. They heard footsteps on the floor above. She set Helen back on her feet. "Get dressed," she whispered.

Helen did not move. Adair put her hands on either side of Helen's face, holding her face as if she could press her remorse into Helen's cheeks. "I am *so sorry*," she breathed.

Tears poured from Helen's eyes, turning her make-up into dark rivulets.

"I thought we were going to die," Adair tried again. "I would never...Helen, I would never, never do that to you. And now we have to run."

Helen ran the heels of her hands across her eyes, her tears receding like the ocean. She pulled her skirt down and kicked off her heels, throwing them under the bed with the wig and the cane. "Let's go."

They ran back to the staircase, but it ended on that floor.

"The windows," Adair said. "They're old." She ran back along the hallway, looking for the loosest sheet of Plexiglas. When she found it, she slid her fingers beneath one corner. Rain blew in on a cold ocean breeze as soon as she lifted one corner of the Plexiglas. Helen grabbed onto the other side of the window. Together they pulled, and, a moment later, the Plexiglas released, sending a shower of plasterboard and splintered wood to the floor.

With the window gone, Adair could see that the entire wing of the hotel stood on wood beams atop stone pilings. She flung one leg and then the other out the window. There was nothing to do but jump and hope she could land on the jagged pile of rocks at the base of the piling. If they could both land without breaking a bone and without tumbling into the ocean below it would be a miracle. She aimed for the flattest rock she could see in the darkness. Then she took one last look at Helen and jumped.

A second later, Adair felt herself sliding along a rock surface that was both slippery and sharp. She clawed at the slime, her hands tangling in kelp. Above her, Helen stood silhouetted in the light of the window. "Jump!" Adair screamed over the sound of the surf, salt water filling her mouth. Dark strands of kelp washed over her hands, like fingers pulling her toward the ocean. "Jump!"

For a second, she thought it would be the last word on her lips and it felt like "love." *I love you, Helen.* A wave hit the piling below her and the icy water crashed over her back. Then her foot caught on a jutting rock. She grabbed a handful of barnacles, as sharp as glass, then clambered to a kneeling position as best she could on the rough rocks. "Now!"

The window behind Helen was very bright. The ocean water was black. Helen wasn't even wearing shoes. Adair raised one hand from the rock, beckoning. "I'll catch you."

When she landed, Helen nearly knocked Adair over, sending them both into the ocean, but Adair held fast to the rock with one hand and caught Helen in her outstretched arm. With strength she'd long forgotten, she pulled Helen to her. For a moment, Helen clung to her, once again pressing her face into Adair's neck. She whispered something that Adair could not hear. Adair had the sense that it was important, and she wanted to know. But there was no time.

Men had appeared in the window above. Someone was yelling. Adair saw the point of a red laser skittering along the rocks beside them. She pulled Helen around the back of the piling, away from the men above. To her relief, the pilings were not entirely water-locked. There was a narrow space between the floor of the hotel and the rocky cliff. It was incredibly dark, but at least the rocks were dry, and they were out of sight.

Together they felt their way along until they emerged from beneath the hotel. They climbed down another promontory, finally reaching a narrow strip of sand between the rocks and the crashing waves. A spotlight crisscrossed the water beyond the hotel, and a sudden profusion of small boats, each heralded by a tiny light at bow and stern, had suddenly appeared on the water.

A moment later, they rounded a promontory and saw the rocks give way to a sandy inlet surrounded by trees. Adair reached for Helen's hand. In the forest, they would be hidden. The highway was only a mile away, maybe less. If they could get to the road, flag down a passing car…

Adair had just formed the thought when she felt a hand clamp over her mouth. An arm circled her waist. She heard Helen scream behind her.

Then a gruff woman's voice said, "It's okay, Hon."

Closer to her own ear, a man said, "You're as good as dead, John."

Chapter Thirty-six

A heavy arm held Helen around the shoulder. "Don't worry," someone whispered to her. "He'll make it quick. You can close your eyes."

The person who held her was also holding a flashlight, training the beam on Adair who was pinned against a tree. A man in a camouflage jacket pressed a rifle to her sternum. "The Lord shall rain down a thousand tongues of fire on the wanton and the lecher." The man spoke so quickly it sounded as though he were reading Miranda rights. "No man shall be saved from the fires of hell but he who renounces sin and accepts Jesus Christ as his personal savior. Do you?"

"Don't hurt her," Helen cried.

The woman at her side—at least she thought the raspy voice belonged to a woman—whispered, "It will all be over soon."

Adair looked like Joan of Arc caught in the crosshairs, her hair shorn, her face childlike in its confusion.

"Do you accept Jesus Christ as your personal savior? You lecher, you defiler of women, you who have wasted your seed in carnal abandon!" The man steadied the rifle on his shoulder. "Do you?"

"Jesus Christ?" Adair blinked in the bright light. "I don't know."

The man adjusted the rifle against his shoulder.

"No!" Helen cried again. "Don't hurt her."

    Karelia Stetz-Waters

The man glanced at her and then back at Adair.

"He's sinned against you," he said.

The woman's grip on Helen's shoulder shifted from that of an assailant to something slightly gentler. A warden. An angry mother. "Look away, child. What he's done to you ain't your fault."

"He…?" Realization sparked in Helen's mind. "No. No. No. She's a woman. Please, listen to me. Don't shoot." The words tumbled from her uncontrolled. She pulled away from the woman and threw herself between Adair and the rifle. "She's a woman." She could feel Adair breathing heavily behind her.

"What are you saying?" the man asked.

Helen pushed the rifle away and frantically lifted Adair's sweatshirt, baring Adair's bound chest. "See?"

The flashlight traveled down the length of Adair's body. The man drew closer to Adair, peering at her. He grabbed one of her hands and held it up to the light. "It's a girl," he said gruffly.

The woman whisked the flashlight beam off Adair's body and into Helen's eyes. Helen was blinded by the bright flash, the imprint of the bulb eating away at the center of her vision. "Please don't shoot us," Helen begged.

"What is this?" the woman demanded. "Are you both running away or did she come here to exercise unnatural passions?"

"We're running away," Helen said. "Please help us."

The flashlight cut off and they stood in the dark. In the distance, Helen could hear the siren calling from the hotel. She thought she heard voices in the woods.

"Do you accept Jesus Christ as your personal

savior?" the man asked. "Do you agree to be guided by his words and to dedicate your life to his works and to make yourself clean in his sight?"

Helen thought of Eliza, praying desperately to Jesus, slowly lowering a pin through the center of her hand because the angels told her to do it. How many times had Helen prayed and raged at the answering silence? "Yes. I always have. Always. And her too," Helen said.

The voices were drawing closer.

"Let's go, Curtis," the woman at her side said. "Let's get these girls into the fold." The woman grabbed Helen's elbow. In front of her, the man muscled Adair along in a similar fashion.

In the distance, Helen saw lights sweeping the bluff. Without the flashlight in her face, she could make out the small cove, a creek spreading out over white sand, and, behind that, a dense pine forest. The coastal highway could not be more than a mile away, but it looked like undiscovered America.

A few minutes later, they entered the forest and the light became even dimmer. Helen could barely see the ground in front of her. Only the sky above distinguished her surroundings from a cave. She was surprised when they stopped, because nothing differentiated this spot from the step before. But their captors—or saviors—seemed to know the woods with a sixth sense.

A second later, the woman turned the flashlight on again, shielding its beam with her hand. In front of her, Helen saw a trailer, so mossy she mistook it for a giant rock. The woman marched Helen up three rickety steps. Inside, it was darker than the night. Helen put her hands in front of her to feel her way.

Her body tensed, waiting for a blow or a plummet downward, but nothing touched her and beneath her feet she felt carpet.

The woman lit a tiny lamp on the far wall and the room was bathed in a night-light glow.

They stood in a small room that clearly served as dining room and living area. Adjacent to the living room, was a miniature kitchen, complete with sink, stove, and a fridge as narrow as a suitcase. Beyond that, an equally narrow hallway led to what Helen guessed must be sleeping quarters.

But what startled Helen was not the size; it was the decoration. Above the dining room table, hung a contorted Jesus, blood drops pooling at his feet, his mouth open in a scream. Plaques depicting Jesus in various settings covered every vertical surface. On the counter rested dozens of sculptures of Jesus in every pose from ominous to maudlin. Like an Indian God with a thousand heads, he looked at them from every angle.

Adair looked pale. Her clothes were drenched, and her face was streaked with mud. She was shivering violently. Helen longed to touch her.

"I am Sister Pammy-Lynne and this is Brother Curtis," the woman said.

They looked about sixty. Both wore work boots, loose fitting jeans, and heavy camouflage jackets. The man's hair was short and uneven as though it had been sheared with kitchen scissors. The woman wore a stocking cap.

Pammy-Lynne said, "Sit down."

The man crossed to the window and put his eye to a crack in the venetian blinds. The woman motioned for Helen and Adair to take a seat in one of the chairs by the kitchen table.

"So what are you doing?" she asked Adair. "You dressed like a boy? You understand, if we find out you're a John, or if you're interfering with this girl in an ungodly way, we have to send you Home."

Helen had a sickening sense that "home" was not an earthly home.

"We're trying to find someone," Adair said. Her eyes were wide.

"At the Pines?" Curtis asked without turning from the window.

Pammy-Lynne got two glasses and filled them with cloudy water from the tap and put them in front of Helen and Adair. The water smelled of soap.

"We were looking for two girls," Helen added. "We thought they might be here."

Pammy Lynne nodded and closed her eyes for a second. "So many lambs," she whispered.

"We think they were abducted. In Massachusetts. We think someone brought them here, and we went in to find them," Helen said.

"What are their names?" Pammy-Lynne asked.

"Charity and Prudence," Helen said, glancing at Adair. Adair was looking around the room with a vacant stare. Helen wondered if she was going into shock.

Pammy-Lynne shook her head.

"We need to call the police," Helen said.

"No use," Pammy-Lynne said.

Helen lowered her voice. "We need to get my friend to a hospital. She's not well."

"We can't alert them," Pammy-Lynne said.

"I don't understand." Helen wrapped her arms around herself because she could not wrap them around Adair. She was shivering too, but somehow it was the tremors in Adair's body that hurt her. *She's so sick!*

"We're crusaders," Pammy-Lynne said. "There's a whole network of us across the country, living by brothels and strip clubs and ports. When a girl runs, we're here to make sure she runs to the right place."

There was one Jesus, among the multitude, who looked compassionate. Helen focused on his face and said a silent prayer.

"On the other side of the cove," Pammy-Lynne continued, "there's Brother Joe and Brother Raymond. If you'd run across the street into the woods, you'd have met Reverend Gunther and Sister Becky. We'll be waiting. We are always waiting in the forest. When we hear the siren, we hear our calling. We've saved twenty-two girls from that place, but we can't have the police coming in here and questioning our ways."

"We don't own this land," Curtis added. "We're not supposed to be here."

"We got ways of disappearing too," Pammy-Lynne added.

Helen tried to catch Adair's eye. "What happens to the girls you rescue?" Helen asked, aware that she was asking what would happen to them.

"We wait until the evacuation," Pammy-Lynne said. "Once the hotel is empty, we take them back to Reverend Mike at the home church, and he cares for them until they relinquish the devil."

"What do you mean empty?" Helen asked.

"You saw those boats," Curtis said, still peering out the window. "Every one of those girls is headed to a different port right now, and their Johns are on a yacht somewhere. The whole brothel is gone. Every single girl in that place, every John, and the sheets they desecrated—all gone.

"The devil makes them clever. Soon as that alarm sounds, the whole place disappears. We've seen it a dozen times. Tomorrow, there won't be one trace of what goes on there. And they're quick as the devil too. Twenty minutes, maybe fifteen, to get everyone out. They like to move the girls around anyways. Keeps them from running. We hardly ever get runaways that haven't been to the Pines at least twice. They don't run their first time, but sometimes, they come back enough times, they see a way out. Then we're waiting for them, here, in the fold."

Helen thought quickly. They had no time to meet Reverend Mike and relinquish the devil. "Can you help us get back to Portland so we can keep looking for our friends?"

"Wait." Adair's voice sounded flat. They all looked at her. "What do you know about 'Ashfelt'?"

Curtis turned from the window. Pammy-Lynne stiffened.

At the table, Helen watched them.

For a moment, they were all silent, then Curtis said, "We knew a girl once, said she was an Ashfelt girl."

Curtis and Pammy-Lynne looked at each other as if passing a secret code.

"Is there anything special about these girls you're looking for?" Pammy-Lynne asked.

Helen nodded infinitesimally.

Curtis took a seat at the table.

"There are sins that go beyond the flesh." His hands balled into fists. "There are sins that are bigger than a man's lust. Most of the men who go to the Pines are fornicators. But there are weak men, and then there are men who have the devil in them. They go to the Pines, and if they have the money, they ask for an Ashfelt girl."

"God rest her soul. They did terrible things to her," Pammy-Lynne said.

"Ungodly things," Curtis said.

Helen felt fear grip her. Adair was shaking. The forest spiked with voices. The search was drawing nearer. Pammy-Lynne and Curtis might yet kill them.

"She fought them off," Curtis said.

"We found her on the beach." Pammy-Lynne continued the story. "But they had already cut her."

"She died that night and we burned her body at sea. We couldn't take her to a hospital. We couldn't risk it. The doctors would ask questions. They would want to know how we found her, and she was already dying," Curtis added. "They'd clear us out if they knew what we were doing, even if it's the Lord's work, even if they say they want the same thing. Like I said, this ain't our land."

Helen tried to keep her face neutral as her mind reeled.

"Do you think they've killed Prudence and Charity?" Adair asked, her voice still flat, her eyes looking everywhere but at Helen.

"They don't always kill them," Curtis said. "More often, they send the Ashfelt girls to Nevada. They have legal brothels there. They keep them there for however long they need to, move them around, put them in the life, then ship them out again. The girls usually have a little fight in them, so they take them to a ranch in Las Vegas and break them."

Curtis looked out the window again. "They're coming."

Chapter Thirty-seven

Adair did not have to ask who.

"This way," the woman named Pammy-Lynne beckoned to Adair and Helen. She led them down the corridor. It was so narrow Adair had to turn sideways. Pammy-Lynne pushed open the door to a small bedroom. An exposed bulb lit the room. Here the depictions of Jesus were interspersed with the Virgin Mary. There was also a faded poster of a kitten dangling from a tree branch. *Hang in there,* the caption read beneath the picture, and Adair cringed. *We burned her body at sea.*

"Get in the closet." Pammy-Lynne opened the door to a closet no deeper than a shoe-box. Shelves were set at regular intervals from floor to low ceiling.

At her side, Helen whispered, "There's no room."

Pammy-Lynne reached inside the closet and fumbled with something on the top shelf. The closet wall swung outward revealing a small chamber, no larger than a bathtub, the floor covered in dirty gray blankets. That was why the hall was so narrow, Adair realized. A false wall had been installed to make this room.

"Get in."

Adair recoiled. She smelled nervous sweat and stale air emanating from the opening. It was as foul as the room on the bottom level of the brothel, sick with the smell of human stench.

"Go!" Pammy-Lynne commanded.

Adair glanced at Helen. Helen's eyes were hollow with fear. Pammy Lynne pushed the palm of her hand into Helen's back, and Helen stumbled in.

"When they come, don't make a sound. Don't move. Don't breathe," Pammy Lynne said.

Adair felt the same firm hand on her back, and then she was inside. The secret panel closed behind them, and the space went black. A second later, she felt Helen's arms around her. She could tell that Helen was crying although she made no sound. Tentatively, she wrapped her arms around her. She wanted to cling to her, to put her body between Helen and any harm that might come, to kiss her once more. But she held her lightly, remembering the spark that had lit her body as she pressed against Helen. She felt it even now, in the dark, in the vibration of Helen's tears. For the first time since she fell ill, she felt desire. Life coursed through her blood. *We're the same, Merrill.*

Helen's silent sobs reverberated in her bones.

"I'm sorry," Adair whispered, "for what I did in the brothel…what I did to you. It was the only way. I couldn't think of anything else."

A tiny bit of light came in through a crack between the fake wall and the ceiling. Adair's eyes adjusted slowly. She could see the tiny cell, the matted blankets. She pulled away from Helen. "Whatever happens…" She lifted Helen's chin with the tips of her finger. "I want you to know, I would not have done that to you if I could have thought of another way." Was it true? Adair's mind had thought of survival, a ruse, a play act, but her animal body had wanted Helen in those last desperate seconds. That was why she was ashamed.

"You thought it was the only way to save us." Helen spoke as though each word hurt her.

"Yes."

"I thought we were going to die," Helen said. "I thought you wanted to fuck me." The word sounded strange on Helen's delicate lips.

"I wouldn't do that to you."

Helen gazed at her, squinting slightly, as if reading a map hung on a distant wall.

It felt to Adair as though she had loved Helen her whole life. She had not *fallen* in love. She had simply recognized Helen as Helen stood on the edge of Carrie Brown's crime scene, haunted and resolute.

"I didn't know what you were thinking," Helen said, "I didn't realize you had a plan. At the very end… of everything, I thought you wanted me."

Adair opened her mouth to speak, then stopped.

"I wanted *you*, Adair," Helen whispered.

This time there was nothing flat or hard in her kiss. She pressed her lips to Adair's, and Adair felt her lips melt into Helen's. Her tongue became Helen's flesh. Her breath became Helen's breath. The cold that had wracked her body warmed like springtime melting the snow on Wyatt's Bluff, sprinkling the rocks with wildflowers. For a moment, Adair felt as though she had taken that final plunge. This was her welcome. This was heaven.

Then the trailer rocked with the sound of pounding.

"Open up!" a man yelled, his voice barely muffled by the thin walls.

Other voices joined the first, all yelling.

"Where are they?"

"We know they're here!"

A door crashed open.

"We'll fucking kill you!"

"I don't know who you're talking about." Pammy-Lynne's voice trembled in response.

"We know you fucking Jesus freaks."

The walls vibrated with the force of their voices. Something crashed to the floor.

"You have three seconds to tell me, and then we're tearing this place apart."

"That's no way to speak to my wife. You need to leave." Curtis's voice sounded old and rusty compared to the men who were screaming at him.

"You're gonna fucking die old man."

"This is the last time."

Then Pammy-Lynne's tearful voice. "They're not here. I swear. We're not like the others. We don't mess with your girls."

Adair heard a shot gun lock. It occurred to her that any bullet fired in the trailer would cut through the fake wall like a paper scrim. There was another crash. Helen flinched.

"There is no one here." It was Curtis.

"If you're lying, I will kill her."

"There's no one here," Pammy Lynne sobbed. "Why won't you leave us alone?"

Adair heard a cacophony of tables crashing and ceramic shattering. A moment later, she heard the bedroom door open. Pammy-Lynne was screaming. Two male voices grunted and swore in between crashes. She heard the closet door open. "Anything in there?" someone yelled.

They were so close, Adair could hear them breathing. Fingernails scraped the fake back of the closet, inches from her head. In the light from the crack in the wall, she saw Helen's face transfixed in terror. Then the man on the other side hit the wall with something hard, the butt of a rifle or a bat.

Adair saw Helen's expression slowly move away from terror. They could have been looking at each other across a conference table. She looked sad but perfectly calm. It was the same expression she wore at Carrie Brown's crime scene. *It has come to this,* she seemed to say. *It always comes to this.* Then Helen closed her eyes as if in prayer.

I love you! Adair mouthed to Helen's closed face.

The wall cracked behind her.

"It's hollow," the voice on the other side yelled.

Adair leapt toward the wall. She pressed her back against the wall where the man had struck it first. Her heart was pounding so hard, she was certain the man on the other side would hear it. She braced herself for the next blow, waiting for the butt of a rifle to splinter the particle board and slam into the small of her back.

The blow came. A swift, hard punch to the wall. It reverberated through her body like a shock wave. She bit her lip to keep from crying. But the particle board held. The blow connected with a dull thud. She had braced the wall.

The man continued down the hall. She heard plasterboard crack in another room. Someone upended a table. A window shattered. Then the sounds died down.

Someone yelled, "Never mind. It's empty."

There was a tromp of feet. Adair heard one more crash, as though someone shattered a lamp just for spite. Then the screen door on the trailer swung shut. And everything was silent. Adair slowly released her breath. In the dim light she saw Helen watching her.

Together they sank to the floor. Helen leaned against Adair and pressed her face against Adair's shoulder.

Adair circled an arm around Helen and rested her cheek against the top of her head, breathing in the smell of her hair and the goodness of her life. "I should never have brought you," Adair whispered.

Helen wrapped her other arm around Adair's waist and pulled her closer. "It's too late."

Then they listened to the rain on the trailer roof, wondering if the man and woman beyond the thin plywood wall were dead.

❧❧❧❧

Sometime in the early morning hours, Adair woke from a shallow sleep. She jerked her head up. Helen lifted her face from Adair's shoulder and glanced around also.

Someone was moving around the trailer.

Adair held her breath. She heard a whisper, then it turned into a prayer. Two voices, and then four, and then a quiet murmur, like a congregation reciting an incantation. A few minutes later, the voices fell silent. Adair heard footsteps in the bedroom beyond, then the sound of a latch releasing. She covered her eyes as light poured into the hidden closet.

Pammy-Lynne was standing in the doorway, her head wrapped in a blood soaked bandage. Behind her stood Curtis and several other men and women. Two of the men held shotguns. One woman held a broom. For a moment, Adair thought they had come for revenge, but a moment later, Pammy-Lynne was putting a hand under her elbow. Another woman took Helen's hand. Someone offered her a glass of water.

As they emerged from the bedroom, Adair could see that the trailer had been wrecked. The table was turned over, the window shattered. Most of the Jesus sculptures had been hurled to the ground. Now they lay in shards staring up at her with half-faces. "I'm sorry," she said.

It looked as though the trailer and all its contents had been churned in the ocean waves.

"You're safe," Pammy-Lynne said. "And that is what God has put us on Earth to do."

A man Adair did not recognize said, "It is a good day when we can serve the Lord."

Curtis introduced the people around them.

"Our church," he said when he had run through the list of names. "They heard the sirens and came this way after the brothel's search party had left. There is some safety in numbers, but we still have to get you out of here. They'll come back when they don't find you."

A few minutes later, one of the men backed a pick-up truck up to the door of the trailer.

"We're going to cut the lights," he said. "You get down the stairs, into the bed of the truck and under the blankets. Don't move until I open the canopy and tell you to get out. The police might stop us, and it's better they don't know about you."

Adair and Helen nodded mutely. A minute later, Adair was feeling her way down the rickety steps and into the bed of the truck. She felt Curtis's rough hand hold her elbow as she climbed in. A second later she heard Helen kneel on the gate and feel her way along the floor of the pick-up bed and under the blankets. From beneath the corner of the blanket, Adair could see the light from the headlights. The engine rumbled to life. Beside her Helen lay very still, her hands tenting the blanket over her face.

When the truck stopped, they were at a gas station. Adair peered out the back to see the man talking to a gray-haired woman in a flannel shirt. Then the man opened the canopy, and instructed them to get into the woman's car as quickly as possible. When Adair tried to thank him, he just shook his head. "Move."

He exchanged a few quick words with the woman, telling her to take Adair and Helen back to Portland.

When they reached the outskirts of Portland, Adair realized the woman probably never drove in the city. She clutched the wheel of the car with white knuckles. But finally, she pulled into the underground parking garage for the Josslin Heights Hotel.

"Don't tell nobody you saw us," the woman said.

Then she was gone.

❦ ❦ ❦ ❦

It was still early in the morning. Thankfully no one was in the elevator. They rode up in silence, their clothes still damp and their faces haggard even in the warped bronze surface of the elevator door. On the top floor, Adair shook the hotel key free from beneath the insole in her shoe. Helen followed her into her suite.

Adair headed straight for the bathroom and downed four Texidol and an oxycodone. Then she dropped onto the foot of the bed. Adrenaline had given way to fatigue. She felt as though a vice gripped her ribcage. She caught her breath in a gasp.

"We should get you to a doctor." Helen looked

worried.

Adair waved her away.

"Are you sure you're all right?"

Adair tried to release the bands she had wrapped around her chest, but the tape was sticky with seawater.

"Let me," Helen said. With deft movements Helen released the end of the bandage and unwound it from her chest, her arms circling Adair as she worked. As the last strips of bandage fell from her skin, Adair doubled over, resting her head between her knees. She felt dizzy. Her vision had blurred to orange.

Slowly she became aware of Helen speaking.

"Did this happen tonight?" She was insistent. "Adair, talk to me? When did this happen?"

Adair sat up. Stars filled her peripheral vision. She blinked. In the dresser mirror she saw Helen watching her. There was a bruise on her arm from where she had fallen against the rocks beneath the Pines. There was probably a bigger bruise where she had braced the wall with her back. She touched her arm. "This?"

"No," Helen whispered. She hovered her hand over Adair's back, tracing the contour of her shoulders down to her waist. "This."

Adair looked in the mirror again. The marks from Cecelia's crop were fading, but they were still visible. She sat up and reached for her sweatshirt, suddenly startled by her own nakedness and loath to sit beneath Helen's gaze. Helen stayed her hand.

"It was consensual," Adair said.

"You let someone do this?"

"I'm sorry." Adair closed her eyes and hung her head. "I'm so sorry."

"I don't understand."

"It was Cecelia." Adair waited for the name to register.

"But she said she loves you." Confusion filled Helen's voice. "Why would she do this to you, if you were sick?"

Adair felt Helen's hand cover the deepest of the bruises. "It's because I was sick. I needed it." Through the numbness of the Texidol, she imagined she felt the warmth of Helen's hand. And Adair remembered something she had not thought of for a long time…the pleasure of being cared for when she was only a little bit sick. It had been years since she had had a lover like that. Adair closed her eyes. In the space behind her eyelids she saw Soledad walking toward her with a cup of steaming tea. It was finals. Adair had a head cold. Soledad's voice spoke to her from the distant past, the lilting Spanish accent still familiar. "You have to rest."

Adair did not know if she answered out loud or in her memory. "No one rests in my family, except my mother, and she's waiting to die."

"You're so dark. Who made you like this?" Soledad asked. Then her memory vanished like a wisp of mist scattered by a breeze.

Drug-induced sleep beckoned to Adair. "I'll never see her again. I promise. Do you know who Cecelia is?" Adair could no longer tell if her eyes were open or closed. All she could see was an orange blur, haunted around the edges by darkness. "You're so sweet, Helen. You think people are good. We can just call the police and be free. Buy a ranch home. Get a dog."

She could almost see it, a little house like Patrick's, Helen standing on the porch with a partner who was healthy. Maybe it would be a man. Someone gentle and thoughtful, maybe an older English professor or a counselor, a weekend gardener, a Sierra Club hiker. Maybe she would choose a woman. Someone whole. Someone who could chew her food without tasting blood. "You'll wear an apron with a ruffle and little roses on it. You'd look so pretty." She was vaguely aware of Helen pulling back the bedspread and guiding her into bed, stroking her hair. "You don't know who she is."

"Shh," Helen whispered.

Now sleep pulled at her, like a creature pulling her into dark water. It had hooked its claws in her chest and she was going under. Still it seemed suddenly vitally important that Helen know everything. "She's Cy's wife." She wasn't sure if she had really spoken.

She thought Helen said, "Who is, love?"

"Cecelia. She's my brother's wife. I love him, and I fucked his wife. I hate her." She heard her voice slurring. "I hate myself. I hate what I did to Cy. But I needed it that much. I needed a pain that I could understand." Adair's eyes flew open. She couldn't see. She couldn't move. In the distance she thought she heard Helen's voice, gentle and insistent.

"If that's what you needed, you could have asked me."

Then she slept.

Chapter Thirty-eight

Helen watched Adair for a long time before crossing the hall to retrieve her cigarettes and her phone. When she returned, she stood in the doorway to Adair's bedroom again, watching her sleep. She lit a cigarette, took a few drags, and tapped the ashes into a coffee cup. Through the floor-to-ceiling windows, Portland woke up like all cities, with a rattle of loading bay doors and the warning beeps of delivery trucks. Helen thought of all the hotels she had slept in. So many conferences. So many receipts. She wandered over to the mini fridge. So many tiny bottles of vodka. She downed one in a gulp, pulled out her phone, and dialed Terri's number. It was still night on the West Coast. "I need to know everything you can find out about a woman named Cecelia Beaucharnel."

"Hello? Who?" The roughness in Terri's voice told her he had been asleep, but it took him only a moment to orient himself. "Where are you, Helen?"

"Maine."

"Why?"

"It doesn't matter." She exhaled a stream of smoke.

"Helen." There was a warning in his voice.

"I went with Adair. She's sick. I need to find out about Cecelia Beaucharnel."

"Okay."

Helen began with the fire at the Grandville

Hotel. She described the trip to the Wilson estate and Cecelia's passionate plea. *Get her to stop.*

Helen went on. "Adair is obsessed with the twins. I think she blames herself for their abduction. But we can't find them, and someone blocked her phone, and I know it was Cecelia."

She could hear her story falling apart as she told it. There were so many things she could not mention. The brothel. The trailer in the woods. *We burned her body at sea.* She should have called the police! Why had she not called the police, even now?

Helen took another bottle from the mini fridge. "Cecelia is Cyrus's wife, and she beat Adair. I saw the bruises on her back, and–"

"How did you see her back?"

"She was sick. I undressed her."

"And you're in Maine? At a hotel?"

"Cecelia Beaucharnel is really Cecelia Wilson, Adair's sister-in-law. She slept with her brother's wife, but not anymore. You have to get me something on her."

Terri's silence told her she had said too much.

"Terri?" she pressed. "I know it sounds crazy."

"You said this woman was Adair's lover while she was missing?"

"Yes."

"And she beat Adair as in domestic assault or *Fifty Shades of Gray*?"

Helen tip-toed over to Adair's room and looked in. Adair slept, one arm thrown across her eyes. Helen closed the door. "She said it was consensual."

On the other end of the line, Terri exhaled a deep breath. "So Adair has a relationship with this woman?"

"I just need some information on Beaucharnel. Something about her…it's just not right."

On the other end of the line, Helen heard Terri moving around. She guessed he was starting a pot of coffee. She waited, sucking the cigarette smoke deep into her lungs where it touched a bit of the Grandville fire and burned. She coughed.

"Helen?" Terri asked, as though she might have put down the phone.

"Yes."

"The answer is no." He sounded sad. "If you're worried about her, talk to her. If she is having an affair with her brother's wife that's messed up." Terri sighed. "But that's just all-American, garden-variety bullshit. Looking up Cecelia's Beaucharnel's DUIs is not going to change that."

"What if there's more than DUIs?"

"What if there's nothing, Helen?"

Helen lit a second cigarette off the tip of her first one. "What are you saying, Terri?"

"I'm saying you're jealous. Adair disappeared without a trace, and now you find out she's been with another woman. Anyone would be jealous, and maybe you should think about whether or not this is the kind of person you want to be with. But *I'm* not going to go fishing around in this woman's personal life because you're jealous of Adair's lover."

Helen remembered the brothel, Adair's hips beating against her as though orgasm might save them from the fate that was so breathlessly close. One final triumph. One stolen joy before the end.

"Cecelia is evil," Helen said.

"You're hurt."

Helen sunk into the sofa. "I just want to know

if she has a criminal record. Has she been involved in any incidents? Is there anything in her background that I should be afraid of."

"That might be public record," Terri said. "But I'm not going to fuel this fire. Take Adair back to New Hampshire or take her back to Pittock. Let this go."

Chapter Thirty-nine

The news of Chastain's death reached Cecelia in a padded envelope with a Florida postmark and no return address. Inside was an obituary clipped from the *Boston Herald*. In excellent health, Dr. Ronald Duthy Chastain had recently run a half marathon. Later that night, he was sitting down to dinner with colleagues from his practice. Chastain had raised a toast to the prosperous future, then died of an aneurism so sudden it had seemed to a friend at the table as though "he simply vanished, like a light switch had been flipped." Another friend added, "A great light has indeed left this world." Included in the padded envelope was a single, white seashell.

Cecelia touched her nose. A smear of red appeared on her finger, and she wiped it on the desk blotter. The cocaine had done nothing to elevate her mood. If anything it touched the panic roiling in her stomach and moved it up into her heart. She paced the length of the hidden office for the hundredth time.

Bolo had the twins. The words kept revolving in her mind, but she couldn't accept them. She did not understand the mechanism by which Chastain had dropped dead of an aneurism, but it was Galloway's work. Whatever secret bullet Galloway's men had trained on Chastain, it was trained on her now. Or it would be in one week when he realized that she had not only lost his prize but had lost them to a man who would almost surely brutalize them. They would be pliable captives, but Bolo did not speak any other language.

She looked at the lines of cocaine on the mirror. It would be so easy. A bad batch cut with too much levamisole. Nothing to trace it back to the reclusive billionaire in the Caribbean. She clenched and unclenched her fists and took another tour around the windowless room.

There had to be a way. Bolo was a fool. She had a week before Galloway returned. She jumped when her phone rang on the encrypted line. "What?" she barked.

"It's Angel." The woman pronounced it with a faint Spanish accent.

It took Cecelia a moment to reorient. Angel and her husband Mikhail ran the Pines from a sumptuous houseboat anchored near Boothbay.

"What do you want?" Cecelia didn't even care if Angel heard the fear in her voice. Let it be a warning to her. They were in danger. The water was cresting the deck. The living were scavenging the teeth of the dead. "Have you found them?"

"No, but there is something I think you should know about the night we shipped out," Angel said.

"If you haven't found them, we don't have anything to talk about. I told Mikhail." Somewhere between the house in Jamaica Plain and the Pines, Bolo had stolen the twins. Nothing else mattered.

"I think we do." Angel had never been one to be bullied. She was one of the few who had made the industry work for her. Sold by impoverished parents in Mexico City, she had been working in a brothel for years before most girls got their period, but she survived. She kept her looks and kept her fight, and somehow got traded up until she reached America and met Mikhail. It wasn't *Pretty Woman*, but she had risen, perhaps because she had already been so low. "The buyer who came that night," Angel went on. "We thought he was a Fed. That's why we cleared out."

"Mikhail said the guy didn't seem right," Cecelia said, tracing a line across the cocaine mirror.

"Mikhail is a fucking pussy. He's afraid to tell you."

"What?" Cecelia licked her finger, savoring the bitterness, the slight numbness, and something else…a plastic taste, the taste of kerosene. *One bad batch.*

"I told him to tell you," Angel continued, her accent growing thicker. "But he says, 'no, it is none of our business. We see the Feds, we ship out. That's all we do.'"

"Get to the point."

"The buyer, he gave two names. I said, 'I do not believe your name. You lie.' He said, 'Okay, I tell you my real name.' The second name he gave was…" Angel pronounced it "Add-hair."

Cecelia froze. "Adair?"

"Yes. Adair. This buyer must have known about the business. He must have known your family owned the Pines. He must have thought he could drop a family name to get in. He must have thought Mikhail and I were just some dumb-shit bouncers." Angel snorted. "Probably thought we still did business in a fucking phone booth. But he didn't know shit. He tried to use Adair's name. Didn't know she was a woman. Thought they were all brothers probably. Montague. Cyrus. Adair. He was going to use one of those names. He did not know…"

"No. She knows." Cecelia set the phone down. "Merrill was at the Pines."

She hung up on Angel and called Marta in Jamaica Plain. "I want all the security camera feeds for the last two weeks. Flag any new clients, any unusual requests. I want everything."

❦ ❦ ❦ ❦

It took three hours for Cecelia to find the footage she was looking for. Merrill sat in the parlor, bantering with Marta. Despite her fear and fatigue, Cecelia felt her body stir as Merrill told Marta she was a collector. "A virgin nun in Guatemala. A vet, just back from Iraq, in a coma. My husband said you would be able to help me find something." In the grainy footage, Merrill leaned back on the sofa, touching her inner thigh, drawing her words out, arguing and seducing at the same time. Twice she looked directly at the camera, and Cecelia was certain Merrill looked at her.

"You know." Cecelia stared at the screen. "You're onto them." She dialed Merrill's number again, but the phone went to voicemail. She hung up. "I need you, Merrill," she said to the dead air. "More now than ever."

Chapter Forty

Adair waited until almost eight in the evening before she ventured out of her suite and knocked on Helen's door. Helen was dressed and coiffed as though she had just come from a business meeting, but somehow Adair had the impression that she, too, had spent the day pacing. "I, um…" The thoughts Adair wanted to speak pushed away any words she could actually imagine uttering.

"Yes," Helen said. Then, seeming to realize that Adair had said nothing to which "yes" was the answer, she added, "I called the police."

"What did they say?"

"They checked out the Pines. They didn't find anything." As if suddenly realizing she was blocking Adair's entrance, Helen stepped quickly away from the door. "They said there was no sign of habitation, not even the homeless. They found your car. No one had touched it. I had it towed back to the hotel. Do you still have the key?"

It took Adair a moment to remember if she had the key or not, to remember that things like that mattered. "I do."

"I told the tow company it was a medical emergency, and you couldn't drive it. They charged a mint, and I had to get the police's permission to have it towed without you present. The concierge at the front desk helped."

"I can pay you back," Adair said.

Helen shook her head. "It doesn't matter."

For a moment they stared at each other. The conversation felt definitely over. There was nothing else to say or do, and yet Adair could not bear to return to her solitary suite. "Would you like to go out to dinner," she blurted. She was not the least bit hungry herself.

"Of course. I'm starving." Helen picked up her purse and her coat, quickly, as though Adair had just told her they were late. "Let's go."

However, on the street, they deliberated over the restaurants like teenagers on a first date, with awkward, over-done tact, each deferring to the other until Helen laughed nervously and said, "We should probably just stop here." She gestured to a dimly lit window and a sandwich-board sign reading "Ray's Best Seafood."

A waiter in a dirty apron led them to a booth by the window and lit a small, oil-burning candle on their table. Helen ordered a glass of wine and drank half of it in one draught.

"How are you feeling?" Helen touched her napkin to her lips. "I mean are you okay…after everything?"

"Yes," Adair said, although when she had woken that evening, she had had the fleeting thought that perhaps, somehow, miraculously, she would wake fully and be cured, as though Helen's touch from the night before might heal her. The disappointment she had felt as she returned to her pain and the metallic taste of Texidol in her mouth had been palpable. "What about you?" She searched Helen's face.

"Shaken up." Helen stared down at the empty plate before her.

"What is it?" Adair asked.

Helen waved vaguely over the table. "I don't know what to do with this."

"I know." She herself had stood in the shower for minutes staring at the tiny shampoo bottles, trying to understand a world that contained the Josslin Heights Hotel and the Pines. *We burned her body at sea.*

Helen must have been thinking the same thing, because she said, "Do you think that woman would have died if they had gotten her to a hospital?"

"I don't know." Adair leaned back in her chair. "What did I say last night?"

"You told me about Cecelia."

Adair sighed. "I'm sorry, Helen. I'm sorry I dragged you into all this. I'm sorry I didn't find you. I'm sorry I let Cecelia…"

"You were sick."

"I've made so many mistakes." Adair looked out the window so she would not have to meet Helen's eyes.

Neither of them spoke, then they both spoke at once.

"You first," Adair said, not even sure what she had been starting to say.

"What was it like growing up in that house with your brothers?"

It was not the question Adair expected, but she thought about it for a moment. "My brothers have always been good to me."

"Really?" Helen looked skeptical.

"Bolo and I used to play together a little bit. His name is Blaine, but everyone calls him Bolo. He's only three years older than me. And Cyrus was a good brother…in a way." The thought pained her. "He taught me how to shoot, and ride a horse, and drive."

"Did he teach you how to drive…like you drive?"

"Of course. I learned how to *drive* at boarding school, but Cyrus taught me how to race."

Helen shook her head.

"That's just Cyrus for you," Adair added. "I don't think he knew what to do with a kid sister. Then there's Monty. Montague junior. He's almost twenty years older than me, and by the time I was old enough to understand the family business, he was already running it with my father."

"What is the family business?"

Adair's water had left a ring on the glass table-top and she spread the water out with the tip of her finger. "Mergers. Commercial real estate. They don't *do* anything. They own things, and that makes money. Although it all seems to take a lot of work."

"Was your mother part of the business?"

"She died when I was twenty, and, no, women like my mother don't work."

"I'm sorry," Helen said. "Twenty. That must have been hard."

Adair shrugged, although the thought of her mother sitting alone by the window in the Grand Hall still sent a pang through her chest. "She was depressed."

The waiter arrived with their meals. Adair stared down at her halibut, knowing it would taste of Texidol. Helen also looked at her plate without picking up her fork.

"Nobody in the family says it was a suicide," Adair said after the waiter left.

Helen reached over and touched Adair's hand. "Was it?"

"It was pills and alcohol. There were so many bottles. Maybe there was something else. Maybe she was sick in a way the doctors didn't know about. Monty found her in her chair by the window. She was always sitting there watching the garden. And then one day she was dead."

Helen kept her hand over Adair's.

"I was home from college," Adair went on. "My…I had fallen in love with a girl. Soledad. We had moved to San Francisco together to work at a women's shelter. Then one day she turned me out. I came back, and she had locked the door, and she was crying, and she said I could never come in again. I had to leave. I called Cyrus for advice." Adair laughed. "I was twenty. I thought he might give me some brotherly pep talk. He said he had chartered a flight, and the driver was around the corner.

"I got home and I stayed in bed for a week. When I got up it was around Easter. Monty and Father were throwing a big party for all the business partners. The house looked gorgeous." Adair did not realize how close she was to tears until her voice cracked. She pulled her hand away from Helen's and wiped her eyes. "I'm sorry. It's the PCPS, the pain. That was years ago." She pressed the heels of her hands into her eyes. "I don't know why…"

"She was your mother," Helen said gently.

Adair held her breath until the reflex to cry had subsided. "On the night of the party, Monty found our mother. He locked the room from the outside, and told the guests she had a migraine. Then he told all of us. He said, 'Don't worry. I've locked the door and none of the servants have the key.' Blaine started to yell at him and cry. Monty just told us it didn't make a difference. She would still be dead in six hours, and there was a client he needed to talk to. I didn't eat for three weeks afterward. I collapsed at college, and Cecelia drove me home. By the time I recovered, Blaine had left for South America. I think he's still there, living in some sort of commune, but we don't know." She let out a bitter laugh. "Maybe I should have followed him. That's even worse than being a lesbian theater professor."

"I thought you said that your brothers supported you."

"Cyrus has been trying to get me to move to Paris for years. He thinks it's where lesbians go. Maybe I should have."

"Because of Cecelia?"

"Because of everything."

The sadness in Helen's eyes made Adair's throat constrict again. "I could never be a kept woman in Paris. My French is awful." She tried to smile. "That's enough about my sordid family." She picked up a slice of lemon and tasted it tentatively. "How's Pittock?"

"Pittock? It's fine. I guess." Helen paused. "No. It's bad. Drummond did a lot of damage to the school's image and people's sense of safety, but he ruined the budget too. He'd been embezzling for years. I thought the school was bad off financially, but I had no idea."

"You've managed to turn it around, though."

"I don't know."

"US News and World Report rated it the seventeenth best private liberal arts college." Adair felt a glow of pride.

"You've been following us," Helen said.

"Of course."

Helen smiled. "Patrick misses you."

"I know." Adair poked her food. "I didn't want him to see me like this."

"Sick?"

"Yes."

"Has it ever occurred to you that that's when your friends want to see you, when you need them?"

A gaggle of young men wearing Bowdoin College sweatshirts strolled past the window and paused to read the menu on the door.

"That's not how my family works," Adair said.

Helen took Adair's hand again. This time she held it tightly. "Your brother left your dead mother in the parlor so he could throw a dinner party. Do you really think that's a good role model?"

Adair was about to explain how in Montague's world, in Cyrus' world, in the world their father built for them, it really wasn't so odd, that it was practicality, not indifference, that their grief had been as tangible at that dinner party as if it had walked, personified, through the hall dragging its chains.

Instead she saw the glint of humor in Helen's eyes and found herself laughing the first real laugh she could remember in months. "I missed you, Helen."

From the Diary of Charity Kimball

The false friend made me swallow a handful of pills, but I know the truth. I know Prudence's illness is in me. She has always been in me. I try to stay awake, but I cannot tell the difference between darknesses. Sometimes I think I am dreaming. Sometimes I am falling into a deep well. Sometimes I open my eyes, and I see shapes dancing before me. It is the end. I do not even pray for forgiveness. Why would I put such a burden on God? Why would I make him bear this truth: that I would have left Oquat even if, like the prophets of old, I had foreseen this end? I would still have chased the sad woman down the mountains and begged her, "Take me."

Chapter Forty-one

The grounds of the Mapleton Psychiatric Hospital were as pleasant as the local country club, but inside there was no concealing the hospital's purpose. Everything was painted a bilious salmon color including the mesh cages that separated the waiting room from the receptionist's desk, and the desk from the wing.

"I'm here to see Marshal Drummond," Cecelia said.

"Name?" The receptionist was a large woman with rough, blotchy skin and hair dyed in alternating shades of burgundy and blond.

"Barbra Shoemaker." She handed the woman an ID. "I'm his niece. I mean, not by blood, but I've always thought of him as an uncle." She forced a smile. "It's so terrible what happened to that poor girl."

The woman hoisted herself out of her chair and made a copy of Cecelia's fake ID. "Visiting hours start at ten. The guard will be here to get you."

There were three other visitors, all women, in the waiting room. Each tried to strike up conversations with her and with each other, but there was nothing to say in that pink cage, and they fell silent. Cecelia stared at the oak tree beyond the barred window.

An hour and a half later, a man in a gray uniform led them down the main hall, opening and closing gates as they went. In a small examination room, they were patted down. In another room, they were each assigned a locker and combination lock for their purses. One woman was asked to remove her underwire bra.

"I'm not going to go in there without a bra," she protested.

"You received the dress code when you requested a visit. I can't allow you to proceed with a potentially dangerous undergarment." The guard's voice droned on like a recording.

Cecelia sighed. These women were going to see loved ones. It was pathetic. She shook her hair out and applied another layer of lipstick.

The guard, a middle-aged man with a crew cut that said *I wanted to be a cop but I never made it*, led them to yet another room where they each produced their ID again and the authorization forms allowing them to visit.

The guard looked at Cecelia's sheet. "Drummond," he read. "Shoemaker. Do you want to meet in the visitation room or on the grounds? Drummond has walking privileges."

Cecelia hid her pleasure. "Is that safe?" She blinked at the guard.

"We'll be nearby. Patients aren't allowed to be more than twenty-five feet from a guard at any time."

❧❧❧❧

The walking path was nothing like the rolling grounds that surrounded the facility. It was just a fenced plot in between two buildings. Men in orange scrubs with the word "patient" printed on the leg and back shuffled around a wood chip path. Several were escorted by guards. One man wore loose shackles. In the corner of the enclosure, a man tongued the wire fence and a guard coaxed him away.

Cecelia scanned the area for Drummond and found him walking alone, his gate slightly off kilter from the prosthetic leg. He too was dressed in orange, but he was still the man Cecelia remembered–Montague's friend from college, a good old boy from a time when there was no need to conceal their antics. The whores. The backdoor deals.

Drummond caught sight of her. "Cecelia!"

Cecelia said, "No, Uncle Marshal. It's me, Barbra. Little Barb. Remember?" She spoke loudly enough for the guards to hear. "You gotta remember." She met Drummond's gaze and held it. "You know me, Uncle Shell."

He nodded twice, slowly. She took his arm and began talking loudly as though he were hard of hearing. "And then you know what little Bebe said? She said, 'Mommy, when Grandpa Jo goes to heaven will the angels have a birthday party for him *every* year, forever and ever?'"

Drummond chuckled.

"Too much?" Cecelia said under her breath.

"Charming," he said, just as quietly. "What do you want?"

"To help you."

They passed a guard and Cecelia said, "I hope they're feeding you well." Then she dropped her voice again. "I've lost something very important. I need it back. You can help me."

A red light fixed on one of the buildings flashed. A prerecorded announcement in a woman's voice said, "Visitation will end in five minutes. Please move toward the exit."

Cecelia bowed her head so her hair fell between her and the guards.

"Right now, Merrill Wilson is at the Josslin Heights Hotel in Portland, Maine. She's looking for twin girls named Charity and Prudence. I need them, and I need her."

"Adair Wilson," Drummond said, his eyes darting to the fence, the guards, the flashing light.

"She's mine," Cecelia said. "But if you can track her down, her and the twins she's looking for, and bring them all to me, I'll get you out of here."

"You'd have to if I'm going to find them."

"I'll get you out, and I'll keep you out. I'll get them to declare you competent."

Their arms were still linked together. Drummond tightened his hold, pulling Cecelia toward him. "Even you know, the second I walk out of this hospital, I'll go straight to prison."

"I'll get you whatever you want," Cecelia murmured without moving her lips. "Enough money to leave the country."

"Hmm." Drummond smiled sloppily at one of the guards.

"And Marshal," Cecelia said, drawing the words out. "Merrill is with Helen Ivers. You find Merrill and you find Helen."

Drummond pulled her even closer.

One of the guards yelled, "Patient, please step away from your guest."

Drummond stepped back.

Cecelia dropped to her knee, pretending to rub at a scuff on her shoe. "And you can do whatever you want with her," she said to the ground in front of her.

"Get me the twins, get me Merrill, and I put you and Helen on a plane to Johannesburg, Bangkok, Moscow, wherever you like."

Drummond turned to her. His lip twitched. She glimpsed his teeth.

A guard stepped to her side. "Visiting time is over, Ms. Shoemaker."

Chapter Forty-two

The following morning Adair woke early, dressed, and walked down to a restaurant near the hotel. It was the kind of charming, grimy place she had once loved. For a long time, she sat staring out the window without drinking her coffee. Cecelia had called a dozen times, but Adair had deleted all the messages unheard. She could not go back to the Wilson estate, and she could not go back to Pittock. Helen cared for her. She knew that, and the thought warmed her like the sunshine slanting through the coffee shop window, but she could not ask Helen to take in an invalid. Still, the plunge from the cathedral roof had lost its siren song.

Perhaps she could rent a villa in some warm place. Perhaps Helen could visit her in the summer. Perhaps a staff of nurses could hide her illness for the week of Helen's visit. She would grow old faster than Helen. Eventually, she would come to think of Helen—ten years her senior—as a child she had loved once and lost. There would be a sweetness in that and a sadness that would cut her to the core.

She opened a browser on her phone and called up a real estate page for rentals in France. They were all beautiful, but she couldn't look. She called up another search field and typed "dicephalic parapagus." There were photographs of famous cases. One set of twins had survived into adulthood and were going to college. In another video, a tiny Chinese baby screamed from its two, perfectly-formed heads. A nurse swabbed mucous from one of its mouths. Another photograph showed an ultrasound of conjoined twins in utero, their eyes blanked out with black bars as if to protect their yet-to-be-born identity. There was nothing about Charity and Prudence.

The barista came by her table to top off her mug. "Working hard?" She shot Adair a flirtatious smile.

"I wish." Adair returned to her real estate search, looking for something that called to her—a bay window, a turquoise cove—but all the photographs looked bright and lifeless.

She flipped back to the previous search and typed "freak show, two-headed, fucked up." The internet disgorged its usual glut: pornography alongside advertisements for get rich quick schemes, weight loss programs, and degree mills. She was about to give up when she found a blog entitled "Hashish, Hookers, and Hookahs." It purported to be written by a twenty-one-year old "party rocker." Adair read,

After a ragin' nite with some sweet ass bitches, stopped for some pancakes at the Shandy Lane Diner. Don't go to that fuckin' shithole. Saw this fucked up shit. Can't see it too good here, but I ain't lying. Bitch had 2 heads. Fuckin viva las vegas.

Below was a photograph of a parking lot outside a pink building. Adair studied it. The figure in question was being ushered into a blue sedan. The whole scene was blurry and far away. A comment below the post read, "It's a pimp and his bitch getting in a car. No big shit. It's Vegas. Sober up muther fucker."

Adair checked the date. It had been posted two days earlier. She turned down the brightness on her phone so she could stare closely at the photograph. It was hard to tell if the figure had two heads, or if she was just seeing a reflection in the car window. What she could see was the distinct shape of the white bonnet covering the woman's hair, concealing her virtue, saving something for the True Reckoning.

Adair did not know what made her look up suddenly or what intuition made her scan the scene outside the window with the same attention she had focused on the phone, but she stared, a shiver of fear tickling her nerves. She felt her vision clear as though a camera lens focused. Everything was sharper. The bricks on the adjacent building. The white outline of a stop sign. The silvery window of a pharmacy. Behind the window, a man strode across the store toward the door. As she watched, the customer emerged. Tall. Upright. With close cropped hair. Gray slacks. A brown sports coat. The man paused to look up at the Josslin Heights, visible above the lower, older buildings that surrounded it.

Terror flooded Adair's body. She knew that man. She recognized his limp, the limp of a one legged man not used to navigating the city streets with his prostheses. The man who had tried to kill her. The man she had tried to kill.

Chapter Forty-three

Helen held the phone gingerly, careful not to let it touch the bathwater. She usually showered vigorously, a habit she had picked up as a young teenager when she first became aware of Eliza's stench. Eliza never bathed, and Helen made up for it by scrubbing her own skin raw. Today she had made an exception and run a gentle bath.

"The shit has hit the fan!" Patrick exclaimed on the other end of the phone. "Where are you?"

"In Maine. I'm with Adair. What is it?" Helen hovered the phone a few inches from her ear.

"It's Duffy. He's accusing you of sexual harassment. He said you seduced him. He said you bargained with sex. He said Adair broke your window with her fist, put a gun to his neck, and said if he hurt you, she'd blow his brains into his asshole."

Helen liked Patrick's voice. She liked the way his lisp got shriller as his agitation mounted. Then at some point it broke, and his real baritone boomed out. The baritone broke through now. "Helen, are you listening?"

"Yes."

"Yes? That's it?"

Her mind was still full of the Pines—*we burned her body at sea*—and of Adair's body pressed against hers, Adair's hand clasping hers across the restaurant table. The candle light. *I missed you, Helen.*

"He tried to rape me." She heard the half-truth tremble in her voice.

Patrick said, "Oh, my God, Helen, are you okay?"

"Yes."

"Are you sure?"

Helen stepped out of the tub and tried to wrap a towel around her with her free hand. "It was awful, but I fought him off, and Adair showed up..." She tried to muster the outrage Patrick expected her to feel.

"Okay," Patrick said slowly.

Helen brushed the steam off the mirror. In its surface, a woman with her face said, "Patrick, I'm coming home in a day or two. Can you just fend off the board? Tell them I've had another death in the family. Tell them I'm sick. Just give me a day or two."

"For what?"

To be with her. "Do you know a woman named Cecelia Beaucharnel?"

Helen could almost hear Patrick's thoughts taking a hard left turn.

"Cyrus Wilson's wife? What about her?"

"Do you think she's dangerous?" The mirror fogged over again.

"I think that whole family's dangerous. I think they eat people like you and me for breakfast. But you've actually got bigger problems right now."

"She's Adair's lover."

"Fuckin' A!" Patrick exclaimed.

"Do you know anything about her?"

"Like what?"

"Does she have a past?"

"Everyone has a past. What's this about?"

Terri's words came back to her. *The answer is no.* "Never mind." Helen sat on the toilet lid, the towel draped over her lap. "I'm sorry. Don't mention it to Adair."

"You're the only one she's talking to, remember?"

"I'm just jealous. It's nothing."

"Okay."

Helen knew the hedge in Patrick's voice.

"If you want conspiracy theories," he said. "Try this one. Thompson got the code off the fire alarm system at the Grandville. Someone turned the sprinklers off before they set a fire inside one of the basement walls directly beneath the only part of the basement that had a wood ceiling instead of concrete." Patrick paused, letting his words sink in. "It looked like an electrical fire because it started near one of the fuse boxes, but Thompson brought in some dog from Boston. I guess it smelled fuel."

"What does that mean?"

"It means it was arson. It means it was someone who knows the building. Thompson thinks he can get a feed off the security camera from the 7-Eleven next door. It was damaged by the smoke, but he thinks he can pull the records. He might get footage of someone entering the building."

"He doesn't think it was Adair, does he?" Helen said, wiping the steam off the mirror again.

"He doesn't want to think it. The fire started between two and three fifteen that afternoon. You were with Adair. Everyone saw her bust into that meeting, and that was at two on the dot. But it didn't help that the two of you disappeared the day after the fire. Thompson also did some research into that cult where the twins came from. Apparently when someone leaves the community without permission, they are 'unborn.' They become 'that which shall not be spoken of.' When the police first asked, the whole town denied their existence."

"Because they had been unborn?"

"Exactly. But finally one of the twins' friends confessed. She even had an old Polaroid of them. So the police are on red alert now. They are looking for them."

"Thank God."

"But Helen," Patrick paused. "You have to get back to Pittock. Thompson's going to want to look Adair in the eye pretty soon, and Duffy's getting ready for war. If he raped you and Adair protected you, you've got to tell someone. Otherwise, it's not going to look good. People are already saying that you may be unfit to be college president."

College president. Helen thought of Adair's back marked by long, red welts. *You could have asked me anything.*

Chapter Forty-four

Adair ran from the coffee shop. If she estimated Drummond's trajectory correctly, he was heading down Market Street to the intersection of Ocean and 8th and toward the Josslin Heights. She paused for only a second, remembering the back entrance to the parking garage. It was farther than the front door, but Drummond would not see her on the parallel street. She could make it. She hoped.

She barely saw the pedestrians blocking her way and then stumbling out of her path as she careened down 11th Street. She dodged a sidewalk cart, breaking through the line of customers waiting for hotdogs. She could see mouths moving in protest, but she could only hear the blood pounding in her ears. She had to get back to the hotel. To Helen.

She was panting in great airless gasps when she finally reached the garage. She ran down the entry lane, ignoring the "No Pedestrians" sign. She was moving so fast, she almost hit the elevator door when she arrived. Doubling over for a second, she was aware of the stitch in her side, but adrenaline kept most of the pain at bay.

She was just about to hit the call button on the elevator when it occurred to her that Drummond would be doing the same thing. He was probably waiting at the bronze doors in the main lobby. There would be no escape if the elevator doors opened on

Drummond. She looked around. There was a service elevator, but it was key operated. Frantic, she grabbed her phone and called Helen, but it went straight to voicemail as always. Adair gasped a warning and then hung up.

She raced for the staircase, pulled open the door and paused for a second, listening. She could hear the mechanism of the elevator creaking. Nothing else. There was nothing to do but to run, praying Drummond chose the elevator, praying it was slow, praying there were guests on every floor waiting to be picked up. Her feet on the concrete stairs kept time with the blood in her ears. She tried to count floors. Two. Seven. Nine. By the time she reached ten, she was so out of breath her vision was fading. She ran on, stumbling upward, falling and hitting her shins, and rising again.

She counted fifteen floors and then abruptly came to a landing, a door, and nothing else. "Fuck!" she swore. There was no staircase to the penthouse. She threw open the door.

It took a moment for her vision to clear. She recognized the hallway with windows on either end and two doors. Of course. There was no 13th floor. This *was* the penthouse. She fell against Helen's door, pounding with her fist.

"What is it?" Helen's hair was wet, her feet bare. She looked stricken.

"Lock the door," Adair gasped. "Your purse. Keys. We have to go."

"Slow down. What's happened?"

Adair clutched her side. Helen put an arm around her shoulders. "Sit down."

Adair shook her head. Behind the sound of her

own heartbeat, she heard the chime of the elevator. She pressed her eye to the spy hole. The elevator doors opened. She almost screamed when she saw Drummond step from the elevator, his face set in a look of determination. "Drummond," she whispered.

Helen's face lost all color. Even her lips seemed translucent as she mouthed, "How?"

Adair put her eye back to the door. Drummond was coming closer, holding two key cards, glancing back and forth between the doors.

Adair froze, keeping her eye to the spy hole. In the hall outside, Drummond glanced back and forth between the doors, then turned to Adair's suite and slid his key card into the lock. Adair waited until the door had closed behind him, then she grabbed Helen's arm.

"Now!" she whispered. "Run to the elevator. Quiet."

Helen did not hesitate. Adair stayed behind just long enough to ease the door closed silently, then she sprinted for the elevator. The wait was interminable. They stood with their backs to the elevator, watching the door into which Drummond had disappeared.

Adair tried to work through a strategy. She had lost her gun at the Pines. She scanned the area around her. A trashcan. A decorative table beneath a painting of poppies. The windows at the far end of the hall… unbreakable. Drummond would probably have a gun. She could run at him swinging the trashcan. She wanted to tell Helen to flee. *When it happens, don't wait for me.* But time had changed, and she was moving in slow motion. Her words came out a senseless drawl like an old record player slowing to a halt.

Behind her the elevator bell sounded as loud as

a gong. It took hours for the doors to pry themselves apart. When they were a few inches open, Adair shoved Helen in, following after her and pounding on the "door-close" button. Farther down the hall, Adair heard a lock rattle. Drummond was coming out.

"Wilson!" his voice shot down the hall like a bullet.

Helen screamed.

Drummond ran toward them, his limp more pronounced, his gait rising and falling like a mechanical spider, a marionette with one tangled string. He reached into his jacket.

A gun.

Adair stepped in front of Helen, pushing her back. In the slow-motion time Adair inhabited, she had time to admire the silencer. She barely heard the bullet leave the chamber. Now it was moving toward her, wobbling a little in its path. Perhaps a defect in the bullet, a slight imperfection in the barrel.

She had no body armor this time. The bullet would pierce the soft flesh of her breast, crack a rib, and send the fragments of bone into her heart. Suddenly she wondered if the last months had been a dream. Perhaps Drummond had only fired one shot—this one. The beautiful week she had spent with Helen: that was the dream of the bullet speeding through air. The agony of the subsequent months was the dream of her blood spilling. There was no way the Kevlar could have held at such short distance. No wonder she could not distinguish the seasons, could not remember, had never really sought out the answers to her questions. Why had Helen left? Why didn't she call? Adair could have driven to Pittock. She could have hired a driver. She could have been there and back a dozen times.

Except that she couldn't because she had always been here. In front of Drummond. Watching this bullet.

⚜ ⚜ ⚜ ⚜

The next thing Adair knew, she was sliding down the side of the elevator wall, and Helen was on top of her, screaming. The bullet was dancing on the floor. There was a dent in the back wall of the elevator. The door was closed. Adair touched her chest. There was no blood. The elevator began to descend. Her senses cleared. Time returned to its normal speed.

Helen was clutching her, screaming, "Adair! Why didn't you move?"

"I didn't…" She touched her chest again. "Did he hit me?"

"No." Helen was sobbing. "What are you thinking?"

She felt the weight of Helen's body on hers, the almost indiscernible pain where her head had hit the back of the elevator.

"You pushed me out of the way," Adair said, the near miss dawning on her slowly.

"Why didn't you move?"

Adair wrapped her arms tightly around Helen.

"If he finds us again," she whispered, "let me take him, Helen. I'll get a gun. Next time I'll kill him."

A moment later, the elevator chimed and the doors opened on the parking garage. They ran for the BMW.

"Get in," Adair gasped, blessing the car that unlocked itself in the mere presence of the key.

"No, I'll drive," Helen said. "You're not well."

A second later, they were speeding backwards up

the in-ramp. Adair heard the sound of plastic breaking as Helen backed into the arm that guarded the ramp. A second later they were in traffic. It was midday and Portland was bustling. Every street presented a new obstacle. Double parked cars waited for a hotel valet. Children streamed out of a local school. Two bicyclists argued with the driver of a red sedan. Helen's hands were tight on the wheel. She kept checking the rearview mirror.

"What is it?" Adair asked.

"I think he's following us."

Adair turned. She recognized the conservative contours of a navy Mercedes four cars back. Helen turned a corner, ran a yellow and lost it, but at the next intersection Adair saw it a block behind them, the sun-visor obscuring the driver's face.

"Helen, I think you're right." Adair wished she had driven. The afternoons she had spent on the Monteith Speedway would serve her well. Still, her vision was fading in and out. Her heart felt like it was going to explode. "You have to lose him," she begged.

"I'm trying." Helen sped up as they approached the sign for the freeway entrance, but it was too late. The Mercedes was behind them. The driver's face was still hidden, but Adair thought she recognized the silhouette. The sports coat. So respectable. The Mercedes came closer, almost tapping the bumper. Once on the freeway, Helen pulled ahead, putting a few cars between them. For a second, the car disappeared, then it reappeared on Helen's left.

Adair could see Drummond gripping the wheel, leaning forward, his face grim and hungry.

"Don't look," Adair said. "Just drive."

Helen kept her eyes focused on the road ahead.

Drummond followed, moving in behind them, closer and closer.

"Shit! He's trying to pit the car," Adair yelled.

They had reached an open stretch of highway. The traffic thinned. Helen hit the accelerator.

"There's a cop. Helen, speed up."

"What?" Helen asked, jerking her head toward the shoulder of the road and then back.

"The police won't follow. It's too dangerous, but he might stop Drummond. Speed up. Speed up. He'll follow if you're doing less than a hundred." It was a gamble. Adair had lost sight of the blue Mercedes. If Drummond was right behind them, they were better off on the interstate putting more distance between them. If the police stopped Drummond, they were safer taking an exit, doubling back, taking a rural highway into New Hampshire. Hiding.

Helen chose speed. Adair could see her arms trembling as she tried to control the car. The highway flew past them. Adair felt sick. She knew that Helen had no idea how much precision and strength it took to drive at this speed. One inadvertent move, one split second of inattention, one car in their lane moving slowly, one mistake, and it was all over.

And Helen drove on. Flawless. Beautiful. Her face as grim as the granite mountains around them.

❧ ❧ ❧ ❧

They had traveled for an hour before Adair felt the adrenaline high wearing off. The pain in her chest reasserted itself. She reached for her bag and the bottle of Texidol. They were gone. The panic that seized her was almost as strong as the panic she had felt when she recognized Drummond in the pharmacy. She grit her teeth. It felt like an invisible hand was twisting her spine, breaking apart the vertebrae. She needed to move, to stand, to pace. The car seat was a prison.

"What is it? What's wrong?" Helen asked.

"I'm fine. Keep driving."

"No, you're not. You're shaking."

Helen slowed the car to the speed of traffic and slid in between two semi-trucks.

"Just let me think," Adair barked. But she already knew the answer. The new, full bottle of Texidol was on the dresser in her suite at the Josslin Heights. She had picked it up on her way to the coffee shop, taken a dose, and then put it back on the dresser instead of putting it in her bag. A small rebellion. She could get a cup of coffee at a diner without clutching the medication to her. She could go an hour without having it on her person. She could pretend.

It was the dinner with Helen that had made her leave it behind. The conversation had been easy, and she had been happy. That night she had pondered questions she had promised herself she would forgo. What if someone found a cure? Maybe in Europe. What if her doctor did not know everything?

Now she paid for her hope.

❧ ❧ ❧ ❧

Adair had lost track of time and distance. She was aware only of the pain. She was breathing heavily, and the iron taste in her mouth was damp. She had bitten her tongue. She faded in and out of consciousness.

When she woke the car had stopped. She was alone. Then she felt Helen's hand under her arm.

Then she was in a bed, and for a moment she thought she was back in Pittock. Then everything went black.

❧ ❧ ❧ ❧

When Adair woke she was in a tiny hotel room. An air conditioning unit rattled in the corner. A blade of light sliced between the closed curtains like a knife.

Helen was speaking to her. "What's the prescription?" she kept asking from her seat on the bed beside Adair. In her hand was a phone and something else. A card. Adair's driver's license. "Your birth date," Helen said, holding up the license. "I just need your pharmacy, the drug, and your doctor's name."

"Texidol." Adair stopped. "There's no pharmacy." She closed her eyes. "It's experimental."

"Tell me the name of your doctor. Who can I call?"

"Chastain. Ronald Chastain. He's the only one. He'll have to ship it. It's not…legal yet."

Chapter Forty-five

I'm so sorry," the receptionist at Doctor Chastain's office said. "We're all very sorry. He was an extraordinary man. Had you been seeing him long?"

Helen tried to explain the situation.

"She lost her medication. She's very sick."

The woman took Adair's full name and birthday reluctantly. "I'm not allowed to give out patient information."

"I don't need information. I just need you to refill her prescription!"

A moment later, the receptionist came back on the line. "If this is a medical emergency, you should dial 911."

"That's not acceptable. She said it's a trial medication. She said a hospital won't have it."

In the bed, Adair groaned and rolled on her back. Her half-open eyes showed only white.

"Listen!" Helen could battle with an incompetent office manager. That part, at least, she understood. "I don't care that Dr. Chastain died. And, frankly, I don't care if he was an extraordinary man. What I care about is that your office has been seeing my friend, and someone prescribed a drug she can't go off, and now you've lost her files. Taking her to the nearest hospital isn't going to help, because they don't have the drug. You're going to find those records, or you're going to transfer me to someone who can."

"One moment please," the woman said.

After a long silence, a man picked up the phone. Helen explained the situation again. The man sighed.

"Have you heard of HIPAA?"

"Of course I've heard of HIPAA."

"You understand that I'm not allowed to discuss…"

"I don't want to *discuss* anything." Helen paced the small hotel room.

"We're not allowed to divulge any patient information including information about patients we are not currently treating."

Helen sensed the man was trying to tell her something, but she could not read his voice. Every time Adair moaned, she felt her heart seize in her chest. She touched Adair's forehead. She felt terribly hot. "I don't have time for this," she hissed to the man on the phone. "She's suffering. She's in pain. She's…"

"We don't have any record of her," he interrupted. "She's never been a patient of Doctor Chastain or anyone at this clinic. I checked Chastain's records for both his practices. We've never seen your friend."

Helen froze.

"We have an impeccable record keeping system." The man sounded calm and untroubled by her agitation. It was the kind of voice Helen hoped for when she had business to conduct. A man who could be kind because he was confident. "Your friend may be confused. If she's being seen for neurological issues, she may not have a clear understanding of her situation. Possibly she read Dr. Chastain's name in the paper and confused him with her doctor."

Adair twisted in the bed.

"We don't lose patients," the doctor said. "And Texidol was pulled from the market over ten years ago because of the side effects. We would never have prescribed it. No one would have prescribed it."

"What happens when someone goes off it?" Helen asked, stroking the damp hair off Adair's forehead.

"You should take your friend to the hospital."

Helen hung up. She touched Adair's forehead again.

"We need to get you to a doctor," she said.

Adair's eyes flew open. "No! He'll find us, Helen."

Helen took her hand. "We'll be safe. We'll be in public."

"They'll be a record. There's always a record. He found you through me. He's looking for you." Adair clutched her hand. "I'd rather die than let him find you." Her eyes flickered closed, and a dream seemed to take hold of her. Her legs twitched and her eyes fluttered behind their lids. "Don't forget the floor-lights," she said, and then in a voice that was all raw panic, "Be careful, Helen!"

Chapter Forty-six

It wasn't really sleep that took Adair, it was more like death, like the heavy uncured skin of a dead animal thrown over her. Time coiled around itself like a snake. Sometimes she woke and she thought she had been lying down for only a minute. Other times it seemed like years.

Sometime in the middle of the day—she assumed it was day because knife-like sun pierced the room—she heard voices. At first they were distant and innocuous. Later she woke again and the voices were in her ear, yelling, *Your brother's wife! You whore!* She rolled over. They followed her, as though they were imbedded in her shoulder. She clawed at the skin. Then she passed out again.

Later she woke, and it was Helen's voice talking earnestly with someone on the phone.

Adair opened her eyes, the room was blessedly dark. Her body felt cold. At the same time, her skin burned. She was vaguely aware of Helen ending her call, setting down the phone, moving around the room.

She tried to speak.

Helen knelt beside her. Something hard and bright reflected in her hand.

"Drink this," Helen said.

The soda was sickeningly sweet. Adair did not have the strength to spit it out, but it dribbled out of her mouth onto the pillow. "I can't."

"Just a little bit more."

Helen tipped a bit of liquid onto Adair's lips. "You're going to be okay."

Adair shook her head a fraction of an inch. She could see Drummond's bullet speeding through the air. "Why does it take so long?" she asked.

Helen put the bottle on the end table. "So long for what?"

"It took months."

"For what, honey?" Helen pressed the back of her hand to Adair's forehead.

"For me to die."

"Shhh. You're going to be okay."

Adair felt Helen's fingers smooth the hair away from her forehead. She flinched, but slowly her body relaxed into the rhythm of Helen's touch. She closed her eyes, then opened them, then closed them again. An orange-gray cloud had covered her vision, hiding the bullet, muffling the voices. She could no longer discern the room around her. All she could feel were Helen's fingertips moving through her hair.

Oddly, she did not *feel* the touch as much as she saw it, like streaks of light moving through her scalp, seen with eyes that were not hers. All her senses had jumbled. Sweet. Orange. Light. Pain. Always pain.

Except where Helen touched her.

"I called Eliza's doctor," Helen murmured. "Another twenty-four hours and the worst will be over."

"Did I die?"

"You won't die."

"How long have I been here?"

"A day and a half." Helen stopped stroking her hair and rose from the bed. The pain reasserted itself as the light faded out of Adair's skin. "Wait," she whispered.

"What is it?" Helen's voice was a tiny drift-boat floating away on the ocean.

Adair couldn't see anything. "Don't leave me," she said, her words getting lost in the ocean.

Helen said nothing, but a moment later, Adair felt the bed sag as Helen lay down beside her. Tentatively, Helen put an arm around her. Everything that touched her skin scraped, as though the outer covering of her skin had been peeled back to reveal the nerves and the red pin pricks of open capillaries. Helen's shirtsleeve ground against her arm. The buttons of her cuff were as cold as liquid nitrogen. She longed to feel Helen beside her, but every touch hurt her. "It's too sharp." She pulled away, only to be flayed by the blankets on the other side.

Vaguely, she remembered the Dore illustrations of Dante's hell, a unique and horrible punishment for each man's crime. The Epicureans trapped in their flaming tombs. Alexander the Great in the river of boiling blood.

Your brother's wife. You whore!

Her punishment was pain, and it was also the isolation. She was like Tantalus, the water just out of reach. The loneliness of her body and her blindness terrifying her. Helen beside her, willing to comfort her.

Then her memories drifted back. She saw her first girlfriend, Soledad, through the bars of a small window. *You have to go, Adair. Don't come back.* She saw Helen, standing naked before her in her flat in the Grandville Hotel, beautiful, untouchable. She saw Cecelia raise her riding crop and bring it down on a horse's flank.

"I know what I did," Adair said.

"Shhh."

"Cyrus loved me." Adair pushed the blankets away. "It's too hot."

"You're shaking," Helen said, trying to pull the blankets over her again.

"I'm burning." Her teeth knocked in her head. "Because of Cecelia. It's my sin."

"No."

Adair felt Helen slip her hands beneath her shoulders and lift her shirt over her head.

"You're okay," Helen repeated over and over, as she unbuttoned Adair's jeans and placed her hands beneath Adair's hips. Then she pulled the jeans down.

It felt as though the heavy denim cut Adair's skin. She cried out. When she tried to open her eyes, she realized they were already open. "I can't see."

"It will come back," Helen murmured.

"I don't know what's happening to me."

"Trust me."

Adair felt the bed sag beneath Helen's weight. A moment later, she felt Helen's body against hers again, only this time it was Helen's bare skin against her own.

"I won't touch you," Helen whispered, although she was cradling Adair's whole body against hers, like an alpine rescuer warming the hypothermia victim, discrete, almost clinical. And naked. Her breasts pressed against Adair's back. Her naked thighs pressed to the back of Adair's legs. "I'm right here."

Adair remained rigid for a long time, afraid to move, but slowly she realized there was nothing sharp in Helen's embrace. She felt the temperature in her body equalize as though Helen's body both warmed and cooled her, dispelling the bone-chill that sent her teeth chattering, soothing the flame that seared her skin. Pain still surrounded her, but it was not *in* her body anymore. It was just in the room, like a haze of smoke.

And everywhere that Helen's body touched her there was light, and the light was also Helen's voice, even though Helen was not speaking. She could hear Helen singing through her skin, an audible finger-print, a portrait drawn in sound and touch. "It's all mixed up," Adair said with more wonder than fear. "I hear you, but it's all light." She gripped Helen's hand for fear she would leave and the pain would reassert itself. "Don't go."

"I won't go anywhere."

Adair felt tears slide down her cheeks, and then she fell into a deep, dreamless sleep.

Chapter Forty-seven

Cecelia slipped into a black Guia La Bruna negligee. A lace panel inset with delicate hand stitching revealed a glimpse of her breasts, her belly, and her navel. In the back, the silk strained against her ass. She had bought the piece in a boutique in Rome for Merrill whose slender, muscular body would have fit it perfectly, but that had just been a passing whim. School girls gave each other nightgowns. Merrill had only ever wanted the tip of her riding crop.

Now Cecelia glided down the hallway, past Monty's smoking lounge, through the Grand Hall, to her husband's office. When they were first married, he had refused to install them in the Wilson estate and had bought a nearby house, a rambling colonial sent into foreclosure by the Silicon Valley bust.

"It's not feudal England," he had grumbled. "And you won't marry my brother if I die."

But I might marry your sister.

Now they were official residents of the house. There were plenty of rooms. She pushed open the door to the office. A fire burned in the fireplace although the air conditioner was still combating the heat. Cyrus sat at his desk, his back to the door. His jacket was slung over the back of his chair. His shirt was damp with sweat. A decanter of cognac sat uncorked by his elbow. A mirror held three lines of cocaine. She felt her nose twitch. He was smoking a cigar. There were also three laptops open on the table. He typed on one, jabbing his thick index fingers at the keyboard.

"Hello Cyrus," she said, closing the door behind her.

He didn't look up.

She stood behind his chair and laid her hands on his back, massaging his shoulders.

"What is it?" he asked, closing the lid of the nearest laptop.

She ran her nails down the back of his neck. "Can I talk to you?"

He swiveled his chair around and surveyed her gown, from the delicate twenty-four karat gold straps to the lace edging. Then he picked up his cigar, pushed his chair away from the desk, and walked over to the sofa. He had his prostitutes. She had hers, on occasion.

She sat across from him.

"What is it?" he asked again.

"I've made a mistake."

He blew a cloud of vile smelling smoke.

"And I'm in trouble." The truth of the words made her hands go cold and her mouth dry. She stood up again and walked over to the desk. An ivory straw lay beside the cocaine. She inhaled two lines. The drug hit her system, and she felt the negligee swirl around her, caressing her legs. "We lost the mine in Idiofa and the one near Ikela." She knew she was stalling. "There's no point in mining coltan if the big five aren't buying. They're calling it a 'conflict mineral'."

Cyrus tucked the cigar in the corner of his mouth and puffed several times in quick succession. "There'll be other mines. Give it a year. You said you wanted to expand into China. Maybe textiles."

"I found a way to make up for the Ikela mine and

more, but I need your help," Cecelia said.

Cyrus had received none of the genetic blessings bestowed on Monty or Merrill. Even Bolo, though she loathed his skinny neck, had his sister's luminous skin and Monty's chiseled jaw. Cyrus was neither lithe nor muscular. His hair had remained a wiry black-and-salt, while Monty's had turned silver. Cyrus had brown eyes, and his skin was perpetually raw. He should have been Bolo: the thug, the ground man.

"Have you heard of Harlow Galloway?" she asked.

"Of course."

Cecelia wrote a sum on a sheet of paper from Cyrus's desk and handed it to her husband. "That's what I've already received, and there will be more."

He sucked on the cigar. "For what?"

"He's a collector, and I acquired an item he wanted."

"An item."

"A woman."

The tip of Cyrus's cigar flared. "I don't like it," he growled.

She had heard it all before. "Who do you think works in your mines for ten cents a day when room and board is twenty?" she spat. "Who gets to leave when the armed guards get a gram of cocaine for every man they catch deserting? That's not slavery?"

"That's industry. What you and Bolo do... abducting girls and selling them around the world like livestock." He shook his head. "It's dirty."

Cecelia sat down beside him this time. She ran her hand down his thigh. "I know you're right, darling." The smoke was cloying. "I should have listened to you." She rested her cheek on his chest. "I found them and we…we took them, and I was supposed to deliver them to Galloway. Please, don't be mad. He's one of the wealthiest men in the world. They were living in a trailer with an outhouse before that. I provided for their transportation. That's all."

"You sold *one* woman to *one* man."

"Not *one* exactly."

"From an undisclosed source to an undisclosed. We agreed on that." Cyrus raised his voice. "Never directly from the family. Never straight to the buyer. No names. No histories. No trace. We agreed."

She whispered the final sum in his ear.

Cyrus leapt up and slammed his cigar into a freestanding ashtray. "And what do you need? Another house? Another one of those vicious horses? What is it you want that you can't already buy?"

An empire.

Merrill.

"Bolo has taken them." There was nothing else to say. "He's gone to another buyer because he wants to marry that sycophantic prom queen. Merrill is the only one who has any idea where they've gone, and I can't reach her. She won't talk to me."

"Merrill!" Cyrus struck the claw-footed ashtray. It crashed to the ground. "You brought her into this?"

"Don't you think it's time she joined the family? Don't you think it's a little antiquated, this idea that women don't work, that you are somehow going to keep Merrill pure by hiding all of this from her?"

Cyrus lunged at her, pinning her to the sofa. His knee knocked the air out of her chest. His hand on her throat stopped her breath. "There will never be a time. Do you understand me, Cecelia? This is not her life. This is ours. This is Monty's. This is Bolo's. But she will never know, like our mother never knew. She will live her whole life and die at peace because there is one thing, one thing…" In his rage, he seemed to have lost his words. "One thing!" He let up on Cecelia's throat.

She gasped. "That's pure?" She rubbed her neck. "She's already in the life, Cy. She just doesn't know it yet."

Chapter Forty-eight

Adair woke with a start. Helen was dressed and reading in a chair by the window. The blinds were closed, the room lit only by an orange table lamp. "What time is it?" she asked, pulling the sheet over her naked body.

"Almost eleven."

"In the morning?"

"In the evening."

The events of the past week flooded back to her: the house in Jamaica Plain, the teenage prostitute, the Pines, Marshal Drummond. She tried to get out of bed. Just as quickly, Helen dropped the book she had been reading, crossed the room, and caught Adair before she fell. "Easy," she said, guiding Adair back to the bed. "You'll be dizzy for a while." Helen pressed a hand to her forehead. "How do you feel?"

Adair took a tentative breath. Her head hurt. Her mouth was dry. But they were familiar pains, like a hangover or the last day of the flu. She knew before she reached for the water glass on the bedside table, that the water would cure her thirst. "I'm hungry." She had forgotten what it felt like.

"Good," Helen said.

Suddenly self-conscious, Adair looked around for her clothes. She smelled of sweat. Her hair was matted to her head. Had they been naked? Or was she remembering their lovemaking from before? "I need to pee," she said, feeling her face flush.

Helen kept an arm around her shoulder as she rose to a sitting position.

"Don't look at me," Adair said.

"You're going to be unsteady for a couple of days." Helen kept her hand on Adair's back as Adair pulled on her jeans and a T-shirt. Then she walked her to the bathroom.

Adair remembered making this trek before with Helen at her side, only then it had been through the cacophony of voices and the blur of her distorted vision. When she finished, Helen urged her to lie down again.

"Are you ready to eat something?" Helen asked.

Adair nodded.

"Don't get up until I get back, okay?" Helen returned moments later with two to-go cartons and a pack of plastic utensils. Adair expected the smell of food to nauseate her. Instead her mouth watered. Helen passed her both boxes, an order of waffles with strawberries and a burger. She set into the breakfast first. Nothing had ever tasted so good. They weren't even real strawberries, more like a strawberry slurry, but the sweetness was so visceral she felt it from her sternum to her groin, as though an artist had painted her body with a long brushstroke that was red and sweet and pleasure all at the same time. It was only after she had finished the carton of food and drank another glass of water that the strangeness of the sensation struck her. She touched her chest where the taste of red was diffusing throughout her body.

Helen watched her. "It's okay if you feel strange. It'll pass."

"Where are we?"

"Oneonta, New York."

"New York? What happened?"

"I drove us." Helen smiled.

"And Drummond?"

Helen's face grew serious. "Rest for a little while. I have a lot to tell you, but I think we're safe for now."

"What happened to me?" Adair rubbed her hands up and down her arms. There was no pain, but she could hear the touch—not the sound of her hand brushing her skin, but a whisper that was the sound of her cells greeting each other. She stumbled over her words.

"I think I know," Helen said. "Drink some more water. You'll be dehydrated for a while."

Adair drank and then took the burger from the second to-go box. She began to eat, more slowly this time. Helen adjusted a pillow against the headboard and took a seat beside her on the bed. In between bites, Adair watched her. She had dark circles under her eyes, but she looked beautiful.

"What do you know about the drug Texidol?" Helen asked when Adair finally set the box aside. She reached over and took Adair's hand.

"Not a lot," Adair confessed. "My doctor prescribed it after…after you left. I was only going to be in New Hampshire for a few days. Then I was going to go back to Pittock. He prescribed it, but the pain kept getting worse."

"How do you feel now?" Helen said, caressing the soft skin of Adair's inner wrist.

"Better. I don't understand. I feel strange but not sick like I was."

"Do you remember if you started to feel sick before you started taking Texidol or after?"

"Before, I guess."

"Are you sure?"

"I can hardly remember. I know it kept getting worse. The doctor said it would. He said it was irreversible." Adair hesitated. "If it comes back, I don't think I can bear it."

"Come here." Helen wrapped her arm around Adair.

Adair slid down in the bed and let her head rest against Helen's chest. She was vaguely aware of her greasy hair and the perspiration that coated her body, but Helen's embrace felt irresistibly good. With the pain dispelled from her bones and Helen's arms wrapped around her, she felt like something newborn and delivered into warm swaddling–helpless and loved.

"I think the strange feelings you're having are a side effect of coming off Texidol," Helen said. "The way you described your symptoms and the way you moved, it reminded me of my sister Eliza when she was on all those medications. She hated them. She said they made her blood hurt. When we got to the hotel, you were so sick. I wanted to call 911, but you begged me not to."

"I don't remember."

"You told me you were already dead, and that Drummond had killed you in the asylum. And you said he would find us if I called for help. I was so scared." Helen pulled Adair closer. "I called Eliza's psychiatrist, Linda. She was the only person I could think of. I told her what had happened. She said Texidol is an old antipsychotic. It was taken off the market, only a few experimental psychiatrists are trying to bring it back. The rest of the medical community says the side effects aren't worth the benefits."

"Am I going mad?"

"Linda thought maybe your doctor prescribed it because your condition was neurological," Helen said slowly. "She wanted me to take you to a hospital, but I also got her to admit there wasn't much they could do except keep you hydrated. Even easing off the drug just prolongs the withdrawal. She said they couldn't give you pain killers because one of the withdrawal symptoms is synesthesia."

"What's that?"

"All your senses get jumbled up. You hear colors. You smell sounds." Helen stroked the back of Adair's T-shirt. "You're going to have residual synesthesia for a few days, maybe longer, but it will go away eventually."

"It's not bad," Adair said. She described the "taste" of the strawberries. "I couldn't feel anything before. I mean nothing good. Not...pleasure." Adair longed to feel Helen's hand on her bare skin.

"Most neuroleptics suppress the dopamine receptors in the brain." Helen slipped her hand under Adair's shirt and rubbed warm, slow circles on her back. "Can you feel that?"

"Yes."

"Is it okay?"

Adair nodded. Helen's touch still left a faint glow on her skin which she could see with eyes that were not eyes.

"How much do you remember of last night?" Helen asked.

"Not a lot."

"I...I took your clothes off." Helen spoke into Adair's hair. "During the worst of it. I didn't know what to do. You were in so much pain. I took my clothes off, and I held you. I just wanted you to know. I didn't want you to think…"

Adair thought Helen might be crying, but she felt so tired she could barely speak. Then she was asleep.

❧❧❧❧

She woke in Helen's arms. Outside the hotel room, a service cart rattled by and two women chatted in Portuguese. Adair rose and brushed her teeth. She was about to step in the shower when Helen knocked on the door.

"Please. I'm afraid you'll fall," Helen said, trying the locked doorknob.

Adair wrapped a towel around her and opened the door.

"Let me run you a bath." Helen said, moving past her into the bathroom. She turned on the water, watched it for several minutes, then tested the temperature with her wrist. Then she held out her hand to steady Adair. Reluctantly Adair released her towel as she stepped over the lip of the tub. Helen closed the lid of the toilet and sat down, watching her.

Adair slid under the water and let it cover her face for a moment before emerging. Over the past months her body had gone soft. She was heavier than she had been, and the flesh on her arms and legs was loose. Flabby. She had lost her tan.

"You're beautiful," Helen said.

Adair rubbed the water out of her eyes. "I can't even remember who I am."

"I can." Helen leaned over and took the small soap from the ledge behind Adair's back. Tentatively, she ran it over Adair's shoulder, holding Adair's gaze.

"I remember *you*," Adair said.

Helen continued to stroke the soap over her shoulders.

"That feels good," Adair whispered.

Helen spread her fingers, the soap in the flat of her palm. She smoothed her hand over Adair's breast. Adair let out a breath as Helen's hand crossed her nipple. The pleasure was visceral. Helen ran her hand down Adair's side and along her thigh, her shirt sleeve trailing in the water. Adair felt her sex wake almost violently. A surge of desire flooded her body, sending a shiver to the tips of her extremities. When Helen drew her hand back along Adair's inner thigh and the water lapped against her sex, Adair groaned. "It's so intense." Her voice was raw.

Helen's smile was gentle and also pleased.

"Eliza's doctor said that's a common side effect. After the worse of the withdrawal is over, your body wakes up."

Adair caught Helen's hand. "You don't have to do this, Helen. You don't owe me anything," she said, although she did not want Helen to withdraw her touch.

Helen's answer was a kiss. She cupped the back of Adair's head with one hand, her mons with the other. Then, holding Adair completely, she kissed her. Hot and deep. Their lips pressed together. Their tongues becoming one. Helen drew back only when they had both run out of air. "Are you okay? Is it too soon?" Helen asked.

From her eyes, Adair knew Helen couldn't bear to wait just as she couldn't. "Please," Adair said.

Helen was still careful helping her out of the tub. She dried her tenderly, wrapping a towel around her before leading her back to the bed. Then she stripped her own clothing without ceremony. A moment later, she was on top of Adair, holding her and kissing her with a fierce, trembling tenderness, as though she wanted to devour her and feared breaking her at the same time.

Adair held her tightly, urging her on. Soon Helen's tender caution melted away into something harder. Every touch expanded throughout Adair's body like concentric circles spreading through water. She felt liquid, hot, open. When Helen kissed her nipples she cried out. When Helen slipped her fingers into Adair's sex, she arched her back off the bed, her cry a song of wanting and receiving. She would have felt self-conscious except that Helen's every move held the same need.

"Oh, God," Helen whispered, pressing her kiss to Adair's neck while sliding her wet fingers around Adair's clit.

Adair bit Helen's shoulder, clutched her buttocks, released a string of words that had only one meaning. Their legs intertwined. Their hips pressed together. Helen pushed the apex of her sex against Adair. Adair felt every fold of her sex become an extension of her clitoris and her clitoris an extension of Helen's body. And everything that was raw and beautiful about sex was in that pressure between their legs.

A second later, Helen cried out as she ascended to orgasm. "I love you." Helen repeated the words with each exhale.

A moment later, Adair came too. For several minutes, she could not speak. She could only breathe. But when she found her voice again, she pulled Helen close and whispered, "I love you, Helen."

Chapter Forty-nine

Helen woke slowly. Sunshine spilled beneath the closed curtains. Outside the room a woman laughed. A car honked. A child splashed into the little pool in the center of the motel complex. Helen felt Adair's arm encircling her waist. She tried not to wake fully. She wanted to float in the warmth of the morning. Perhaps, when she checked her phone, she would learn that Thompson had apprehended Drummond. Perhaps the twins had been found. Even now, their faces might be splayed across every morning news program. Perhaps everything she needed to tell Adair was mute. She pulled Adair closer and dozed again.

When she woke again, Adair was watching her.

"Good morning, beautiful," Helen said sleepily.

Adair stroked her fingers down Helen's arm, raising a trail of goose bumps. "Good morning."

Helen rolled toward her, and Adair snuggled close. They lay together for several minutes.

"You said there were things you needed to tell me," Adair said finally.

Reluctantly, Helen rolled out of Adair's arms and reached for her phone. There were no new messages. She took a deep breath. She had made several phone calls while Adair was sick: Terri, Patrick, Thompson, Eliza's doctor. Except for the doctor's assurance that Adair would live through the withdrawal, none of the news was good.

"Are you sure you're ready? I should give you a couple of days to rest," Helen said.

"I'm ready," Adair said.

"Okay." Helen took a deep breath. "Unless things have changed, here it is. I called Thompson. Drummond was released. Somehow there was a mix-up, and the hospital let him go. They don't know where he is."

Adair nodded.

"You're not surprised."

"Men like Drummond don't go down for life," Adair said matter-of-factly. "They don't lose."

"No one at the state hospital is willing to take responsibility except to fire the man who actually walked Drummond off the grounds, but he was just following orders. The paperwork all said Drummond was free to be released." Helen stared up at the ceiling. "Thompson thinks Drummond may have had something to do with the fire at the Grandville, even though he was still in the hospital at that time. He thinks he might have found a way to pay someone on the outside. They're trying to recover video footage from the minimart next door. The store was damaged by smoke, but they think they'll have the video within a day or two. He's going to send it to us if there's anything on it. One of the cameras pointed to the back door of the Grandville." The reality of their situation hit Helen again and her voice trembled. "Tyron says Drummond is obsessed with me. He says Drummond may have commissioned the fire to get you out of the way. He sees you as a threat to his 'relationship' with me."

"I am." Adair took her hand. "I'm going to kill

him."

"Don't say that! You'd go to jail. I'd never see you again."

Adair leaned over and kissed Helen's forehead. "Don't worry. I'm just as well connected as he is."

"But your brother…His wife."

"Cyrus doesn't know." Adair looked away. "Cecelia won't tell him. It's not to her advantage to tell him. Anyway, we're still family."

It sounded ominous to Helen. "Don't. Please. Promise me, you won't do anything like that. Unless he's coming at you, and it's self-defense. I can't lose you again."

"If I hadn't been so sick, I would have killed him already. Now that I'm better, there is no world in which I don't find him and kill him."

"You're reckless." Helen squeezed Adair's hand. "I love that about you, but you can't do that. I won't let you. That's not who you are."

"It's who I would be for you."

"I don't want that." Helen lifted Adair's hand to her mouth and pressed her lips to Adair's knuckles. "You can't murder a man. It would destroy you."

"If I kill him, we'll be free."

Helen met Adair's pale blue eyes. Blue the color of ice under moving water, of winter storms, of the sky where it thins on the horizon. It seemed to Helen that nothing else had ever mattered, and that she would follow Adair to any end.

❧ ❧ ❧ ❧

An hour later, Helen had showered and changed into a pair of jeans and a blouse she bought at the Wal-

Mart down the street from their motel. She emerged from the bathroom. Adair was dressed in similar fashion and sitting on the bed staring at her phone.

"What is it?" Helen sat beside her.

Adair didn't say anything for a moment, then she gave the phone to Helen. "What does that look like to you?"

Helen squinted at the screen. "Are those the twins?"

"I saw this online right before I saw Drummond."

Helen read the text below the photograph. "Las Vegas. That's where Curtis and Pammy-Lynne said they took girls to break them in."

"I should never have taken them out of Utah." Adair sighed. "I've made mistakes before. I've hurt students' feelings. I've ignored policies and gotten other people in trouble. And my brother Cyrus, he's sued everyone who's ever crossed me. He's like the grim reaper. But I've never done anything like this. I've never been the *one* person responsible for something this awful."

Helen put her arm around Adair, relishing the warmth of Adair's body even as she chose her next words carefully. "You weren't the one person. Remember, I asked you. And Cecelia thought it would be good for you. And the donor, whoever he is, got it through his head that he could play God with these girls just because he missed his dead sisters. All donors are egotists. It's too bad we live off them." Helen ran her fingers down Adair's back.

Adair shivered and said nothing for a long time. Outside, the noises of ordinary life carried on insensitive to the intimate heat of the little hotel room. Finally Adair said, "They ran to me. They wanted to leave, at least Charity wanted to leave. They risked everything."

Helen caressed Adair's cheek, then ran her hand down Adair's neck and across her back. She could feel the architecture of Adair's body. Despite her illness, her bones felt strong like the ribs of a gothic cathedral. And her face, when she turned to Helen, was more beautiful than any magazine cutout, not because of her straight nose or high cheekbones, but because of her soul flashing in her eyes. *I have never loved anyone else.* "Thompson says we can keep moving if that feels safer," Helen said slowly. "He says there are risks. In Pittock, the police know to look for Drummond. The whole town knows. On the road, they're working with local police who have no idea who Drummond is or who we are, and they've got their own crises to deal with. But, Thompson also said that Drummond is smart. He's probably connected. The best protection may be going places he simply wouldn't expect."

"Like where?" Adair asked, her voice mournful.

Helen took a breath. "Las Vegas."

"To look for Charity and Prudence?"

"We have to stay in touch with Thompson and with the local police wherever we are," Helen said. "We have to do things by the book with the help of the police and the local agencies. But we could ask around…if you want. If that would make you feel better."

"You would do that for me?"

The wonder in Adair's face was the only prize that had ever mattered to Helen. "You have to promise not to do anything reckless," she said, knowing that she herself was throwing away all caution for a taste of the same dark exhilaration that had spiced the days surrounding Carrie Brown's death.

Chapter Fifty

Adair and Helen made love again, and Adair worshiped every cell of Helen's body with her kiss, her tongue, her own unbroken body, with the self that had been returned to her whole. Then they ate another meal out of cartons on the bed, then they slept.

They decided to travel at night so left the hotel at midnight and hurried to the car. The fear of encountering Drummond made every shadow a knife, every noise a footstep. Still, mixed in with the fear was a giddiness that caught Adair's heart like a light breeze taking a kite. She was well. She could stretch without feeling her vertebrae pulling apart. She could lounge in the seat of the BMW without the urge to crawl out of her skin. And beside her, Helen sat in the driver's seat, easing the car into traffic and onto the freeway.

Helen touched her knee. "How are you doing?"

For a second, the image of Drummond's face flashed across her mind, but even he could not disrupt the happiness that surrounded her like a golden spotlight. If there was only this moment, then she would live in it. She rolled down her window and breathed in the smell of night air. "I feel wonderful."

❧❧❧❧

It was about 5 a.m. on the third day, when Adair

saw the lights of Las Vegas, first a glow in the sky, then an orange carpet of light in the distant valley.

"I've never been to Vegas," Helen said idly, leaning forward in the passenger seat.

"It's all right." Adair was driving. She tapped the steering wheel with her fingertips, trying to think of something to show Helen. She wished it was Rome or Venice, someplace to equal Helen's beauty, someplace sacred. "It's just as plastic as everyone says on the strip, and then you get off on a side street and it's just…another place."

"Does anything impress you?" Helen asked, stroking Adair's leg.

Adair chuckled. "You do."

Helen clicked her tongue dismissively.

Adair leaned forward for a better view of the city. "Oquat impressed me."

A billboard on the side of the road flashed a line of women's legs in red heels. "Strut your stuff at Passion's Adult Emporium" the headline read.

"When were you in Vegas last?" Helen asked.

"I came here to talk to one of the architects who works for the Josslin Heights. He was doing a renovation. I wanted to talk to him about the Grandville." Adair stopped, thinking of the beautiful white building.

"I'm sorry," Helen said.

"I am glad Ulysses got out." She hadn't thought about the giant mastiff for months. "Patrick still has him, doesn't he?"

Helen nodded. "Of course."

"Monty says he'll build another hotel." Adair shook her head. "I think Cyrus has rented me a flat in Paris. But the Grandville felt like home. You know that feeling?"

Helen glanced at her with a strange half-smile. "No."

❧ ❧ ❧ ❧

Their first stop in Las Vegas was a charity called Stand United. It was located in a dusty strip mall, in between a sandwich shop and a tanning salon. The name was stenciled in peeling letters on the front of the window. A yellow paper shade obscured the interior. Adair pushed the flimsy glass door open and a bell jangled. Inside, four metal chairs sat against one wall. A tattered poster warned against child abuse. In one corner a Christmas cactus in a plastic pot had dried away to a gray skeleton. Adair tapped the bell on the counter. In the back she heard a chair slide.

The woman who appeared at the front counter was surprisingly polished for her surroundings, with short gray hair, a navy blazer over a white T-shirt, and trim jeans. She wore a large belt with a silver buckle and a matching bolo tie at her throat.

"Can I help you?" the woman asked.

Helen shook her hand. "Helen Ivers. President of Pittock College." She held her hands up in polite deference. "It's in Massachusetts. You've probably not heard of it."

"I have. I went to Amherst," the woman said.

Helen smiled, and Adair saw the perfect administrator assert herself. So polished. So gracious.

"This is Adair Wilson." Helen gestured to her. "We'd love a little bit of your time. We're looking for someone."

"A woman?"

Helen nodded. "Two students. We think they've been abducted."

"Prostitution?"

Helen nodded again.

"Come on back," the woman said.

Her office was more commodious than the front room. The walls were textured stucco, painted a rustic orange. The window behind the woman's desk was shaded with heavy venetian blinds. The houseplants were lush and well-tended. On the desk sat a picture of the woman smiling next to a gray haired man and two smiling girls. The woman introduced herself as Chris Hillsmith, a social worker and the director of Stand United.

Helen outlined the story, starting with the offer of the scholarship, the twins, and their disappearance, and taking her through the brothel in Maine. She described the picture Adair had seen online, and Adair produced her phone. Helen did not mention Marshal Drummond. When she finished narrating the events, she added, "There are a lot of reasons why we both feel responsible."

"Have you contacted the police?"

"I have," Helen said.

Adair glanced at her.

"This morning, when you were sleeping," Helen added.

She nodded to Helen. "Thank you."

Helen smiled. To Chris, Helen added, "They filed a report and said they would keep an eye out. They also said that if the girls had been abducted, their captor would keep them secreted. As soon as someone sees them, they'll be all over the internet."

Chris steepled her fingers on the desk before her.

"You were actually in the brothel in Maine? You're lucky you got out."

"I know." Helen nodded.

Adair added, "We think the girls were taken by a group of people who call themselves the Ashfelt club. The word Ashfelt seems to be some kind of password that got us access to the brothel in Maine."

"We talked to other activists who'd heard of the Ashfelt Club," Helen said.

It took Adair a moment to realize that Helen was talking about Curtis and Pammy-Lynne. "They said the Ashfelt Club sold girls to individual buyers. They mentioned an occasion when a girl was purchased and…killed. They thought they used the legal brothels as a kind of cover."

Chris nodded solemnly. "I've heard of that." She opened up her computer file and scanned through a few screens. "I have one idea," she said, looking up and then going back to her computer. "I know a woman. She co-owns one of the brothels. She doesn't like our agency, but she's smart, and I think she's bored. She might talk to you."

Adair glanced at Helen.

"You want to try?" Helen asked.

"We don't have to," Adair added, but Helen's face said, *we already are.*

Chris rose from her office chair and picked up a set of keys from the table behind her desk. "Let's go then."

Helen hesitated. "Don't you have to be here?" she asked the social worker.

Chris was already heading for the door, grabbing a white Stetson from a peg by the door. "I wait until someone comes and says they need my help. Then I help." She turned and shot them a frank smile.

Adair wondered what it would be like to live without any secrets. A few minutes later, she was sandwiched between Helen and Chris in the cab of a dusty pick-up truck. The ride took over an hour. They said little. Eventually they arrived at a place called the Lonely Star Ranch. The brothel consisted of squat, windowless, white buildings surrounded by a hurricane fence. The entrance was a white, picket fence gate incongruously set in chicken wire. A short, wheelchair ramp led up to the nearest door. Beyond that the desert was barren rock framed on one side by a distant mountain range. It was both less sinister and less glamorous than Adair had imagined.

"Wait here," Chris said. She got out of the car and walked over to the intercom at the gate.

A moment later, the gate swung open. Chris got back in the truck and drove them to the other side of the complex. There they waited at a backdoor, like the employee entrance for some B-grade strip mall. Eventually, the door opened, and a man in a white polo shirt ushered them inside.

Once inside, the Lonely Star Ranch looked like a cross between a cheap hotel and a dorm. They were in a hallway, with brown carpet and beige walls. Every few feet, there was a door. Unlike the standard hotel doors, most were decorated. The one closest to Adair had a red feather boa pinned to the molding. Farther down, she saw a drape of black satin embellished with the outline of a woman's body stitched in red sequins. Another door bore a series of nude photographs, while the one across the hall bore snap shots of the Grand Canyon and a collage of words cut out of a magazine. *Every day is precious*, the motto read. A white-board plaque on the wall by each door bore a name written in colorful ink: Candy, Poshy, Amber-Ann, Tiger.

"Who comes here?" Adair asked.

Chris glanced at their guide.

The man in the polo shirt shrugged. "Everyone."

As they moved down the hall, they crossed paths with a girl wearing a tennis skirt and no shirt. Catching their eye, the girl kicked her leg up in a cheerleader's dance move, revealing a shaved pudendum. Adair looked away.

"Is all of this legal," Helen whispered to Chris.

"Yep," the guide answered instead. "It's the only place in the United States, but it's only legal in the rural counties and only legal in the brothels."

Adair glanced back at the girl who was disappearing into one of the bedrooms. "Why would anyone…?" Adair's unfinished question hung in the air.

"A woman can make fifty or sixty thousand a year here," Chris said, and Adair could hear the weight in Chris's voice.

"Or more," the guide said without turning to look at them. "The ranch is divided into three sections," he went on. "Right now we're on the veterans' side. They call it the Silver Wing. These women have all been with the ranch for over a year. Then there is the cafeteria, and on the other side is Copper Canyon. That's for the new girls and the hoppers."

"Girls who move from brothel to brothel for better wages or to get away from a John they don't like," Chris clarified.

"And the Lonely Stars are women who have all been here for over ten years," the guide added.

"Ten years!" Adair exclaimed.

Their guide shrugged. "I've been here for eight."

It did not seem like the same thing, but Adair felt Helen's hand on her arm and said nothing.

The guide led the trio out of the long hallway and outside into the white heat. They were clearly at the center of the complex. The Lonely Stars' cabins were five small, sun-bleached cabins surrounding an empty swimming pool. One palm tree stood at the head of the pool, a red hose snaking away from its base and disappearing behind one of the cabins.

"You go ahead," Chris said. "I'll wait over there." She pointed to a table with a tattered patio umbrella. "Katherine and I don't see eye to eye, obviously."

❧ ❧ ❧ ❧

Tentatively Adair knocked on Katherine's door. There was a rustle inside the cabin, then the sound of a lock releasing. A moment later, a voice from within called, "Come in."

Pushing the door open, Adair felt like she had walked onto the set of a stage play. There was nothing particularly unusual about the room. It was a small living-room and open kitchen with one door leading off to the bedroom. The curtains were drawn, but enough light poured in around the edges to illuminate the scene. A leather sofa. Two slightly worn leather easy chairs. A Turkish rug. Silk palms. A vase of red roses stood on the coffee table in the center of the room. Nothing else. The items in the room were countable. Sofa, chair, chair, rug, palm, palm, vase: seven. If the stage manager had to clear them off for another performance, it would be easy to inventory them. Nowhere did Adair see signs of real inhabitation. No pile of keys. No magazines. No bit of plastic packaging left over from a recent purchase. In that way, it reminded her of the Wilson Estate.

The woman who greeted them had clearly unlocked the door and then arranged herself on the sofa, a navy blue kimono pooling around her. "I'm Katherine," she said as they entered. She held out her hand to shake, and Adair had the fleeting impression Katherine expected her to kneel and kiss it.

"May I get you a martini?" Katherine asked without moving. Her voice was as smooth as chocolate. Long golden curls cascaded over her shoulders.

She was fifty at least, probably older, her face handsome but lined.

"Were you expecting an eighteen-year-old whore?" Katherine's eyes were piercing. "Then you only understand half our work," she added as though Adair had answered the question.

A breeze stirred closed curtains, revealing nothing.

"Sit." Katherine said.

Adair settled into the leather sofa. It felt like skin. Helen sat beside her.

As if performing a quick recalculation, Katherine pointed a long finger at Adair and then at Helen. "How long have you two been sleeping together? A year? No, just a few days, but you've wanted it for a long time."

Helen coughed. Adair stared at Katherine, trying to read the real woman behind the act, but there seemed to be nothing there.

"This my profession." Katherine smiled. "I would be remiss if I couldn't smell lust when it walks into my house. Or is it love?" A queen on her throne, Katherine tapped long, pearlescent nails on the arms of her chair and eyed Helen.

"It's love," Helen whispered.

"And this quest of yours has something to do with whatever you two are carrying around. 'Love,' as she calls it." Katherine waved a hand in Helen's direction.

The truth of her statements grated on Adair more than simple rudeness would have.

"We just want to ask you a few questions." Adair began to lay out the story.

Katherine put up a hand.

"I didn't say I would answer your questions. I said I would *see* you. They said a college president and some sort of activist professor were looking for Siamese twins. That's more interesting than the usual."

"The usual?" Adair asked.

"Some housewife from Bakersfield looking for her daughter who ran away with a boy with too many tattoos," Katherine said. "Now she thinks her daughter is a whore. Funny how quickly a mother jumps to that conclusion. Probably because she remembers the conception."

"So you do know something about the twins?" Adair pressed. "I think they've been taken by something called the Ashfelt Club. It's some sort of… service that caters to men who are looking for strange sex and violent sex. If they're still alive, we might not have a lot of time."

"You're like all the new girls. You just want to get down to business," Katherine said, rising from her chair. "I'd like to get to know you a little before I tell you all my secrets." Her expression was *all* secrets.

From a small bookshelf, she withdrew a heavy, leather-bound album. The cover was well worn. "My vita," she said, handing it to Adair.

Adair opened the first page and gasped. A faded magazine clipping showed a girl spread-eagle and flirting with the camera, one skinny finger tucked between her lips. "It's a child!" Adair said, the horror she felt filling her voice. It was like looking at a crime scene photograph. The crime was already over, and yet she had the urge to scream, "No, stop!"

Katherine laughed. "I was nineteen. My manager said that body was gold." The pride in Katherine's voice made Adair want to rip the page out and shred it to pieces.

"I was in the film industry too," Katherine said. "That was back when it was *film*, and you couldn't get everything online. We had real fans."

Adair turned the page. Another magazine clipping read, "Katherine Fenning takes Miss Barely Legal for the second time. Apparently she's found the secret to youth because Katherine 'the wren' Fenning just gets younger every year."

"This is sick," Adair said, momentarily forgetting the twins.

"It's not child pornography," Katherine said, as though they were discussing mild weather.

Adair was vaguely aware of Helen's hand on her arm again.

"What if men look at this and think it's okay?" Adair could not stop herself. "What if someone… you're feeding into this! It doesn't matter if you were nineteen. You don't look nineteen."

"I was twenty in that photograph," Katherine said as though that explained everything.

Adair slammed the book shut. "And now?"

Katherine brushed her hand in front of her face

as if waving away a gnat. "Now I provide conversation and company to the highest class of men."

"I don't think the highest class of men visit prostitutes." Adair felt her face flush.

Helen whispered, "Shh."

Katherine turned her gaze to Helen. "You would do well here. Your friend is prettier." Katherine gestured to Adair. "But that's not what it's about, is it? That's not why men choose you."

"Men don't choose Helen!" Adair shot back. She saw Duffy emerging from the stairwell.

"Every woman is a whore." Katherine's voice was so smooth it almost sounded like a benediction. "Don't you agree, Miss Ivers? Unless of course she's a dyke, and they're probably whores too." She shot Adair a withering look. "I just wouldn't know, myself."

Adair leapt to her feet.

"It's okay," Helen said. "Sit down."

"It's not." Adair raised her voice. "Two innocent girls who know nothing about sex have been kidnapped. If you know anything about this, you have a duty to tell us, but you don't know, do you? You're just bored. Maybe your men *would* prefer an eighteen-year-old. So you sit here in a hut, in the dark, in the middle of fucking nowhere, making every woman out to be a whore, because you want to justify your lifestyle."

"Oh I think you're the one with the 'lifestyle'," Katherine shot back.

"Let's go." Adair turned to Helen. "We're wasting our time."

But Helen's eyes were fixed on Katherine. The two regarded each other across the room as if across a boardroom table.

"You know, don't you?" Helen said.

Katherine broke their stare and turned away with a little flounce of her robe. "I know nothing."

Adair grabbed Helen's hand. "Let's get out of here."

Helen looked shaken.

"By the way," Katherine called after them. "If you're looking for the Ashfelt Club, ask any lot lizard. She's heard of it. You can make a thousand an hour at the Ashfelt Club. And all your little college boy mongers, they've been there too, from LA to New York. You can have anything you want at the Ashfelt Club, and the girls do it for free because they love the work. Every new fish is looking for the Ashfelt Club, her and her nineteen-year-old 'souteneur'." Her voice was a snarl curled around velvet rope. "Ashfelt is a myth. It's an urban legend. It's just a way of saying you're desperate, and you don't know shit about the world."

Chapter Fifty-one

Helen, I love Adair just as much as you do, but you have to get back here." Patrick's voice rattled out of Helen's cell phone.

I doubt that. Helen was sitting in Adair's car, the engine running to keep the interior at a bearable eighty degrees. Outside, the parking lot of their latest hotel cooked in the one-hundred-sixteen-degree sun even though it was almost seven in the evening. The sign for the hotel stood a story and a half higher than anything else on the block. *Almost Home Comfort Plaza.* Beyond the hotel, a block of fast food restaurants and gas stations crumbled into the desert. It was their fifth hotel in seven days.

"You're going to lose your job." He wasn't playing the meddling secretary anymore. He was angry.

"Tell them I've had a death in the family." Helen scanned the parking lot. Nothing moved.

"Who Helen? You don't have any family. Everyone knows that. I told them it was an aunt, but that's wearing thin. It's been almost two weeks."

"People take more than two weeks bereavement. Jonas from biology was gone for a month, Tanya from purchasing…"

"*You* don't. You took one week when your provost tried to kill you. I can't lie to them anymore. And you can't lose your job. Remember, you're not made of money like Adair."

Helen ran her finger along the seam in the dashboard. Everything was covered in a fine layer of dust. "It doesn't matter." Helen could not explain to him that nothing mattered except the communion of her body and Adair's behind the standard-issue curtains of a cheap motel. She could not even remember her office in Pittock.

"Talk to me, Helen. Off the record. What the hell are you doing?"

"We're looking for the twins." The leather interior of the car felt hot.

"Why?" Patrick demanded.

So far they had visited three police stations, two women's shelters, three agencies that specialized in human-trafficking, a sexual health clinic, and sixteen churches that advertised "anti-prostitution" and "sexual morality" programming. No one had seen or heard anything to suggest the twins had been in Las Vegas.

"Adair feels responsible."

"Bruno Duffy is going to fuck you up the ass!" Patrick's voice soared. "I mean it. He's going to have you fired. You've got to pull it together."

Helen looked up at their hotel window. Behind the closed curtains, Adair was showering. She was changing into some drab, loose-fitting clothes they had bought at the Wal-Mart. It didn't matter. The sweat pants and the "I love Las Vegas" T-shirt did nothing to hide her beauty. Even the bloat of the Texidol could not do that, and now that she was off the drug, her face had slimmed and her body seemed to have lengthened. Men watched her as she walked. In the nonprofits, frank crew-cut women with eyes like little shards of desert rock shook Adair's hand and thanked her for her work. The way they handed Adair their cards—Helen saw it—they wanted her. "I love her," Helen said.

"I get it. You think she's the one. But she can be *the one* back at Pittock."

"I haven't seen Eliza," Helen said. "Since Adair came back."

"We can work with that."

She could tell Patrick was trying to calm himself down.

"If you tell the board you're having a mental breakdown, it might help. It's an explanation. They can't fire you for mental health issues."

"But I'm fine." Helen searched her memory for the mental health section of the college's ADA policy. "They probably could fire me. But the college is in better shape now than it's been in ten years. I have given my life to that school. I have vacation time. Tell the board and tell Duffy, they can fucking wait. I'm on holiday."

"You can't go on holiday." Patrick was not easily cowed.

"Just do your job, Patrick!"

"I'm not running interference for you."

Their anger simmered in the static between phones and then burned out.

"I'm sorry, Patrick," Helen said.

"Helen, talk to me. Why are you doing this? You've got so much to lose."

"I'm forty-seven," Helen said slowly. "I love her. Maybe this is my chance."

"For what?"

Life.

"It's not just about you." Patrick pressed the words to her ear, one by one. "If you don't come back here and say something, Duffy's going to press charges against Adair. He says she held him at gun point. She could go to jail, Helen."

❧ ❧ ❧ ❧

When Helen returned to the hotel room, Adair was flopped on the bed, her arms flung over her head. Somewhere she had found a pair of scissors and cut the dye out of her hair. Now she looked like a high fashion model in some edgy shoot, the dreary hotel and the mangled haircut all highlighting her beauty like a simple setting for a rare gem.

"Who were you talking to?" Adair looked up at Helen as she entered.

"Patrick."

"I miss him," Adair said absently.

"He misses you too, although he says he's going to kill you if he sees you again."

Adair sighed. "That's Patrick." Adair sat up, wrapped her arms around Helen's waist, and ran her hands under Helen's shirt. She pressed her lips to Helen's breast.

Through her bra, Helen could feel Adair's teeth teasing the edge of her nipple. A shiver ran through her body.

"We've done enough for today," Adair said. "Take this off." She unbuttoned Helen's shirt and pushed it off her shoulders. "That's better." She slipped her hands down Helen's back, then slid her pants and underwear off in one practiced move. "Lie down."

Helen tried not to think, only to feel as she

stretched out on the bed. In the past days, the fervor of Adair's search for the twins had been matched only by her passion in bed. The past week had been a blur of hot days spent waiting in cramped nonprofit offices and nights spent lovemaking, their senses heightened by the fear that kept them both on edge.

Now Adair pulled Helen onto the bed. Quickly, deftly, and with a tenderness that was all restrained strength, Adair removed the rest of Helen's clothes. Helen's body responded instantly. The desire she felt told her she had never known want before Adair. The few dull pangs of sexual need she had experienced before her, were like a small fluorescent bulb held up to the sun. Before Helen realized what she was doing, she had spread her legs, and Adair was caressing her inner thighs, then trailing her tongue along the side of Helen's labia, missing her clitoris deliberately. Helen gasped. "Please!" She pressed her hips up, but then, in the back of her mind, she heard Patrick's voice. *She could go to jail, Helen.*

Adair slipped her tongue beneath Helen's clit.

"There," Helen gasped. "No. Higher."

Adair shifted slightly. Helen felt her whole body tense, but her mind drifted away. She heard Bruno Duffy say, *So you want to fuck Adair Wilson. You and half this college.* Helen willed her body to relax.

Adair slipped her fingers inside Helen and pressed on her clitoris from behind as she sucked harder.

Duffy's going to press charges against Adair. The pleasure ebbed away. Suddenly Helen felt trapped and numb. "Please stop. I'm sorry. I can't."

"Did I hurt you?" Adair climbed onto the bed beside her, brushing the slight sheen off her chin.

"No."

"I'm so sorry." Adair rested a protective hand over Helen's pubic hair, not touching her sex. "It was too much, wasn't it? I should have waited. I should have gone slowly."

"No." Helen shook her head. "You're wonderful." She squeezed her eyes closed.

"What is it, baby?" Adair lay down beside her and cradled Helen in her arms.

Helen hesitated for a long minute. "I have to go back to Pittock." Outside the room, the day was easing into night. The light coming in under the curtains was fading. In the distance a motorcycle revved to life. A dog in the next room barked twice.

"I'm sorry." Adair rested her cheek on Helen's chest. "I've already dragged you into too much."

"It's not that." Helen stroked Adair's hair. She saw Duffy entering her foyer. She felt his hair run through her fingers. She remembered the skin of his cock and his weight as he tried to force himself on her. *I asked him!* Her mind reeled. *I propositioned him.* "I've made a mistake."

"What is it?"

Helen hesitated. "Duffy."

"He's a bastard!"

Helen opened her eyes and stared up at the ceiling. "Katherine said all women are whores."

"Katherine is a whore and a narcissist." Adair raised up on one elbow and looked at her. "She's a child pornographer, whatever she says."

Helen was still trying to think of what to say when she blurted out the words. "I said I would fuck him."

"What?" Adair sat fully upright.

Now that Helen had begun, the words felt inevitable. "I told him I'd fuck him for your job. I couldn't keep it open." Helen sat up, cross-legged in the bed, her head bowed. "I know I'm the president, but I don't have any jurisdiction over hires. The president is just a figurehead. I tried to get the board to keep your position open and they agreed, but eventually Duffy overruled me. Then I saw you at Pittock, and I knew I would do anything to keep you close. I told him what I wanted, and we made a deal. It was so… easy."

"I don't need that job, Helen. I never did." Adair pressed a hand to Helen's cheek, catching her first tear.

"I didn't do it because *you* need a salary. I did it to keep you close. I never thought you would stay for me." Helen did not meet Adair's eyes, but she reached up and touched the diamond stud in Adair's ear. *I still don't.* "But I thought you might stay for your students. Then we got upstairs, and I realized what I had done. He was naked. I hated him." Helen traced the curve of Adair's ear. "Then you walked in with your hand bleeding, and *he* came down, and I thought, she'll never have me if she knows what I was going to do."

"It doesn't matter what you've done. We've all done things."

"But it does." Helen let her hand fall to her lap. "Duffy told the board I propositioned him. It's sexual harassment. It's a textbook case. I have to go back and tell the board what happened, otherwise he's going to press charges against you. Unless they know he tried to force me they'll charge you with assault."

"This is nothing." Adair shrugged. "We'll get a lawyer. I'll call Monty."

Helen shook her head. "It doesn't work that way for real people."

Adair looked confused.

Helen remembered Adair striding across the Pittock quad. It was winter, her long coat flaring out behind her, her breath crystallizing in the cold air, the flash of her lipstick the only real color in the winter gray. That rare beauty. *She doesn't understand,* Helen thought and loved her all the more for her simple, aristocratic innocence. "I would have gone through with it," Helen added, "if I thought it would have worked. I only stopped because I realized you can't buy that. You can't sell it."

"What?"

"Love."

"I'm not worth it," Adair said gently.

"But you are." Helen felt tears cover the surface of her eyes and then spill down her cheeks. She closed her eyes and let Adair pull her into an embrace. When she cried, she cried for the months she had waited for Adair's phone call. And she cried for Adair's tragic letter. She cried for her own body that she had been willing to waste on Bruno Duffy, and for Adair's suffering, and for the fear that now edged every minute with red. "I'm sorry," she choked out.

Adair moved to her side and put her arms around Helen. "Can I tell you something?" she asked eventually.

Helen swallowed a sob. "Of course."

"Can I tell you about Cecelia?"

Despite Adair's arms around her, Helen stiffened. Cecelia was beautiful, and she came from the same extravagant wealth that surrounded Adair. It was easy to be jealous. "You can tell me anything," she said.

"You saw the marks on my back."

"Yes." Helen clutched Adair.

"It started when I was twenty, after Soledad left me and my mother died. I was so unhappy. The doctors called it anorexia, but it was so much bigger than that." She rocked Helen gently as she spoke. "I had this vision of a croquet party. Me and my family and everyone we knew except for Soledad, were on a lawn playing and drinking lemonade. But at the edge of the lawn was a cliff. No one saw it but me, and when I looked over the edge, there was nothing. We were just tiny, meaningless figurines surrounded by nothingness. I went back to college, but I stopped eating. Soledad was gone. My mother was gone. Blaine had left home." Adair twined her fingers loosely through Helen's hair.

"What happened?" Helen asked, not wanting to hear the answer but certain she had to ask.

"Cyrus sent me to a facility. The family told everyone I was studying abroad. The doctors fed me with a tube and showed me pictures of fat women and told me they were beautiful. They were beautiful, but that wasn't the point." Adair went on, her voice calm as though she were recounting a film that she had watched. "None of them understood. Then one day Cecelia arrived. She took me out on a day pass and rented a hotel room. She blindfolded me and tied me." Adair's voice grew distant. "There is a state called subspace. It's a kind of trance where you disappear. You float away. Who you are becomes just your skin, or your back, or lips, or nothing. Even pain becomes a kind of meditation. She took me there. It was like floating into that void at the edge of the cliff and finding there were only clouds and space. She hurt me too, but it didn't matter."

A tiny voice in the back of Helen's mind whispered, *they come from the same world.*

"After several visits, I started eating again. The facility said it was a miracle cure."

"Do you still want that?" Helen whispered.

Outside the hotel room, the sounds of real life rattled like coins in a box. A garbage truck. A housekeeping cart.

"It was never sexual with Cecelia," Adair said. "It can be, but it wasn't with her. Not for me. As soon as I was released, I broke it off. I didn't think she would care. I needed what she gave me, but she was cruel too, and I didn't want that cruelty to follow me."

"Isn't that the point?" Helen asked. "To be cruel?"

"No. It's the opposite. You're supposed to care for the person in subspace. They say you can't consent when you're in that state. You're helpless. And being a dominant…a top…doesn't mean you want to abuse people. At least it shouldn't. I remember lying there, bound. I couldn't let myself think about what it would be like with someone who…loved me. There was no give and take with her. There was no understanding. She always pushed too far." Adair seemed to be figuring something out. Finally, she added, "I don't know why she married Cyrus."

Helen felt tears pushing at her eyes again. "Do you still love her?" she blurted out. "Do you still want her?"

Adair seemed surprised. She pulled Helen closer, speaking into her hair. "No! I never loved her. I never wanted her. Never," she said vehemently. She drew a breath to speak and then stopped. "I'm sorry. I shouldn't have said anything."

"What *are* you saying?" Helen sat up and looked at her.

Adair hesitated. "With Cecelia...it was wrong. She was never kind. But with someone who loves you..."

Helen gazed into Adair's pale blue eyes. The color of sky. The strange eyes of an arctic dog. She knew that Adair had posed a question, and there would only ever be one answer. She nodded.

"Let me show you. Lay back." Adair arranged the pillows behind Helen's head. "Put your hands here."

She guided Helen's arms above her head. Then she rose and rummaged around in her small satchel of clothing. A moment later, she held a bandana in her hand. She knelt beside Helen on the bed, folded the cloth, and laid it gently over Helen's eyes. "I'm yours, and there's nothing else," Adair said. She secured the bandana behind Helen's head.

A second later, Helen felt the weight of a belt draped across her wrists.

"You can't move," Adair said. She did not tie the belt, just rested it on Helen's wrists. "Because this is holding you down. Okay?"

"Okay." Helen felt her tears recede as Adair began to stroke her body.

"I should have come to you, even though I was sick," Adair said quietly. "I should never have left you."

Goose bumps shivered across Helen's skin.

"I love you, Helen."

The darkness behind the blindfold heightened her senses.

"You don't do anything unless I tell you." Adair's voice took on a deeper tenor.

Helen pressed her hips toward Adair.

"Don't move," Adair said, and Helen felt oddly comforted by the commanding tone. She relaxed into the bed as Adair straddled her, barely touching her body then leaned down, clasping Helen's wrists in her hands and kissing her with just her lips. The combination of the weight of Adair's hands pinning her down and the gentleness of her kiss made Helen's pulse pound between her legs, and yet she felt strangely calm. Her body was swimming behind the blindfold, losing its form as Adair began to massage her breasts.

"Are you comfortable?" Adair asked.

Helen's yes was a sigh.

"Do you trust me?"

"Yes."

Helen felt Adair readjust the belt, looping it around her wrists and buckling it firmly. "Is that okay?"

Helen nodded.

For a moment, Adair's body left hers. She gasped.

"I'm here," Adair said. She slid her hand down Helen's ribs, across her belly, and between her legs. Helen felt the length of her body expand with Adair's touch. Then Adair began to explore her sex. She strained against her bonds.

"Shh," Adair whispered. "I get to enjoy you, and I'll tell you when it's time to come, but you can tell me what you want." Adair's voice was deep and full of love. "I might give you what you want."

Helen barely heard the words because she had forgotten words. She had forgotten thoughts. She had lost all the coordinates that held her to her real life. All she knew was Adair's touch as Adair ran her fingers in and over and around her sex in a myriad of different patterns, each one eliciting a new incarnation of pleasure, like a hundred different flowers opening in time lapse photography.

Finally, the circles Adair traced on her body grew smaller and smaller, and lighter and lighter, until she circled the very tip of Helen's clitoris with a touch as gentle as sunlight and as powerful.

"Do you want to come?"

Helen could almost feel Adair's smile against her skin.

"Yes."

Adair slid down her body, kissing her breasts, her belly, her inner thighs, murmuring words Helen could not decipher. For a long moment, Adair teased the mouth of her sex with her breath and then her tongue. Then she drew Helen's clitoris into her mouth. The darkness filled with stars. The pleasure of Adair's kiss bordered on an exquisite pain that Helen wanted to last and to last because nothing else existed. She was Eve before daybreak. She was the first cell dividing. Then the orgasm surged through her body, and she did not know how she had lived before this pleasure.

Chapter Fifty-two

The next morning, Adair watched as Helen sat on the bed and packed her little duffle. Adair had already packed her own bag.

Helen tucked her toothbrush into her bag and zipped it up. "I am sorry I have to go back to Pittock, but I have to tell the board what happened. I can't let Thompson think you attacked Duffy for no reason. And I can't go on making Patrick lie for me."

"I know." Adair sat down beside Helen. "I'll come back with you. I won't leave you alone, not while Drummond is free. Not ever. We can install a security system. I'll teach you how to shoot." Adair exhaled heavily. Suddenly, she felt tired of the drab hotel room. "I can't believe we didn't find anything. I can't believe they're just…gone."

"Drummond's looking for me. We're looking for the twins." Helen sounded resigned.

"I failed." Adair leaned her elbows on her knees. "I used to worry about failing my students by giving a bad lecture or going too easy on a young actor who wasn't trying. I didn't know what it felt like to really *fail.*"

"You didn't fail." Helen put an arm around Adair's shoulders. "Do you really think Katherine knew nothing?"

"Katherine? That woman was vile." Adair looked up and searched Helen's face. "Do you think she knew something?"

"I don't know." Helen seemed to ponder for a moment. "Before I leave. Before I go back to Pittock, if you want, I'll go talk to her again. Alone."

"I'm not letting you go anywhere alone."

"You're a hothead." Helen punctuated her words with a kiss to Adair's cheek. "But you know that right?" Helen smoothed a hand over Adair's hair. Adair relaxed into the touch, closing her eyes. "You piss people off for all the right reasons. I love that," Helen added. "But sometimes you can get more out of people if you don't tell them what you think."

"What makes you think she knows something?"

"Just let me do this for you. If you come back to Pittock, I know you're coming back for me. Let me at least try to talk to Katherine." Helen kissed Adair.

Adair felt her body expand.

"I don't want you to feel like you failed," Helen said when she drew away. "Ever."

⚜ ⚜ ⚜ ⚜

That afternoon Adair waited in the Stand United office with Chris while another social worker drove Helen out to the Lonely Star Ranch. Chris and her colleague had agreed it would be best if Helen went unaccompanied. "Katherine will hold a grudge," Chris said. "If Helen thinks she has a rapport with her, you can't be there."

Twenty minutes after the pick-up pulled out of the parking lot, Adair started checking her phone.

"It's an hour to get out there," Chris said kindly, sitting down next to Adair on one of the plastic waiting-room chairs. "They haven't even gotten out of

Las Vegas yet. And she'll be fine. I have my reservations about the brothels, but they are highly regulated. She's as safe as she would be at the state fair."

Adair rested her chin on her knuckles, glaring at the linoleum floor. "That doesn't mean much."

Chris leaned forward. "What is it?"

Adair wanted to rip the fading posters off the wall, hurl the desiccated houseplant through the window. Helen had been so casual, as though she was just paying Katherine a social visit. *Just let me do this for you.* Adair had agreed. She had even thanked Helen. Now every cell in her bloodstream hated her decision. "I should never have let her go."

"Why?"

"She's being stalked." It came out sounding like an accusation, but even so the words sounded paltry compared to the terror of Marshal Drummond's bullet. "We both are."

Chris nodded and Adair could see her professional persona slide into place. The social worker. The careful listener. "Tell me more."

She does this all the time. The thought made Adair shudder. "How many women have you actually found?"

"Some," Chris said in a modulated voice. "Tell me about your situation with Helen?"

Adair ran her hands over her face. The room was hot. "Helen and I met about a year ago." She remembered the first time she had seen Helen. She had missed the open forum interviews with the presidential candidates, assuming Drummond would take the position regardless of the other applicants' qualifications. Then one day she had been walking across campus with friends. Helen had strode across their path, her navy suit a sharp contrast to the comfortable denims and tweeds worn by the faculty.

"Who's that?" Adair had asked her friend from the film department.

"You don't know?"

Another friend laughed and pretended to punch her on the arm. "Is she your type?"

The next time Adair saw Helen, she was standing in the forest near Carrie Brown's crime scene, her eyes full of the world's grief. Adair glanced up at Chris's professional concern. "She was my type," Adair said.

Then she told her about the murders at Pittock, about the asylum, and finally about Drummond's appearance in Maine. "God! Why did I let her go? Looking for the twins was *my* idea." Adair checked her phone again. "I should have given her a gun. I need to call her to tell her to come back." It was so clear now.

Chapter Fifty-three

Entering Katherine's room again, Helen had the impression that nothing had moved. The same slit of sunlight escaped the closed curtains. The same roses stood on the table. Katherine sat in the same navy blue kimono, her face composed in the same appraising stare. "You came back." Only her lips moved. "But without your dyke lover."

Helen drew in a deep breath. She would not be goaded. "Yes."

"You disapprove of me so much. Why come back?"

"Adair disapproves." Helen took a seat without invitation, leaning back and regarding Katherine. "But she's young."

Katherine's smile was as sharp as the barbed roses. "You must be in love."

The heat and the darkness were oppressive. Nothing lived there. It was as dry and dead as the empty pool outside.

"I think you know where the twins are," Helen said.

"Why do you say that?"

Helen had lain awake the night before, writing and rewriting this conversation in her mind. "I think you know a lot that goes on." She made a vague gesture toward the ceiling, implying the brothel, the desert, Las Vegas. "I think you're like a spider at the center of her web." It was a gamble.

Katherine frowned, and Helen thought she had misjudged. Then Katherine let out a practiced laugh. "As are you, I presume, in your own little country club life."

"Maybe." Helen smoothed her hand across the sofa's upholstery so that she would not clench her hands into fists.

"And now you want me to do you a favor," Katherine said.

"Yes."

"Why should I?" Katherine's body remained languid. "What could possibly make me want to help you? Even if it didn't mean betraying a client, even if I had nothing to lose? I'd let them take those twins just because you want to find them."

Helen must have recoiled because Katherine said, "Yes. You. And women like you. You come in here with your ideals and this notion that you know something about my life." Katherine rose.

Helen caught a glimpse of navy stilettos etched with red embroidery.

"I know what you think. You think you understand me because you once slept with the wrong man. Maybe it was your sister's boyfriend, back in college?" She stepped in front of Helen. "But you don't get it. You and I are just the same, but it's not because you got drunk once and fucked some low class trucker. It's in your board meetings and your country club, that's where I am." She looked down on Helen, drawing out each word. Helen could imagine Katherine taking the same stance before a man. "Now you want to come in here and tell me to do right because there's still a bit of good in me. You're no better than I am." Katherine stepped closer until her kimono caressed Helen's shoes. Helen could smell her perfume, and beneath that the smell of latex and an artificial strawberry scent.

"I don't think you're that good," Helen said.

"Should I tell your dyke lover because she's so noble?" Katherine asked with a sneer.

"Yes," Helen said quietly.

Katherine laughed.

Helen looked up at her, willing herself not to flinch as Katherine shifted her weight in a practiced movement and revealed a fleeting glimpse of her pale flesh.

"You know, I don't care if they're dead." Helen did not know the truth of the words until she spoke them. "I really don't. But it matters to her." The twins and their legendary innocence, the cheap, hard city with its glittering arteries and its sunburnt hotels with slot machines in every lobby bar. None of it mattered except that it mattered to Adair.

"Twins." Katherine still stood over her, her crotch at Helen's eye level. "Isn't that what we all want? Our other half. Someone who understands *everything*."

"I've never even met them," Helen said. "They're children. They're virgins. They'll suffer. I suffered. But she cares. And if you know the answer, you don't deserve to keep it from her."

"Because I'm a whore?"

"Because you're not her."

"And because you've suffered so much in love," Katherine mocked.

Helen rose quickly, forcing Katherine to take a step back. "Yes!"

In her heels, Katherine stood at least three

inches taller than Helen, but Helen held her stare, her chin tilted up to Katherine's face so close they could have kissed. In the distance beyond the cottage, a man yelled. Then two other voices joined his. A gate clanged. "Yes. I have suffered in love." Helen had not practiced the words that flowed from her. Before she realized what she was saying she was racing through the details of Eliza's death and the Pittock murders, skipping parts that held the story together in a logical chronology, racing from horror to horror. Eliza on the floor. The blood. The coroner's report: she cut her eye out. The photographs of Carrie Brown's severed legs. Marshal Drummond in the asylum. The gun.

"And you think I haven't suffered?" She raised her voice. "Her family kept us apart. Her doctor poisoned her because he was curious, because she was a medical anomaly, because he and some pharmaceutical company thought they could repackage an old drug, but we finally found each other, and there was some hope. If we could find the twins, help the police…I had this dream that she would love me in this simple way that I don't even think exists anymore. I thought we'd buy a house. We'd grow dahlias and go skiing. But Marshal Drummond is after us now, and he'll always be waiting. And even if he does get caught, I've ruined the life I had there, because I *am* like you, and they've found out. But I can give her *this*. She needs to know. She needs closure. She thinks it's her fault, and the sad thing is…the sad *fucking* thing is that it'll be easier to find them than to convince her she's innocent. So, goddamn it, if you know where they are then tell me because I swear to god, I will find every federal agent in the country and bring them crashing down on this hole because what you do may be legal, but there's something here that stinks, and I will find it."

Outside, there was a rumble of wheels on dust.

Helen's gaze was a saber bared.

Katherine blinked. "Okay." She stepped closer. Suddenly her lips were on Helen's. Helen couldn't breathe. Then Katherine pulled away. "His name is Bi Jiao Hui, but he's a white American. He took the name when he moved to China. He's buying the twins to fulfill some vendetta. There's another man. There always is. He wants them more. So Bi Jiao hired some bottom to steal them from his purveyor. There's going to be a drop at an abandoned airstrip called the Minotaur. It's outside of Reno, about a hundred miles in the desert. It used to be for military practice. It's not on the map, but you can see it in the satellite pictures. It's going to happen within the week, and then it's going to be war."

An engine roared outside. They both glanced at the door.

"How do you know?" Helen asked.

"Because Bi Jiao Hui is my lover."

There was a knock on the door, then the sound of someone rattling the doorknob. Katherine did not move. Something large and heavy hit the wooden door.

Helen gasped.

"Is that for you?" Katherine asked.

The door frame jumped as someone threw their weight against it.

"Adair?" Helen whispered.

The deadbolt released its shallow grip on the doorframe. Helen screamed.

Katherine stepped back. "Is it him?" Katherine yelled, her voice losing its practiced cadence and becoming the voice of a woman in fear.

Chapter Fifty-four

The depth of Adair's anxiety must have affected Chris because they both jumped when Adair's phone rang. Adair answered.

"Please come back, Helen," she begged as soon as she heard a breath on the other end. "I don't want you out there. I should never have let you go."

"It's not Helen." The social worker's voice sounded distant and tinny.

Adair felt the air leave the room. "Where's Helen?"

"Someone followed us out here." Even through the bad connection, Adair could hear the woman's voice shake. "They turned off before the ranch, so we thought it was nothing."

Adair heard a police siren in the background.

"What happened? Where's Helen?"

There was a burr of static, then the social worker said, "There was a man. I think...I think he killed Katherine. He took Helen with him."

The next thing Adair was aware of was Chris prying the phone from her hand.

"I've called the police," Chris said. "They're looking for her. Can you hear me?"

Adair let go of the phone and fell to her knees. She was too shocked to cry. Her head felt light, and her chest hurt as though Drummond's bullet had pierced her. She thought maybe she was having a heart attack.

Chris knelt beside her. "I've called the police," she said again. "Everyone is looking for her right now."

Time seemed to expand between breaths. "They won't find her." Adair's despair was as deep as the pain in her chest. "Oh, my God. He's going to cut off her legs. I have to find her. Did he kill her?"

"No. The police say he killed Katherine, but he took Helen alive. They're in a white van, and the police are looking for them. The police are trained in this kind of rescue." Chris was reciting a litany she had said before. Adair looked up at her face. A good face. A kind face. A woman who had spent her life counseling grieving mothers and tearful fathers.

"How many have you saved?" Adair whispered.

"A lot."

"How many?"

"The police are going to update us hourly."

"How many girls have you saved?" Adair yelled.

"Eight." Chris's lips pressed into a frown. "They're going to find her."

"I need my phone." There was only one thing to do, one chance. She dialed. "Monty, I need you."

On the other end of the line, Adair heard a phone switch to speaker.

"Hello, sweetheart," Cecelia said.

"Wait," Adair called to her brother, but the sound on the other end told her he had left the room.

"Is it time to come home?" Cecelia's voice was treacle sweet, and in the depths of the black treacle was a knife aimed at Adair's heart.

There was nothing she could do but beg.

"Drummond has Helen. You said you know someone, a man in the FBI who found people." Static crackled on Cecelia's speaker phone, and Adair heard her own voice broadcast a half-second after she spoke.

"I suppose you want me to find your precious twins too, go dedicate myself to charity, live a godly life," Cecelia said.

Adair rose and walked to the window. "Just find Helen."

"Why should I help your little secretary when you know I love you?"

"If you loved me, you would help me." Adair touched her fingertips to the window, meeting her own panicked reflection.

"Charming." Cecelia chuckled. "Did you hear that in a Disney movie? Love doesn't mean lying down in the road like a dog while your lover fucks some blue collar whore."

"You kept her from me!"

"She's common," Cecelia snapped.

"None of this would have happened if it weren't for you." The waste of it all hit her like a physical blow. If Doctor Chastain had not prescribed the Texidol, she would never have fallen for the simple ruse of a blocked area code. She would have gotten on her motorcycle and been in Helen's arms. Helen would never have felt compelled to fuck Bruno Duffy. Adair would never have been bored—as Cecelia called that liminal state between hope and suicide—and Cecelia would never have sent her to Oquat. The twins would have remained with their family, the scholarship unclaimed.

With utter clarity, Adair saw the life she could have had. Days spent laughing with her students. Nights in the theater surrounded by the familiar smells of sweat and grease paint. Helen would sit for opening night and afterward she would appear like a vision on the edge of whatever party Adair had been dragged to. The whole campus would know. The gay students would smile when they passed. They would have kept their relationship a secret for a year or two. Then perhaps they would have had a wedding in the quad, bought a house together, and slowly forgotten Drummond because he would never have been released.

"How did you lose your Cinderella? So careless," Cecelia said.

"She thought she could find out where the twins were."

"Did she?" Curiosity sparked in Cecelia's voice. "Does she know where they are?"

"I don't know."

"But you think she knows?" Cecelia pressed.

"She went to see a prostitute named Katherine. She thought Katherine knew. She was with Katherine when Drummond took her. Please, Cecelia, I'll do anything to get her back," Adair sobbed.

"Anything?" Cecelia asked.

Chapter Fifty-five

The stillness struck Cecelia even before she noticed the blood. She had wondered why Cyrus decided to retire to his private study in the middle of the day, especially since Monty and Belinda were traveling. They had the estate to themselves, not that they made use of it in the way other couples might. Now she understood. Even in death, the Wilsons had a sense of decorum. She loved that about the family, loved the way Merrill wore an evening gown to dinner, even though she dressed like an action movie heroine the rest of the time. And she loved that Cyrus had shot himself in his own room, at his own desk, far away from the army of staff that Monty and Belinda employed.

She tiptoed into the room.

It was still shocking. Men were more emphatic about these things. The way his face rested on the table told her the exit wound had taken off most of his jaw. The blood that pooled around his chair was still tacky. His Glock lay on the floor. She walked around the splatter. On the desk, a note rested in a plastic Ziploc bag. He had not taken any chances. *Cecelia,* it read in his heavy, block print.

I have very little to write to you now at the end. You are vile, and I have always loathed you, as I loathe our family and our profession. You know the request I would beg of you if I had any hope that you possessed an ounce of integrity. Mine, I realize, is only nostalgia.

I used to watch her running through the fields by the creek. She played with imaginary horses when we had a real stable. She built castles out of willow branches when we lived in a castle.

I think, if I had been born to another family, I would have loved her as a man, and she would have saved me. As it was, I tried to protect her as a brother. I failed.

Cyrus

"I didn't know you were such a poet," Cecelia said. Still the air pressed on her like a shroud. She could smell his blood. She could see Merrill running through the fields, her flaxen hair the color of thistle tufts in sunlight. "Fuck you, Cyrus," she said out loud. Then she left the room, locking the door from the inside. In the hall outside, she dialed her housekeeper. "I'll be traveling for the next week. We won't need anyone."

"And Mr. Wilson?"

"He's out of town."

Chapter Fifty-six

Helen woke to the pain in her head. She could see nothing. She blinked her eyes to make sure they were open. Then she touched the gash where Drummond had hit her. The memory came back to her in pieces like photographs tumbling from a police file...he had hit her with a heavy baton. Across the chest. Then he had sprung on Katherine. "Where are they?" he had yelled.

When Katherine recoiled, he hit her across the face.

"You know!" he yelled.

Panicking, Katherine poured out the same information she had told Helen.

"Is that what you want?" Katherine pleaded. "Is that what you've come for?"

Then Drummond struck Katherine across the neck. Helen heard a crack. Katherine opened her mouth. A sickening gurgle escaped her lips. She dropped to the floor as though her legs had been cut out beneath her. Helen lunged for the door. A second later, Drummond had hit her across the head. That was the last thing she remembered.

Now Helen struggled to a sitting position. Her chest ached. Her head throbbed. She was desperately thirsty. It was dark. The air was stifling. She could tell she was in a vehicle traveling over rough terrain. Every bump sent a bolt of pain through her temple.

She felt around. The floor was corrugated plastic. The walls were hot metal.

She felt panic rising in her chest. She couldn't breathe. She had to get out. He was going to torture her. The pain in her head foretold the future. She stood up, stumbling as the vehicle—a van she guessed—hit another bump. She fell toward the door, fumbling for a latch. Anything would be better than the heat, and the darkness, and the future. She would hurl herself onto the road. It didn't matter. She would probably die. It was better than this blackness. Her hands clawed the metal door, yanking on every exposed bolt, scratching at a coffin lid. Her breath came faster. Suddenly the darkness was full of orange spirals, like the pattern behind closed eyes, only sharper, like saw blades rotating with clockwork precision. Wheels within wheels. Some disassociated part of her wondered if she had a concussion. She knew the signs. Headaches. Confusion. Lack of coordination. Did you need water for a concussion or was that heat stroke?

She sunk to the floor, curling into the fetal position. Her mouth felt like it had been pasted shut. For a long time she did not know if she were living or dead. She thought she had stopped breathing, but her mind still existed.

I think therefore I am.

She remembered a lecture hall. She saw it, suddenly. The long tables curved around a podium at the center of the amphitheater. She was a freshman. Her notes scrawled across every inch of her notebook page, but she did not understand the lesson.

"Kierkegaard writes that every man must be an end onto himself," the professor said in a monotone.

The girl in the row behind her leaned over,

her thick brown hair brushing Helen's shoulder. She handed Helen her own notebook. There was a sketch of a woman chewing on her pencil. It took Helen a moment to realize the drawing was of her.

Then it was Adair at the podium. Helen could not make out all the words, but she could hear the cadence. She caught the word "diaspora," then a pause. Adair chuckled. "Surprisingly, we've come to know this as Shakespearean," Adair said. Helen knew, without knowing, that this joke was meant for her, and that its secret was their lovemaking.

She uncurled from the fetal position. The floor of the van was warm, and she felt very relaxed. A voice startled her. *Help me, Helen.* It was Eliza. She covered her ears with her hands, trying to slip back into the dream about Adair. Eliza's voice grew louder and more serious. It seemed to be coming from very far away, yet it filled the whole space around her.

Wake up, Helen!

Helen cradled her head in her arms. "Go away." She had promised herself she would never answer. If she did not answer, they were just memories. But it didn't matter now. The only thing that mattered was dreaming of Adair.

No! Eliza answered. *It won't help.*

"What won't?" Helen whimpered.

Wake up. He's coming. I love you. Wake up.

"I love you?" Helen sat up. "Eliza?"

Helen reached out as though Eliza might be sitting in front of her.

It doesn't matter, Eliza hissed in her ear. *He's coming.*

Helen felt around. The space was very close. She was surrounded by what felt like boxes. They seemed to shift with the movement of the van, sometimes pressing against her side, sometimes knocking against her back.

You have to get out, Helen. He's coming.

Helen stood. This time she braced herself against something. A crate. She felt around. The back half of the van was definitely filled with boxes. Some were loose and others strapped to the walls by ropes or bungee cords. She felt the door again. There were no catches or handles, but there was a window blackened by paint. She scratched it with her fingernail. It made no mark. She tried for several minutes. Finally a fleck of paint chipped off, letting in a pinprick of light, but it was not enough to illuminate her surroundings. She continued to work at the spot until a massive jolt sent her sprawling.

She landed hard, jamming her wrist against the floor, but she also touched something familiar: a crate wrapped in plastic. She felt the object again. It was a flat of bottles, the kind she had often ordered for meetings on campus. She stretched the plastic wrap and pulled out one of the bottles and drank.

There has to be a way out, Eliza whispered.

Helen felt her way to another box. Her fingers were raw from scraping at the window. Her head hurt. Her side ached with every jolt in the road. Slowly, carefully, methodically, she felt the surface of the box until she touched tape. She followed the tape until she reached a seam. It took her minutes to loosen an edge of tape and strip it off the box, but once she removed the first strip, the cross tape came away easily. She reached inside the box and felt around.

Inside there were more boxes. The first one she pulled out contained only a piece of fabric. The next one held a row of tiny bottles. It was only when she reached the box of syringes that she realized she was unpacking a box of medical supplies. Gauze. Surgical tape. Medicine. Novocain? Or just an anticoagulant? Terror washed over her again. She screamed, but she did not recognize her own voice. She opened her mouth, and it was there, like wind rushing through a tunnel.

Behind her she heard Eliza.

There has to be a saw.

❧ ❧ ❧ ❧

Helen did not know if she stopped screaming or if the sound of the engine simply ate up her voice. In the back of her mind, she heard Eliza whispering, her voice gaining and losing volume as the engine rumbled.

A saw so he can cut off your legs. Find it, Helen. Find it.

Suddenly, the van stopped.

Not yet, Eliza whispered.

Helen froze. Should she scream? She could pound on the door. Someone might hear her. But the van was tilted at an angle as though it had hit a rut. They could be miles from the nearest human being. If he heard her moving around, he would tie her up. He would have a gun. He would strike her again. She had to find a weapon.

A second later, the engine started. The van rocked backward and forward several times, throwing Helen against the walls. Then it resumed its course, and she resumed her search. She was not sure how much time passed, only that the pinprick of light in the painted window went black. It was hard to move around the van. Everywhere she stepped, she stepped on something she had unpacked: a tarp, a box of cans, a pack of batteries, a contraption she guessed was a camping stove.

She had drunk most of the water and urinated once in the corner of the van like an animal. She could smell her own fear. Of course Drummond hadn't left the saw. He hadn't left her a gun either. The search was just a distraction. She hadn't been able to fight him off in the Pittock Asylum when it was daylight and she was well. She would not be able to do it now, bloodied, exhausted, in the desert. He would cut her. She would suffer. And then she would die. For a moment, her rage at the unfairness surpassed her fear. She wanted to live. She thought of the weeks she had spent with Adair—not even weeks, just days. "Is that all?" she cried.

She loves you. Eliza's voice whispered so close to her ear it was inside her head.

The van lurched and the motion sent Helen sprawling. Then the van slowed. He had heard her. She tore at the nearest box, scraping her fingers, throwing bits of cardboard on the floor. There had to be something!

Then she found it. A heavy plastic box with latches on the side. She pried them open, her hands clumsy in the darkness. Inside, she felt hard foam and nestled in the foam: sticks. She pulled one out and ran her fingers up its length. The blade at the end was so fine and sharp she did not feel it cut her finger. She had to taste the blood to know. It was a box of scalpels.

So easy, the voice in her ear said.

The van jerked to a stop. Helen fell backward,

losing her hold on the box. Still she had one scalpel in her hand. She touched the blade again. *So soft*. She could feel Eliza's hand curling over hers.

The driver's side door slammed. She heard footsteps on the side of the van.

I love you. Cut out his eyes. Eliza's voice grew high with panic. *It's so easy. You just follow the bone and then...pluck. Do it now, Helen. Now!*

The door to the back of the van rattled. Drummond was trying to put a key in the lock. She could hear the rage in his movements.

Now.

Helen gripped the scalpel.

The key clicked into place, teeth to jaw. Drummond turned it. She heard a door handle release.

You can win, Helen. You always win.

The door flew open. It was night time, and there was not a light visible anywhere on the horizon, but Helen had been in darkness for hours. The black sky was her day. She saw everything. Drummond peered into the chaos she had wreaked on the van, his teeth set in a grimace, the baton in one hand, a gun in the other.

Deeper, Eliza hissed. *Cut him.*

Helen lunged forward, the scalpel raised in her fist like a knife. The first blow was clumsy. She struck Drummond where his neck joined his shoulder. The tiny blade glanced off his shirt. She didn't know if she had drawn blood. She raised the scalpel again and plunged it at his face. He yelped. She felt the blade hit bone. It was a tiny knife, meant for detail work, but it was strong. She struck again, this time grazing his lips.

He's watching, Eliza hissed. *Cut out his eyes.*

Helen heard the gun drop as Drummond reached

up to cover his eyes. Her fourth blow hit his hands. She sliced between his fingers, searching. A scream and the feel of hard rubber beneath the blade told her, she had connected with his eye. She kicked wildly at the ground until she felt the gun skitter away. Then she wrestled the baton away from Drummond's hand. She took a step away so she could wield it. He had the advantage of height, but his face was bleeding. She could see everything in the moonlight like a black and white movie. He wiped at the blood. She struck his arm with the baton.

The keys, Eliza said.

Helen struck Drummond again across the face. She dropped the scalpel. With her free hand she felt the side of his leg, his pocket. A key, on a little plastic tab as though he had just come from the repair shop or the rental agency. Just another tourist.

She ran to the front of the van, clasping the key with a death grip. She fumbled with the lock. Her whole body was shaking. Finally she got it in and pulled on the handle. The door swung open. She climbed inside, slamming the door shut and pushing down the peg lock on both sides.

A second later Drummond's face appeared in the window, pale and dripping blood.

He pounded on the window. Helen feared the glass would break.

"You're mine!" he screamed.

Helen jammed the key into the ignition. For a sickening second, it would not turn over. They were out of gas. The battery had died. It would only take Drummond minutes to find the gun. She would have to fight him until he shot her. She wondered if she should try to leap out the other side of the van and get the gun before he did. Then the engine coughed and revved to life. She pushed the van into second and lurched forward. Drummond slid away from the window.

All around her was desert. She had only a quarter tank of gas. She could hear the supplies spilling out behind her as she drove. The back doors clanged. In the rearview mirror Drummond stood silhouetted against the sky, his arms raised, limping after her like a runner on the last leg of some marathon in hell.

❧❧❧❧

By the time the sun was up, Helen was out of gas. The needle reached orange and then red. A gas can icon lit up on the dusty dashboard. Then the van sputtered to a stop. She didn't realize the air conditioning had been on. It had probably been on, even in the back of the van. It could not have been more than six in the morning, but the heat was stunning. She stepped out, shielding her eyes. Everything was white dirt and blue sky. The horizon shimmered. She walked around to the back of the van. Most of the supplies had been lost, but a few bottles of water remained in a cardboard pallet strapped to the wall. She took a bottle and drank it in the shade of the van's interior. Twenty-four bottles in a case. There were eight left.

She remembered a disaster preparedness presentation at Pittock. Three gallons of water per day per person in case of emergency. Did she have enough for one day? In the desert, it had to be more. She scanned the horizon for Drummond. She wanted to lock herself in the cab in case he found her, but the heat was suffocating. In the locked cab, she would die within minutes.

She lay down on the floor of the van. She was very tired.

❧ ❧ ❧ ❧

Helen did not know how long she had slept. When she woke the sun was slicing across her face, and she felt sick. Her lips were cracked. The blood had dried on the back of her head where Drummond had hit her as she tried to flee Katherine's house. Now the skin felt swollen and tight. She tried to open another bottle of water, but her hands felt like they were encased in shells. She fumbled with it. In her mind she was crying but there was not enough moisture in her body to release tears.

Slowly she became aware of a noise in the distance, the rumble of an engine. She stared out at the white heat beyond the van. She could see nothing. She held up one hand and peered through her fingers. There was a spot on the horizon. Then it was gone. Then it reappeared, closer this time. Then it veered off into the undulating heat and disappeared. She watched the horizon for a long time, and then she slept again.

Chapter Fifty-seven

The day had passed like the end of the world. Hours turned into eternities while Adair sat in the hotel room, the news garbling in the background, mixing Helen's tragedy with trivia about the weather. Chris had offered to let Adair stay with her family, but Adair could not bear their comfort or the thought than anyone in the world would survive this tragedy and keep on living. Even the children playing kickball in the hotel parking lot had seemed hateful, their shrill voices announcing their indifference to the world. When the news had announced that the search for Helen Ivers had passed the critical twenty-four hour mark, Adair stumbled to the bathroom and vomited until her throat was raw.

Now she lay on the bed, the television playing on mute. The knock on the door did not even startle her. "It's open," she called out.

Cecelia stepped into the room, clearing the stale air with her sharp perfume. She wore a cream pant suit with a low cut blouse and a necklace of diamonds on a thin gold chain. She sniffed. "You're a wreck. This place smells." Cecelia picked Helen's blouse off the back of a chair and threw it onto the bed. She sat down, eyeing Adair. "You look like hell."

Adair closed her eyes.

"You know this would all be more pleasant if you acted halfway glad to see me. Grateful even." Cecelia rose again and threw the curtains open. It was almost dawn. Adair had not slept in forty-eight hours.

"I am grateful," she said.

"Are you?" Cecelia sat down and draped her arms over the sides of her chair. She crossed her ankle over her knee. "I hope you understand how grateful I expect you to be. Come here."

Adair knew. She stood.

"Kiss me."

Adair glanced at the window.

"We can do business in the open, can't we?" Cecelia said, her eyes flashing like sharks deep beneath the surface. "Because that's what this is, isn't it? Business. You want my FBI operative, I want..." She paused for an infinitesimal second in which some truth slipped into her voice. "I want you as I always have." She spread her arms. "Let me see if you're still as good as I remember."

Adair knelt before her. She felt sick. The smell of Cecelia's perfume cut away at her heart. She leaned forward. Cecelia's lips were dry. Her tongue tasted of chartered airplane mini-bars and cocaine. Adair wrapped her arms around Cecelia and leaned in. She tried to think only of the performance, allowing her body to slip into the familiar rhythm, allowing the weight of her chest against Cecelia's knees to signal desire she did not feel. Cecelia's kiss was dry, flat, and empty, like the road outside. Like the desert. Another horror, like the horror of watching the news cut from Helen's abduction to a detergent commercial. Adair glanced at the open curtains. She wanted a stranger to walk by. *See me,* she begged the unyielding universe. *Save me.* After an obligatory minute, she pulled back.

Cecelia's smile was mixed with irritation. "You'll

have to do a little bit better than that."

"Help me find, Helen," Adair said. "Then I'll do whatever you want. I'll come back to New Hampshire. I'll do anything. But first we have to find her."

"How do I know you're going to fulfill your end of the bargain?" Cecelia asked. "What if I bring your precious Helen back and you decide to run off into the sunset?"

"I promise, Cecelia. I promise you anything, anything you want. But if we get there and it's too late, I swear to God I will kill you myself."

"Fine." Cecelia pushed Adair back and stood. "What kind of car are you driving?"

"The M6."

"Christ. We'll have to rent something rugged. They're way out in the desert."

"The FBI already found her?" Adair asked.

Cecelia turned, her dark eyes flashing. "There is no FBI."

⁂

"Where are we going?" Adair asked as they got into Cecelia's rented Escalade. "If you know where they are, we should call the police."

Cecelia sighed. "You really have been in the country too long. They'll head straight over with a helicopter. They have to. What's the liability if they know where she is and they don't take action? As soon as Marshal sees the lights, he'll kill her, or he'll go deeper into hiding. He'll disappear like a rattlesnake." Cecelia threw a GPS up on the dashboard, tapping a set of coordinates onto the screen. "Let's get your little Cinderella."

"What did you mean 'there's no FBI'?" Adair asked.

Cecelia put her hand on Adair' leg, moving it slowly up her thigh until her long nails brushed the seam of Adair's jeans. "I mean I already know where they are."

Adair closed her eyes, trying to divorce herself from her body, trying to calm the terror that welled up in her like blood in an open artery. Helen could be bleeding. She could be dead. Adair tried not to think about what rusty instruments Marshal would use or how little would be left of Helen's soul if they found her maimed in the desert.

In some ways, death would be better. Adair did not know, as they drove along the narrow, desert road, whether she could even hope to find Helen alive now. Perhaps the only grace permitted now was to find that Helen had died a fast, blinding death.

❧❧❧❧

Adair and Cecelia drove for several hours at an excruciatingly slow speed. There was no road, only flat, cracked earth dotted at regular intervals with tufts of gray vegetation. Occasionally, they got up to twenty-five miles per hour. Then the Escalade would hit a deep crack or a patch of rocks and Cecelia would slow down to a crawl.

"Can't you go faster?" Adair pleaded as she watched the speedometer drop below ten miles per hour.

"If one of these rocks flies up and hits the coolant, we'll lose the AC."

"I don't care about the AC."

Cecelia cocked her head. "Without the AC, we die. Knock out the coolant and we're stranded here, and we're dead within the hour."

Adair checked her cell phone. She had no signal. She stared out the window. She could see for miles in every direction. She knew that somewhere there were cities and mountains and people going about their normal lives, but she could only see a faint white haze on the horizon. If Helen were out here, she could not escape. The open space would be her prison. "How do you know where she is? Adair asked, glancing at Cecelia."

"You asked me to know." Cecelia smiled. Half an hour later Cecelia spoke again. "It's around here." She slowed to a stop.

"Here?"

"There." Cecelia pointed.

Indeed there was something on the horizon. Through the shimmer of heat, Adair thought she made out a shack and something white.

"Stay here. You can leave the AC running," Cecelia said. She opened her door. The heat that rushed into the SUV was smothering. She walked around to the back. Adair heard her rattle something in the trunk. A moment later she reappeared wearing a wide, elegant sun hat.

"I'll come with you." Adair got out.

Cecelia drew her gun and trained it on the shack as though testing the distance. "No. I know Marshal. I can talk to him. He'll kill you." Cecelia slipped the gun into the pocket of her slacks.

Adair saw now that Cecelia had dressed for the day. Everything she wore was white, and the loose sleeves of her jacket covered her hands.

"You have a gun I presume?" Cecelia said. "In case something happens. You *are* Cy's prodigy."

Adair reached for the familiar weight of the Glock in her waistband, then remembered the brothel in Maine. "I lost it. How did you know he was here?"

"How inconvenient." Cecelia smiled. "If you just carried your gun in your purse like a woman. But you have to be so butch."

Adair stared out into the vast desert. She did not have the energy to explain that she hadn't lost her gun the way people misplace their keys. She had fled for her life, dragging Helen behind her, every step a step towards Helen's death.

"Stay here. I'll go talk to Marshal about your precious Helen," Cecelia said. "He'll kill her the minute he sees you. That's the whole point."

Adair wanted to fling herself behind the wheel and race toward the shack. She didn't care about the coolant or the heat. If she could be there now! She imagined the blade poised over Helen's thigh. Would he use a knife, or an electric saw that could cut the flesh in seconds? The first would be more painful, but the second would be so fast. "Helen!" Adair cried.

"Shut up." Cecelia strode around the hood of the SUV and grabbed Adair's arm with a tight grip. "Listen to me. If you want to see her alive, you wait here. No heroics. You've tried that before."

"You have to save her. You have to hurry."

"Sit in the fucking car. There's water in the back." Slowly, Cecelia released Adair's arm. Then she leaned up on tiptoe and kissed her quickly. "I love you, Merrill."

❧❧❧❧

The sunset, when it came, was unjustly beautiful, a canvass of gold and pink, mocking Adair's grief. She wondered how far it was until the next tourist town. How many travelers were pulling out their cameras and memorializing the sunset as it darkened from pink to scarlet? There was another life in which she stood at the rim of some highway viewpoint with Helen. They took an ill-framed picture together, Adair holding the camera out in front of them. There was a life that had slipped through her fingers before she even realized it was hers. She closed her eyes and hated the glory of the sky.

✦✦✦✦

Cecelia had still not returned by the time it got dark, but in the distance, Adair saw a spark of light. There was someone at the campsite. It occurred to Adair that perhaps Cecelia had been too bold. She said she knew Drummond. Adair also knew Drummond. She knew how easily he could project the persona of a respectable, antiquated gentleman. He was J. Alfred Prufrock. He was a minor Shakespearean nobleman tottering off the stage. And then he was Marshal Drummond, and the bullet was speeding toward her heart.

She stepped out of the SUV. Far away, she could hear the buzz of a helicopter. She scanned the horizon. Above the hills, silhouetted against the last slash of sunset, she could see it hover like a horsefly. She waved her arms in its direction, then dropped them. It was a ridiculous attempt. The helicopter was miles away.

I love you. Helen's face swam before her eyes.

She checked her cell phone again. There was still no signal. She began to walk in the direction Cecelia had gone. It was farther than she had expected and rockier. Several times she stumbled, tripping over a stone or turning her ankle in a crack in the dry earth. When she was close enough to see her destination clearly, she knelt down. Then on second thought, she lay flat on her belly. She felt the rocks beneath her. A slight breeze stirred the dust around her. She blinked it away.

Before her stood a makeshift encampment built around a dilapidated shed. It could have been a gold-rush homestead long abandoned and preserved by the heat. The small wooden shack leaned to one side. The windows were gaping holes. The door hung ajar. A little farther off, a fire had charred a circle on the ground, but there was no fire now. The area rested in shadow. It took Adair's eyes a moment to adjust to the dimness and see the tableau before her. When she did, she froze.

Near the blackened fire, a man lay face down in the dirt.

A moment later, Cecelia emerged from the shed, her white suit bright against the dark doorway. She stretched her arms and sighed theatrically. "I'm getting rather tired of this game." Her words traveled across the desert.

The man groaned. It was Drummond. "You'll kill me," he said, clawing at the dust.

"You're already dying." Cecelia sounded irritated.

Adair inched forward, cursing the crackle of dry vegetation.

"You can die here, now, as you've clearly planned

on doing, or you can take a risk. Tell me where they are." Cecelia stretched again and yawned, but there was something taut in her casualness. "Tell me where they're going to do the drop, and you'll live."

"Get me some water," Drummond croaked.

Cecelia reached into the satchel thrown over her shoulder and withdrew a bottle of water, cracked the seal, and took a sip. Then she drizzled water onto the sand near his head. He rolled toward it.

"Leave it." Cecelia's voice had lost its breezy tone. She inserted a booted toe under his shoulder and delivered a forceful push, rolling the upper half of his body over, leaving his waist at an odd, broken angle. "Bastard."

Adair crawled closer. She could see Drummond's face. His eyes sunk into hollow cheeks. His mouth hung open. His lips receded. His teeth bared. His chest rose and fell quickly.

"Where are they?" Cecelia demanded. "You said she knew. Tell me, and I might let you live." Cecelia kicked a swift blow to the juncture between shoulder and neck. Drummond convulsed. "But if you wait me out, and they're gone, I swear to God I'll cut your other leg off and leave you here to die."

"Water," he gasped.

She knelt down beside him.

"I will kill you." This time her voice was poisonously sweet, but there was fear in it too. This mattered to Cecelia. There was something wrong. "Now tell me." She stood up again. Her white suit glowed. She sipped the water and then spat it in Drummond's face. "Tell me!"

Cecelia delivered another kick to Drummond's shoulder and then one to his head.

Drummond mumbled something else. "I don't remember."

"I don't believe you."

"Take me back to town, and I'll tell you," Drummond said.

"So you *do* remember." She stepped forward and must have stepped on Drummond's hand because he let out a howl. "Do you know what I remember? I remember that we had a deal." Cecelia must have stepped down harder, because Drummond screamed again. "You give me the twins, I give you Helen."

Adair's heart seized. A voice in her mind screamed along with Drummond. *No!* She pressed her chest to the ground.

You give me the twins, I give you Helen.

Cecelia twisted her booted foot.

"Outside Reno." Drummond convulsed.

"Where?"

"An airstrip."

"Where!" Cecelia yelled.

"They call it the Minotaur." Drummond rose up, struggled for a moment, then fell back again. "Stop!"

Cecelia stepped back. "Now that wasn't so hard. When is the drop?"

Adair had always known Cecelia was jealous.

I'll call Doctor Chastain about increasing your dosage.

"And who is the buyer?" Cecelia kicked Drummond again.

Why do I love you, and you never love me back?

"Some American with a Chinese name."

"Samuel Buchannan?"

She doesn't want you broken.

"I don't know," Drummond pleaded.

I love you, Merrill.

"And you thought you could step in and get some of that money for yourself," Cecelia said. "Did you think that? Did you think you could strike a deal with Samuel Buchannan?"

"I didn't. I only wanted Helen. I don't care about the money. I don't care about the twins."

Cecelia looked up. Even in the darkness Adair knew when Cecelia's eyes met hers. A slow smile spread over Cecelia's face. She readjusted the grip of her gun. It was a Browning Medalist .22. Adair had seen it up close. It was a beautiful gun. The thought flashed through her mind, a tiny piece of detritus shaken loose by the storm. Cecelia had customized the pistol with elegant filigrees engraved on the silver slide. Cyrus would have called it a woman's gun.

Cecelia turned toward Drummond. "Thank you, Marshal."

And as Adair watched, Cecelia leaned over Drummond, turned her face away as though from the opening door of an oven, and shot him, point blank, in the head.

She didn't have a silencer on the .22. Still the shot didn't seem loud enough to kill a man. It was just a ping, a rock hitting the windshield, a little puff of air, and Marshal Drummond was dead.

"I'm sorry, Merrill," Cecelia called out. "Did you want the honor?"

You give me the twins, I give you Helen.

Adair rose and stumbled toward the blackened campfire. "Where is she?" Adair cried, rushing past Cecelia and staggering into the shed, nearly pulling the door off its rusty hinges. "Helen!" The room was dark. There was something on the floor. She fell to her knees, feeling the shape, but it was only an empty sleeping bag. She looked around. There was an empty jug and a can of coffee, nothing else. She ran outside, glancing frantically back and forth for a sign.

"She's not here," Cecelia called.

"No!" If Helen was not there, then Drummond was the only one who knew where she was. Adair fell to the ground by his side and pressed her hands to the bullet wound in Drummond's forehead. "He knows," she screamed. "Where is she?"

She tried to compress his heart while still holding her left hand to his forehead. Blood exploded on the ground behind him. She smelled his urine and feces, or maybe it was hers. "Where is she?" she sobbed.

She beat his chest with her fists, pummeling him, screaming obscenities although no words were deplorable enough. Then she lurched to her feet and kicked Drummond's head as hard as she could, feeling bone crack beneath her boot, and feeling the impotence of every blow. He was just sand now.

Slowly she became aware of Cecelia speaking. It was not to her. A radio crackled. Every once in a while, Cecelia paused as though someone responded to her. Adair heard the whir of a helicopter. She turned toward Cecelia. "How could you?" she asked.

Cecelia pocketed a small transmitter, tucked the Browning Medalist in her satchel, and struck Adair across the face with the flat of her hand. "Better?" she asked mildly.

Adair flew at her, ready to pummel her like she had pummeled Drummond's body, but she was blinded by tears. Cecelia dodged out of her way. Adair's foot caught on the edge of a stone. She pitched forward onto her knees. A second later, she felt a blow to her stomach and she doubled over. "Why, Cecelia?" she said with the last air in her lungs.

The helicopter that had been buzzing in the background was right above their heads. Cecelia's words were almost lost in the rhythmic beating of the propeller, but she did not need to hear the voice to hear the words.

I love you, Merrill.

The helicopter landed in a rain of dust. In the dark, it looked like a medieval beast with one staring eye, the headlight fixed on the scene of Drummond's death.

"Now get up." Cecelia grabbed Adair by the arm and moved her toward the helicopter.

As they approached, two men—one white, one black—jumped to the ground. The white man carried a semiautomatic rifle and a heavy, rubber bag the size of a small man. The black man carried a medical kit. The red cross glowed on its pale surface.

Adair turned. Even as Cecelia pushed her toward the helicopter, she saw the man with the rifle pause and survey Drummond's body. Then he whirled his rifle around and struck Drummond's mouth with the butt end.

"Get in," Cecelia called over the noise.

The helicopter was nothing like the Sikorsky the Wilsons owned. The Sikorsky came complete with curtains, calf-leather seats, and private bathroom. Here the entire interior seemed to be made of black plastic. Six seats were bolted to the floor like an afterthought. Straps, headsets, and nets hung from the ceiling. At the front of the helicopter, two men sat strapped into the pilots' seats, with pads on either side of their heads as though to prevent whiplash. Neither of them turned, but one of them, a ruddy blond man with a heavy South African accent, asked, "Who is she?"

He and the other man exchanged a few words in a language Adair did not recognize.

"She's coming with us," Cecelia said. She pointed to a seat made of mesh and steel rods. "Sit," she told Adair.

The two men conversed in their own language. Then the co-pilot, a skinny man with the same impossibly dark skin as the doctor outside, said, "No. She is not." He moved a pistol from his lap to his hand and held it loosely, pointed in Adair's direction. "No."

"She was not part of the original agreement," the white South African added.

"She is part of every agreement," Cecelia said.

"Then who is she?" the white man demanded.

Cecelia leaned forward. Her voice spoke straight to the gun. "She's the purveyor."

Chapter Fifty-eight

A few minutes later, the other two men hauled the rubber bag onto the floor of the helicopter. Adair tried not to look.

Once they were airborne, Cecelia gestured to Adair to put on a headset. Adair obeyed as if in a trance. Inside the quiet of the large earphones she could hear the pilot talking in his own language. The other men remained motionless watching her with weapons ready. Cecelia lowered the microphone attached to her headphones.

"You didn't really think we'd find her, did you?" Cecelia asked.

Adair turned to the window, her back to Cecelia.

"He told me what happened," Cecelia continued, her voice close in Adair's ear. "He tried to do it as soon as he got her into the desert, before he set up all that phony medical equipment. He just couldn't resist."

Adair said nothing.

"He hit an artery on the first cut. He was so eager, he didn't tie the tourniquet. She bled out in minutes."

Below them the desert sparked with one light and then another, then a little cluster of lights in a tiny grid. Some small town, some dusty outpost.

"You should be happy," Cecelia added. "She didn't suffer much."

"What did he do with her body?" Adair couldn't hear her own voice in the headset. She remembered being in the sound booth at the Pittock theater and turning off the speakers that connected the booth to the stage. *Another life.*

"In the desert," Cecelia said.

"And what is all this?" Adair asked without looking at her. She felt very cold. In the back of her mind, it occurred to her that she was probably going into shock.

"You'll see," Cecelia said.

❧ ❧ ❧ ❧

Less than an hour later, they flew into the opulent glow of Las Vegas. All the attractions were visible like a light-up version of the world's fair. The Eiffel Tower. The Sphinx. The London Ferris wheel. At the heart of it, the strip glared up at them, like a neon gash in the crust of the earth.

The pilot spoke to the radio. "UD1 Black, VFR entering Las Vegas airspace. South at or below 500 feet." His accent had disappeared. "Landing with permission at 35.0900° North, 125.1242° West."

The radio crackled a response. "UD1 Black, approved."

A few minutes later, they were honing in on a building located on a bluff outside the town. The pilot deftly landed the helicopter on a roof, avoiding the vents and chimneys that jutted through the tarry surface. The guards nodded to each other and bagged their guns in black nylon duffle bags. From a compartment in the side of the helicopter, they removed blue polo shirts with the words "Mansfield Security Co." printed in white capitals on the breast. These they put on over their camouflage.

Adair was struck by how quickly they went from foreign mercenaries to respectable paramilitary. She could almost imagine them strolling the grounds of the Wilson estate, flirting with the maids and making obsequious conversation with her brothers. Only they weren't. One man had her by the elbow. The other positioned himself on her other side. Close. Almost touching. They were making sure she did not run. She glanced back at Cecelia although she did not know if it was fear or familiarity that made her seek out Cecelia's face.

"Let's go," Cecelia said to the guards.

One of the men unlatched the door. He held Adair's elbow as she descended. The air outside was warm, but not as hot as the desert. From where they had landed, Adair could not see the city below, but she could see its glow, like a chemical fire burning in the valley. The man on her right gestured toward a small concrete bunker built on top of the roof.

"Where are we going?" Adair tried pulling away.

"Be quiet, Merrill," Cecelia hissed. "These aren't my men."

Behind them the helicopter's propellers sped up, their sound displacing the air around them. The guard to her right held her tightly. The guard on her left raised two fingers in salute to the pilot. The helicopter lifted and a second later they were left in silence: the three armed guards, Cecelia, and herself.

The third guard unlocked the door to the bunker. Inside a blue fluorescent light came on, illuminating a stairwell. Their feet rang out on the concrete as they descended one flight of stairs. When the man opened the door at the bottom of the stairs, Adair stumbled back in surprise. She had not recognized the Josslin

Heights Las Vegas from above, but she had been in this suite before. It was the executive suite. It looked like the one in Maine. The same kitchenette. The same faux fireplace. She could almost see Helen standing before the floor-to-ceiling windows, her hair smooth, her forehead creased with worry. *You could have asked me.*

"Come in. Rest, Merrill," Cecelia said as though they were merely tourists. She turned to the guards. "Don't disturb us." She led Adair to the bedroom.

"I won't fuck you," Adair said when the door closed behind them. "I'd rather die."

"You're so melodramatic."

Adair walked over to the window. The hotel was located above Las Vegas. Somehow her brothers had bought an unobstructed view of the city. The lights spread out before them. "I used to be," she said.

"You really should clean yourself up, Merrill."

Cecelia looked fresh in her white suit, although when Adair looked closely she could see Drummond's blood spray on the cuff of her pants.

"Why are we here?"

"Why? Because Marshal told me where we'd find your precious twins. Because I've employed those men to ensure we recoup them safely. Because we can wait here while they do that. Because you asked me to come."

"Who are they?"

"They're on loan from a business partner, a man named Harlow Galloway. Do you know him?"

"No."

Cecelia leaned in so that her lips were an inch from Adair's. "Would you really rather die? You know, it's actually kind of romantic. We're bound together. Even your death is part of who we are."

"Are you going to kill me?" Adair asked.

"Of course not. I'll never let you go." She touched Adair's cheek.

Adair grabbed her wrist and twisted it back. She could see Cecelia's eyes widen as the pain startled her, but Cecelia did not pull away. Adair searched her face. She had known Cecelia since she was fourteen. She had laid beneath her. She had let Cecelia beat her. She had let Cecelia save her. "Why did you kill Marshal Drummond?" Adair asked, searching her eyes.

"He's a predator. You can't trust the courts to protect you. I won't let him hurt you." Cecelia was too smart to look away when she lied, but Adair saw the lie in her pupils like coins dropped in a dark well.

"You don't know where Helen is!" The thought struck her suddenly. Hope filled her lungs. "She wasn't there. You don't know if he lied." She twisted Cecelia's arm back.

Cecelia cried out.

"What did he really tell you?" Adair reached for Cecelia's other arm, to pin it back, to throw her to the floor, but Cecelia was faster. She raised her arm, out of Adair's reach, then slashed it down. Adair caught the movement out of the corner of her eye. Too late, she realized there was something in Cecelia's hand. She felt the blow hit the juncture between her neck and her shoulder. A split second later, she felt the sting of a needle entering her muscle. She heard the hiss of an auto-injector. The dose of Texidol was larger than any she had ever taken, but she recognized the pain as soon as the drug hit her bloodstream. It seized her from inside. She dropped Cecelia's wrist and tried to scream. Then she hit the floor and the world went black.

Chapter Fifty-nine

When Helen woke it was dark and the engine noise was louder. She opened her eyes to see headlights. They were close and fixed on her like the eyes of a predator. She crawled to the back of the van. She wanted to grab something, to fight, but her body felt like an empty grain sack. She couldn't stand. She was desperately thirsty.

A second later, the vehicle stopped, its lights illuminating her. It was Drummond. He had come back to get her, she knew, although she could not see anything in the glare of the headlights. She opened her mouth. Nothing came out. Someone got out of the car and walked across the beams, a huge shadow in the shape of a man.

Hold on, Eliza said quietly. *I love you.*

❧❧❧❧

When Helen jerked awake she found an IV skewered her wrist. She tried to pull it out, but a man's hand stopped her. She opened her mouth to scream.

"You're safe," the man said. He had a heavy Spanish accent.

Helen looked around. If it weren't for the IV, she could have been at a retreat center. The room reminded her of a monastery where she had stayed during a leadership conference. It was pleasant and light. The furnishings were simple–an icon, a wooden chair, a small writing table, a window seat lined with faded cushions.

Helen stretched her legs beneath the blanket. Her body was intact. "Where am I?"

The man sitting beside her had a sun-worn face and eyes so narrow they disappeared in his cheeks. He held a cowboy hat in his lap. On his button front shirt, he wore a silver badge.

"The nurses said you might be frightened when you woke up, so I stayed. You're at the Hermosa Madre Medical Clinic outside of Las Vegas." He toyed with the cowboy hat in his hands. "I'm Sheriff Jimenez. I found you. Do you remember what happened?"

A nurse in a simple white dress and wimple entered. "You'll have to let her rest."

"No, wait." Helen sat up. "You need to call my friend! Adair Wilson. You have to find her."

The nurse touched a dial on the IV.

"Adair…" A moment later, Helen felt herself pulled into a deep and dreamless sleep.

✿ ✿ ✿ ✿

When Helen woke again, the sheriff was sitting on the window seat, his cowboy hat still in his lap. At the foot of the bed stood two uniformed police officers. The nurse stood in the corner, her face set in a slight frown. Helen watched the door, waiting for Adair to appear, waiting to see the smile spread across her face. She was surprised that Adair had not already sent some ridiculously extravagant bouquet, and her surprise was quickly turning to fear. "What happened?" She looked at the sheriff.

"Is she well enough to talk?" he asked the nurse.

"For a few minutes."

Jimenez leaned forward. "Everyone heard the bulletin about your abduction." He spoke slowly. "I knew a man down on Pahrump Valley Road. He runs a little country store for the folks out there and the mountain climbers who want to climb Spring Mountain. He said a man had been coming around. It wasn't what he bought." Jimenez shook his head. "Randy said it was what he *didn't* have. No kids. No buddies. And he was an older guy, not tough enough to go desert camping, not the right supplies either. Just didn't seem right. Randy never got a license or a make on the guy's car. He always walked in from down the road."

"You're a lucky woman," one of the police officers said. He was a heavyset man of about fifty, with a face that must once have been handsome and had now slid into kindliness. "We had reports of a white van heading toward Henderson. We had a search party spreading out from Henderson to Boulder City to Sloan, but he doubled back, headed toward Pahrump and Ash Meadows Wildlife Preserve. Jimenez knows that area."

"These guys were right behind me when I headed out," Jimenez said modestly. "But I know what happens in the desert. I had to get to you as soon as I could. Didn't know if you had water."

Helen touched her head. A gauze pad covered the place where Drummond had hit her.

"They have you on fluids," Jimenez added. "And you got a bad bump on your head, bruises on your chest. But they took an X-ray. No fractures."

The kind-faced police officer cleared his throat.

"The doctor performed a rape kit. The results were negative."

Helen opened her mouth to speak, but words eluded her.

"I'm Officer Collins," he added, "and this is my partner Officer Dayne. If you're up to it, we'd like to ask you a few questions."

Helen nodded.

Collins took a note book from his shirt pocket and made a few notes, then asked Helen to spell her name. "How did you know your assailant?"

In a shaky voice, Helen recounted the events, starting with Carrie Brown's murder and ending with Drummond breaking down the door of Katherine's cabin. She kept waiting for a moment to ask about Adair, but the police officer's questions flowed one to the next.

"And did you make a positive visual ID on Marshal Drummond?" Collins asked, making a note in his book.

"Did you see his face?" his partner clarified.

"Yes," Helen said.

"At approximately what time did you see him enter Katherine Fenning's lodging at the Lonely Star Ranch?" Collins asked.

"About noon." Helen hesitated. "I don't know. Maybe it was still morning. My friend Adair, she was waiting for me at the Stand United office. Is she here?"

"Did he say anything to you?" Collins asked.

"He asked about the twins. It was like he was looking for them too, and Katherine knew where they were. She said she was sleeping with a man named…I can't remember. He had a Chinese name, but she said he was a white American. Has anyone come to see me?"

Collins fidgeted with something on his belt.

"He's still out there, isn't he?" She looked at the sheriff. "That's why you're here. To protect me from him."

"No," Jimenez said.

"Did you catch him?" Helen did not dare to hope. Then another thought pushed all others aside. "He got Adair, didn't he?" Helen felt as though a vice had squeezed her chest.

Collins cleared his throat. "Marshal Drummond appears to have been murdered."

If I had killed him, we'd be free. "Murdered?" Helen's heart did not slow its frantic beating. She glanced from Jimenez to Collins to Dayne. The officers remained impassive.

Jimenez leaned over and placed a hand on Helen's wrist. "He's dead."

It took Helen several seconds to speak. "He's really dead?"

"After you escaped," Collins continued, "he remained in the desert near Ash Meadows. He suffered heatstroke and some blood loss. But he was alive when someone shot him at about eighteen hundred hours last night."

"Dead," Helen said again, her thoughts flying to Adair. "Do you know who did it?"

"There were tire tracks leading to the location and an SUV rented under the name of John Chambers," Collins went on, "but no signs of anyone remaining in the area. No footprints leaving the area." He coughed quietly into his hand. "I know you will probably not mourn his death, but anything you can tell us that would shed light on his murder…"

     Karelia Stetz-Waters

Adair had been the first thing on Helen's mind when she woke. She had been anxious to ask about her. Now she was mute.

"Do you know anyone who would want to kill him?" Collins asked.

The nurse stepped forward and placed a hand on Helen's shoulder. "Will you be done soon, Officer?"

"Yes. Of course. Ms. Ivers needs to rest," Collins said apologetically. He turned back to Helen. "Are you sure you can't think of anyone who might have a grudge against Marshal Drummond? Someone who hated him enough to want him dead? We've contacted Carrie Brown's parents, but they don't seem likely candidates."

"No," Helen said quietly. "No one."

"Thank you," Collins said. "Is there anyone you'd like us to call?"

"Just my secretary, Patrick Jayce at Pittock College. He can let everyone else know what they need to know."

After the sheriff and the police officers left, Helen asked the nurse for a telephone. The woman brought in an old push button phone, placed it on the table beside Helen's bed and plugged the cord into a phone jack on the wall.

"It's long distance," Helen said apologetically.

"Don't worry." The nurse patted her arm. "You've earned it."

When the nurse left, Helen dialed Adair's number and got her voicemail. She rattled off a message. "The police have been here to ask me about Drummond. He's been murdered. I told them I didn't know anyone who would want to do that." A few minutes later, Helen jumped at the sound of the phone ringing, but it was only Patrick.

"The whole town is talking about you, and Duffy has come off looking like a complete asshole. He said you'd skipped town to get away from the sexual harassment charge. Next thing you know, the board turns on the TV, and there you are on *every* channel. The woman who fought off Marshal Drummond and lived. They think you missed the board meeting because you were in the back of Drummond's van fighting for your life."

"Have you heard from Adair?" Helen interrupted.

"I know. I know. I'm chopped liver. But no, why?"

Helen lowered her voice. "I haven't heard from her since…Drummond. It must have been in the news. She must know that I'm okay, but she hasn't come to see me. And Drummond's dead, Patrick. Someone killed him. Do you understand what I'm saying? Adair is missing, and someone killed Drummond."

"Shh. Shh," he lisped. "Don't go there. She's crazy, but she's not *crazy*. I'll find her. You're new to this gay thing. They probably didn't let her into the hospital because she's not family. Welcome to conservative America. I'll get her in there. Just don't French kiss her if she says she's your sister."

From the Diary of Charity Kimball

I woke to the sound of Prudence's thoughts stirring like winter bears waking in the spring. We lay in an enormous bed. Only in the sad woman's home have I felt a bed as soft. It was like lying on a cloud, and for a moment, I thought we were in heaven. Indeed, when I looked to my side, I again saw the tablet that is like a miracle, for it is a window to distant places. Again the man named Harlow gazed out at us like an angel.

Prudence was still sleeping, although I could hear her dreams again. I reached out toward the man, careful not to wake her. "Are you real," I asked. My voice was very weak. I could not tell if he heard me.

"Good morning, my darling." His voice was like sunshine. "How are you feeling?"

"I am well," I said because the Apostles of the True Reckoning do not lament the pains of the flesh.

"You will be," he said. "What do you remember?"

"The darkness," I said.

"Only the darkness?" He looked worried.

I tried to think back, to relate to him the first memory that preceded the darkness, to please him with my answer.

But he said, "Shh. You are tired. Rest. I've been looking for you for a long time."

I felt as though his love reached across the continents and enveloped me.

"Do you want to pray?" he asked.

I shook my head a tiny bit. He did not scowl the way Prudence scowled when the apostles prayed in church, and I let my mind walk away from their prayers.

"Is there anything you need?" he asked. "Anything you want?"

I could not tell him that I wanted only for him to look at me.

"I will come for you soon," he said. "I am already traveling toward you."

Chapter Sixty

Patrick still had not located Adair when the doctor released Helen from the clinic. Sheriff Jimenez was waiting for her when they wheeled her out. Several reporters were also waiting, but the sheriff took her arm and escorted her into the front seat of his white LeSabre cruiser. *Nye County* it read on the side below the crest. "Where can I take you?" he asked.

"We were at the Almost Home Comfort Plaza. I don't know if they held the room," Helen said.

"We asked the hotel owner to keep it for you until you got out."

That meant Adair had not been there.

Jimenez went on. "Carl's a good guy. He made sure he was the only one with a key, so none of the staff got curious and went snooping."

Helen was not listening.

Moments later, they pulled up in front of the hotel.

"Are you sure there's nothing else we can do for you?" Jimenez asked, handing Helen a keycard.

"No. Thank you for everything."

When the hotel room door closed behind her, a sob escaped her lips. She tried to remember the room as she had left it. It looked both familiar and strange. Her shirt was tossed on the bed. Adair's leather jacket hung in the closet. "Where are you?" she asked the empty room. She searched for a note, turning over the plastic mat on the desk and leafing through the Gideon's Bible. There was nothing.

She fell to the bed and buried her face in the pillow. "How could you leave me?"

❧❧❧❧

Around midnight, Helen walked to the mini-mart down the road from the hotel and bought a bottle of vodka and a pack of cigarettes. She looked for some place to sit. She did not want to be in the hotel with the remnants of Adair's life drifting around her. She did not want to be with people.

It wasn't hard to find a place as desolate as her mood. A quarter of a mile from the mini-mart, the shopping plazas and fast food restaurants gave way to vacant lots and then open desert. She found the remains of a broken concrete wall in the middle of a cracked and overgrown parking lot and sat with her back against it. She lit a cigarette.

The sound of brakes squealing in the distance made her stand up quickly, ready to flee. Then she remembered. *He's dead.* That nightmare was over. The twins were in the hands of God, or the police, or fate. She didn't care. The stars belonged to her again. She looked up. "Is that the price?" she asked out loud. She took a deep drag on her cigarette and washed the taste of smoke away with alcohol.

Adair had been ready to do it once. *There is no world in which I don't find him and kill him.* Adair's words came back to her. *You forget. I'm just as well connected as he is.*

The air was crisp. Helen took another swig of vodka. A car passed on the road, slowed, and then took off again. "There was supposed to be another way." She looked up at the stars as though they might answer.

In her pocket her phone buzzed. She leapt to answer it, but it was Terri. "How are you?" he asked.

She crushed her cigarette on the ground. She could not even answer.

"Helen?"

She did not want to tell him the whole story. She did not want to reassure him she was fine, pressing her assurances against his repeated query. *Are you sure? Are you all right?* As though asking again and again would get at the truth.

"Patrick called me. Are you all right?" Terri pressed.

She reached for another cigarette. "I don't want to talk."

"Helen, it's me."

Her lighter sparked with her anger. "I can't talk about it, not with you, not with anyone."

"Are you up to listening for a little while?" he asked.

She stared out at the desert. It had seemed so hellish from the vantage of Drummond's van. Now it seemed forlorn, a beautiful stretch of darkness beyond the glitter of town, lonely and fragile.

"I talked to your friend Patrick," Terri continued without her answer. "He really is as good as you say. He got me all the records on the Kimball scholarship. He gave me the donor's name: Peter Reynolds Barr, born August 14, 1970. Supposedly he had lived in a little town called Wishbone, Montana and had twin sisters, Lucy and Patricia Barr, dicephalic parapagus conjoined twins. They died when they were eleven after spending the last year of their life bedridden."

"I know." Helen sighed. "I'll tell the alumni association to wait a year and then hit him up for a donation in their honor."

"No. Listen. That's what you were told, but there is no record of a Peter Reynolds Barr born in Montana. The closest we could find was a Peter Ryan Barr born in North Dakota in 1959."

"It doesn't matter."

"It might." Terri spoke quickly. She could hear his breath in the phone. "Since Peter Reynolds Barr was a fiction, I went digging a little deeper. If there's no donor, where did the money come from? Supposedly, Barr was a rancher and he and his family owned a small chain of grocery stores. SpelMart Groceries. Well, there was a chain of SpelMart Groceries. The money from the sale of those stores was still floating around in some corporate trust owned by something called the Feldmore Conglomerate."

Only their many years of friendship kept Helen from simply ending the call.

"Feldmore is an international commercial real estate company," Terri went on. "But commercial real estate doesn't begin to describe it. They own property all over North America, but the bulk of the money is in mines overseas, mostly Africa, mostly coltan—that's columbo-tantalite or tantalum—operations in the Congo."

Helen touched "speaker" on her phone and set it on the ground beside her. She leaned her head against the concrete behind her and exhaled into the stars. "Where are you going with this?"

"Most tantalum comes from Canada, Brazil, or Australia, but they've got it in the Congo too, and no one's charted how much. They use it to make the components that control the flow of current inside circuit boards. It's in your cell phone and every computer, game console, and tablet in the world. There's money there if the established markets run dry or raise their prices. A lot of people are interested."

"Terri, I don't want to talk about this." Helen ran her hand through the gravel and sand on the ground beside her, raising up a little handful and letting it sift back to earth. *Ashes to ashes. Dust to dust.*

"Listen, Helen. Listen. Feldmore had to close down half of their mines. Amnesty International and the UN wanted them to clean up the operation, and their buyers went to Canada because of the bad press. Blood phones, they're calling them. A lot of people are saying the Feldmore Conglomerate profited from the political instability in the Congo and ran their mines with slave labor. Miners worked for food and lodging, and if they tried to leave the compound they were shot."

"This doesn't have anything to do with the twins." Helen had lost the thread of the conversation. *It doesn't have anything to do with me.*

Terri was not deterred. "Here's the connection. I think someone with access to Feldmore money created the scholarship, but they were sloppy because they didn't find a real donor. The money trail is right, but the people are all wrong. I also think the Feldmore Conglomeration is looking for a new source of revenue, and they have a history of human trafficking."

"So someone wanted Charity and Prudence to work in a mine? In the Congo? You know you're in the perfect line of work." Helen sipped the vodka. She was tired. She did not like the thrill of excitement that entered Terri's voice when he talked about research. "This isn't some celebrity scandal."

"No it's not. Here's the last piece."

Finally. "What?" Helen sighed.

"A small subsidiary of the Feldmore Conglomerate called Insurant National Supplies Inc. owns the Josslin Heights."

"No. The Wilsons own the Josslin Heights."

"I know, Helen. I know the Wilsons own the Josslin Heights."

⁂

"Upgrading?" the cabby asked when Helen directed him toward the Josslin Heights Las Vegas. He peered up at the sign above the Almost Home Comfort Plaza.

"Yes."

"Nice night, isn't it? Not as hot as last night."

Helen said nothing.

"Say, aren't you that woman on the news?" the cabby asked, turning out of the parking lot.

Helen clutched her purse tighter. "No."

When they reached the Josslin Heights, Helen paid the man with a hundred dollar bill. He searched his wallet for change.

"Keep it." Helen turned briefly to watch the cab disappear behind the fountain in the center of the circular drive. Lights mounted in the basin produced fireworks of color in ever-changing patterns, but the light was nothing compared to the view of the city at night.

She walked into the hotel. If Adair was still in the city, she would be in the penthouse. Helen took the elevator up six stories. The hotel was smaller than the one in Portland, clearly a refurbished antique, but the view and the vintage grandeur made it seem finer. The elevator opened onto a foyer on the top floor. Over-stuffed leather furniture basked in the dim glow of Tiffany lamps while a chandelier of a thousand icicles glittered overhead without shedding any real light. At the end of the foyer, facing the elevator, stood a massive set of double doors carved from dark wood.

Helen took a deep breath, crossed the space, and knocked. "Adair?" she called out.

A security camera mounted in the corner followed her movements.

"Are you there?"

Chapter Sixty-one

Adair woke with an intense headache and the sense that someone was watching her. She rubbed her eyes. She was in a Josslin Heights. She recognized the company logo woven into the pillow sham beside her head. Then it all came back to her, and she wished she could sink back into the drug induced sleep. Helen was dead or stranded somewhere in the desert. The man who knew where she was was dead, his body mutilated and disposed of by the fierce guards who were, almost certainly, waiting outside the room with Cecelia.

"Is she awake?" someone whispered.

"Let her sleep. She's sick," another voice said.

Adair rolled over and blinked. Her vision was blurry. For a moment she was not sure if she saw the room or if she simply remembered rooms like this. The elegant but unexceptional furniture. The heavy brocade curtains hanging over some high-rent view. The ornamental palms, live but replaced weekly. The massive dose of Texidol had left her nauseous and dazed. She closed her eyes again, but the voices continued.

"But he's coming. She will want to see him."

"It is a glory."

She rubbed her eyes. For a moment, the pressure of her fists on her eyelids turned the whole world into a swirl of color. Then her vision cleared. Standing before the closed curtains like two porcelain dolls stood Charity and Prudence.

"You must see him," Charity said. "He's so beautiful."

"We have been praying for you," Prudence said. They moved toward her.

Vertigo consumed Adair as she rose, but she still managed to open her arms to the twins and draw them into a hug. Their torso was almost twice the breadth of hers. Their arms encircled her. Each girl pressed a cheek against Adair's. She could smell their freshly-washed hair.

"I thought you were dead." Adair held them tightly. This was one small mercy. She wanted to cry. "She really found you." Adair drew back to look at them. They were beautiful and serene as the Oquat Mountains, their eyes almost black, their faces pale. They showed no sign of fear. It was as though nothing had happened to them. They were like a still pool that absorbed all movement. "Are you all right?" she asked.

"We are going to meet our benefactor," Prudence said.

"Our helpmate," Charity added. "He has been looking for us."

"He would never leave us," Prudence said.

They spoke in such perfect alternation, it could have been one voice. Adair's heart sank. There was madness in their melodic chant.

"We are his."

"We are destined."

"He is coming."

"He is already here."

"The Purveyor has asked you to accompany us. Come. God has made us for him." Prudence's voice was full of eerie joy.

Adair sank back down on the bed and put her head in her hands.

"Do not be sad. God has chosen this for us." Charity put her hand on Adair's shoulder.

Adair looked up. Deep in Charity's eyes she thought she saw a spark of hunger beneath the placid surface. "What happened?"

"It doesn't matter. He's coming," Prudence said.

"He's already here."

"Come. Now."

The girls took her hands and pulled like little children eager to share a secret.

"He's upstairs."

"He's outside."

"He's in the light."

Confused, half blinded by Texidol, Adair followed. The girls led her out of the bedroom. In the common area, the three soldiers stood at attention, positioned around the room, their rifles held against their chests. Four other men sat at the table. She thought she recognized one of them as Cyrus's driver. No one moved.

"This way," Charity said. She pulled Adair toward the small utility staircase through which they had entered the suite.

"Come." Prudence released Adair's hand and pulled the door open.

No alarm sounded. Adair expected the guards to stop them, but they remained motionless. The girls bounded up the stairs and flung open the door to the roof. Outside the blue glow of pre-dawn mixed with the city's orange halo. Adair mounted the last steps and stepped out onto the roof where they had landed the night before. She presumed it was the night before. Perhaps days had passed.

The roof was covered in undulating waves of tar paper, interrupted by exhaust vents.

"Finally," a voice behind her said.

Adair turned.

Cecelia stood with her back against the wall of the small brick bunker that housed the top of the stairwell. She wore black leather riding pants and a dark blouse that revealed her cleavage. A ruby winked at her throat. "I found them," Cecelia said. "Just where Marshal said they would be. Just where Blaine took them."

A light breeze blew her words across the open space.

"Blaine?" Adair said.

Cecelia pushed herself off the wall. Almost hidden in her curls, she wore a headset. Now she pulled the microphone down and spoke into it. "Not yet." To Adair she added. "Do you see that helicopter?"

Adair squinted at the indigo sky. On the horizon, where dawn was turning the dark blue gold, a helicopter hovered.

"Do you want to understand?" Cecelia took Prudence's hand but kept her eyes trained on Adair. "I'm not sure you do, but it's time."

"He's coming," Prudence said.

Adair felt weak.

"Does the name Harlow Galloway mean anything to you?" Cecelia did not wait for an answer. "He is a very private man and one of the wealthiest in the world. He's a collector." She looked at the girls. "Of rare things, and for the rarest he is willing to pay a sum the ordinary world cannot imagine, a price even

God cannot match."

"Is that him?" Charity asked.

"Yes," Cecelia said. "He is there."

The first lip of the sun rose over the horizon. The girls stared into it unblinking.

"What are you saying?" Adair asked.

Cecelia dropped Prudence's hand and took a step toward Adair. Quickly she wrapped an arm around Adair's waist and pulled her in, kissing her hard on the lips. "Your brothers protected you. Your father did too. Your innocence is a tribute to *their* power."

"I don't have time for games," Adair said, pulling away. "What is this?"

Helen could still be out in the desert. The twins were broken, staring into the sun. She had to get out. She had to find Helen. She had to tell someone. She staggered as fear and Texidol warred for control of her body.

"You have nothing but time," Cecelia said, languidly.

"Let me go!"

Cecelia stepped between Adair and the door to the stairwell, drawing the Browning Medalist from the back of her waistband. She shook her head. "It's too late for that." Cecelia aimed the gun at the back of Charity's head. "I could kill them both with one shot, you know. That's their fate. They are forever intertwined. Like us."

"What do you want?"

"I want to tell you a story." The gun remained steady in Cecelia's outstretched hand. "I want to tell you a story about a company called the Feldmore Conglomerate."

"I don't want to hear it."

Cecelia ignored her. "In Zaire they found it was more profitable to pay the warlords than the workers. It's amazing what people will do when someone holds a gun to their mother's head or their son's."

"What are you talking about?" Adair asked.

"You're father's legacy."

"My father never…"

"It's so awkward." Cecelia lowered the gun, but kept her body in between Adair and the door that led off the roof. "No one wants to say it. But slave labor is how great societies rise. Egypt. America. It works. It's how dynasties are built. The trade isn't in natural resources. It is in *the* natural resource–people. For sex. For labor. You can't steal a coal mine. You can't make diamonds walk to their new owners. But there are a million hungry girls who will do anything for a promise or a gun at their back, and no one will ever miss them. Your little social service agencies know. They say there are twenty-five million slaves out there right now. What they don't see is how many more there could be. There is a cornucopia, and it's ours." Cecelia gestured with the gun. "The fruit is so heavy. But peasants gather. That's what I realized." Cecelia looked at the twins who now stood near the edge of the building. "They're different."

"You poisoned me. You poisoned my family." Adair's confusion crystallized into rage. "You're mad."

"Because I slept with you? Because I married Cyrus when I didn't love him?" Cecelia laughed. "Who would love Cyrus?"

Adair thought of Cyrus standing beside her at the shooting range, a large boulder of a man teaching a nine-year-old girl to handle a Glock 45. "I love him," she said.

"He's dead now. Blaine too. And your precious Cinderella."

"You're lying."

Cecelia cupped the back of Adair's head in her hand. She pressed the gun to Adair's neck almost tenderly.

"Cyrus found out what I'd done," she said, "what we'd done. I told him everything. It was just too much for him. He's still in his office, you know. Just like your mother. No need to let the dead interfere with business. They can wait. Do you want to know what happened? Do you want to know why he killed himself?"

"No!" Adair struggled in Cecelia's grip.

"He was a troubled man," Cecelia went on. "He didn't like the things we did, but he did them, and he thought if he kept you pure, it might save his soul. It didn't, of course."

"I don't believe anything you say!" Adair shot back.

Cecelia pushed the gun harder against her neck. Instinctively, Adair leaned her head away from the cold metal. "You won't kill me," she said through clenched teeth, but the Texidol in her blood told another story.

"In just a minute Harlow Galloway is going to land here and collect his prize," Cecelia said. "The girls you brought him."

The helicopter was drawing nearer. Adair looked from Cecelia to the girls. Before she even knew she was going to act, she lunged at Cecelia, reaching for the gun in her hand. But her movements were slowed by the Texidol. Cecelia dodged out of the way, striking Adair in the temple with the butt of the gun. Adair stumbled, tripped over an exhaust vent on the roof top, and went sprawling.

"There was no scholarship." Cecelia said, leaping on Adair and pinning her hand. "I called little Helen's school and told them there was so much money. If only they had someone good enough, gentle enough to lure the twins away. Helen suggested it herself. She sent you."

Adair struggled.

Cecelia was breathing heavily from the exertion of keeping her pinned. "It was something for you to do," Cecelia said between gasps. "She wanted a way to get you back, so she sent you to convince them to leave Oquat."

For a second, Adair's vision faded to black. Before she could blink her way back into the world, she felt the bite of metal on her wrist. Cecelia clamped a handcuff tight against her skin. Adair kicked at Cecelia, trying to grab the gun with her free hand, but it was no use.

"I thought you would stop for my men at the bottom of the mountain, but you dodged them," Cecelia yelled over the noise of the approaching helicopter. "Harlow is not a showy man. He wants them a secret. I thought we'd lost everything, but then you brought them all the way to Pittock without anyone seeing. You were perfect."

Adair tried to roll away, but Cecelia struck her chin with the gun. In the seconds it took her body to register the new pain, Cecelia had cuffed her other hand. "For old times' sake," Cecelia said. With one hand she held the gun just above Adair's eye. With the other she held the handcuff chain against the roof.

"I thought your work was done," Cecelia went on. "But Blaine decided he would undercut me. He found another buyer and thought he could keep the profits to himself. We would have lost them, but you and your little secretary found them again. Don't be mad. I only sent Drummond after you because you had stopped talking to me."

Adair did not want to listen, but she did, held as much by the story as by the gun and the handcuffs. Both horrible. Both irrefutable.

"You're so childish sometimes." Cecelia leaned over and kissed Adair's cheek, still holding the gun to her face. "He was never going to hurt you. We had a deal. He was supposed to find you and the location of the twins and I would give him Helen. Except that he couldn't wait." Cecelia's eyes were wild. Her hair seethed around her face, and the jewel at her throat hung like a drop of blood suspended on a spider web. "He was supposed to wait for me before he took her. He's ruled by his appetite, but we took care of that, didn't we? And Blaine too. I'm sorry. You haven't seen him in years, and now you won't, but he was a stupid pimp anyway."

"What do you want?" Adair grit her teeth.

"I want you to understand who you are," Cecelia said, suddenly calmer, almost conversational.

Adair lay pinned beneath Cecelia's knee. She closed her eyes.

"Listen to me, Merrill. When Harlow takes the twins we become the richest women in the world. You and me. We rise. Cyrus is dead. Blaine is dead. We own Monty. We are the pinnacle. We are the natural law. You don't despise the leopard for its bite. It's God's will." Cecelia spoke into her headset. "We're ready."

Over Cecelia's shoulder, Adair could just barely see the twins.

"He's coming," they said in unison. As they spoke, they raised their hands.

Then the helicopter was there, blowing a storm of dust across the roof. The door opened. A set of stairs unfolded. A man in a white suit stepped out, the dawn shining off the pale material. He frowned at Cecelia.

Adair thought she heard him say, "Really, my dear. You are as rough as your trade."

And even bound and pressed to the hot tar roof, Adair was struck by the man's beauty. Like the twins, he seemed to hold something of the sky in him. He held out his hands to the girls, and they moved toward him.

"Don't!" Adair cried, but her voice did not reach his beauty. "He's a bad man. He'll hurt you." Adair could not hear over the roar of the helicopter, but she could read Charity's lips.

He loves me.

"No!" Adair screamed. "God, please, no!"

The twins moved toward the man and embraced him. Then they turned and mounted the steps into the helicopter, their heads bowed as if in prayer.

Cecelia bent down, kneeling her entire weight on Adair's chest until Adair thought her sternum would crack. "It's just like on television," Cecelia said. "There's always a special guest." To the microphone, she added, "Bring her up."

※ ※ ※ ※

Behind Adair's head the door to the stairwell opened. Cecelia released a little bit of the pressure on Adair's chest. Adair craned her neck to see. The guards exited. Between them, half carried, half dragged, hands bound behind her back, a gag tied across her mouth, was Helen.

Suddenly the strength that had eluded Adair filled her limbs like fire. Cecelia was kneeling above her, holding Adair's cuffed hands to the ground. Adair jerked her arms and unbalanced Cecelia. Cecelia toppled off her. Adair pounced on her. Adair's hands were still cuffed, but the chain that bound them together was a weapon. She pressed it to Cecelia's neck.

"Let Helen go," Adair cried.

Cecelia pried at the chain, her face turning red.

"I don't care if you love me. I don't care that you're jealous," Adair yelled. "This isn't a game."

One of the men leapt forward and pulled Adair away, throwing her onto the ground and sticking his rifle in her chest.

Cecelia coughed and stood, brushing off her pants. "Isn't it all just a game?" She picked her gun up off the roof and pointed it at Helen. "Leave the woman with us," she said to the men. "And leave us."

"Are you sure ma'am?" the guard barked.

"I'm sure," Cecelia said. "She won't hurt me now that I have her lover."

One guard closed the door to the stairwell behind them and locked it. He tossed the key to Cecelia who pocketed it. Then the guards vaulted into the helicopter with a natural grace.

"Don't try anything," Cecelia said to Adair. "My men are downstairs waiting for us. Plus I'll kill her if you blink." She walked toward Helen and pointed her gun at Helen's chest.

Adair scrambled to her feet and threw herself between them.

"How noble," Cecelia said. "The first bullet would rip through the two of you."

Adair looked around. They were alone on the rooftop, and there were no buildings near enough to witness the scene. The helicopter was lifting off. Adair searched for a fire escape. It had to be there. She remembered touring the Josslin Heights Las Vegas before retrofitting the Grandville. She had liked the architect. He felt about his work the way she felt about her tenants. He was a steward, a protector. It would be hard for Helen to make it down the fire escape with her hands tied, but she could do it.

Slowly, Adair turned to Cecelia. "You wanted to tell me a story," Adair said, holding Cecelia's gaze. "It's Genesis, isn't it." She stepped forward. "Where I come from. Who I am."

Cecelia smiled.

"Okay." Adair let her eyes drift shut. She drew in the smell of Cecelia's breath—a slight acidity, a hint of mint—and with it a new life. She released everything she had been, her love, her dreams, because that was what actors did. They emptied themselves of the real and the past, and became only the story. "Make me a leopard," Adair said.

"Shoot her."

"Who?"

"You know."

"Free me." Adair held out her cuffed hands.

"I can't trust you."

"Have you ever?" Adair pressed her words to Cecelia's lips, then bit Cecelia's lower lip, a hard sharp bite. "Do you want to trust me? Do you want a ranch home in the suburbs? Or do you want Helen to watch us fuck before I kill her?"

Cecelia laughed. "Merrill," her voice purred.

Adair turned to Helen. This was the instant that mattered. "Do you remember that night we sat on the fire escape at the Grandville?" Adair asked.

They had never sat on the fire escape.

Her eyes held Helen's. *Say yes.*

Helen nodded.

Adair looked sharply over Helen's shoulder, her best guess for the location of the hidden fire escape.

"We sat on the fire escape." She repeated the glance. "And I told you that I loved you, but I didn't. You were a whim. You were a life I thought I'd try on for a day. What would it be like to be poor and pay a mortgage and grow dahlias in a bucket because they're so pretty?" She filled her voice with Cecelia's scorn. "And take up knitting at fifty because I was old."

She saw tears well up in Helen's eyes.

Adair shot another look in the direction of the fire escape. *Understand me.* Every fiber of her body longed to take Helen in her arms. *You know I love you.* She felt her own eyes fill with tears as she realized what she was about to do. Helen could not get away in time if Cecelia was alive. Cecelia held the gun. Cecelia could summon her men in a second. In the end, the final plunge would not be out of despair–it would be out of love. There was no other way. She wanted to weep, but she was an actor, and the tears dried on her eyes like fleur de sel harvested from the Dead Sea.

"A secretary," Adair hissed. "A pawn. A spinster. Did you really think I would love you?" Adair turned back to Cecelia, plunging her tongue into Cecelia's mouth.

Cecelia moaned.

The gun and Adair's cuffed hands were pinned

between their bodies. As it had always been, Adair thought. Her bondage. Cecelia's power. She thrust her hips against Cecelia.

The sun was up now, its light partially blocked by the helicopter that continued to hover a few yards beyond the edge of the building. She stepped forward, driving Cecelia back with the force of her kiss. Cecelia had always controlled their sex, but now Adair was in control. Despite the handcuffs, despite the gun. It was her tongue driving into Cecelia's mouth. It was her hips setting their rhythm.

With one hand Cecelia clasped Adair's back.

Adair knew Cecelia would only abandon herself for a second. "I want you," Adair growled. She kissed Cecelia again, pushing her back toward the unprotected edge of the roof.

Another twenty feet.

There might be unforeseen casualties when they hit the ground–a couple on their honeymoon, an old gambler walking into the hotel. Adair did not care. Helen would have a minute, maybe two, to reach the fire escape, run down, crash through the window on the floor below, and throw herself on the mercy of whatever maid or tourist she saw first.

Fifteen feet.

Their kissed deepened. Adair lifted her arms over her head, so that she could loop her handcuffed wrists around Cecelia's back, binding them together.

Ten feet.

The papers would love it. The hotel's popularity would soar.

Five feet.

"I want you, Cecelia. I've always wanted you."

The light coming over the edge of the building

was blinding. Cecelia's back was to the drop. Cecelia did not know how close she was, but Adair knew. They were right on the edge. She felt Cecelia's body against hers, their legs intertwined, their tongues locked. The manacles holding Adair's hands together held her to Cecelia. Cecelia tried to draw back, but she could not. Out of the corner of her eye Adair saw Helen fall to her knees, screaming through her gag.

And Adair kissed Cecelia, for Cecelia's lies and for the sudden certainty that they were not lies. For Cyrus and Monty and Blaine. For her mother. For the beauty of the Wilson estate. For the spring time. For the soft skin of Helen's sex. For her own suffering. For the dawn that would rise without her.

And then Adair Wilson stepped forward into the light.

From the diary of Charity Kimball

He was lovelier than I could have imagined, with silver hair and skin the color of sunshine in autumn. He helped us into the helicopter, and I loved him. I knew Prudence loved him too. He could be her savior and my lover. I saw that in his eyes.

I could not believe the miracle of flight as we lifted off the roof. I thought, *this must be how the angels see the world.* The noise was incredible which I had not expected, but then the angels are never as we anticipate. Also there were dark Negro men in the helicopter. Each one held a strange rifle. Perhaps they were angels too. They yelled at each other in strange codes I did not understand. Then our savior raised his hand, and they fell silent.

I looked out the window. On the rooftop, I saw the sad woman. Adair, her name is. Like Adar from the Bible. She was bound at the wrists, and she was doing what is surely a sin, for she was kissing the dark-haired woman who brought us to the basement and brought the doctor when we were sick. She was kissing her, and pushing her toward the edge of the roof. I knew that she would hurl their bodies into the sky. I knew her mind, because I knew her loneliness. Behind her, another woman was bound at the wrists and the mouth. She was weeping.

Even from where I sat, hovering in the air, I could tell the exact minute when the dark haired woman knew what Adair planned. Those were the kisses of Jael before she stabbed Sisera through the head with a tent peg. The dark haired woman and Adair struggled on the edge. The weeping woman stumbled forward, her hands tied, her eyes screaming.

Adair yelled, "Run!"

I could hear her over the noise.

"I love you. Run!" Adair yelled.

Her friend's eyes said *no, no, no* but she could not speak through the gag. I could see her tears.

My heart went out to Adair—*Adar*, whose name means high or eminent—and her friend, the weeping woman. The weeping woman fell to her knees, crying to her God. Prudence cannot imagine that God. Prudence does not know the God Who Does Not Answer, but I know. I have prayed, and I am angry that God is so often silent.

I turned to our savior, my Gabriel.

There was a Negro sitting beside him with a strange, black rifle.

"May I hold it?" I asked.

The Negro said, "She'll shoot us, boss."

"Perhaps," our savior said. "One always runs that risk."

He took the rifle from the Negro and handed it to me.

I lifted Prudence with me, and we stood by the small window of the helicopter. We were only twenty feet away, but the chasm between the helicopter and the roof was the chasm that would swallow up Adair and the dark haired woman.

"Go!" Adair screamed.

The weeping woman did not run.

I raised the rifle. It was lighter than I expected. I

did not need to speak to Prudence. In life and in death we are one. She is my sister, my flesh, my soul.

The first bullet shattered the window. A sudden apocalypse of wind hit my face. The Negroes screamed. But I could feel our savior watching us, motionless. We raised the rifle again. It was not as windy as a night on the Nesqonquet Range. We blended our vision into one, then one by one we closed our eyes, until only my right eye was open, trained on the dark-haired woman, for I knew in whose likeness we were made.

Then we fired.

Chapter Sixty-two

For a moment, Adair stood perfectly upright, pressed against Cecelia. She felt her mind separating from her body, like the moment when orgasm becomes inevitable. She would step forward, push Cecelia backwards off the roof, and plunge down with Cecelia beneath her. Nothing she or Cecelia could do could stop that now. Even Cecelia's panicked step forward—she realized!—was sending them over. Time slowed. She saw Cecelia shake her head as she tried to forestall the inevitable. Overhead, the helicopter beat the air in a slow dirge. Adair cried out for Helen to run.

Then she heard a shot.

Suddenly the side of her head collided with the tar roof. There was blood everywhere. The noise of the helicopter doubled. A bullhorn blared. "UD1 Black, this is an FBI escort." Adair tried to move. She was on the ground. Cecelia pinned her down. Adair tried to raise her head to get out of the blood, but it was pouring across her cheek, down her chin, into her mouth.

Then everything was moving. Men in black suits like armored beetles covered the space around her. She could see their boots, the tips of rifles, the movement of men running low to the ground. The helicopter noise had been replaced by men yelling in bursts.

"Clear."

"Over here."

"Medic!"

"One dead, one injured."

"Shot appears to have been fired from helicopter."

"Grey Rider 84, do not pursue. Copy."

A radio blared. "Copy."

Something jabbed her shoulder. "Put your hands on your head."

Adair lifted her hands off Cecelia's back. "Help me," she whispered.

"Don't move this is the FBI. Put your hands where I can see them."

Adair tried to pull herself from beneath Cecelia's dead weight, but the tip of a rifle stopped her.

"Helen," Adair cried, her mouth full of Cecelia's hair. "Help me."

A moment later, a man in pale blue scrubs appeared at her side. He was yelling but not at her. "Move her. She's dead, man. Look at her!"

For a moment, Adair thought he meant her. Then someone moved Cecelia's body. The blood that had been pouring across Adair's face stopped.

The man in the blue uniform knelt beside her. "Can you hear me?"

Adair nodded.

"What is your name?"

"Adair Merrill Wilson."

He pressed a gloved finger to her throat. To someone far above them he called, "She has a strong pulse. We need fluids and a stretcher." Then to Adair he said. "I need you to tell me if you're in pain."

Adair tried to rise, but he held her down. "Where's Helen?" she asked, frantically trying to see through the sea of men. "You have to find her."

Chapter Sixty-three

The knock on her hotel door startled Helen like gunfire. The doctor who had examined her after the raid on the Josslin Heights had offered her a sedative, but she refused. "I need to see Adair," she had told the doctor.

"They're questioning her now," the doctor said apologetically. "We can't allow you to contact her."

"But she didn't do anything," Helen begged. "She's the victim." Now Helen leapt from her bed and pressed her eye against the spy hole in the hotel door. A familiar face looked back. "Let him in," she said to the guard standing outside. She heard a key in the lock, and the door swung open.

Terri stood before her, a short man in a pink oxford shirt open over a spotless white T-shirt. He was pushing seventy, but he had broad shoulders and a good tan. His gray hair was tousled as though he had just stepped off a boardwalk in Santa Cruz. He smiled and shrugged.

She fell into his arms.

"How are you, my dear?" he said, enclosing her in a hug.

"They've locked me in this hotel room, and they won't let me talk to Adair," she said when he released her. "They won't tell me anything. I don't even know if she's okay."

"But you're okay?" Terri asked. "You're not hurt?"

"I'm alive." She sank into a chair. "They think Adair killed Marshal Drummond."

"Don't worry." Terri patted her arm and pulled up a chair in front of her. "No one thinks Adair killed Marshal Drummond."

"But they won't let me see her."

"Precautions." Terri dismissed the word with a wave of his hand. "Someone is dotting their i's and crossing their t's. You and Adair are on every television station in America. The *Sun* is calling you, the new face of American crime fighting." He turned on the television and shook the remote a couple of times. The screen remained black. "Probably for the best," he added.

"What happened?" Helen asked. "Was this all the Wilsons?"

Terri's face grew serious. "They haven't talked to you about it yet?"

"No. There was Drummond, and then I went to find Adair, and Cecelia Beaucharnel was there. Then these men tied me up. I was on the roof. There were police. It was like a dream."

"They'll talk to you soon," Terri said. "They didn't put any restrictions on my visit, so I think they're going to release you."

"And Adair?"

"Don't worry. I've got one of the best lawyers in the country on her case. Pro bono too. He just wants the exposure. This is going to be big."

"She didn't do anything."

"They know that, but it's always good to be careful. Listen, here's what I know so far. That raid on the Josslin Heights, that was Cyrus's doing. He killed himself."

Helen pressed her hand to her lips. "Oh, God! Poor Adair."

"But before that, he made an incredibly thorough accounting of the family's business. It looks like the Wilsons have been involved in human trafficking for generations. Holdings in the Belgian Congo. Coltan mines. Child labor in textile mills in Bangladesh. But it wasn't until recently that Cecelia Beaucharnel and Blaine Wilson started trafficking directly."

"Buying slaves?"

"Mostly sex trafficking. It started abroad when Blaine—they call him Bolo—was in Venezuela. But the twins were different. The man in the helicopter who took them off the roof, his name is Harlow Galloway, and he requested them specifically. Cecelia Beaucharnel abducted them, and she sold them to Galloway, with some complications along the way. I guess Blaine wanted in on the action and tried to sell them to his own buyer. Cyrus got wind of it all and told the FBI where they could find Cecelia and what she was doing. Then he killed himself. The feds were just a bit late or just on time, depending on how you look at it. The twins say they saw Cecelia hold Adair at gunpoint on the roof of the Josslin Heights. They fired from twenty feet away and shot her through the side of the head."

Helen stared at Terri.

"You're not sufficiently impressed," Terri added. "That's a one in a billion shot. They were in a moving helicopter. Adair and Cecelia were struggling at the edge of the roof. They would have fallen off except that the force of the shot knocked them back."

Helen saw Adair silhouetted against the sun. "Adair was trying to save me. She told me to run."

"I always liked her." Terri winked.

Helen leaned back in her chair.

"It's a lot to take in, I know," Terri said. "Let me make you a coffee."

He rattled around in the kitchenette, and a minute later the smell of coffee filled the room. Before he handed her a cup, he produced a flask from his pants pocket. "I thought you might need a little something." He poured a shot into Helen's coffee and handed it to her.

"Did they catch Galloway?" Helen asked.

"No. They got the twins though. They caught up with them at a private airstrip in New Mexico. There was no trace of the helicopter, no money trail that they could find in time to arrest him, and no record of any communication with Cecelia. They apprehended the girls because the girls claimed to be seventeen, and they were leaving the country with no valid ID or passport. They've been taken into state custody until New Mexico DHS can figure out what to do with them. As you can imagine, the media is all over them, and they are putting on a good show."

"What do you mean?" she swallowed a gulp of coffee that was more rum than Folgers.

"They say it was all consensual. They say that God means Harlow Galloway to be their 'helpmate,' their savior, and that it's God's will they be with him and spread the message of inseparable love."

"Did anyone explain to them that he *bought* them?"

"*Slaves obey your earthly masters.* Ephesians 6:5." Terri shrugged. "Galloway got away. They had Adair's word that he was a buyer and that Beaucharnel had tricked her into getting the twins out of Utah, but she had a wound to the head—don't worry, she'll be fine—and she was in shock. She wasn't much of a witness. The twins, on the other hand, said they got a hold of an iPad, contacted Galloway on the internet, and asked him to come get them. Galloway offered to let the FBI look at all his bank accounts. They know they'll find the money somewhere, but there wasn't enough to hold him now. He's not a US citizen."

"What about Adair?" Helen clasped the cup so her hands would not shake.

"Cyrus sent the FBI a detailed record of his efforts to keep Adair out of the trade. He went as far as separating out all her money, all her holdings. She inherited a lot of her money from her mother whose family made their fortune in hydroelectric power. They were some of the original investors in the Tucuruí Dam in Brazil. They weren't doing it out of charity, but it was clean money. The forensic accountant says it looks like Cyrus had been concerned about this for a long time. These weren't the records a man collects right before he spills his brains on his laptop."

"Christ!"

"Sorry. Too graphic. But that's what happened, and this was a lifetime of evidence against his brothers, against Cecelia Beaucharnel, against himself, and in defense of Adair."

"She said he always wanted her to move to Paris."

Terri leaned forward. "He said that in the suicide letter he sent to the FBI. He said he had done everything he could to drive her away. He even said that he married Cecelia Beaucharnel because he knew Adair and Cecelia had been lovers. He thought somehow by doing that he could protect Adair from Cecelia. He said Cecelia had bribed and then threatened to kill the family of Adair's first girlfriend."

"Soledad." Helen finished her coffee and set the mug down on an end table.

"Soledad Plascensia," Terri clarified. "Now that Cecelia is dead, she's willing to testify."

Soledad. "Adair loved her." Helen felt sick.

"That was a long time ago," Terri said, as though reading her thoughts. "Soledad is married with three kids. She's milking the press for all it's worth. I don't think you have to worry."

"When can I see Adair?" Helen asked.

"I'll talk to the agent in charge of the case." Terri nodded as though he had already settled the matter. "Neither of you are under arrest. Supposedly you are in protective witness custody. We'll lawyer up if we have to. I don't think it'll be a problem. Even the FBI watches TV."

"What do you mean?"

Terri stood, stretching. "Every media outlet across America is saying that you're heroes."

⁂

It was dark and Helen had been lying awake in bed for hours when she heard another knock on the door. She got up quickly and opened it. The guard was gone. Adair stood before her in unfamiliar clothes. A gash on her temple had been secured with thin strips of surgical tape. Her eyes seemed to stare through Helen into an outer distance much larger than the hotel room.

"Come in," Helen said. She felt suddenly shy.

"They say we're free to go, but they want us to stay until tomorrow for a debriefing." Adair's voice was a monotone. "I don't know what that means."

Helen led her to the bed and sat down beside her. "I'm so sorry, Adair. Terri told me everything."

Adair's eyes remained fixed on something outside the room. "Cyrus is dead."

"I know."

"And Blaine. Cecelia's men shot Blaine. They arrested Monty in the Heathrow Airport. I've done everything wrong," Adair whispered.

Helen put a tentative hand on Adair's shoulder. She looked like a sleepwalker. Helen wondered if she had accepted the doctor's sedatives. "But you didn't know about any of this."

"No."

"Then you weren't a part of it. The FBI will see that. They just have to be careful. They have to ask the questions."

"But it's my family." Adair pressed her face to the pillow. Helen could barely make out what she said next. "My whole life," Adair mumbled. "My money, my family. Of course Cyrus wanted me to move to Paris. I thought I was so…but everything I touched, everything I ate, was bought with someone else's blood."

"Terri says your money comes from a different source," Helen pleaded.

Adair sat up. "It doesn't matter. My *life* came from them. Who I *am* came from them."

Helen wanted to press her body against Adair's and be comforted by its warmth. She wanted to shake Adair and cry for her to come back to her old self. But when she closed her eyes, she saw Adair silhouetted against the rising sun, stepping forward, pushing Cecelia toward the brink. She felt, with utter clarity, that this was Adair's catastrophe. There was no way she could stand in for everything Adair had lost. She sat beside her, her hand resting on Adair's for a long time. Finally Adair's eyes began to close, and she curled up wordlessly on top of the covers and slept.

⁂

For Helen, the first days back at Pittock passed in a blur of fear and boredom. Every sound made her jump, and yet the days dragged on as she moved around the Pittock House, putting down books and deleting emails unread. Neither she nor Adair went out. They silenced their phones. Helen ate little. Adair ate less and said almost nothing. Her eyes remained focused on her thoughts, and at night she lay motionless in their bed like a stranger.

A few weeks into their self-imposed siege, Patrick called to tell Helen that the college had reopened Adair's position in the theater. Later Helen lay in bed with Adair and asked if she would reapply. "I know they want you to get it," Helen said. "If you apply, they'll pick you."

Adair lay with her back to Helen and stared at the wall. "I can't go out there."

"You can." Helen touched Adair's hip. "The twins are going to be here next week. Admissions voted to give them a full scholarship plus room and board. You could be their teacher."

They were ill-prepared for college, but they had nowhere else to go.

"I can't," Adair said simply.

Helen hesitated. "In a few days, I have to go in front of the board. Because of Bruno Duffy."

Adair said nothing.

"I may lose my job."

Adair did not move.

Helen watched her motionless back.

"I know," Adair said finally. Then she was silent for so long Helen thought she was asleep, but when she tried to put an arm around her, Adair said, quietly, "Don't."

Helen rose. Downstairs she sat on the white sofa and clutched one of the pillows to her chest as she cried. Somewhere deep behind her tears she heard Eliza's voice. *I'm sorry I can't help you, Helen.* Then Eliza drifted away, and she was alone.

⁂

On the morning of her hearing, Helen dressed in her best suit. The sharp tailored creases felt unfamiliar. Then she set out across campus to her trial. The board sat in a semicircle at the front of the board room. High narrow windows let in light but no view. Patrick's assistant, Stephanie, sat behind a laptop, her pink fingernails poised to record the exact details of Helen's demise. Helen knew all the board members by name: Debby, Cadence, Bruce, Frank, Lucile, and the chairman John Cleland. Now they looked at her like strangers.

Cleland spoke first. "Do you understand why you're here?"

"Yes."

Stephanie typed three quick clicks with her candy-colored nails.

"For the record," the chairman said. "Dean Bruno Duffy alleges that Helen Ivers invited him to her house for the purpose of soliciting a favor—the reinstatement of Adair Wilson to the position of Associate Professor of Dramatic Arts—in exchange for sex. He said that he refused whereupon Adair Wilson held him at gunpoint. He has not pressed formal charges against Adair Wilson." Cleland stopped and folded his hands. "What is your response?"

Helen took a deep breath. "I did invite Bruno Duffy to my house."

The board had the decency to look surprised.

"Go on," Cleland said.

He reminded Helen of her father. He was an alum, about 70, smart but not academic, compassionate, but not warm. He understood the role of the board as an advisory committee. He had never had to make use of the board's role as the president's direct supervisor.

"I gave him a glass of wine," Helen said. There were no decisions to make now. She was simply telling the truth. It was a relief in a way. "I did ask him for that favor, but by the time we had gone upstairs, I knew I had made a mistake. I told him it was wrong and that we should stop. It was a terrible lapse in judgment. I don't expect you to excuse me because I changed my mind. But I did, and he…tried to force me. I called for help. When Professor Wilson heard me, Bruno Duffy was trying to rape me."

"And what was your relationship with Adair Wilson at the time?" Cleland asked.

Helen swallowed.

The chairman continued. "Let me put it this way. If you continue as the president of this college, will you seek out a consensual sexual relationship with Adair Wilson?"

"Yes."

"Are you aware that she has applied for the position of Professor of Dramatic Arts?"

Helen had not seen Adair near a computer. Hope sparked in her heart. She shook her head. "I did not know that."

"And if she were hired, would you still want to continue your relationship with her?"

Helen nodded.

Cleland glanced at the board members lined up behind their laptops and their bottled water. Bruce looked at the wall clock. Lucile cleaned something from beneath her fingernail. Debby stretched her neck. They were waiting for lunch.

"You may wait outside while the board deliberates," Cleland concluded.

Helen stepped outside. She sat down on a bench. In town, a church bell struck the hour. Students poured from the academic buildings, their backpacks flapping. A moment later, Patrick approached, clearly looking for her. When he saw her, he quickened his pace and plopped down beside her.

"I'll miss all this," Helen said, watching the quad empty as the students found their way to their next classes.

"Adair didn't come?" Patrick asked.

"No."

"That's bullshit. She should have." Patrick folded his arms over his chest and stretched his legs out. "How'd it go in there?"

"You don't bounce back from something like this."

Patrick bumped her shoulder with his. "Don't pack it in yet."

"What can they say? I just hope they listen

about Adair. After everything she's been through, she doesn't need some trumped up charge from Duffy."

"I can't promise anything," Patrick drawled. "No one ever tells the secretaries anything." He elbowed Helen again. "But I heard from an undisclosed source in HR that Duffy's going to resign."

"Because of this?" Helen asked.

"Funny. No." Patrick unfolded his arms and leaned in, his voice dropping to a baritone. "Apparently he's been visiting a work-study student in the computer lab. Night shift. I guess she's just a luscious little thing." Patrick waved his hands in the shape of an hourglass. "Duffy kept coming around. What he didn't know…" Patrick grinned "…was that her hippy, anti-establishment boyfriend is a film major. His professor got a look at his film project, and it's quite, shall we say, arresting." Patrick reached into his pocket and handed Helen his cell phone. "I'm no attorney, but if things don't go your way, show them this. Now I've got to get back to the office to triage your inbox."

Your inbox. "Thank you, Patrick. For everything."

She watched him strut away then cued up the video. Creative splicing made Duffy "dance" to a heavy backbeat. It was adolescent and ludicrous and entirely damning, because there was no soundtrack over the part where Duffy told the girl he could help her keep her scholarship despite her failing grades.

"But I'm not failing." Even in the video her breasts were ridiculously large. "I have a 3.97."

Duffy leaned in. "I can change that in ten keystrokes, sweetheart. Think about." The techno music cut in again, and Duffy jittered across the screen.

Helen shook her head. "Fucking bastard." She closed the browser, and stared out across the quad. She hoped the film professor would be on the theater's hiring committee. Helen did not know the woman well, but she was about Adair's age, with a passion for activist journalism and several awards for her documentaries on factory farming. She would vote for Adair. If Helen left and Adair stayed, she might be a friend for Adair. Along with Patrick, the students, and the other faculty—with all their peculiar obsessions and quirky habits—Adair could heal here.

"Excuse me," someone called.

Helen looked over. For a moment, she did not recognize the elegant woman dressed in slacks and a long black coat with a mandarin collar. Adair had shaved her head. She wore lavender lipstick drawn in a vertical stripe through the center of her lips, giving her an otherworldly quality, like a science fiction heroine.

"Shouldn't you be in class?" Adair asked, her lips lifting in a half-smile.

Helen rose, speechless.

"I'm sorry," Adair said, opening her arms. "I should have been here."

Helen fell into her embrace. Adair held her, and, for the first time in weeks, Helen felt like Adair's soul was present.

"How did it go in there?" Adair asked.

The door to the building opened. "We're ready," Stephanie called.

"I don't know," Helen said.

Adair released her. "Am I too late?"

Helen took her hand. "No. You're not too late." Together they walked into the board room.

Cleland read from his notes, summarizing Duffy's accusations and Helen's claims. The recitation felt interminable. Finally he added, "President Ivers claims that this was a momentary lapse of judgment on her part, amounting to only a matter of minutes. She also stated for the record that Adair Wilson was only trying to protect her. Ivers states that, if reinstated, she would continue to seek a consensual relationship with Adair Wilson."

Adair squeezed her hand.

"Is this an accurate recording of the hearing?"

"It is," Helen said.

"In that case, the board has elected to suspend you, without pay, for two weeks, during which time you are entitled to remain in your campus lodging, but not to participate in any administrative duties. You will also undergo sexual harassment training and mandatory counseling for up to one year."

Helen scanned the board members' faces. Debby, the youngest member of the board, was smiling.

"In light of the events of the past year and a half, including the murder of Carrie Brown and the rescue of the Kimball twins, the board would like to note that Helen Ivers has been under a kind of pressure unprecedented by a position of this type, and that she has served the college admirably." Now Cleland smiled. "Adair Wilson," he went on, "will be required to review the college weapons policy and sign an affidavit saying she will not carry a firearm on campus under any circumstances."

Frank touched Cleland's shoulder and said, "Provided she is rehired."

"Provided she is rehired," Cleland repeated.

Everyone on the board was smiling.

At the far end of the table, Debby said, "Oh, what the hell." She stood and clapped. A moment later, the whole board rose and joined in her applause.

"Welcome back," Cleland said.

⚛ ⚛ ⚛ ⚛

That night, Helen and Adair walked down to the Craven Bar and Grill. The subterranean bar had not changed since Helen sat there, talking to Terri about the beautiful young professor who was so alluring and so utterly unsuitable for her.

Now Adair sat across from Helen studying the menu.

"You have beautiful eyes," Helen said.

Adair's smile flashed for a second and then vanished.

"Please eat something," Helen said.

"The food here was never good," Adair said.

When the waitress arrived, Adair ordered a cup of tomato soup. Helen watched her stir it and taste only the tiniest bit. Around them, townies clinked glasses and cheered a college football game on television. In the kitchen, someone dropped a plate. Everything Helen wanted to say was too big for the cramped bar with its low ceiling and Saint Pauli girl posters, but she feared Adair's silence.

Helen's food arrived, and she offered Adair a bite of beef stroganoff.

Adair declined.

"I know." Helen looked at the brown slurry. "Why do we always eat here?"

"It's the only place in town."

"It hasn't changed a bit," Helen said. *But we*

have.

They both jumped as someone yelled, "Prof A!"

It was Adair's student Marcus Billing with a crowd of friends.

A red haired girl at his side said, "It's Wilson!"

Suddenly their table was surrounded. Marcus and the red haired girl both talked at once. "I heard you were back. You *have* come back, haven't you? We can't *live* without you."

Adair smiled shyly.

"Slater is a total douche bag. He gave me a B!" Marcus complained.

"He tried to rewrite *My Fair Lady* to be a communist critique of modern commercialism," another girl said.

"You have to save us." Marcus clasped his hands to his chest dramatically.

"Professor Wilson was the best," the red haired girl said to their younger companions. "She did stuff nobody thought you could do on stage."

Helen remembered the night they had made love on the stage.

"Why don't you guys sit down," Helen said, surprising herself. "Adair, come over here." She motioned for Adair to scoot around the semi-circular booth. She put a hand on Adair's knee.

Marcus shot her a knowing smile.

Helen wondered if he, like Patrick, knew infinitely more than he was supposed to. Helen caught the waitress's eye and ordered two plates of the appetizer sampler which was a hideous smorgasbord of everything that could possibly be filled with cream cheese and deep fried. The smell was nauseating. The students dove in immediately, thanking her through mouthfuls of fried mushrooms.

Helen felt Adair's leg tense as the students jostled around in the booth. They talked constantly and simultaneously, and the girl with the red hair had a laugh like a cannon. Adair jumped every time it went off. But slowly, Helen felt her relax. Finally as the students talked and laughed and recited passages from their latest productions, Helen saw Adair pick up one of the jalapeno poppers, examine it, and tentatively put it into her mouth.

Chapter Sixty-four

That night, in the bedroom of the Pittock House, Adair watched Helen undress. She had a beautiful body, gracefully curved like a Lefebvre nude, neither lean nor fat, unapologetically feminine.

Helen looked over her shoulder at Adair, and for a moment her gaze was all invitation. Then she held her silk nightgown up to her breasts and looked away. "We don't have to do anything you don't want to," Helen whispered.

Adair did not know how to tell her she wanted to. She wanted Helen to take her, to hold her down, to make her receive pleasure. She wanted Helen to make pleasure the only answer because otherwise her own guilt sat in a chair by the wall. The coltan. The mines in Idiofa. So much money. So many accounts.

Helen edged a little bit closer. It occurred to Adair that Helen moved like someone approaching a wild animal. But Adair did not know how to soften her face to say "yes." She was still fully dressed. She saw the fear in Helen's eyes. *She thinks I'm going to turn her away.* "I want you," Adair said. "I just...how can I deserve this after what my family has done?"

Helen dropped the nightgown and stood before Adair naked. A lamp, shaded by pearlescent pink glass, lit her body with a soft light. Helen's silk nightgown lay pooled on the floor. Behind her, the bed floated in piles of white eiderdown blankets. "I love you."

Helen put her hands on Adair's cheeks. "What your family did does not change who you are." Her voice was tight, but her touch was soft. "Do you understand that? Do you believe me?" Then Helen pressed her lips to Adair's.

Adair felt desire race through her. She ran her hands through Helen's hair, drawing her closer. Helen's kiss went deeper. Helen pulled their hips together. Adair felt Helen's nakedness through her own clothes.

"Tell me what you want," Helen whispered.

Adair's animal body dampened and swelled, but she felt transfixed, like a teenager, breathlessly aroused, yet frightened at the same time.

"Anything," Helen urged.

Adair hesitated. "Tie me?"

Helen nodded solemnly. "I won't hurt you like she did."

"I don't want that. I just..." Adair trailed off.

"You want to forget," Helen said.

Adair stood for a moment, not knowing what to do next.

"Shh," Helen said gently. Slowly, she unbuttoned Adair's blouse and draped it carefully over a chair. Then she loosened Adair's bra and cast that away. When Adair was topless, Helen led her to the bed. Adair lay down, closed her eyes, raised her hands over her head, and grabbed the metal filigree of the headboard. Helen clasped her wrists with a strength Adair did not know she possessed and pinned her down. For a moment, Cecelia's face flashed before Adair's eyes, and she felt the tar paper roof beneath her back. Then Helen slid her leg between Adair's, sending an exquisite wave of pleasure through Adair's body, and the past disappeared.

As if from thin air, Helen produced a silk Hermes scarf and wrapped it around both of Adair's wrists, then around the metal work in the headboard. "Like that?" she asked.

"Tighter."

Helen pulled the bonds harder.

"Yes," Adair breathed out.

Helen pulled Adair's pants off, caressing the length of her body as she did. When Adair was naked, Helen retrieved another long scarf and surveyed Adair. Her eyes lingered on the apex of Adair's legs, and Adair felt her glance like a physical touch. One quick touch, one flick of Helen's tongue, and she would catch fire. Helen took the scarf and looped it around Adair's ankles, binding her feet together.

"Have you done this before?" Adair gasped.

"Only with you." Helen pressed one hand to Adair's racing heart. "How will I know when it's over? Do you have a word?"

"Home," Adair said.

Helen kissed Adair playfully. "Like homerun?"

Adair smiled and shook her head. "Just home." Then conscious thoughts fled Adair's mind as Helen mounted her, kissing her, stroking her chest, and then twisting her nipples so the sensation skittered along the fault line between pleasure and pain. Then she tightened her grip and the pain became a sweet, hot flame that brought Adair into her body, while it seared away all memory of the past. Adair's hips bucked. She clenched the muscles in her sex, pushing her clitoris toward Helen. Helen put a hand on her hip bone. "Don't move or I'll stop."

Adair took a trembling breath and relaxed into

Helen's touch. Slowly Helen slid down her body. She kissed the curls that covered Adair's pubis. Then she speared Adair's clit with her tongue. Adair tried to spread her legs but the bonds held her.

"Don't move," Helen said, her voice stern and strong but also full of love. "Relax."

Helen's breath teased her sex. When Adair settled back on the bed, Helen began again, licking as much of Adair's labia as she could reach with Adair's legs pressed together, her tongue pushing into the tight folds until Adair's whole consciousness distilled down to a single point, Helen's tongue pressing down on her clit, Helen's fingers massaging her mons, reaching a deep inner fiber of pleasure. Then there it was. The orgasm she had been waiting for raced up her spine and down her legs and turned the space behind her eyelids into pinwheels of red and gold. She heard herself cry out.

Helen released her.

Adair felt another orgasm pressing her clitoris from inside. "Wait. Yes." Adair's eyes flew open. "Please." She struggled against the bonds that held her, pressing her hips toward Helen's lips.

"Again?" Helen stroked Adair's bound legs.

"Yes."

Helen freed her ankles. Then she spread Adair's legs wide and kissed Adair's open sex and pressed her fingers deep inside Adair's body, stretching her body, holding her entirely, inside and out. Adair threw her head back, her mouth open in a moan.

"Is that too much?" Helen asked quietly, lifting her head from Adair's body.

"Yes. I don't know. Don't stop." Adair could not articulate the collision of desire and fragility she felt.

She wanted Helen's kiss so deeply, she felt the need in her bones, but her clitoris was so sensitive each kissed seared her.

"Rest," Helen said. Very tenderly she began licking the junction between Adair's outer labia and her thigh. As Adair relaxed, Helen moved her tongue inward, making long deep strokes, dipping into the opening to Adair's sex, leaving her clit untouched. She repeated the kisses on the other side, then asked, "Are you ready?"

"Please."

Helen pulled Adair's clit into her mouth and sucked. Adair's cry was half laughter as she felt the fierce pull. She felt as if Helen sucked the orgasm from deep within her. It rose slowly, luxuriously, washing away fear and disappointment and shame, like the sun rising slowly and breaking across the landscape. Helen kept her tongue pressed to Adair's sex just long enough. Then when the pressure became too much, she released her. When Adair's body stopped heaving, Helen kissed Adair's stomach just below her belly button. "Are you home?" Helen asked.

"I'm home."

Epilogue

Two Years Later

Helen and Adair stared at the floral arrangement that had landed in the clutter behind the Ventmore stage. It was the size of a small car, comprised entirely of white flowers: roses, lilies, snowball hydrangeas, and other species Helen did not recognize. Orchid-like blooms the size of dinner plates. A chain of tiny white bells.

"Who brought this?" Adair called to a student manning the curtains.

"Some florist from Boston," the boy called back. "Took two people to get it in here, and then we had to help them get it onto a table."

Another boy said, "It's almost seven. President Ivers, I need to check your mic." A moment later he was carefully threading the line to her lapel mic under her collar. Meanwhile, a girl with a pixie haircut dusted powder over Adair's face. "Don't rub it off," the girl told Adair, glancing in Helen's direction. The boy with the mic released Helen. She walked around the flowers. A large white envelope poked out between roses.

"There's a card." Helen removed it from the envelope and read, "To Helen and Adair, congratulations on opening night." Included was a photograph. Harlow Galloway stood on a white beach, his linen trousers rolled up to his ankles, his feet just touching the Caribbean blue water. Slightly behind him, Charity and Prudence stood in the surf, their heads covered in white bonnets, their long skirts heavy with sea water. They were all beaming.

Helen remembered the day, almost a year ago, when Galloway had called her. "I do not want there to be any misunderstandings when my driver comes for them," he had said. "They are adults in full possession of their faculties, and they are joining me of their own free will."

He had called Chief Thompson with the same message.

Adair had cried a little bit as she watched the twins wave to their dorm mates and then duck into the back of a black limousine. They carried no luggage.

Now Adair eyed the flowers. "I failed them," she said, cupping her hand around a white rose.

"No you haven't." Helen was not going to let the silence consume Adair again. "They know what happened. They know who Galloway is and what he did. And they know that if they wanted to stay here, no one would force them to leave. Galloway is a rich, beautiful man. He wants to give them everything, and they said yes."

"But they've been indoctrinated," Adair said.

"There's real abuse out there, real slavery, but this isn't it." Helen touched Adair's waist, drawing her away from the flowers. "In the end they *chose* him. I wouldn't have. You wouldn't have. But they *did*. Do we have a right to say anything else?"

Adair pulled a ball of hydrangea off the arrangement and crushed it in her hand. "Do you think this is a threat then?"

"No," Helen said. She didn't realize how certain she felt until she spoke. "I think it's a greeting."

"Come on," The girl with the pixie haircut touched Helen's elbow. "You're on."

Helen stepped from the side curtains and took her place at the center of the stage. The Ventmore Theater was packed and not only with students. Terri sat in the audience with a colleague from LA. Patrick and his husband, David, waved from the front row. There were a lot of townies as well as men and women in evening wear that suggested they had come from larger cities where theater was a fancier affair.

"Good evening," Helen began. "It is my great pleasure to welcome you to the opening night of Adair Wilson's original play, *Sold*. A script that, I understand, will soon be made into a feature length movie."

There was a round of applause.

"*Sold* looks at the breadth and complexity of the human trafficking problem in the world today and draws heavily on Wilson's experiences untangling her own family's ties to modern slavery. Adair Wilson has been commended by numerous anti-trafficking organizations for her work on her family's case, her donation of the family's unencumbered funds to anti-trafficking efforts, and her work on this groundbreaking play. And now I would like to introduce to you, the playwright, and, as of two o'clock this afternoon at the Pittock courthouse..."

Terri and Patrick grinned. A pocket of students in the middle of the theater cheered, reminding Helen how quickly secrets traveled on a small campus.

"...my wife, Mrs. Adair Merrill Wilson."

About the author

Karelia Stetz-Waters is an English professor by day and writer by night (and early morning). Her work includes the thriller, The Admirer, and a YA novel, Forgive Me If I've Told You This Before (coming Fall 2014). She lives with her beloved wife, Fay, her pug dog, Lord Byron, and her cat, Cyrus the Disemboweler. Her interests include large snakes, conjoined twins, corn mazes, lesbians, popular science books on neurology, and any roadside attraction that purports to have the world's largest ball of twine. She would love to hear from her readers.

Learn more about Karelia at

Home page: www.kareliastetzwaters.com

Other books by Karelia

The Admirer - **ISBN - 978-1-939062-42-0**

A serial killer "makes" perfect women by amputating their legs. A troubled girl walks knowingly into the killer's arms. An ambitious college president spirals toward madness.

Helen Ivers is still reeling from her sister's recent suicide when she takes a position as the president of Pittock College. The isolated campus seems like a good place to recover, but shortly after she arrives, two severed human legs are found bound to the train tracks. The local police explain away the gruesome occurrence, but Helen is convinced the police chief, and maybe the whole town, is covering for a killer.

She embarks on her own investigation, but she begins to doubt herself as nightmares of her sister's suicide become waking hallucinations and everyone discounts her fears. The only person who shares her apprehensions is a young professor whose aggressive sexual advances are as frightening and alluring as impending madness – a woman who is either Helen's only ally or the killer.